Praise for Debbie Macomber's Christmas Stories

"Macomber offers fans a stocking stuffer
for the Christmas season...[a] feel-good,
PG-rated contemporary romance."
—*Publishers Weekly* on *The Christmas Basket*

"[A] sweet traditional romance that
celebrates the power of love and friendship."
—*Booklist* on *The Christmas Basket*

"A fast, frothy fantasy for those looking to add some
romance to their holidays."
—*Publishers Weekly* on *The Snow Bride*

"Macomber spins another pure-from-the-heart romance
giddy with love and warm laughter—
a get-you-set-for-Christmas treat that's
as yummy as divinity melting on the tongue."
—*BookPage* on *The Snow Bride*

"Readers looking for a holiday fairy tale
will find plenty of reasons to cheer."
—*Publishers Weekly* on *When Christmas Comes*

"[A] fast-paced, light-hearted and charming Christmas
story, a tale as joyful as the season itself."
—*Booklist* on *When Christmas Comes*

"Macomber's take on *A Christmas Carol*...
adds up to another take of romance in the lives
of ordinary people, with a message that life is
like a fruitcake: full of unexpected delights."
—*Publishers Weekly* on *There's Something About Christmas*

"*There's Something About Christmas* is a wonderfully funny
and at times heartwrenching story of finding the right
person to love at the most delightful time of the year."
—*Times Record News,* Wichita Falls, TX

Dearest Friends,

As you might have guessed from the number of Christmas books I've written, I'm a real Christmas person. Every year I decorate my house and office with boughs, holly, Christmas trees (yes, plural) and Nativity scenes. I simply love Christmas!

When my children were young they'd leaf through catalogs, study each page, then make their lists of Christmas wishes. When they were finished—and they'd narrowed their lists down to under a hundred items each—they'd present them to me. Come to think of it, they still do that.

I have a list of Christmas wishes for you, my dear readers. I wish you joy and peace and love, not just in this season but throughout the year. I wish you good health and prosperity. And I wish you laughter and contentment. (If these two stories bring you a chuckle or a smile, if they leave you with a feeling of warmth, I'll know I've achieved my goal.)

Rainy Day Kisses has been updated, with a new prologue and epilogue. I wrote this in 1990, but it's still one of my all-time favorites. *Christmas Letters* was published in hardcover last year and is based (loosely!) on all the holiday letters I wrote through the years.

I hope you'll grab a cup of hot chocolate (or eggnog!), make yourself comfortable and enjoy these stories. And may all your Christmas Wishes come true this holiday season!

Debbie Macomber

I love to hear from readers. You can reach me through my Web site at www.DebbieMacomber.com or at P.O. Box 1458, Port Orchard, WA 98366.

DEBBIE MACOMBER

Christmas Wishes

MIRA®

MIRA

ISBN-13: 978-0-7783-2506-2
ISBN-10:   0-7783-2506-7

CHRISTMAS WISHES

Copyright © 2007 by MIRA Books.

The publisher acknowledges the copyright holder
of the individual works as follows:

CHRISTMAS LETTERS
Copyright © 2006 by Debbie Macomber.

RAINY DAY KISSES
Copyright © 1990 by Debbie Macomber.

www.MIRABooks.com

Printed in U.S.A.

Contents

Christmas Letters

To Katherine Orr

Better known as K.O.

for her encouragement and support
through the years

Prologue

Zelda O'Connor Davidson
76 Orchard Avenue
Seattle, Washington
Christmas, 2006

Dear Family and Friends:
Merry Christmas, everyone!
Let me warn you—this Christmas letter won't be as clever as last year's. My sister, Katherine (whom you may know better as K.O.), wrote that one for me but, ironically, she hasn't got time to do this year's. Ironic because it's due to the popularity of that particular letter that she's managed to start a little business on the side—

writing Christmas letters for other people! (She offered to write mine, of course, but I know that between her work doing medical transcriptions, her job search and her Christmas letters, it would be a real stretch to find the time.)

So, here goes. The twins, Zoe and Zara, have recently turned five. They're looking forward to starting kindergarten next September. It's hard to believe our little girls are almost old enough for school! Still, they keep themselves (and us!) busy. So do our assorted pets—especially the dogs, two Yorkies named Zero and Zorro.

I'm still a stay-at-home mom and Zach's still working as a software programmer. This year's big news, which I want to share with all of you, has to do with a wonderful book I read. It changed my family's life. It's called *The Free Child* and it's by Dr. Wynn Jeffries. My sister scoffs at this, but Dr. Jeffries believes that children can be trusted to set their own boundaries. He also believes that, as parents, we shouldn't impose fantasies on them—fantasies like Santa Claus. Kids are capable of accepting reality, he says, and I agree! (See page 146 of *The Free Child*.)

So, this Christmas will be a different kind of experience for us, one that focuses on family, not fantasy.

Zach and the girls join me in wishing all of you a wonderful Christmas. And remember, a free child is a happy child (see page 16).

Love and kisses,
Zelda, Zach, Zoe and Zara
(and a wag of the tail from Zero & Zorro)

Chapter

1

It *was* him. Katherine O'Connor, better known as K.O., was almost positive. She squinted just to be sure. He looked identical to the man on the dust jacket of that ridiculous book, the one her sister treated like a child-rearing bible. Of course, people didn't really look like their publicity photos. And she hadn't realized the high and mighty Dr. Wynn Jeffries was from the Seattle area. Furthermore, she couldn't imagine what he was doing on Blossom Street.

She'd never even met him, but she distrusted him profoundly and disliked him just as much. It was because of Dr. Jeffries that she'd been banned from a local bookstore. She'd had a small difference of opinion with the manager on the subject of Wynn's book. Apparently the bookseller was a personal friend of his, because she'd leaped to Dr. Jeffries's defense and had ordered K.O. out of the store. She'd even suggested K.O. take her future book-purchasing business elsewhere, which seemed unnecessarily extreme.

"K.O.," Bill Mulcahy muttered, distracting her. They sat across from each other at the French Café, filled to capacity during the midmorning rush. People lined up for coffee, and another line formed at the bakery counter. "Did you get all that?" he asked.

"Sure," K.O. said, returning her attention to him. "Sorry—I thought I saw someone I knew." Oh, the things she was willing to do for some extra holiday cash. One witty Christmas letter written on her sister's behalf, and all of a sudden K.O. was the most sought-after woman at her brother-in-law's office. They all wanted her to write their Christmas letters. She'd been shocked to discover how much they'd willingly plunk down for it, too. Bill Mulcahy was the third person she'd met with this week, and his letter was the most difficult so far. Leno or Letterman would've had a hard time finding anything amusing about this man's life.

"I don't know what you're going to write," Bill continued. "It's been an exceptionally bad year. As I explained earlier, my son is in a detention home, my daughter's living with her no-good boyfriend and over Thanksgiving she announced she's pregnant. Naturally, marriage is out of the question."

"That *is* a bit of a challenge," K.O. agreed. She widened her eyes and stared again at the man who waited in the long line at the cash register. It *was* him;

she was convinced of it now. The not-so-good doctor was—to put it in appropriately seasonal terms—a fruitcake. He was a child psychologist who'd written a book called *The Free Child* that was the current child-rearing rage.

To be fair, K.O. was single and not a mother. The only child-rearing experience she'd had was with her identical twin nieces, Zoe and Zara, whom she adored. Until recently, anyway. Overnight the five-year-olds had become miniature monsters and all because her sister had followed the "Free Child" rules as set out by Dr. Jeffries.

"My wife," Bill said, "is on the verge of a breakdown."

K.O. pitied the poor woman—and her husband.

"We've written Christmas letters for years and while life wasn't always as perfect as we—well, as we implied…" He let the rest fade away.

"You painted the picture of a model family."

"Yes." Bill cleared his throat and offered her a weak smile. "Patti, that's my wife, chose to present a, shall we say, rosier depiction of reality." He exhaled in a rush. "We never included family pictures and if you met my son, you'd know why. Anyone looking at Mason would know in a minute that this kid isn't a member of the National Honor Society." He released his breath again and shook his head sadly. "Mason's into body piercing," Bill added. "He pierced his eyebrows, his nose, his lips, his tongue, his nipples—"

K.O. stopped him before he went any lower. "I get it."

"You probably don't, but that's lucky for you. Oh, and he dyed his hair green."

"Green?"

"He wears it spiked, too, and he...he does this thing with paint." Bill dropped his voice.

K.O. was sure she'd misunderstood. "I beg your pardon?"

"Mason doesn't call it paint. It's some form of cosmetic he smears across his face. I never imagined that my son would be rummaging through his mother's makeup drawer one day."

"I suppose that is a bit disconcerting," K.O. murmured.

"I forget the actual significance of the black smudges under his eyes and across his cheeks," Bill said. "To me it looks like he's some teenage commando."

Yes, this letter would indeed be a challenge. "Have you thought about skipping your Christmas letter this year?" K.O. asked hopefully.

"Yeah, I'd like to, but as I said, Patti's emotional health is rather fragile. She claims people are already asking about our annual letter. She's afraid that if we don't send it the same as we do every year, everyone will figure out that we're pitiful parents." His shoulders drooped. "In other words, we've failed our children."

"I don't think you've necessarily *failed*," K.O. assured him. "Most teenagers go through a rebellious stage."

"Did you?"

"Oh, sure."

"Did you pierce anything?"

"Well, I had my ears pierced...."

"That's not the same thing." He peered at her earrings, visible through her straight blond hair, which she wore loosely tied back. "And you only have one in each ear—not eight or ten like my son." He seemed satisfied that he'd proved his point. "Then you'll write our Christmas letter and smooth over the rough edges of our year?"

K.O. was less and less confident that she could pull this off. "I don't know if I'm your person," she said hesitantly. How could she possibly come up with a positive version of such a disastrous year? Besides, this side job was supposed to be fun, not real work. It'd begun as a favor to her sister and all of a sudden she was launching a career. At some stage she'd need to call a halt—maybe sooner than she'd expected.

Her client shifted in his seat. "I'll pay you double what you normally charge."

K.O. sat up straight. Double. He said he'd pay double? "Would four days be enough time?" she asked. Okay, so she could be bought. She pulled out her Day-Timer, checked her schedule and they set a date for their next meeting.

"I'll give you half now and half when you're finished."

That seemed fair. Not one to be overly prideful, she held out her hand as he peeled off three fifty-dollar bills. Her fingers closed around the cash.

"I'll see you Friday then," Bill said, and reaching for his briefcase, he left the French Café carrying his latte in its takeout cup.

Looking out the windows with their Christmas garland, she saw that it had begun to snow again. This was the coldest December on record. Seattle's normally mild climate had dipped to below-freezing temperatures for ten days in a row. So much for global warming. There was precious little evidence of it in Seattle.

K.O. glanced at the coffee line. Wynn Jeffries had made his way to the front and picked up his hot drink. After adding cream and sugar—lots of both, she observed—he was getting ready to leave. K.O. didn't want to be obvious about watching him, so she took a couple of extra minutes to collect her things, then followed him out the door.

Even if she introduced herself, she had no idea what to say. Mostly she wanted to tell him his so-called Free Child movement—no boundaries for kids—was outright lunacy. How could he, in good conscience, mislead parents in this ridiculous fashion? Not that she had strong feelings on the subject or anything. Okay, so maybe she'd gone a little overboard at the bookstore that day, but she couldn't help it. The manager had been touting the benefits of Dr. Jeffries's book to yet another unsuspecting mom. K.O. felt it was her duty to let the poor woman know what might happen if she actually followed Dr. Jeffries's advice. The bookseller had strenuously disagreed and from then on, the situation had gotten out of hand.

Not wanting him to think she was stalking him, which she supposed she was, K.O. maintained a careful distance. If his office was in Seattle, it might even be in this neighborhood. After the renovations on Blossom Street a few years ago, a couple of buildings had been converted to office space. If she could discreetly discover where he practiced, she might go and talk to him sometime. She hadn't read his book but had leafed through it, and she knew he was a practicing child psychologist. She wanted to argue about his beliefs and his precepts, tell him about the appalling difference in her nieces' behavior since the day Zelda had adopted his advice.

She'd rather he didn't see her, so she dashed inconspicuously across the street to A Good Yarn, and darted into the doorway, where she pretended to be interested in a large Christmas stocking that hung in the display window. From the reflection in the window, she saw Dr. Jeffries walking briskly down the opposite sidewalk.

As soon as it was safe, she dashed from the yarn store to Susannah's Garden, the flower shop next door, and nearly fell over a huge potted poinsettia, all the while keeping her eyes on Dr. Jeffries. He proved one thing, she mused. Appearances were deceiving. He looked so...so normal. Who would've guessed that beneath that distinguished, sophisticated and—yes—handsome exterior lay such a fiend? Perhaps *fiend* was too strong a word. Yet she considered Wynn Jeffries's thinking to be nothing short of diabolical, if Zoe and Zara were anything to judge by.

No way!

K.O. stopped dead in her tracks. She watched as Wynn Jeffries paused outside her condo building, her very own building, entered the code and strolled inside.

Without checking for traffic, K.O. crossed the

street again. A horn honked and brakes squealed, but she barely noticed. She was dumbfounded.

Speechless.

There had to be some mistake. Perhaps he was making a house call. No, that wasn't right. What doctor made house calls in this day and age? What psychologist made house calls *ever*? Besides, he didn't exactly look like the compassionate type. K.O. bit her lip and wondered when she'd become so cynical. It'd happened around the same time her sister read Dr. Jeffries's book, she decided.

The door had already closed before she got there. She entered her code and stepped inside just in time to see the elevator glide shut. Standing back, she watched the floor numbers flicker one after another.

"Katherine?"

K.O. whirled around to discover LaVonne Young, her neighbor and friend. LaVonne was the only person who called her Katherine. "What are you doing, dear?"

K.O. pointed an accusing finger past the elegantly decorated lobby tree to the elevator.

LaVonne stood in her doorway with her huge tomcat, named predictably enough, Tom, tucked under her arm. She wore a long shapeless dress that was typical of her wardrobe, and her long graying hair was drawn back in a bun. When K.O. had first met her, LaVonne had reminded her of the character Auntie Mame. She still did. "Something wrong with the elevator?" LaVonne asked.

"No, I just saw a man..." K.O. glanced back and

noticed that the elevator had gone all the way up to the penthouse suite. That shouldn't really come as a shock. His book sales being what they were, he could easily afford the penthouse.

LaVonne's gaze followed hers. "That must be Dr. Jeffries."

"You know him?" K.O. didn't bother to hide her interest. The more she learned, the better her chances of engaging him in conversation.

"Of course I know Dr. Jeffries," the retired accountant said. "I know everyone in the building."

"How long has he lived here?" K.O. demanded. She'd been in this building since the first week it was approved for occupation. So she should've run into him before now.

"I believe he moved in soon after the place was renovated. In fact, the two of you moved in practically on the same day."

That was interesting. Of course, there was a world of difference between a penthouse suite and the first-floor, one-bedroom unit she owned. Or rather, that the bank owned and she made payments on. With the inheritance she'd received from her maternal grandparents, K.O. had put a down payment on the smallest, cheapest unit available. It was all she could afford at the time—and all she could afford now. She considered herself lucky to get in when she did.

"His name is on the mailbox," LaVonne said, gesturing across the lobby floor to the mailboxes.

"As my sister would tell you, I'm a detail person." It was just the obvious she missed.

"He's a celebrity, you know," LaVonne whispered conspiratorially. "Especially since his book was published."

"Have you read it?" K.O. asked.

"Well, no, dear, I haven't, but then never having had children myself, I'm not too concerned with child-raising. However, I did hear Dr. Jeffries interviewed on the radio and he convinced me. His book is breaking all kinds of records. Apparently it's on all the bestseller lists. So there must be *something* to what he says. In fact, the man on the radio called Dr. Jeffries the new Dr. Spock."

"You've got to be kidding!" Jeffries's misguided gospel was spreading far and wide.

LaVonne stared at her. "In case you're interested, he's not married."

"That doesn't surprise me," K.O. muttered. Only a man without a wife and children could possibly come up with such ludicrous ideas. He didn't have a family of his own to test his theories on; instead he foisted them on unsuspecting parents like her sister, Zelda, and brother-in-law, Zach. The deterioration in the girls' behavior was dramatic, but Zelda insisted this was normal as they adjusted to a new regimen. They'd "find their equilibrium," she'd said, quoting the book. Zach, who worked long hours, didn't really seem to notice. The twins' misbehavior would have to be even more extreme to register on him.

"Would you like me to introduce you?" LaVonne asked.

"No," K.O. responded immediately. Absolutely

not. Well, maybe, but not now. And not for the reasons LaVonne thought.

"Do you have time for tea?" LaVonne asked. "I wanted to tell you about the most recent class I attended. Fascinating stuff, just fascinating." Since her retirement, LaVonne had been at loose ends and signed up for a variety of workshops and evening classes.

"I learned how to unleash my psychic abilities."

"You're psychic?" K.O. asked.

"Yes, only I didn't know it until I took this class. I've learned so much," she said in wonder. "So much. All these years, my innate talent has lain there, unused and unfulfilled. It took this class to break it free and show me what I should've known all along. *I can see into the future.*" She spoke in a portentous whisper.

"You learned this after one class?"

"Madame Ozma claims I have been blessed with the sight. She warned me not to waste my talents any longer."

This *did* sound fascinating. Well...bizarre, anyway. K.O. would have loved to hear all about the class, but she really needed to start work. In addition to writing Christmas letters—which she did only in November and December—she was a medical transcriptionist by training. It paid the bills and had allowed her to put herself through college to obtain a public relations degree. Now she was searching for a job in PR, which wasn't all that easy to find, even with her degree. She was picky, too. She wanted a job with a salary that would actually meet her expenses. Over the years she'd grown accustomed to a few luxuries, like regular meals and flush toilets.

Currently her résumé was floating around town. Anytime now, she was bound to be offered the perfect job. And in the meanwhile, these Christmas letters gave her some useful practice in creating a positive spin on some unpromising situations—like poor Bill Mulcahy's.

"I'd love a cup of tea, but unfortunately I've got to get to work."

"Perhaps tomorrow," LaVonne suggested.

"That would be great."

"I'll call upon my psychic powers and look into your future if you'd like." She sounded completely serious.

"Sure," K.O. returned casually. Perhaps LaVonne could let her know when she'd find a job.

LaVonne's eyes brightened. "I'll study my class notes and then I'll tell you what I *see* for you."

"Thanks." She reached over and scratched Tom's ears. The big cat purred with pleasure.

With a bounce in her step, LaVonne went into her condo, closing the door with a slam that shook her Christmas wreath, decorated with golden moons and silver stars. K.O. headed for her own undecorated door, which was across the hall. Much as she disapproved of her sister's hero, she could hardly wait to tell Zelda the news.

Chapter

2

K.O. waited until she'd worked two hours straight before she phoned her sister. Zelda was a stay-at-home mom with Zoe and Zara, who were identical twins. Earlier in the year Zelda and Zach had purchased the girls each a dog. Two Yorkshire terriers, which the two girls had promptly named Zero and Zorro. K.O. called her sister's home the Land of Z. Even now, she wasn't sure how Zelda kept the girls straight, let alone the dogs. Even their barks sounded identical. *Yap. Yap* and *yap* with an occasional *yip* thrown in for variety, as if they sometimes grew bored with the sound of their own yapping.

Zelda answered on the third ring, sounding frazzled and breathless. "Yes?" she snapped into the phone.

"Is this a bad time?" K.O. asked.

"Oh, hi." The lack of enthusiasm was apparent. In addition to everything else, Dr. Jeffries's theories had placed a strain on K.O.'s relations with her younger sister.

"Merry Christmas to you, too," K.O. said cheerfully. "Can you talk?"

"Sure."

"The girls are napping?"

"No," Zelda muttered. "They decided they no longer need naps. Dr. Jeffries says on page 125 of his book that children should be allowed to sleep when, and only when, they decide they're tired. Forcing them into regimented nap- and bedtimes, is in opposition to their biological natures."

"I see." K.O. restrained the urge to argue. "Speaking of Dr. Jeffries..."

"I know you don't agree with his philosophy, but this is the way Zach and I have chosen to raise our daughters. When you have a family of your own, you can choose how best to parent your children."

"True, but..."

"Sorry," Zelda cried. It sounded as if she'd dropped the phone.

In the background, K.O. could hear her sister shouting at the girls and the dogs. Her shouts were punctuated with the dogs' yapping. A good five minutes passed before Zelda was back.

"What happened?" K.O. asked, genuinely concerned.

"Oh, nothing."

"As I started to say, I saw Dr. Jeffries."

"On television?" Zelda asked, only half-interested.

"No, in person."

"Where?" All at once she had Zelda's attention.

"On Blossom Street. You aren't going to believe this, but he actually lives in my building."

"Dr. Jeffries? Get out of here!"

Zelda was definitely interested now. "Wait—I heard he moved to Seattle just before his book was published." She took a deep breath. "Wow! You really *saw* him?"

"Uh-huh."

"Oh, my goodness, did you talk to him? Is he as handsome in person as he is in his photo?"

Feeling about him the way she did, K.O. had to consider the question for a moment. "He's fairly easy on the eyes." That was an understatement but looks weren't everything. To her mind, he seemed stiff and unapproachable. Distant, even.

"Did you tell him that Zach and I both read his book and what a difference it's made in our lives?"

"No, but..."

"K.O., could you... Would it be too much to get his autograph? Could you bring it on the fifteenth?"

K.O. had agreed to spend the night with the twins while Zelda and Zach attended his company's Christmas party. Her sister and brother-in-law had made arrangements to stay at a hotel downtown, just the two of them.

"All the mothers at the preschool would *die* to have Dr. Jeffries's autograph."

"I haven't met him," K.O. protested. It wasn't like she had any desire to form a fan club for him, either.

"But you just said he lives in your building."

"Yes."

"Are you sure it's him?"

"It looks like him. Anyway, LaVonne said it was."

Zelda gave a small shout of excitement. "If LaVonne says it's him, then it must be. How could you live in the same building as Dr. Jeffries and not know it?" her sister cried as though K.O. had somehow avoided this critical knowledge on purpose. "This is truly amazing. I've *got* to have his autograph."

"I'll...see what I can do," K.O. promised. This was not good. She'd hoped to find common ground with her sister, not become a...a go-between so Zelda could get her hero's autograph. Some hero! K.O.'s views on just about everything having to do with parenting were diametrically opposed to those purveyed by Dr. Wynn Jeffries. She'd feel like a fraud if she asked for his autograph.

"One more thing," Zelda said when her excitement had died down. "I know we don't agree on child-rearing techniques."

"That's true, but I understand these are your daughters." She took a deep breath. "How you raise them isn't really any of my business."

"Exactly," Zelda said emphatically. "Therefore, Zach and I want you to know we've decided to downplay Christmas this year."

"Downplay Christmas," K.O. repeated, not sure what that meant.

"We aren't putting up a tree."

"No Christmas tree!" K.O. sputtered, doing a poor

job of hiding her disapproval. She couldn't imagine celebrating the holiday without decorating a tree. Her poor nieces would be deprived of a very important tradition.

"I might allow a small potted one for the kitchen table." Zelda seemed a bit doubtful herself. She *should* be doubtful, since a Christmas tree had always been part of their own family celebration. The fact that their parents had moved to Arizona was difficult enough. This year they'd decided to take a cruise in the South Pacific over Christmas and New Year's. While K.O. was happy to see her mother and father enjoying their retirement, she missed them enormously.

"Is this another of Dr. Jeffries's ideas?" K.O. had read enough of his book—and heard *more* than enough about his theories—to suspect it was. Still, she could hardly fathom that even Wynn Jeffries would go this far. Outlaw Christmas? The man was a menace!

"Dr. Jeffries believes that misleading children about Santa does them lasting psychological damage."

"The girls can't have Santa, either?" This was cruel and unusual punishment. "Next you'll be telling me that you're doing away with the tooth fairy, too."

"Why, yes, of course. It's the same principle."

K.O. knew better than to argue with her sister. "Getting back to Christmas..." she began.

"Yes, Christmas. Like I said, Zach and I are planning to make it a low-key affair this year. Anything that involves Santa is out of the question."

Thankfully her sister was unable to see K.O. roll her eyes.

"In fact, Dr. Jeffries has a chapter on the subject. It's called 'Bury Santa Under the Sleigh.' Chapter eight."

"He wants to bury Santa Claus?" K.O. had heard enough. She'd personally bury Dr. Jeffries under a pile of plowed snow before she'd let him take Christmas away from Zoe and Zara. As far as she was concerned, his entire philosophy was unacceptable, but this no-Santa nonsense was too much. Here was where she drew her line in the snow—a line Wynn Jeffries had overstepped.

"Haven't you been listening to *anything* I've said?" Zelda asked.

"Unfortunately, I have."

Her doorbell chimed. "I need to go," K.O. told her sister. She sighed. "I'll see what I can do about that autograph."

"Yes, please," Zelda said with unmistakable gratitude. "It would mean the world to me if you could get Dr. Jeffries's autograph."

Sighing again, K.O. replaced the receiver and opened the door to find her neighbor LaVonne standing there. Although *standing* wasn't exactly the right word. LaVonne was practically leaping up and down. "I'm sorry to bother you but I just couldn't wait."

"Come in," K.O. said.

"I can't stay but a minute," the retired CPA insisted as she stepped over the threshold, clutching Tom. "I did it!" she exclaimed. "I saw the future." She squealed with delight and did a small jig. "I saw the future of your love life, K.O. It happened when I went to change the kitty litter."

"The...kitty litter." That was fitting, since it was where her love life happened to be at the moment. In some kind of toilet, anyway.

"Tom had just finished his business," LaVonne continued, gazing lovingly at her cat, "and there it was, plain as day."

"His business?" K.O. asked.

"No, no, the future. You know how some people with the *gift* can read tea leaves? Well, it came to me in the kitty-litter box. I know it sounds crazy but it's true. It was right there in front of me," she said. "You're going to meet the man of your dreams."

"Really?" K.O. hated to sound so disappointed. "I don't suppose you happened to see anything in the kitty litter about me finding a job?"

LaVonne shook her head. "Sorry, no. Do you think I should go back and look again? It's all in the way it's arranged in the kitty litter," she confided. "Just like tea leaves."

"Probably not." K.O. didn't want to be responsible for her neighbor sifting through Tom's "business" any more than necessary.

"I'll concentrate on your job prospects next."

"Great." K.O. was far more interested in locating full-time employment than falling in love. At twenty-eight she wasn't in a rush, although it *was* admittedly time to start thinking about a serious relationship. Besides, working at home wasn't conducive to meeting men. Zelda seemed to think that as a medical transcriptionist K.O. would meet any number of eligible physicians. That, however, hadn't turned out to be the case. The only person in a white coat she'd encountered in the last six months had been her dentist, and he'd been more interested in looking at her X-rays than at her.

"Before I forget," LaVonne said, getting ready to leave. "I'd like you to come over tomorrow for cocktails and appetizers."

"Sure." It wasn't as if her social calendar was crowded. "Thanks."

"I'll see you at six." LaVonne let herself out.

"Concentrate on seeing a job for me," K.O. reminded her, sticking her head in the hallway. "The next time you empty the litter box, I mean."

LaVonne nodded. "I will," she said. As she left, she was mumbling to herself, something K.O. couldn't hear.

The following morning, K.O. set up her laptop on a window table in the French Café, determined to wait for Dr. Jeffries. Now she felt obliged to get his autograph, despite her disapproval of his methods. More importantly, she had to talk to him about Christmas. This clueless man was destroying Christmas for her nieces—and for hundreds of thousands of other kids.

She had no intention of knocking on his door. No, this had to seem unplanned. An accidental meeting. Her one hope was that Wynn Jeffries was hooked on his morning latte. Since this was Seattle, she felt fairly certain he was. Nearly everyone in the entire state of Washington seemed to be a coffee addict.

In an effort to use her time productively, K.O.

started work on the Mulcahy Christmas letter, all the while reminding herself that he was paying her double. She had two ideas about how to approach the situation. The first was comical, telling the truth in an outlandish manner and letting the reader assume it was some sort of macabre humor.

Merry Christmas from the Mulcahys, K.O. wrote. She bit her lip and pushed away a strand of long blond hair that had escaped from her ponytail. *Bill and I have had a challenging year. Mason sends greetings from the juvenile detention center where he's currently incarcerated. Julie is pregnant and we pray she doesn't marry the father. Bill, at least, is doing well, although he's worried about paying for the mental care facility where I'm receiving outpatient therapy.*

K.O. groaned. This *wasn't* humorous, macabre or otherwise. It was difficult to turn the Mulcahys' disastrous year into comedy, especially since the letter was purportedly coming from them.

She deleted the paragraph and tried her second approach.

Merry Christmas from the Mulcahys, and what an—interesting? unexpected? unusual?—year it has been for our lovely family. K.O. decided on *eventful. Bill and I are so proud of our children, especially now as they approach adulthood. Where have all the years gone?*

Mason had an opportunity he couldn't turn down and is currently away at school. Our son is maturing into a fine young man and is wisely accepting guidance from authority figures. Our sweet Julie is in her second year of college. She and her boyfriend have decided to deepen their relationship. Who knows, there might be wedding bells—and perhaps even a baby—in our daughter's future.

So intent was she on putting a positive spin on the sad details of Bill Mulcahy's year that she nearly missed Wynn Jeffries. When she looked up, it was just in time to see Dr. Jeffries walk to the counter. K.O. leaped to her feet and nearly upset her peppermint mocha, an extravagance she couldn't really afford. She remained standing until he'd collected his drink and then straightening, hurried toward him.

"Dr. Jeffries?" she asked, beaming a winsome smile. She'd practiced this very smile in front of the mirror before job interviews. After her recent cleaning at the dentist's, K.O. hoped she didn't blind him with her flashing white teeth.

"Yes?"

"You are Dr. Jeffries, Dr. Wynn Jeffries?"

"I am." He seemed incredibly tall as he stood in front of her. She purposely blocked his way to the door.

K.O. thrust out her hand. "I'm Katherine O'Connor. We live in the same building."

He smiled and shook her hand, then glanced around her. He seemed eager to escape.

"I can't tell you what a surprise it was when LaVonne pointed out that the author of *The Free Child* lived in our building."

"You know LaVonne Young?"

"Well, yes, she's my neighbor. Yours, too," K.O. added. "Would you care to join me?" She gestured toward her table and the empty chairs. This time of day, it was rare to find a free table. She didn't volunteer the fact that she'd set up shop two hours earlier in the hope of bumping into him.

He checked his watch as if to say he really didn't have time to spare.

"I understand _The Free Child_ has hit every bestseller list in the country." Flattery just might work.

Wynn hesitated. "Yes, I've been most fortunate."

True, but the parents and children of America had been most _un_fortunate in her view. She wasn't going to mention that, though. At least not yet. She pulled out her chair on the assumption that he wouldn't refuse her.

He joined her, with obvious reluctance. "I think I've seen you around," he said, and sipped his latte.

It astonished her that he knew who she was, while she'd been oblivious to his presence. "My sister is a very big fan of yours. She was thrilled when she heard I might be able to get your autograph."

"She's very kind."

"Her life has certainly changed since she read your book," K.O. commented, reaching for her mocha.

He shrugged with an air of modesty. "I've heard that quite a few times."

"Changed for the _worse_," K.O. muttered.

He blinked. "I beg your pardon?"

She couldn't contain herself any longer. "You want to take Santa away from my nieces! _Santa Claus._ Where's your heart? Do you know there are children all over America being deprived of Christmas because of _you_?" Her voice grew loud with the strength of her convictions.

Wynn glanced nervously about the room.

K.O. hadn't realized how animated she'd become until she noticed that everyone in the entire café had stopped talking and was staring in their direction.

Wynn hurriedly stood and turned toward the door, probably attempting to flee before she could embarrass him further.

"You're no better than...than Jim Carrey," K.O. wailed. She meant to say the Grinch who stole Christmas but it was the actor's name that popped out. He'd played the character in a movie a few years ago.

"Jim Carrey?" He turned back to face her.

"Worse. You're a...a regular Charles Dickens." She meant Scrooge, darn it. But it didn't matter if, in the heat of her anger, she couldn't remember the names. She just wanted to embarrass him. "That man," she said, stabbing an accusatory finger at Wynn, "wants to bury Santa Claus under the sleigh."

Not bothering to look back, Wynn tore open the café door and rushed into the street. "Good riddance!" K.O. cried and sank down at the table, only to discover that everyone in the room was staring at her.

"He doesn't believe in Christmas," she explained and then calmly returned to the Mulcahys' letter.

The confrontation with Wynn Jeffries didn't go well, K.O. admitted as she changed out of her jeans and sweater later that same afternoon. When LaVonne invited her over for appetizers and drinks, K.O. hadn't asked if this was a formal party or if it would be just the two of them. Unwilling to show up in casual attire if her neighbor intended a more formal event, K.O. chose tailored black slacks, a white silk blouse and a red velvet blazer with a Christmas tree pin she'd inherited from her grandmother. The blouse was her very best. Generally she wore her hair tied back, but this evening she kept it down, loosely sweeping up one side and securing it with a rhinestone barrette. A little lip gloss and mascara, and she was ready to go.

A few minutes after six, she crossed the hall and rang LaVonne's doorbell. As if she'd been standing there waiting, LaVonne opened her door instantly.

K.O. was relieved she'd taken the time to change. Her neighbor looked lovely in a long skirt and black jacket with any number of gold chains dangling around her neck and at least a dozen gold bangles on her wrists.

"Katherine!" she cried, sounding as though it'd been weeks since they'd last spoken. "Do come in and meet Dr. Wynn Jeffries." She stepped back and held open the door and, with a flourish, gestured her inside.

Wynn Jeffries stood in the center of the room. He held a cracker raised halfway to his mouth, his eyes darting to and fro. He seemed to be gauging how fast he could make his exit.

Oh, dear. K.O. felt guilty about the scene she'd caused that morning.

"I believe we've met," Wynn said stiffly. He set the cracker down on his napkin and eyed the door.

Darn the man. He looked positively gorgeous, just the way he did on the book's dust jacket. This was exceedingly unfair. She didn't *want* to like him and she certainly didn't want to be attracted to him, which, unfortunately she was. Not that it mattered. She wasn't interested and after their confrontation that morning, he wouldn't be, either.

"Dr. Jeffries," K.O. murmured uneasily as she walked into the room, hands clasped together.

He nodded in her direction, then slowly inched closer to the door.

Apparently oblivious to the tension between them, LaVonne glided to the sideboard, where she had wine and liquor bottles set on a silver platter. Sparkling wineglasses and crystal goblets awaited their decision. "What can I pour for you?" she asked.

"I wouldn't mind a glass of merlot, if you have it," K.O. said, all the while wondering how best to handle this awkward situation.

"I do." LaVonne turned to Wynn. "And you, Dr. Jeffries?"

He looked away from K.O. and moved to stand behind the sofa. "Whiskey on the rocks."

"Coming right up."

"Can I help?" K.O. asked, welcoming any distraction.

"No, no, you two are my guests." And then as if to clear up any misconception, she added, "My *only* guests."

"Oh," K.O. whispered. A sick feeling attacked the pit of her stomach. She didn't glance at Wynn but suspected he was no more pleased at the prospect than she was.

A moment later, LaVonne brought their drinks and indicated that they should both sit down.

K.O. accepted the wine and Wynn took his drink.

With her own goblet in hand, LaVonne claimed the overstuffed chair, which left the sofa vacant. Evidently Dr. Jeffries was not eager to sit; neither was K.O. Finally she chose one end of the davenport and Wynn sat as far from her as humanly possible. Each faced away from the other.

"Wynn, I see you tried the crab dip," LaVonne

commented, referring to the appetizers on the coffee table in front of them.

"It's the best I've ever tasted," he said, reaching for another cracker.

"I'm glad you enjoyed it. The recipe came from Katherine."

He set the cracker down and brushed the crumbs from his fingers, apparently afraid he was about to be poisoned.

K.O. sipped her wine in an effort to relax. She had a feeling that even if she downed the entire bottle, it wasn't going to help.

"I imagine you're wondering why I invited you here this evening," LaVonne said. Phillip, her white Persian, strolled regally into the room, his tail raised, and with one powerful thrust of his hind legs, leaped into her lap. LaVonne ran her hand down the length of his body, stroking his long, white fur. "It happened again," she announced, slowly enunciating the words.

"What happened?" Wynn asked, then gulped his drink.

Dramatically, LaVonne closed her eyes. "The sight."

Obviously not understanding, Wynn glanced at K.O., his forehead wrinkled.

"LaVonne took a class this week on unleashing your psychic abilities," K.O. explained under her breath.

Wynn thanked her for the explanation with a weak smile.

LaVonne's shoulders rose. "I have been gifted with the sight," she said in hushed tones.

"Congratulations," Wynn offered tentatively.

"She can read cat litter," K.O. told him.

"That's not all," LaVonne said, raising one hand. "As I said, it happened again. This morning."

"Not with the litter box?" K.O. asked.

"No." A distant look came over LaVonne as she fixed her gaze on some point across the room.

Peering over her shoulder, K.O. tried to figure out what her neighbor was staring at. She couldn't tell—unless it was the small decorated Christmas tree.

"I was eating my Raisin Bran and then, all of a sudden, I knew." She turned slightly to meet K.O.'s eyes. "The bran flakes separated, and that was when two raisins bobbed to the surface."

"You saw...the future?" K.O. asked.

"What she saw," Wynn muttered, "was two raisins in the milk."

LaVonne raised her hand once more, silencing them. "I saw the *future*. It was written in the Raisin Bran even more clearly than it'd been in the cat litter." She pointed a finger at K.O. "Katherine, it involved *you*."

"Me." She swallowed, not sure whether to laugh or simply shake her head.

"And you." LaVonne's finger swerved toward Wynn. Her voice was low and intent.

"Did it tell you Katherine would do her utmost to make a fool of me at the French Café?" Wynn asked. He scooped up a handful of mixed nuts.

As far as K.O. was concerned, *nuts* was an appropriate response to her neighbor's fortune-telling.

LaVonne dropped her hand. "No." She turned to K.O. with a reproachful frown. "Katherine, what did you do?"

"I..." Flustered she looked away. "Did...did you know Dr. Jeffries doesn't believe in Santa Claus?" There, it was in the open now.

"My dear girl," LaVonne said with a light laugh. "I hate to be the one to disillusion you, but there actually *isn't* a Santa."

"There is if you're five years old," she countered, glaring at the man on the other end of the sofa. "Dr. Jeffries is ruining Christmas for children everywhere." The man deserved to be publicly ridiculed. Reconsidering, she revised the thought. "He should be censured by his peers for even *suggesting* that Santa be buried under the sleigh."

"It appears you two have a minor difference of opinion," LaVonne said, understating the obvious.

"I sincerely doubt Katherine has read my entire book."

"I don't need to," she said. "My sister quotes you chapter and verse in nearly every conversation we have."

"This is the sister who asked for my autograph?"

"Yes," K.O. admitted. Like most men, she concluded, Dr. Jeffries wasn't immune to flattery.

"She's the one with the children?"

K.O. nodded.

"Do you have children?"

LaVonne answered for her. "Katherine is single, the same as you, Wynn."

"Why doesn't that surprise me?" he returned.

K.O. thought she might have detected a smirk in his reply. "It doesn't surprise me that you're single, either," she said, elevating her chin. "No woman in her right mind—"

"My dears," LaVonne murmured. "You're being silly."

K.O. didn't respond, and neither did Wynn. "Don't you want to hear what I saw in my cereal?"

Phillip purred contentedly as LaVonne continued to stroke his fluffy white fur.

"The future came to me and I saw—" she paused for effect "—I saw the two of you. Together."

"Arguing?" Wynn asked.

"No, no, you were in love. Deeply, deeply in love."

K.O. placed her hand over her heart and gasped, and then almost immediately that remark struck her as the most comical thing she'd ever heard. The fact that LaVonne was reading her future, first in cat litter and now Raisin Bran, was ridiculous enough, but to match K.O. up with Wynn— It was too much. She broke into peals of laughter. Pressing her hand over her mouth, she made an effort to restrain her giggles.

Wynn looked at her curiously.

LaVonne frowned. "I'm serious, Katherine."

"I'm sorry. I don't mean to be rude. LaVonne, you're my friend and my neighbor, but I'm sorry, it'll never happen. Never in a million years."

Wynn straightened. "While Katherine and I clearly don't see eye to eye on any number of issues, I tend to agree with her on this."

LaVonne sighed expressively. "Our instructor, Madam Ozma, warned us this would happen," she said with an air of sadness. "Unbelievers."

"It isn't that I don't believe you," K.O. rushed to add. She didn't want to offend LaVonne, whose friendship she treasured, but at the same time she found it difficult to play along with this latest idea of hers. Still, the possibility of a romance with just about anyone else would have suited her nicely.

"Wynn?" LaVonne said. "May I ask how you feel about Katherine?"

"Well, I didn't officially meet her until this morning."

"I might've given him the wrong impression," K.O. began. "But—"

"No," he said swiftly. "I think I got the right impression. You don't agree with me and I had the feeling that for some reason you don't like me."

"True…well, not exactly. I don't know you well enough to like *or* dislike you."

LaVonne clapped her hands. "Perfect! This is just perfect."

Both K.O. and Wynn turned to her. "You don't really know each other, isn't that correct?" she asked.

"Correct," Wynn replied. "I've seen Katherine around the building and on Blossom Street occasionally, but we've never spoken—until the unfortunate incident this morning."

K.O. felt a little flustered. "We didn't start off on the right foot." Then she said in a conciliatory voice, "I'm generally not as confrontational as I was earlier today. I might've gotten a bit…carried away. I apologize." She did feel guilty for having embarrassed him and, in the process, herself.

Wynn's dark eyebrows arched, as if to say he was pleasantly surprised by her admission of fault.

"We all, at one time or another, say things we later regret," LaVonne said, smiling down on Phillip. She raised her eyes to K.O. "Isn't that right, Katherine?"

"Yes, I suppose so."

"And some of us," she went on, looking at Wynn, "make hasty judgments."

He hesitated. "Yes. However in this case—"

"That's why," LaVonne said, interrupting him, "I took the liberty of making a dinner reservation for the two of you. Tonight—at seven-thirty. An hour from now."

"A dinner reservation," K.O. repeated. Much as she liked and respected her neighbor, there was a limit to what she was willing to do.

"It's out of the question," Wynn insisted.

"I appreciate what you're doing, but…" K.O. turned to Wynn for assistance.

"I do, as well," he chimed in. "It's a lovely gesture on your part. Unfortunately, I have other plans for this evening."

"So do I." All right, K.O.'s plans included eating in front of the television and watching *Jeopardy,* and while those activities might not be anything out of the ordinary, they did happen to be her plans.

"Oh, dear." LaVonne exhaled loudly. "Chef Jerome Ray will be so disappointed not to meet my friends."

If Wynn didn't recognize the name, K.O. certainly did. "You know Chef Jerome Ray?"

"Of Chez Jerome?" Wynn inserted.

"Oh, yes. I did his taxes for years and years. What most people don't realize is that Jerome is no flash in the pan, if you'll excuse the pun. In fact, it took him twenty years to become an overnight success."

The Seattle chef had his own cooking show on the Food Network, which had become an immediate hit. His techniques with fresh seafood had taken the country by storm. The last K.O. had heard, it took months to get a reservation at Chez Jerome.

"I talked to Jerome this afternoon and he said that as a personal favor to me, he would personally see to your dinner."

"Ah…" K.O. looked at Wynn and weighed her options.

"Dinner's already paid for," LaVonne said in an encouraging voice, "and it would be a shame to let it go to waste."

A nuked frozen entrée and *Jeopardy*, versus one dinner with a slightly contentious man in a restaurant that would make her the envy of her friends. "I might be able to rearrange my plans," K.O. said after clearing her throat. Normally she was a woman of conviction. But in these circumstances, for a fabulous free dinner, she was willing to compromise.

"I think I can do the same," Wynn muttered.

LaVonne smiled brightly and clapped her hands. "Excellent. I was hoping you'd say that."

"With certain stipulations," Wynn added.

"Yes," K.O. said. "There would need to be stipulations."

Wynn scowled at her. "We will *not* discuss my book or my child-rearing philosophies."

"All right," she agreed. That sounded fair. "And we'll...we'll—" She couldn't think of any restriction of her own, so she said, "We refuse to overeat." At Wynn's frown, she explained, "I'm sort of watching my weight."

He nodded as though he understood, which she was sure he didn't. What man really did?

"All I care about is that the two of you have a marvelous dinner, but I know you will." LaVonne smiled at them both. "The raisins have already assured me of that." She studied her watch, gently dislodged Phillip and stood. "You'll need to leave right away. The reservation's under my name," she said and ushered them out the door.

Before she could protest or comment, K.O. found herself standing in the hallway with Wynn Jeffries, her dinner date.

Chapter

4

I f nothing else, K.O. felt this dinner would afford
her the opportunity to learn about Wynn. Well, that
and an exceptional dining experience, of course.
Something in his background must have prompted a
child-rearing ideology that in her opinion was completely impractical and threatened to create a generation of spoiled, self-involved brats. Although she didn't
have children of her own, K.O. had seen the effect on
her nieces ever since Zelda had read that darn book. She
was astonished by how far her sister had been willing to
go in following the book's precepts, and wondered if
Zach understood the full extent of Zelda's devotion to
The Free Child. Her brother-in-law was quite the worka-
holic. He was absorbed in his job and often stayed late
into the evenings and worked weekends.

Chez Jerome was only a few blocks from Blossom Street, so K.O. and Wynn decided to walk. She retrieved a full-length red wool coat from her condo while Wynn waited outside the building. The moment she joined him, she was hit by a blast of cold air. A shiver went through her, and she hunched her shoulders against the wind. To her surprise, Wynn changed places with her, walking by the curb, outside the shelter of the buildings, taking the brunt of the wind. It was an old-fashioned gentlemanly action and one she hadn't expected. To be fair, she didn't know *what* to expect from him. With that realization came another. He didn't know her, either.

They didn't utter a single word for the first block.

"Perhaps we should start over," she suggested.

Wynn stopped walking and regarded her suspiciously. "You want to go back? Did you forget something?"

"No, I meant you and me."

"How so?" He kept his hands buried in the pockets of his long overcoat.

"Hello," she began. "My name is Katherine O'Connor, but most people call me K.O. I don't believe we've met."

He frowned. "We did earlier," he said.

"This is pretend." Did the man have to be so literal? "I want you to erase this morning from your memory and pretend we're meeting for the first time."

"What about drinks at LaVonne's? Should I forget that, too?"

"Well." She needed to think this over. That hadn't

been such a positive experience, either. "Perhaps it would be best," she told him.

"So you want me to act as if this is a blind date?" he asked.

"A blind date," she repeated and immediately shook her head. "I've had so many of those, I need a Seeing Eye dog."

He laughed, and the sound of it was rich and melodious. "Me, too."

"You?" A man this attractive and successful required assistance meeting women?

"You wouldn't believe how many friends have a compulsion to introduce me to *the woman of my dreams.*"

"My friends say the same thing. *This* is the man you've been waiting to meet your entire life. Ninety-nine percent of the time, it's a disaster."

"Really? Even you?" He seemed a little shocked that she'd had help from her matchmaking friends.

"What do you mean *even you?*"

"You're blond and beautiful—I thought you were joking about those blind dates."

She swallowed a gasp of surprise. However, if that was the way he saw her, she wasn't going to argue.

He thrust out his hand. "Hello, Katherine, my name is Jim Carrey."

She laughed and they shook hands. They continued walking at a leisurely pace, and soon they were having a lively conversation, exchanging dating horror stories. She laughed quite a few times, which was something she'd never dreamed she'd do with Wynn Jeffries.

"Would you mind if I called you Katherine?" he asked.

"Not at all. Do you prefer Wynn or Dr. Jeffries?"

"Wynn."

"I've heard absolutely marvelous things about Chez Jerome," she said. Not only that, some friends of K.O.'s had recently phoned to make dinner reservations and were told the first available opening was in May.

"LaVonne is certainly full of surprises," Wynn remarked. "Who would've guessed she had a connection with one of the most popular chefs in the country?"

They arrived at the restaurant, and Wynn held the door for her, another gentlemanly courtesy that made her smile. This psychologist wasn't what she'd expected at all. After hearing his theories about Christmas, she'd been sure he must be a real curmudgeon. But in the short walk from Blossom Street to the restaurant, he'd disproved almost every notion she'd had about him. Or at least about his personality. His beliefs were still a point of contention.

When Wynn mentioned LaVonne's name to the maître d', they were ushered to a secluded booth. "Welcome to Chez Jerome," the man said with a dignified bow.

K.O. opened her menu and had just started to read it when Jerome himself appeared at their table. "Ah, so you are LaVonne's friends."

K.O. didn't mean to gush, but this was a real honor. "I am so excited to meet you," she said. She could hardly wait to tell Zelda about this—even though her sister would be far more impressed by her meeting Wynn Jeffries than Jerome.

The chef, in his white hat and apron, kissed her hand. The entire restaurant seemed to be staring at them and whispering, wondering who they were to warrant a visit from the renowned chef.

"You won't need those," Jerome said and ostentatiously removed the tasseled menus from their hands. "I am preparing a meal for you personally. If you do not fall in love after what I have cooked, then there is no hope for either of you."

Wynn caught her eye and smiled. Despite herself, K.O. smiled back. After a bit of small talk, Jerome returned to the kitchen.

Once the chef had gone, Wynn leaned toward her and teased, "He makes it sound as if dinner is marinated in Love Potion Number Nine." To emphasize the point, he sang a few lines from the old song.

K.O. smothered a giggle. She hated to admit it, but rarely had she been in a more romantic setting, with the elegant linens, flattering candlelight and soft classical music. The mood was flawless; so was their dinner, all four courses, even though she couldn't identify the exact nature of everything they ate. The appetizer was some kind of soup, served in a martini glass, and it tasted a bit like melted sherbet. Later, when their waiter told them the soup featured sea urchin, K.O. considered herself fortunate not to have known. If she had, she might not have tasted it. But, in fact, it was delicious.

"Tell me about yourself," she said to Wynn when the soup dishes were taken away and the salads, which featured frilly greens and very tart berries, were delivered.

He shrugged, as though he didn't really have anything of interest to share. "What would you like to know?"

"How about your family?"

"All right." He leaned back against the luxurious velvet cushion. "I'm an only child. My mother died three years ago. My father is Max Jeffries." He paused, obviously waiting to see if she recognized the name and when she didn't, he continued. "He was a surfer who made a name for himself back in the late sixties and early seventies."

She shook her head. Surfing wasn't an activity she knew much about, but then she really wasn't into sports. Or exercise, either. "My dad's the captain of his bowling team," she told him.

He nodded. "My parents were hippies." He grinned. "True, bona fide, unreconstructed hippies."

"As in the Age of Aquarius, free love and that sort of thing?" This explained quite a bit, now that she thought about it. Wynn had apparently been raised without boundaries himself and had turned out to be a successful and even responsible adult. Maybe he figured that would be true of any child raised according to his methods.

Wynn nodded again. "Dad made it rich when he was awarded a patent for his surfboard wax. Ever heard of Max's Waxes?" He sipped his wine, a lovely mellow pinot gris. K.O. did, too, savoring every swallow.

"I chose my own name when I was ten," he murmured.

It was hardly necessary to say he'd lived an unconventional life. "Why did you decide on Wynn?" she asked, since it seemed an unusual first name.

"It was my mother's maiden name."

"I like it."

"Katherine is a beautiful name," he commented. "A beautiful name for a beautiful woman."

If he didn't stop looking at her like that, K.O. was convinced she'd melt. This romantic rush was more intense than anything she'd ever experienced. She wasn't even prepared to *like* Wynn, and already she could feel herself falling for this son of a hippie. In an effort to break his spell, she forced herself to look away.

"Where did you grow up?" she asked as their entrées were ceremoniously presented. Grilled scallops with wild rice and tiny Brussels sprouts with even tinier onions.

"California," he replied. "I attended Berkeley."

"I lived a rather conventional life," she said after swooning over her first bite. "Regular family, one sister, two parents. I studied to become a medical transcriptionist, worked for a while and returned to college. I have a degree in public relations, but I'm currently working from home as a transcriptionist while looking for full-time employment. I'd really like to work as a publicist, but those jobs are rare and the pay isn't all that great." She closed her eyes. "Mmm. I think this is the best meal I've ever had." And she wasn't referring *just* to the food.

He smiled. "Me, too."

A few minutes later, he asked, "Your sister is married with children?"

"Identical twin girls. Zoe and Zara. I'm their godmother." When she discussed the twins, she became animated, telling him story after story. "They're delightful," she finally said. Dessert and coffee arrived then. An unusual cranberry crème brûlée, in honor of the season, and cups of exquisite coffee.

"So you like children?" Wynn asked when they'd made serious progress with their desserts.

"Oh, yes," she said, then added a qualifier, "especially well-behaved children."

His eyebrows arched.

Seeing how easy it was to get sidetracked, she said, "I think children are a subject we should avoid."

"I agree." But Wynn's expression was good-natured, and she could tell he hadn't taken offense.

Even after a two-and-a-half-hour dinner, K.O. was reluctant to leave. She found Wynn truly fascinating. His stories about living in a commune, his surfing adventures—including an encounter with a shark off the coast of Australia—and his travels kept her enthralled. "This has been the most wonderful evening," she told him. Beneath the polished exterior was a remarkable human being. She found him engaging and unassuming and, shock of shocks, *likeable.*

After being assured by Jerome that their meal had already been taken care of, Wynn left a generous tip. After fervent thanks and a protracted farewell, they collected their coats. Wynn helped K.O. on with hers, then she wrapped her scarf around her neck.

When they ventured into the night, they saw that snow had begun to fall. The Seattle streets were decorated for the season with sparkling white lights on the bare trees. The scene was as festive as one could imagine. A horse-drawn carriage passed them, the horse's hooves clopping on the pavement, its harness jingling.

"Shall we?" Wynn asked.

K.O. noticed that the carriage was traveling in the opposite direction from theirs, but she couldn't have cared less. For as long as she could remember, she'd wanted a carriage ride. "That would be lovely." Not only was Wynn a gentleman, but a romantic, as well, which seemed quite incongruous with his free-and-easy upbringing.

Wynn hailed the driver. Then he handed K.O. into the carriage before joining her. He took the lap robe, spread it across her legs, and slipped his arm around her shoulders. It felt like the most natural thing in the world to be in his embrace.

"I love Christmas," K.O. confessed.

Wynn didn't respond, which was probably for the best, since he'd actually put in writing that he wanted to bury Santa Claus.

The driver flicked the reins and the carriage moved forward.

"It might surprise you to know that I happen to feel the same way you do about the holidays."

"But you said—"

He brought a finger to her lips. "We agreed not to discuss my book."

"Yes, but I *have* to know...."

"Then I suggest you read *The Free Child*. You'll understand my philosophies better once you do. Simply put, I feel it's wrong to mislead children. That's all I really said. Can you honestly object to that?"

"If it involves Santa, I can."

"Then we'll have to agree to disagree."

She was happy to leave that subject behind. The evening was perfect, absolutely perfect, and she didn't want anything to ruin it. With large flakes of snow drifting down and the horse clopping steadily along, the carriage swaying, it couldn't have been more romantic.

Wynn tightened his arm around her and K.O. pressed her head against his shoulder.

"I'm beginning to think LaVonne knows her Raisin Bran," Wynn whispered.

She heard the smile in his voice. "And her cat litter," she whispered back.

"I like her cats," he said. "Tom, Phillip and…"

"Martin," she supplied. The men in her neighbor's life all happened to be badly spoiled and much-loved cats.

The carriage dropped them off near West Lake Center. Wynn got down first and then helped K.O. "Are you cold?" he asked. "I can try to find a cab if you'd prefer not to walk."

"Stop," she said suddenly. All this perfection was confusing, too shocking a contrast with her previous impressions of Dr. Wynn Jeffries.

He frowned.

"I don't know if I can deal with this." She started walking at a fast pace, her mind spinning. It was difficult to reconcile this thoughtful, interesting man with the hardhearted destroyer of Christmas Zelda had told her about.

"Deal with *what?*" he asked, catching up with her.

"You—you're wonderful."

He laughed. "That's bad?"

"It's not what I expected from you."

His steps matched hers. "After this morning, I wasn't sure what to expect from you, either. There's a big difference between the way you acted then and how you've been this evening. *I* didn't change. You did."

"I know." She looked up at him, wishing she understood what was happening. She recognized attraction when she felt it, but could this be real?

He reached for her hand and tucked it in the crook of his arm. "Does it matter?" he asked.

"Not for tonight," she said with a sigh.

"Good." They resumed walking, more slowly this time. She stuck out her tongue to catch the falling snow, the way she had as a child. Wynn did, too, and they both smiled, delighted with themselves and each other.

When they approached their building on Blossom Street, K.O. was almost sad. She didn't want the evening to end for fear she'd wake in the morning and discover it had all been a dream. Worse, she was afraid she'd find out it was just an illusion created by candlelight and gorgeous food and an enchanting carriage ride.

She felt Wynn's reluctance as he keyed in the door code. The warmth that greeted them inside the small lobby was a welcome respite from the cold and the wind. The Christmas lights in the lobby twinkled merrily as he escorted her to her door.

"Thank you for one of the most romantic evenings of my life," she told him sincerely.

"I should be the one thanking you," he whispered. He held her gaze for a long moment. "May I see you again?"

She nodded. But she wasn't sure that was wise. "When?"

K.O. leaned against her door and held her hand to her forehead. The spell was wearing off. *"I don't think this is a good idea."* That was what she'd *intended* to say. Instead, when she opened her mouth, the words that popped out were, "I'm pretty much free all week."

He reached inside his overcoat for a PDA. "Tomorrow?"

"Okay." How could she agree so quickly, so impulsively? Every rational thought told her this relationship wasn't going to work. At some point—probably sooner rather than later—she'd have to acknowledge that they had practically nothing in common.

"Six?" he suggested.

With her mind screaming at her to put an end to this *now,* K.O. pulled out her Day-Timer and checked her schedule. Ah, the perfect excuse. She already had a commitment. "Sorry, it looks like I'm booked. I have a friend who's part of the Figgy Pudding contest."

"I beg your pardon?"

"Figgy Pudding is a competition for singing groups. It's a fund-raising event," she explained, remembering that he was relatively new to the area. "I told Vickie I'd come and cheer her on." Then, before she could stop herself, she added, "Want to join me?"

Wynn nodded. "Sure. Why not."

"Great." But it wasn't great. During her most recent visit with Vickie, K.O. had ranted about Dr. Jeffries for at least ten minutes. And now she was going to be introducing her friend to the man she'd claimed was ruining America. Introducing him as her...*date?*

She had to get out of this.

Then Wynn leaned forward and pressed his mouth to hers. It was such a nice kiss, undemanding and sweet. Romantic, too, just as the entire evening had been. In that moment, she knew exactly what was happening and why, and it terrified her. She liked Wynn. Okay, *really* liked him. Despite his crackpot theories and their total lack of compatibility. And it wasn't simply that they'd spent a delightful evening together. A charmed evening. No, this had all the hallmarks of a dangerous infatuation. Or worse.

Wynn Jeffries! Who would've thought it?

Chapter
5

The phone woke K.O. out of a dead sleep. She rolled over, glanced at the clock on her nightstand and groaned. It was already past eight. Lying on her stomach, she reached for the phone and hoped it wasn't a potential employer, asking her to come in for an interview that morning. Actually, she prayed it *was* a job interview but one with more notice.

"Good morning," she said in her best business-like voice.

"Katherine, it's LaVonne. I didn't phone too early, did I?"

In one easy motion, K.O. drew herself into a sitting position, swinging her legs off the bed. "Not at all." She rubbed her face with one hand and stifled a yawn.

"So," her neighbor breathed excitedly. "How'd it go?"

K.O. needed a moment to consider her response. LaVonne was obviously asking about her evening with Wynn; however, she hadn't had time to analyze it yet. "Dinner was incredible," she offered and hoped that would satisfy her friend's curiosity.

"Of course dinner was incredible. Jerome promised me it would be. I'm talking about you and Wynn. He's very nice, don't you think? Did you notice the way he couldn't take his eyes off you? Didn't I tell you? It's just as I saw in the kitty litter and the Raisin Bran. You two are *meant* for each other."

"Well," K.O. mumbled, not knowing which question to answer first. She'd prefer to avoid them all. She quickly reviewed the events of the evening and was forced to admit one thing. "Wynn wasn't anything like I expected."

"He said the same about you."

"You've talked to him?" If K.O. wasn't awake before, she certainly was now. "What did he say?" she asked in a rush, not caring that LaVonne would realize how interested she was.

"Exactly that," LaVonne said. "Wynn told me you were nothing like he expected. He didn't know what to think when you walked into my condo. He was afraid the evening would end with someone calling the police—and then he had a stupendous night. That was the word he used—*stupendous.*"

"Really." K.O. positively glowed with pleasure.

"He had the look when he said it, too."

"What look?"

"The *look*," LaVonne repeated, emphasizing the word, "of a man who's falling in love. You had a good time, didn't you?"

"I did." K.O. doubted she could have lied. She *did* have a wonderful evening. Shockingly wonderful, in fact, and that made everything ten times worse. She wanted to view Wynn as a lunatic confounding young parents, a grinch out to steal Christmas from youngsters all across America. How could she berate him and detest him if she was in danger of falling in love with him? This was getting worse and worse.

"I knew it!" LaVonne sounded downright gleeful. "From the moment I saw those raisins floating in the milk, I knew. The vision told me everything."

"Everything?"

"Everything," LaVonne echoed. "It came to me, as profound as anything I've seen with my psychic gift. You and Dr. Jeffries are perfect together."

K.O. buried her face in her hand. She'd fallen asleep in a haze of wonder and awakened to the shrill ring of her phone. She couldn't explain last night's feelings in any rational way.

She wasn't attracted to Wynn, she told herself. How could she be? The man who believed children should set their own rules? The man who wanted to eliminate Santa Claus? But she was beginning to understand what was going on here. For weeks she'd been stuck inside her condo, venturing outside only to meet Christmas-letter clients. If she wasn't transcribing medical records, she was filling out job applications. With such a lack of human contact, it was only natural that she'd be swept along on the tide of romance LaVonne had so expertly arranged for her.

"Wynn told me you were seeing him again this evening," LaVonne said eagerly.

"I am?" K.O. vaguely remembered that. "Oh, right, I am." Her mind cleared and her memory fell into place like an elevator suddenly dropping thirteen floors. "Yes, as it happens," she said, trying to think of a way out of this. "I invited Wynn to accompany me to the Figgy Pudding event at West Lake Plaza." She'd *invited* him. What was she thinking? *What was she thinking?* Mentally she slapped her hand against her forehead. Before this afternoon, she had to find an excuse to cancel.

"He's very sweet, isn't he?" LaVonne said.

"He is." K.O. didn't want to acknowledge it but he was. He'd done it on purpose; she just didn't know *why*. What was his purpose in breaking down her defenses?

She needed to think. She pulled her feet up onto the bed and wrapped one arm around her knees. He *had* been sweet and alarmingly wonderful. Oh, he was clever. But what was behind all that charm? Nothing good, she'd bet.

"I have more to tell you," LaVonne said, lowering her voice to a mere whisper. "It happened again this morning." She paused. "I was feeding the boys."

K.O. had half a mind to stop her friend, but for some perverse reason she didn't.

"And then," LaVonne added, her voice gaining volume, "when I poured the dry cat food into their bowls, some of it spilled on the floor."

"You got a reading from the cat food?" K.O. supposed this shouldn't surprise her. Since LaVonne had taken that class, everything imaginable provided her with insight—mostly, it seemed, into K.O.'s life. Her love life, which to this point had been a blank slate.

"Would you like to know how many children you and Wynn are going to have?" LaVonne asked triumphantly.

"Any twins?" K.O. asked, playing along. She might as well. LaVonne was determined to tell her, whether she wanted to hear or not.

"Twins," LaVonne repeated in dismay. "Oh, my goodness, I didn't look that closely."

"That's fine."

LaVonne took her seriously. "Still, twins are definitely a possibility. Sure as anything, I saw three children. Multiple births run in your family, don't they? Because it might've been triplets."

"Triplets?" It was too hard to think about this without her morning cup of coffee. "Listen, I need to get off the phone. I'll check in with you later," K.O. promised.

"Good. You'll give me regular updates, won't you?"

"On the triplets?"

"No," LaVonne returned, laughing. "On you and Wynn. The babies come later."

"Okay," she said, resigned to continuing the charade. Everything might've been delightful and romantic the night before, but this was a whole new day. She was beginning to figure out his agenda. She'd criticized his beliefs, especially about Christmas, and now he was determined to change hers. It was all a matter of pride. *Male* pride.

She'd been vulnerable, she realized. The dinner, the wine, Chef Jerome, a carriage ride, walking in the snow. *Christmas.* He'd actually used Christmas to weaken her resolve. The very man who was threatening to destroy the holiday for children had practically seduced her in Seattle's winter wonderland. What she recognized now was that in those circumstances, she would've experienced the same emotions with just about any man.

As was her habit, K.O. weighed herself first thing and gasped when she saw she was up two pounds. That fabulous dinner had come at a price. Two pounds. K.O. had to keep a constant eye on her weight, unlike her sister. Zelda was naturally thin whereas K.O. wasn't. Her only successful strategy for maintaining her weight was to weigh herself daily and then make adjustments in her diet.

Even before she'd finished putting on her workout gear, the phone rang again. K.O. could always hope that it was a potential employer, but caller ID informed her it was her sister.

"Merry Christmas, Zelda," K.O. said. This was one small way to remind her that keeping Santa away from Zoe and Zara was fundamentally wrong.

"Did you get it?" Zelda asked excitedly. "Did you get Dr. Jeffries's autograph for me?"

"Ah…"

"You didn't, did you?" Zelda's disappointment was obvious.

"Not exactly."

"Did you even *talk* to him?" her sister pressed.

"Oh, yes, we did plenty of that." She recalled their conversation, thinking he might have manipulated that, too, in order to win her over to his side. The dark side, she thought grimly. Like Narnia without Aslan, and no Christmas.

A stunned silence followed. "Together. You and Dr. Jeffries were together?"

"We went to dinner...."

"You went to dinner with Dr. Wynn Jeffries?" Awe became complete disbelief.

"Yes, at Chez Jerome." K.O. felt like a name-dropper but she couldn't help it. No one ate at Chez Jerome and remained silent.

Zelda gasped. "You're making this up and I don't find it amusing."

"I'm not," K.O. insisted. "LaVonne arranged it. Dinner was incredible. In fact, I gained two pounds."

A short silence ensued. "Okay, I'm sitting down and I'm listening really hard. You'd better start at the beginning."

"Okay," she said. "I saw Wynn, Dr. Jeffries, in the French Café."

"I already know that part."

"I saw him again." K.O. stopped abruptly, thinking better of telling her sister about the confrontation and calling him names. Not that referring to him as Jim Carrey and Charles Dickens was especially insulting, but still... "Anyway, it's not important now."

"Why isn't it?"

"Well, Wynn and I agreed to put that unfortunate incident behind us and start over."

"Oh, my goodness, what did you do?" Zelda demanded. "What did you say to him? You didn't embarrass him, did you?"

K.O. bit her lip. "Do you want to hear about the dinner or not?"

"Yes! I want to hear *everything*."

K.O. then told her about cocktails at LaVonne's and her neighbor's connection with the famous chef. She described their dinner in lavish detail and mentioned the carriage ride. The one thing she didn't divulge was the kiss, which shot into her memory like a flaming dart, reminding her how weak she really was.

As if reading her mind, Zelda asked, "Did he kiss you?"

"Zelda! That's private."

"He did," her sister said with unshakable certainty. "I can't believe it. Dr. Wynn Jeffries kissed my sister! You don't even like him."

"According to LaVonne I will soon bear his children."

"What!"

"Sorry," K.O. said dismissively. "I'm getting ahead of myself."

"Okay, okay, I can see this is all a big joke to you."

"Not really."

"I don't even know if I should believe you."

"Zelda, I'm your sister. Would I lie to you?"

"Yes!"

Unfortunately Zelda was right. "I'm not this time, I swear it."

Zelda hesitated. "Did you or did you not get his autograph?"

Reluctant though she was to admit it, K.O. didn't have any choice. "Not."

"That's what I thought." Zelda bade her a hasty farewell and disconnected the call.

Much as she hated the prospect, K.O. put on her sweats and headed for the treadmill, which she kept stored under her bed for emergencies such as this. If she didn't do something fast to get rid of those two pounds, they'd stick to her hips like putty and harden. Then losing them would be like chiseling them off with a hammer. This, at least, was her theory of weight gain and loss. Immediate action was required. With headphones blocking outside distractions, she dutifully walked four miles and quit only when she was confident she'd sweated off what she'd gained. Still, a day of reduced caloric intake would be necessary.

She showered, changed her clothes and had a cup of coffee with skim milk. She worked on the Mulcahys' Christmas letter, munching a piece of dry toast as she did. After that, she transcribed a few reports. At one o'clock LaVonne stopped by with a request.

"I need help," she said, stepping into K.O.'s condo. She carried a plate of cookies.

"Okay." K.O. made herself look away from the delectable-smelling cookies. Her stomach growled. All she'd had for lunch was a small container of yogurt and a glass of V8 juice.

"I hate to ask," LaVonne said, "but I wasn't sure where else to turn."

"LaVonne, I'd do anything for you. You know that."

Her friend nodded. "Would you write my Christmas letter for me?"

"Of course." That would be a piece of cake. Oh, why did everything come down to food?

"I have no idea how to do this. I've never written one before." She sighed. "My life is pitiful."

K.O. arched her brows. "What do you mean, pitiful? You have a good life."

"I do? I've never married and I don't have children. I'm getting these Christmas letters from my old college friends and they're all about how perfect their lives are. In comparison mine is so dull. All I have are my three cats." She looked beseechingly at K.O. "Jazz up my life, would you? Make it sound just as wonderful as my girlfriends' instead of just plain boring."

"Your life is *not* boring." Despite her best efforts, K.O. couldn't keep her eyes off the cookies. "Would you excuse me?"

"Ah…sure."

"I'll be back in a minute. I need to brush my teeth."

Her neighbor eyed her speculatively as K.O. left the room.

"It's a trick I have when I get hungry," she explained, coming out of the bathroom holding her toothbrush, which was loaded with toothpaste. "Whenever I get hungry, I brush my teeth."

"You do what?"

"Brush my teeth."

Her friend regarded her steadily. "How many times have you brushed your teeth today?"

"Four...no, five times. Promise me you'll take those cookies home."

LaVonne nodded. "I brought them in case I needed a bribe."

"Not only will I write your letter, I'll do it today so you can mail off your cards this week."

Her friend's eyes revealed her gratitude. "You're the best."

Ideas were already forming in K.O.'s mind. Writing LaVonne's Christmas letter would be a snap compared to finishing Bill Mulcahy's. Speaking of him... K.O. glanced at her watch. She was scheduled to meet him this very afternoon.

"I've got an appointment at three," she told her friend. "I'll put something together for you right away, drop it off, see Bill and then stop at your place on my way back."

"Great." LaVonne was still focused on the toothbrush. "You're meeting Wynn later?"

She nodded. "At six." She should be contacting him and canceling, but she didn't know how to reach him. It was a weak excuse—since she could easily ask LaVonne for his number. Actually, she felt it was time to own up to the truth. She wanted to see Wynn again, just so she'd have some answers. *Was* she truly attracted to him? *Did* he have some nefarious agenda, with the intent of proving himself right and her wrong? Unless she spent another evening with him, she wouldn't find out.

"Are you..." LaVonne waved her hand in K.O.'s direction.

"Am I what?"

LaVonne sighed. "Are you going to take that tooth-brush with you?"

"Of course."

"I see." Her neighbor frowned. "My psychic vision didn't tell me anything about that."

"No, I don't imagine it would." K.O. proceeded to return to the bathroom, where she gave her teeth a thorough brushing. Perhaps if Wynn saw her foaming at the mouth, he'd know her true feelings about him.

Chapter 6

K.O. had fun writing LaVonne's Christmas letter. Compared to Bill Mulcahy's, it was a breeze. Her friend was worried about how other people, people from her long-ago past, would react to the fact that she'd never married and lacked male companionship. K.O. took care of that.

Merry Christmas to my Friends, K.O. began for LaVonne. *This has been an exciting year as I juggle my time between Tom, Phillip and Martin, the three guys in my life. No one told me how demanding these relationships can be. Tom won my heart first and then I met Phillip and how could I refuse him? Yes, there's a bit of jealousy, but they manage to be civil to each other. I will admit that things heated up after I started seeing Martin. I fell for him the minute we met.*

I'm retired now, so I have plenty of time to devote to the demands of these relationships. Some women discover love in their twenties. But

it took me until I was retired to fall into this kind of happiness. I lav-
ish attention and love on all three guys. Those of you who are con-
cerned that I'm taking on too much, let me assure you—I'm woman
enough to handle them.

I love my new luxury condo on Blossom Street here in Seattle. And
I've been continuing my education lately, enhancing my skills and ex-
ploring new vistas.

K.O. giggled, then glanced at her watch. The afternoon had escaped her. She hurriedly finished with a few
more details of LaVonne's year, including a wine-tast-
ing trip to the Yakima Valley, and printed out a draft
of the letter.

The meeting with Bill Mulcahy went well, and he
paid her the balance of what he owed and thanked her
profusely. "This is just perfect," he said, reading the
Christmas letter. "I wouldn't have believed it, if I wasn't
seeing it for myself. You took the mess this year has
been and turned it all around."

K.O. was pleased her effort had met with his satisfaction.

LaVonne was waiting for her when she returned,
the Christmas letter in hand. "Oh, Katherine, I don't
know how you do it. I laughed until I had tears in my
eyes. How can I ever thank you?"

"I had fun," she assured her neighbor.

"I absolutely insist on paying you."

"Are you kidding? No way." After everything La-
Vonne had done for her, no thanks was necessary.

"I love it so much, I've already taken it down to the
printer's and had copies made on fancy Christmas

paper. My cards are going out this afternoon, thanks to you."

K.O. shrugged off her praise. After all, her friend had paid for her dinner with Wynn at Chez Jerome and been a good friend to her all these months. Writing a simple letter was the least she could do.

K.O. had been home only a short while when her doorbell chimed. Thinking it must be LaVonne, who frequently stopped by, she casually opened it, ready to greet her neighbor.

Instead Wynn Jeffries stood there.

K.O. wasn't ready for their outing—or to see him again. She needed to steel herself against the attraction she felt toward him.

"Hi." She sounded breathless.

"Katherine."

"Hi," she said again unnecessarily.

"I realize I'm early," he said. "I have a radio interview at 5:30. My assistant arranged it earlier in the week and I forgot to enter it into my PDA."

"Oh." Here it was—the perfect excuse to avoid seeing him again. And yet she couldn't help feeling disappointed.

He must've known, as she did, that any kind of relationship was a lost cause.

"That's fine, I understand," she told him, recovering quickly. "We can get together another time." She offered this in a nonchalant manner, shrugging her shoulders, deciding this really was for the best.

His gaze held hers. "Perhaps you could come with me," he said.

"Come with you?" she repeated and instantly recognized this as a bad idea. In fact, as bad ideas went, it came close to the top. She hadn't been able to keep her mouth shut in the bookstore and had been banned for life. If she had to listen to him spout off his views in person, K.O. didn't know if she could restrain herself from grabbing the mike and pleading with people everywhere to throw out his book or use it for kindling. Nope, attending the interview with him was definitely *not* a good plan.

When she didn't immediately respond, he said, "After the interview, we could go on to the Figgy Pudding thing you mentioned."

She knew she should refuse. And yet, before she could reconsider it, she found herself nodding.

"I understand the radio station is only a few blocks from West Lake Plaza."

"Yes…" Her mouth felt dry and all at once she was nervous.

"We'll need to leave right away," he said, looking at his watch.

"I'll get my coat." She was wearing blue jeans and a long black sweater—no need to change.

Wynn entered her condo and as she turned away, he stopped her, placing one hand on her arm.

K.O. turned back and was surprised to find him staring at her again. He seemed to be saying he wasn't sure what was happening between them, either. Wasn't sure what he felt or why… Then, as if he needed to test those feelings, he lowered his mouth to hers. Slowly, ever so slowly… K.O. could've moved away at any point. She didn't. The biggest earthquake of the century could've

hit and she wouldn't have noticed. Not even if the building had come tumbling down around her feet. Her eyes
drifted shut and she leaned into Wynn, ready—no, more
than ready—*eager* to accept his kiss.

To her astonishment, it was even better than the
night before. This *couldn't* be happening and yet it was.
Fortunately, Wynn's hands were on her shoulders,
since her balance had grown unsteady.

When he pulled away, it took her a long time to
open her eyes. She glanced up at him and discovered
he seemed as perplexed as she was.

"I was afraid of that," he said.

She blinked, understanding perfectly what he
meant. "Me, too."

"It was as good as last night."

"Better," she whispered.

He cleared his throat. "If we don't leave now, I'll be
late for the interview."

"Right."

Still, neither of them moved. Apparently all they
were capable of doing was staring at each other. Wynn
didn't seem any happier about this than she was, and
in some small way, that was a comfort.

K.O. forced herself to break the contact between
them. She collected her coat and purse and was halfway to the door when she dashed into the bathroom.
"I forgot my toothbrush," she informed him.

He gave her a puzzled look. "You brush after every
meal?" he asked.

"No, before." She smiled sheepishly. "I mean, I
didn't yesterday, which is why I have to do it today."

He didn't question her garbled explanation as she dropped her toothbrush carrier and toothpaste inside her purse.

Once outside the building, Wynn walked at a fast pace as if he already had second thoughts. For her part, K.O. tried not to think at all. To protect everyone's peace of mind, she'd decided to wait outside the building. It was safer that way.

By the time they arrived at the radio station, K.O. realized it was far too frigid to linger out in the cold. She'd wait in the lobby.

Wynn pressed his hand to the small of her back and guided her through the impressive marble-floored lobby toward the elevators.

"I'll wait here," she suggested. But there wasn't any seating or coffee shop. If she stayed there, it would mean standing around for the next thirty minutes or so.

"I'm sure they'll have a waiting area up at the station," Wynn suggested.

He was probably right.

They took the elevator together, standing as far away from each other as possible, as though they both recognized the risk for potential disaster.

The interviewer, Big Mouth Bass, was a well-known Seattle disk jockey. K.O. had listened to him for years but this was the first time she'd seen him in person. He didn't look anything like his voice. For one thing, he was considerably shorter than she'd pictured and considerably...rounder. If she had the opportunity, she'd share her toothbrush trick with him. It might help.

"Want to sit in for the interview?" Big Mouth asked.

"Thank you, no," she rushed to say. "Dr. Jeffries and I don't necessarily agree and—"

"No way." Wynn's voice drowned hers out.

Big Mouth was no fool. K.O. might've imagined it, but she thought a gleam appeared in his eyes. He hosted a live interview show, after all, and a little controversy would keep things lively.

"I insist," Big Mouth said. He motioned toward the hallway that led to the control booth.

K.O. shook her head. "Thanks, anyway, but I'll wait out here."

"We're ready for Dr. Jeffries," a young woman informed the radio personality.

"I'll wait here," K.O. said again, and before anyone could argue, she practically threw herself into a chair and grabbed a magazine. She opened it and pretended to read, sighing with relief as Big Mouth led Wynn out of the waiting area. The radio in the room was tuned to the station, and a couple of minutes later, Big Mouth's booming voice was introducing Wynn.

"I have with me Dr. Wynn Jeffries," he began. "As many of you will recall, Dr. Jeffries's book, *The Free Child*, advocates letting a child set his or her own boundaries. Explain yourself, Dr. Jeffries."

"First, let me thank you for having me on your show," Wynn said, and K.O. was surprised by how melodic he sounded, how confident and sincere. "I believe," Wynn continued, "that structure is stifling to a child."

"*Any* structure?" Big Mouth challenged.

"Yes, in my opinion, such rigidity is detrimental to a child's sense of creativity and his or her natural ability to develop moral principles." Wynn spoke eloquently, citing example after example showing how structure had a negative impact on a child's development.

"No boundaries," Big Mouth repeated, sounding incredulous.

"As I said, a child will set his or her own."

Just listening to Wynn from her chair in the waiting room, K.O. had to sit on her hands.

"You also claim a parent should ignore inappropriate talk."

"Absolutely. Children respond to feedback and when we don't give them any, the undesirable action will cease."

Big Mouth asked a question now and then. Just before the break, he said, "You brought a friend with you this afternoon."

"Yes..." All the confidence seemed to leave Wynn's voice.

"She's in the waiting area, isn't she?" Big Mouth continued, commenting more than questioning. "I gathered, during the few minutes in which I spoke to your friend, that she doesn't agree with your child-rearing philosophy."

"Yes, that's true, but Katherine isn't part of the interview."

Big Mouth chuckled. "I thought we'd bring her in after the break and get her views on your book."

"Uh..."

"Don't go away, folks—this should be interesting.

We'll be right back after the traffic and weather report."

On hearing this, K.O. tossed aside the magazine and started to make a run for the elevator. Unfortunately Big Mouth was faster than his size had led her to believe.

"I...I don't think this is a good idea," she said as he led her by the elbow to the control booth. "I'm sure Wynn would rather not..."

"Quite the contrary," Big Mouth said smoothly, ushering her into the recording room, which was shockingly small. He sat her next to Wynn and handed her a headset. "You'll share a mike with Dr. Jeffries. Be sure to speak into it and don't worry about anything."

After the traffic report, Big Mouth was back on the air.

"Hello, Katherine," he said warmly. "How are you this afternoon?"

"I was perfectly fine until a few minutes ago," she snapped.

Big Mouth laughed. "Have you read Dr. Jeffries's book?"

"No. Well, not really." She leaned close to the microphone.

"You disagree with his philosophies, don't you?"

"Yes." She dared not look at Wynn, but she was determined not to embarrass him the way she had in the French Café. Even if they were at odds about the validity of his Free Child movement, he didn't deserve to be publicly humiliated.

"Katherine seems to believe I'm taking Christmas away from children," Wynn blurted out. "She's wrong, of course. I have a short chapter in the book that merely suggests parents bury the concept of Santa."

"You want to *bury Santa?*" Even Big Mouth took offense at that, K.O. noticed with a sense of righteousness.

"My publisher chose the chapter title and against my better judgment, I let it stand. Basically, all I'm saying is that it's wrong to lie to a child, no matter how good one's intentions."

"He wants to get rid of the Tooth Fairy and the Easter Bunny, too," K.O. inserted.

"That doesn't make me a Jim Carrey," Wynn said argumentatively. "I'm asking parents to be responsible adults. That's all."

"What does it hurt?" K.O. asked. "Childhood is a time of make-believe and fairy tales and fun. Why does everything have to be so serious?"

"Dr. Jeffries," Big Mouth cut in. "Could you explain that comment about Jim Carrey?"

"I called him that," K.O. answered on his behalf. "I meant to say the Grinch. You know, like in *How the Grinch Stole Christmas.* Jim Carrey was in the movie," she explained helplessly.

Wynn seemed eager to change the subject. He started to say something about the macabre character of fairy tales and how they weren't "fun," but Big Mouth cut him off.

"Ah, I see," he said, grinning from ear to ear. "You two have a love/hate relationship. That's what's *really* going on here."

K.O. looked quickly at Wynn, and he glared back.

The "hate" part might be right, but there didn't seem to be any "love" in the way he felt about her.

"Regrettably, this is all the time we have for today," Big Mouth told his audience. "I'd like to thank Dr. Jeffries for stopping by this afternoon and his friend Katherine, too. Thank you both for a most entertaining interview. Now for the news at the top of the hour."

Big Mouth flipped a switch and the room went silent. So silent, in fact, that K.O. could hear her heart beat.

"We can leave now," Wynn said stiffly after removing his headphones.

Hers were already off. K.O. released a huge pent-up sigh. "Thank goodness," she breathed.

Wynn didn't say anything until they'd entered the elevator.

"That was a disaster," he muttered.

K.O. blamed herself. She should never have accompanied him to the interview. She'd known it at the time and still couldn't resist. "I'm sorry. I shouldn't have gone on the air with you."

"You weren't given much choice," he said in her defense.

"I apologize if I embarrassed you. That wasn't my intention. I tried not to say anything derogatory—surely you could see that."

He didn't respond and frankly, she didn't blame him.

"The thing is, Katherine, you don't respect my beliefs."

"I don't," she reluctantly agreed.

"You couldn't have made it any plainer." The elevator doors opened and they stepped into the foyer.

"Perhaps it would be best if we didn't see each other again." K.O. figured she was only saying what they were both thinking.

Wynn nodded. She could sense his regret, a regret she felt herself.

They were outside the building now. The street was festive with lights, and Christmas music could be heard from one of the department stores. At the moment, however, she felt anything but merry.

The Figgy Pudding contest, which was sponsored by the Pike Market Senior Center and Downtown Food Bank as an annual fund-raiser, would've started by now and, although she didn't feel the least bit like cheering, she'd promised Vickie she'd show up and support her efforts for charity.

K.O. thrust out her hand and did her utmost to smile. "Thank you, Wynn. Last night was one of the most incredible evenings of my life," she said. "Correction. It was *the* most incredible night ever."

Wynn clasped her hand. His gaze held hers as he said, "It was for me, too."

People were stepping around them.

She should simply walk away. Vickie would be looking for her. And yet…she couldn't make herself do it.

"Goodbye," he whispered.

Her heart was in her throat. "Goodbye."

He dropped his hand, turned and walked away. His steps were slow, measured. He'd gone about five feet when he glanced over his shoulder. K.O. hadn't moved. In fact, she stood exactly as he'd left her, biting her lower lip—a habit she had when distressed. Wynn stopped abruptly, his back still to her.

"Wynn, listen," she called and trotted toward him. "I have an idea." Although it'd only been a few feet, she felt as if she was setting off on a marathon.

"What?" He sounded eager.

"I have twin nieces."

He nodded. "You mentioned them earlier. Their mother read my book."

"Yes, and loved it."

There was a flicker of a smile. "At least *someone* in your family believes in me."

"Yes, Zelda sure does. She thinks you're fabulous." K.O. realized she did, too—aside from his theories. "My sister and her husband are attending his company Christmas dinner next Friday, the fifteenth," she rushed to explain. "Zelda asked me to spend the night. Come with me. Show me how your theories *should* work. Maybe Zelda's doing it wrong. Maybe you can convince me that the Free Child movement makes sense."

"You want me to come with you."

"Yes. We'll do everything just as you suggest in your book, and I promise not to say a word. I'll read it this week, I'll listen to you and I'll observe."

Wynn hesitated.

"Until then, we won't mention your book or anything else to do with your theories."

"Promise?"

"Promise," she concurred.

"No more radio interviews?"

She laughed. "That's an easy one."

A smile came to him then, appearing in his eyes first. "You've got yourself a deal."

Yes, she did, and K.O. could hardly wait to introduce Zoe and Zara to Dr. Wynn Jeffries. Oh, she was sincere about keeping an open mind, but Wynn might learn something, too. The incorrigible twins would be the true crucible for his ideas.

K.O. held out her hand. "Are you ready for some Figgy Pudding?" she asked.

He grinned, taking her mittened hand as they hurried toward the Figgy Pudding People's Choice competition.

Chapter 7

The Figgy Pudding People's Choice event was standing room only when Wynn and K.O. arrived. Vickie and her friends hadn't performed yet and were just being introduced by a popular morning-radio host for an easy-listening station. K.O. and Vickie had been friends all through high school and college. Vickie had married three years ago, and K.O. had been in her wedding party. In fact, she'd been in any number of wedding parties. Her mother had pointedly asked whether K.O. was ever going to be a bride, instead of a bridesmaid.

"That's my friend over there," K.O. explained, nodding in Vickie's direction. "The one in the Santa hat."

Wynn squinted at the group of ladies huddled together in front of the assembly. "Aren't they all wearing Santa hats?"

"True. The young cute one," she qualified.

"They're all young and cute, Katherine." He smiled. "Young enough, anyway."

She looked at Wynn with new appreciation. "That is such a sweet thing to say." Vickie worked for a local dentist as a hygienist and was the youngest member of the staff. The other women were all in their forties and fifties. "I could just kiss you," K.O. said, snuggling close to him. She looped her arm through his.

Wynn cleared his throat as though unaccustomed to such open displays of affection. "Any particular reason you suddenly find me so kissable?"

"Well, yes, the women with Vickie are…a variety of ages."

"I see. I should probably tell you I'm not wearing my glasses."

K.O. laughed, elbowing him in the ribs. "And here I thought you were being so gallant."

He grinned boyishly and slid his arm around her shoulders.

Never having attended a Figgy Pudding event before, K.O. didn't know what to expect. To her delight, it was enchanting, as various groups competed, singing Christmas carols, to raise funds for the Senior Center and Food Bank. Vickie and her office mates took second place, and K.O. cheered loudly. Wynn shocked her by placing two fingers in his mouth and letting loose with a whistle that threatened to shatter glass. It seemed so unlike him.

Somehow Vickie found her when the singing was over. "I wondered if you were going to show," she said, shouting to be heard above the noise of the merry-go-round and the crowd. Musicians gathered on street corners, horns honked and the sights and sounds of Christmas were everywhere. Although the comment was directed at K.O., Vickie's attention was unmistakably on Wynn.

"Vickie, this is Wynn Jeffries."

Her friend's gaze shot back to K.O. "Wynn Jeffries? Not *the* Wynn Jeffries?"

"One and the same," K.O. said, speaking out of the corner of her mouth.

"You've got to be joking." Vickie's mouth fell open as she stared at Wynn.

For the last two months, K.O. had been talking her friend's ear off about the man and his book and how he was ruining her sister's life. She'd even told Vickie about the incident at the bookstore, although she certainly hadn't confided in anyone else; she wasn't exactly proud of being kicked out for unruly behavior. Thinking it might be best to change the subject, K.O. asked, "Is John here?"

"John?"

"Your husband," K.O. reminded her. She hadn't seen Wynn wearing glasses before, but she hoped his comment about forgetting them was sincere, otherwise he might notice the close scrutiny Vickie was giving him.

"Oh, *John*," her friend said, recovering quickly. "No, he's meeting me later for dinner." Then, as if inspiration had struck, she asked, "Would you two like to join us? John got a reservation at a new Chinese restaurant that's supposed to have great food."

K.O. looked at Wynn, who nodded. "Sure," she answered, speaking for both of them. "What time?"

"Nine. I was going to do some shopping and meet him there."

They made arrangements to meet later and Vickie went into the mall to finish her Christmas shopping.

"I'm starving now," K.O. said when her stomach growled. Although she had her toothbrush, there really wasn't a convenient place to foam up. "After last night, I didn't think I'd ever want to eat again." She considered mentioning the two pounds she'd gained, but thought better of it. Wynn might not want to see her again if he found out how easily she packed on weight. Well, she didn't *really* believe that of him, but she wasn't taking any chances. Which proved that, despite everything, she was interested. In fact, she'd made the decision to continue with this relationship, see where their attraction might lead, almost without being aware of it.

"How about some roasted chestnuts?" he asked. A vendor was selling them on the street corner next to a musician who strummed a guitar and played a harmonica at the same time. His case was open on the sidewalk for anyone who cared to donate. She tossed in a dollar and hoped he used whatever money he collected to pay for music lessons.

"I've never had a roasted chestnut," K.O. told him.

"Me, neither," Wynn confessed. "This seems to be the season for it, though."

While Wynn waited in line for the chestnuts, K.O. became fascinated with the merry-go-round. "Will you go on it with me?" she asked him.

Wynn hesitated. "I've never been on a merry-go-round."

K.O. was surprised. "Then you have to," she insisted. "You've missed a formative experience." Taking his hand, she pulled him out of the line. She purchased the tickets herself and refused to listen to his excuses. He rattled off a dozen—he was too old, too big, too clumsy and so on. K.O. rejected every one.

"It's going to be fun," she said.

"I thought you were starving."

"I was, but I'm not now. Come on, be a good sport. Women find men who ride horses extremely attractive."

Wynn stopped arguing long enough to raise an eyebrow. "My guess is that the horse is generally not made of painted wood."

"Generally," she agreed, "but you never know."

The merry-go-round came to a halt and emptied out on the opposite side. They passed their tickets to the attendant and, leading Wynn by the hand, K.O. ushered him over to a pair of white horses that stood side by side. She set her foot in the stirrup and climbed into the molded saddle. Wynn stood next to his horse looking uncertain.

"Mount up, partner," she said.

"I feel more than a little ridiculous, Katherine."

"Oh, don't be silly. Men ride these all the time. See? There's another guy."

Granted, he was sitting on a gaudy elephant, holding a toddler, but she didn't dwell on that.

Sighing, Wynn climbed reluctantly onto the horse,

his legs so long they nearly touched the floor. "Put your feet in the stirrups," she coaxed.

He did, and his knees were up to his ears.

K.O. couldn't help it; she burst out laughing.

Wynn began to climb off, but she stopped him by leaning over and kissing him. She nearly slid off the saddle in the process and would have if Wynn hadn't caught her about the waist.

Soon the carousel music started, and the horses moved up and down. K.O. thrust out her legs and laughed, thoroughly enjoying herself. "Are you having fun yet?" she asked Wynn.

"I'm ecstatic," he said dryly.

"Oh, come on, Wynn, relax. Have some fun."

Suddenly he leaned forward, as if he were riding for the Pony Express. He let out a cry that sounded like sheer joy.

"That *was* fun," Wynn told her, climbing down when the carousel stopped. He put his hands on her waist and she felt the heat of his touch in every part of her body.

"You liked it?"

"Do you want to go again?" he asked.

The line was much longer now. "I don't think so."

"I've always wanted to do that. I felt like a child all over again," he said enthusiastically.

"A Free Child?" she asked in a mischievous voice.

"Yes, free. That's exactly what my book's about, allowing children freedom to become themselves," he said seriously.

"Okay." She was biting her tongue but managed

not to say anything more. Surely there were great rewards awaiting her in heaven for such restraint.

"Would you like to stop at the bookstore?" he asked.
"I like to sign copies when I'm in the neighborhood."

"You mean an autographing?" She hoped it wouldn't
be at the same bookstore that had caused all the trouble.

"Not exactly an autographing," Wynn explained.
"The bookseller told me that a signed book is a sold
book. When it's convenient, authors often visit book-
stores to sign stock."

"Sort of a drive-by signing?" she asked, making a
joke out of it.

"Yeah." They started walking and just as she feared,
they were headed in the direction of *the* bookstore.

As they rounded the corner and the store came
into sight, her stomach tightened. "I'll wait for you
outside," she said, implying that nothing would please
her more than to linger out in the cold.

"Nonsense. There's a small café area where you can
wait in comfort."

"Okay," she finally agreed. Once she'd made it past
the shoplifting detector K.O. felt more positive. She
was afraid her mug shot had been handed out to the
employees and she'd be expelled on sight.

Thankfully she didn't see the bookseller who'd
asked her to leave. That boded well. She saw Wynn
chatting with a woman behind the counter. He followed her to the back of the store. Some of the tension eased from K.O.'s shoulder blades. Okay, she
seemed to be safe. And she didn't have to hide behind

a coffee cup. Besides, she loved to read and since she was in a bookstore, what harm would it do to buy a book? She was in the mood for something entertaining. A romantic comedy, she decided, studying a row of titles. Without much trouble, she found one that looked perfect and started toward the cashier.

Then it happened.

Wynn was waiting up front, speaking to the very bookseller who'd banished K.O. from the store.

Trying to be as inconspicuous as possible, K.O. set the book aside and tiptoed toward the exit, shoulders hunched forward, head lowered.

"Katherine," Wynn called.

With a smile frozen in place, she turned to greet Wynn and the bookseller.

"It's you!" The woman, who wore a name tag that identified her as Shirley, glared at K.O.

She timidly raised her hand. "Hello again."

"You two know each other?" Shirley asked Wynn in what appeared to be complete disbelief.

"Yes. This is my friend Katherine."

The bookseller seemed to have lost her voice. She looked from Wynn to Katherine and then back.

"Good to see you again," K.O. said. She sincerely hoped Shirley would play along and conveniently forget that unfortunate incident.

"It *is* you," Shirley hissed from between clenched teeth.

"What's this about?" Wynn asked, a puzzled expression on his face. "You've met before?"

"Nothing," K.O. all but shouted.

"As a matter of fact, we have met." Shirley's dark

eyes narrowed. "Perhaps your *friend* has forgotten. I, however, have not."

So it was going to be like that, was it? "We had a difference of opinion," K.O. told Wynn in a low voice.

"As I recall, you were permanently banned from the store."

"Katherine was *banned* from the store?" Wynn asked incredulously. "I can't believe she'd do anything deserving of that."

"Maybe we should leave now," K.O. suggested, and tugged at his sleeve.

"If you want to know," Shirley began, but K.O. interrupted before she could launch into her complaint.

"Wynn, please, we should go," she said urgently.

"I'm sure this can all be sorted out," he murmured, releasing his coat sleeve from her grasp.

Shirley, hands on her hips, smiled snidely. She seemed to take real pleasure in informing Wynn of K.O.'s indiscretion.

"This *friend* of yours is responsible for causing a scene in this very bookstore, Dr. Jeffries."

"I'm sure no harm was meant."

K.O. grabbed his arm. "It doesn't matter," she said, desperate to escape.

"Katherine does tend to be opinionated, I agree," he said, apparently determined to defend her. "But she's actually quite reasonable."

"Apparently you don't know her as well as you think."

"I happen to enjoy Katherine's company immensely."

Shirley raised her eyebrows. "Really?"

"Yes, really."

"Then you might be interested to know that your so-called friend nearly caused a riot when she got into an argument with another customer over *your* book."

Wynn swiveled his gaze to K.O.

She offered him a weak smile. "Ready to leave now?" she asked in a weak whisper.

K.O.'s doorbell chimed, breaking into a satisfying dream. Whatever it was about seemed absolutely wonderful and she hated to lose it. When the doorbell rang again, the sound longer and more persistent, the dream disappeared. She stumbled out of bed and threw on her flannel housecoat.

Reaching the door, she checked the peephole and saw that it was LaVonne. No surprise there. Unfastening the lock, K.O. let her in, covering a yawn.

"What time did you get home last night?" her neighbor cried as she hurried in without a cat—which was quite unusual. "I waited up as long as I could for you." LaVonne's voice was frantic. "I didn't sleep a wink all night," she said and plopped herself down on the sofa.

K.O. was still at the front door, holding it open. "Good morning to you, too."

"Should I make coffee?" LaVonne asked, leaping to her feet and flipping on the light as she swept into the kitchen. Not waiting for a response, she pulled out the canister where K.O. kept her coffee grounds.

K.O. yawned again and closed the front door. "What time is it?" Early, she knew, because her eyes burned and there was barely a hint of daylight through her living room windows.

"Seven-twenty. I didn't get you up, did I?"

"No, I had to answer the door anyway." Her friend was busy preparing coffee and didn't catch the joke. "How are the guys?" K.O. asked next. LaVonne usually provided her with daily updates on their health, well-being and any cute activities they'd engaged in.

"They're hiding," she said curtly. "All three of them." She ran water into the glass pot and then poured it in the coffeemaker.

Katherine wondered why the cats were in a snit but didn't have the energy to ask.

"You haven't answered my question," LaVonne said as the coffee started to drip. She placed two mugs on the counter.

"Which one?" K.O. fell into a kitchen chair, rested her arms on the table and leaned her head on them.

"Last night," LaVonne said. "Where were you?"

"Wynn and I were out—"

"*All* night?"

"You're beginning to sound like my mother," K.O. protested.

LaVonne straightened her shoulders. "Katherine, you hardly know the man."

"I didn't sleep with him, if that's what you think." She raised her head long enough to speak and then laid it down on her arms again. "We went out to dinner with some friends of mine after the Figgy Pudding contest."

"It must've been a very late dinner." LaVonne sounded as if she didn't quite believe her.

"We walked around for a while afterward and went out for a drink. The time got away from us. I didn't get home until one."

"I was up at one and you weren't home," LaVonne said in a challenging tone. She poured the first cup of coffee and took it herself.

"Maybe it was after two, then," K.O. said. She'd completely lost track of time, which was easy to do. Wynn was so charming and he seemed so interested in her and her friends.

Vickie's husband, John, was a plumbing contractor. Despite Wynn's college degrees and celebrity status, he'd fit in well with her friends. He'd asked intelligent questions, listened and shared anecdotes about himself that had them all laughing. John even invited Wynn to play poker with him and his friends after the holidays. Wynn had accepted the invitation.

Halfway through the meal Vickie had announced that she had to use the ladies' room. The look she shot K.O. said she should join her, which K.O. did.

"That's really Wynn Jeffries?" she asked, holding K.O.'s elbow as they made their way around tables and through the restaurant.

"Yes, it's really him."

"Does he know about the bookstore?"

K.O. nodded reluctantly. "He does now."

"You didn't tell him, did you?"

"Unfortunately, he found out all on his own."

Vickie pushed open the door to the ladies' as K.O. described the scene from the bookstore. "No way," her friend moaned, then promptly sank down on a plush chair in the outer room.

K.O.'s face grew red all over again. "It was embarrassing, to say the least."

"Was Wynn upset?"

What could he say? "He didn't let on if he was." In fact, once they'd left the store, Wynn seemed to find the incident highly amusing. Had their roles been reversed, she didn't know how she would've felt.

"He didn't blow up at you or anything?" Vickie had given her a confused look. "This is the guy you think should be banned from practicing as a psychologist?"

"Well, that might've been a bit strong," she'd said, reconsidering her earlier comment.

Vickie just shook her head.

"He rode the merry-go-round with me," K.O. said aloud, deciding that had gone a long way toward redeeming him in her eyes. When she glanced up, she realized she was talking to LaVonne.

"He did what?" LaVonne asked, bringing her back to the present.

"Wynn did," she elaborated. "He rode the carousel with me."

"Until two in the morning?"

"No, before dinner. Afterward, we walked along the waterfront, then had a glass of wine. We started walking again and finally stopped for coffee at an all-night diner and talked some more." He seemed to want to know all about her, but in retrospect she noticed that he'd said very little about himself.

"Good grief," LaVonne muttered, shaking her head, "what could you possibly talk about for so long?"

"That's just it," K.O. said. "We couldn't *stop* talking." And it was even more difficult to stop kissing and to say good-night once they'd reached her condo. Because there was so much more to say, they'd agreed to meet for coffee at the French Café at nine.

LaVonne had apparently remembered that Katherine didn't have any coffee yet and filled her mug. "Just black," K.O. told her, needing a shot of unadulterated caffeine. "Thanks."

"Why were you waiting up for me?" she asked after her first bracing sip of coffee. Then and only then did her brain clear, and she understood that LaVonne must have something important on her mind.

"You wrote that fantastic Christmas letter for me," her neighbor reminded her.

"I did a good job, didn't I?" she said.

"Oh, yes, a good job all right." LaVonne frowned. "I liked it so much, I mailed it right away."

"So, what's the problem?"

"Well…" LaVonne sat down in the chair across from K.O. "It was such a relief to have something clever and…and exciting to tell everyone," LaVonne said, "especially my college friends."

So far, K.O. didn't see any problem at all. She nodded, encouraging her friend to get to the point.

LaVonne's shoulders sagged. "If only I'd waited," she moaned. "If only I'd picked up my own mail first."

"There was something in the mail?"

LaVonne nodded. "I got a card and a Christmas letter from Peggy Solomon. She was the president of my college sorority and about as uppity as they come. She married her college boyfriend, a banker's son. She had two perfect children and lives a life of luxury. She said she's looking forward to seeing me at our next reunion." There was a moment of stricken silence. "Peggy's organizing it, and she included the invitation with her card."

"That's bad?"

"Yes," LaVonne wailed. "It's bad. How am I supposed to show up at my forty-year college reunion, which happens to be in June, without a man? Especially *now*. Because of my Christmas letter, everyone in my entire class will think I've got more men than I know what to do with."

"LaVonne, you might meet someone before then."

"If I haven't met a man in the last forty years, what makes you think I will in the next six months?"

"Couldn't you say it's such a tricky balancing act you don't dare bring any of them?"

LaVonne glared at her. "Everyone'll figure out that it's all a lie." She closed her eyes. "And if they don't, Peggy's going to make sure she tells them."

Another idea struck K.O. "What about your psychic powers? Why don't you go check out the litter box again?" On second thought, maybe that wasn't such a great idea.

"Don't you think I would if I could?" she cried, becoming ever more agitated. "But I don't see anything about myself. Trust me, I've tried. So far, all my insights have been about you and Wynn. A lot of good my newfound talent has done *me*. You're being romanced night and day, and I've just made a complete fool of myself."

"LaVonne…"

"Even my cats are upset with me."

"Tom, Phillip and Martin?" K.O. had never understood why her neighbor couldn't name her feline companions regular cat names like Fluffy or Tiger.

"They think *I'm* upset with *them*. They're all hiding from me, and that's never happened before."

K.O. felt guilty, but she couldn't have known about the college reunion, any more than LaVonne did. "I'm sure everything will work out for the best," she murmured. She wished she had more than a platitude to offer, but she didn't.

"At this point that's all I can hope for." LaVonne expelled her breath and took another sip of coffee. That seemed to relax her, and she gave K.O. a half smile. "Tell me about you and Wynn."

"There's not much to say." And yet there was. She honestly liked him. Vickie and John had, too. Never would K.O. have guessed that the originator of the Free Child movement she so reviled would be this warm, compassionate and genuinely nice person. She would've been happy to settle for *one* of those qualities.

Despite everything K.O. had done to embarrass him, he was attracted to her. And it went without saying that she found Wynn Jeffries compelling and smart and...wonderful. But she was afraid to examine her feelings too closely—and even more afraid to speculate about his.

"You've spent practically every minute of the last two days together," LaVonne said. "There's got to be something."

Shrugging, K.O. pushed her hair away from her face.

"You were with him until two this morning."

"And I'm meeting him at the café in about an hour and a half," she said as she glanced at the time on her microwave.

"So what gives?" LaVonne pressed.

"I like him," she said simply. K.O. hadn't been prepared to have any feelings for him, other than negative ones. But they got along well—as long as they didn't discuss his book.

Overjoyed by her confession, LaVonne clapped her hands. "I knew it!"

K.O. felt it would be wrong to let her friend think she really believed in this psychic nonsense. She'd cooperated with LaVonne's fantasy at first but now it was time to be honest. "Wynn said he asked you about me before you introduced us."

LaVonne looked away. "He did, but it was just in passing."

"He knew I lived in the building and had seen me around."

Her neighbor shifted in her seat. She cleared her

throat before answering. "All right, all right, I was aware that he might be interested." She paused. "He asked me if you were single."

Really? Wynn hadn't told her that. "When was this?"

"Last week."

"Was it before or after you discovered your psychic talents?"

"Before."

Aha.

"Why didn't he just introduce himself?"

"I asked him that, too," LaVonne said. "Apparently he's shy."

"Wynn?"

LaVonne raised one shoulder. She frowned over at the phone on the counter. "You've got a message."

It'd been so late when she finally got to bed that K.O. hadn't bothered to check. Reaching over, she pressed the play button.

"K.O.," Zelda's voice greeted her. "Good grief, where are you? You don't have a date, do you?" She made it sound as if that was the last thing she expected. "Is there any chance it's with Dr. Jeffries? Call me the minute you get home." The message was followed by a lengthy beep and then there was a second message.

"Katherine," Zelda said more forcefully this time. "I don't mean to be a pest, but I'd appreciate it if you'd get back to me as soon as possible. You're out with Dr. Jeffries, aren't you?" Zelda managed to make that sound both accusatory and improbable.

Another beep.

"In case you're counting, this is the third time I've phoned you tonight. Where can you possibly be this late?"

No one ever seemed to care before, K.O. thought, and now her sister and LaVonne were suddenly keeping track of her love life.

Zelda gave a huge sigh of impatience. "I won't call again. But I need to confirm the details for Friday night. You're still babysitting, aren't you?"

"I'll be there," K.O. muttered, just as if her sister could hear. *And so will Wynn.*

Zelda added, "And I'd really like it if you'd get me that autograph."

"I will, I will," K.O. promised. She figured she'd get him to sign Zelda's copy of his book on Friday evening.

LaVonne drained the last of her coffee and set the mug in the sink. "I'd better get back. I'm going to try to coax the boys out from under the bed," she said with a resigned look as she walked to the door.

"Everything'll work out," K.O. assured her again—with a confidence she didn't actually feel.

LaVonne responded with a quick wave and left, slamming the door behind her.

Now K.O. was free to have a leisurely shower, carefully choose her outfit...and daydream about Wynn.

Wynn had already secured a window table when
K.O. arrived at the French Café. As usual, the
shop was crowded, with a long line of customers waiting to place their orders.

In honor of the season, she'd worn a dark-blue
sweater sprinkled with silvery stars and matching star
earrings. She hung her red coat on the back of her chair.

Wynn had thoughtfully ordered for her, and there was
a latte waiting on the table, along with a bran muffin,
her favorite. K.O. didn't remember mentioning how
much she enjoyed the café's muffins, baked by Alix
Townsend, who sometimes worked at the counter. The
muffins were a treat she only allowed herself once a
week.

"Good morning," she said, sounding a little more

breathless than she would've liked. In the space of a day, she'd gone from distrust to complete infatuation. Just twenty-four hours ago, she'd been inventing ways to get out of seeing Wynn again, and now... now she could barely stand to be separated from him.

She broke off a piece of muffin, after a sip of her latte in its oversize cup. "How did you know I love their bran muffins?" she asked. The bakery made them chock-full of raisins and nuts, so they were deliciously unlike blander varieties. Not only that, K.O. always felt she'd eaten something healthy when she had a bran muffin.

"I asked the girl behind the counter if she happened to know what you usually ordered, and she recommended that."

Once again proving how thoughtful he was.

"You had one the day you were here talking to some guy," he said flippantly.

"That was Bill Mulcahy," she explained. "I met with him because I wrote his Christmas letter."

Wynn frowned. "He's one of your clients?"

"I told you how I write people's Christmas letters, remember?" It'd been part of their conversation the night before. "I'll write yours if you want," she said, and then thinking better of it, began to sputter a retraction.

She needn't have worried that he'd take her up on the offer because he was already declining. He shook his head. "Thanks, anyway." He grimaced. "I don't want to offend you, but I find that those Christmas letters are typically a pack of lies!"

"Okay," she said mildly. She decided not to argue.

K.O. sipped her coffee again and ate another piece of muffin, deciding not to worry about calories, either. "Don't you just love Christmas?" she couldn't help saying. The sights and sounds of the season were all around them. The café itself looked elegant; garlands draped the windows and pots of white and red poinsettias were placed on the counter. Christmas carols played, just loudly enough to be heard. A bell-ringer collecting for charity had set up shop outside the café and a woman sat at a nearby table knitting a Christmas stocking. K.O. had noticed a similar one displayed in A Good Yarn, the shop across the street, the day she'd followed Wynn. Christmas on Blossom Street, with its gaily decorated streetlights and cheerful banners, was as Christmassy as Christmas could be.

"Yes, but I had more enthusiasm for the holidays before today," Wynn said.

"What's wrong?"

He stared down at his dark coffee. "My father left a message on my answering machine last night." He hesitated as he glanced up at her. "Apparently he's decided—at the last minute—to join me for Christmas."

"I see," she said, although she really didn't. Wynn had only talked about his parents that first evening, at Chez Jerome. She remembered that his parents had been hippies, and that his mother had died and his father owned a company that manufactured surfboard wax. But while she'd rattled on endlessly about her own family, he'd said comparatively little about his.

"He didn't bother to ask if I had other plans, you'll notice," Wynn commented dryly.

"Do you?"

"No, but that's beside the point."

"It must be rather disconcerting," she said. Parents sometimes did things like that, though. Her own mother often made assumptions about holidays, but it had never troubled K.O. She was going to miss her parents this year and would've been delighted if they'd suddenly decided to show up.

"Now I have to go to the airport on Sunday and pick him up." Wynn gazed out the window at the lightly falling snow. "As you might've guessed, my father and I have a rather...difficult relationship."

"I'm sorry." She wasn't sure what to say.

"The thing is," Wynn continued. "My father's like a big kid. He'll want to be entertained every minute he's here. He has no respect for my work or the fact that I have to go into the office every day." Wynn had told her he met with patients most afternoons; he kept an office in a medical building not far from Blossom Street.

"I'm sorry," she said again.

Wynn accepted her condolences with a casual shrug. "The truth is, I'd rather spend my free time with you."

He seemed as surprised by this as K.O. herself. She sensed that Wynn hadn't been any more prepared to feel this way about her than she did about him. It was all rather unexpected and at the same time just plain wonderful.

"Maybe I can help," K.O. suggested. "The nice thing about working at home is that I can choose my own hours.". That left her open for job interviews, Christmas letters and occasional babysitting. "My transcription work is really a godsend while I'm on my job quest. So I can help entertain him if you'd like."

Wynn considered for a moment. "I appreciate your offer, but I don't know if that's the best solution." He released a deep sigh. "I guess you could say my father's not my biggest fan."

"He doesn't believe in your child-rearing ideas, either?" she teased.

He grinned. "I wish it was that simple. You'll know what I mean once you meet him," Wynn said. "I think I mentioned that at one time he was a world-class surfer."

"Yes, and he manufactures some kind of special wax."

Wynn nodded. "It's made him rich." He sighed again. "I know it's a cliché, but my parents met in San Francisco in the early 70s and I think I told you they joined a commune. They were free spirits, the pair of them. Dad hated what he called 'the establishment.' He dropped out of college, burned his draft card, that sort of thing. He didn't want any responsibility, didn't even have a bank account—until about fifteen years ago, when someone offered to mass-produce his surfboard wax. And then he grabbed hold with both hands."

K.O. wondered if he realized he was advocating his parents' philosophy with his Free Child movement. However, she didn't point it out.

"In the early days we moved around because any money Dad brought in was from his surfing, so the three of us followed the waves, so to speak. Then we'd periodically return to the commune. I had a wretched childhood," he said bleakly. "They'd called me Radiant Sun, Ray for short, but at least they let me choose my own name when I was older. They hated it, which was fine by me. The only real family I had was my maternal grandparents. I moved in with the Wynns when I was ten."

"Your parents didn't like your name?"

"No, and this came from someone who chose the name Moon Puppy for himself. Mom liked to be called Daffodil. Her given name was Mary, which she'd rejected, along with her parents' values."

"But you—"

"My grandparents were the ones who saw to it that I stayed in school. They're the ones who paid for my education. Both of them died when I was a college senior, but they were the only stable influence I had."

"What you need while your father is here," K.O. said, "is someone to run interference. Someone who can act as a buffer between you and your father, and that someone is me."

Wynn didn't look convinced.

"I want to help," she insisted. "Really."

He still didn't look convinced.

"Oh, and before I forget, my sister left three messages on my phone. She wants your autograph in the worst way. I thought you could sign her copy of *The Free Child* next Friday when—" It suddenly occurred to her that if Wynn's father was visiting, he wouldn't be able to watch the twins with her. "Oh, no," she whispered, unable to hide her disappointment.

"What's wrong?"

"I— You'll have company, so Friday night is out." She put on a brave smile. She didn't actually need his help, but this was an opportunity to spend time with him—and to prove that his theories didn't translate into practice. She might be wrong, in which case she'd acknowledge the validity of his Free Child approach, but she doubted it.

Wynn met her eyes. "I'm not going to break my commitment. I'll explain to my father that I've got a previous engagement. He doesn't have any choice but to accept it, especially since he didn't give me any no- tice."

"When does he arrive?" K.O. asked. She savored another piece of her muffin, trying to guess which spices Alix had used.

"At four-thirty," Wynn said glumly.

"It's going to work out fine." That was almost iden- tical to what she'd told LaVonne earlier that morning.

Then it hit her.

LaVonne needed a man in her life.

Wynn was looking for some way to occupy his fa- ther.

"Oh, my goodness." K.O. stood and stared down at Wynn with both hands on the edge of the table.

"What?"

"Wynn, I have the perfect solution!"

He eyed her skeptically.

"LaVonne," she said, sitting down again. She was so sure her plan would work, she felt a little shiver of delight. "You're going to introduce your father to LaVonne!"

He frowned at her and shook his head. "If you're thinking what I suspect you're thinking, I can tell you right now it won't work."

"Yes, it will! LaVonne needs to find a man before her college reunion in June. She'd—"

"Katherine, I appreciate the thought, but can you honestly see LaVonne getting involved with an ex-hippie who isn't all that ex—and is also the producer of Max's Wax?"

"Of course I can," she said, refusing to allow him to thwart her plan. "Besides, it isn't up to us. All we have to do is introduce the two of them, step back and let nature take its course."

Wynn clearly still had doubts.

"It won't hurt to try."

"I guess not..."

"This is what I'll do," she said, feeling inspired. She couldn't understand Wynn's hesitation. "I'll invite your father and LaVonne to my place for Christmas cocktails."

Wynn crossed his arms. "This is beginning to sound familiar."

"It should." She stifled a giggle. Turnabout was fair play, after all.

"Maybe we should look at the olives in the martinis and tell them we got a psychic reading," Wynn joked.

"Oh, that's good," K.O. said with a giggle. "A drink or two should relax them both," she added.

"And then you and I can conveniently leave for dinner or a movie."

"No...no," K.O. said, excitedly. "Oh, Wynn this is ideal! We'll arrange a dinner for *them*."

"Where?"

"I don't know." He was worrying about details too much. "We'll think of someplace special."

"I wonder if I can reach Chef Jerome and get a reservation there," Wynn murmured.

K.O. gulped. "I can't afford that."

"Not to worry. My father can."

"That's even better." K.O. felt inordinately pleased with herself. All the pieces were falling into place. Wynn would have someone to keep his father occupied until Christmas, and LaVonne might find a potential date for her class reunion.

"What are your plans for today?" Wynn asked, changing the subject.

"I'm meeting Vickie and a couple of other friends for shopping and lunch. What about you?"

"I'm headed to the gym and then the office. I don't usually work on weekends, but I'm writing a follow-up book." He spoke hesitantly as if he wasn't sure he should mention it.

"Okay." She smiled as enthusiastically as she could. "Would you like me to go to the airport with you when you pick up your father?"

"You'd do that?"

"Of course! In fact, I'd enjoy it."

"Thank you, then. I'd appreciate it."

They set up a time on Sunday afternoon and went their separate ways.

K.O. started walking down to Pacific Place, the mall where she'd agreed to meet Vickie and Diane, when her cell phone rang. It was Wynn.

"What day?" he asked. "I want to get this cocktail party idea of yours on my schedule."

"When would you suggest?"

"I don't think we should wait too long."

"I agree."

"Would Monday evening work for you?"

"Definitely. I'll put together a few appetizers and make some spiked eggnog. I'll pick up some wine—and gin for martinis, if you want." She smiled, recalling his comment about receiving a "psychic" message from the olives.

"Let me bring the wine. Anything else?"

"Could you buy a cat treat or two? That's in case LaVonne brings Tom or one of her other cats. I want her to concentrate on Moon Puppy, not kitty."

Wynn laughed. "You got it. I'll put in a call to Chef Jerome, although I don't hold out much hope. Still, maybe he'll say yes because it's LaVonne."

"All we can do is try. And there are certainly other nice places."

Wynn seemed reluctant to end the conversation. "Katherine."

"Yes."

"Thank you. Hearing my father's message after such a lovely evening put a damper on my Christmas."

"You're welcome."

"Have fun today."

"You, too." She closed her cell and set it back in her purse. Her step seemed to have an extra bounce as she hurried to meet her friends.

Saturday afternoon, just back from shopping, K.O. stopped at LaVonne's condo. She rang the doorbell and waited. It took her neighbor an unusually long time to answer; when she did, LaVonne looked dreadful. Her hair was disheveled, and she'd obviously been napping—with at least one cat curled up next to her, since her dark-red sweatshirt was covered in cat hair.

"Why the gloomy face?" K.O. asked. "It's almost Christmas."

"I know," her friend lamented.

"Well, cheer up. I have great news."

"You'd better come inside," LaVonne said without any real enthusiasm. She gestured toward the sofa, although it seemed to require all the energy she possessed just to lift her arm. "Sit down if you want."

"Wouldn't you like to hear my good news?"

LaVonne shrugged her shoulders. "I guess."

"It has to do with you."

"Me?"

"Yup. I met Vickie and Diane at Pacific Place, and we had lunch at this wonderful Italian restaurant."

LaVonne sat across from her, and Martin automatically jumped into her lap. Tom got up on the chair, too, and leisurely stretched out across the arm. She petted both cats with equal fondness.

"I ordered the minestrone soup," K.O. went on to tell her, maintaining her exuberance. "That was when it happened." She'd worked out this plan on her way home, inspired by Wynn's joke about the olives.

"What?"

"I had a psychic impression. Isn't that what you call it? Right there with my two friends in the middle of an Italian restaurant." She paused. "It had to do with romance."

"Really?" LaVonne perked up, but only a little.

"It was in the soup."

"The veggies?"

"No, the crackers," K.O. said and hoped she wasn't carrying this too far. "I crumbled them in the soup and—"

"What did you see?" Then, before K.O. could answer, LaVonne held out one hand. "No, don't tell me, let me guess. It's about you and Wynn," her neighbor said. "It must be."

"No...no. Remember how you told me you don't have the sight when it comes to yourself? Well, apparently I don't, either."

LaVonne looked up from petting her two cats. Her gaze narrowed. "What did you see, then?"

"Like I said, it was about *you*," K.O. said, doing her best to sound excited. "You're going to meet the man of your dreams."

"I am?" She took a moment to consider this before her shoulders drooped once more.

"Yes, you! I saw it plain as anything."

"Human or feline?" LaVonne asked in a skeptical voice.

"Human," K.O. announced triumphantly.

"When?"

"The crackers didn't say exactly, but I felt it must be soon." K.O. didn't want to tell LaVonne too much, otherwise she'd ruin the whole thing. If she went overboard on the details, her friend would suspect K.O. was setting her up. She needed to be vague, but still implant the idea.

"I haven't left my condo all day," LaVonne mumbled, "and I don't plan to go out anytime in the near future. In fact, the way I feel right now, I'm going to be holed up in here all winter."

"You're overreacting."

Her neighbor studied her closely. "Katherine, you *really* saw something in the soup?"

"I did." Nothing psychic, but she wasn't admitting that. She'd seen elbow macaroni and kidney beans and, of course, the cracker crumbs.

"But you didn't take the class. How were you able to discover your psychic powers if you weren't there to hear the lecture from Madam Ozma?" she wanted to know.

K.O. crossed her fingers behind her back. "It must've rubbed off from spending all that time with you."

"You think so?" LaVonne asked hopefully.

"Sure." K.O. was beginning to feel bad about misleading her friend. She'd hoped to mention the invitation for Monday night, but it would be too obvious if she did so now.

"There might be something to it," LaVonne said, smiling for the first time. "You never know."

"True...one never knows."

"Look what happened with you and Wynn," LaVonne said with a glimmer of excitement. "The minute I saw those two raisins gravitate toward each other, I knew it held meaning."

"I could see that in the crackers, too."

This was beginning to sound like a church revival meeting. Any minute, she thought, LaVonne might stand up and shout *Yes, I believe!*

"Then Wynn met you," she burbled on, "and the instant he did, I saw the look in his eyes."

What her neighbor had seen was horror. LaVonne couldn't have known about their confrontation earlier that day. He'd clearly been shocked and, yes, horrified to run into K.O. again. Especially with the memory of her ranting in the café so fresh in his mind.

"You're right," LaVonne said and sat up straighter. "I shouldn't let a silly letter upset me."

"Right. And really, you don't even know how much of what your college friend wrote is strictly true." K.O. remembered the letter she'd written for Bill Mulcahy. Not exactly lies, but not the whole truth, either.

"That could be," LaVonne murmured, but she didn't seem convinced. "Anyway, I know better than to look to a man for happiness." LaVonne was sounding more like her old self. "Happiness comes from within, isn't that right, Martin?" she asked, holding her cat up. Martin dangled from her grasp, mewing plaintively. "I don't need a man to be complete, do I?"

K.O. stood up, gathering her packages as she did. Toys and books for the twins, wrapping paper, a jar of specialty olives.

"Thanks for stopping by," LaVonne said when K.O. started toward the door. "I feel a hundred percent better already."

"Keep your eyes open now," she told LaVonne. "The man in the soup could be right around the corner." Or on the top floor of their condo building, she added silently.

"I will," her neighbor promised and, still clutching Martin, she shut the door.

Sunday afternoon Wynn came to K.O.'s door at three, his expression morose.

"Cheer up," she urged. "Just how bad can it be?"

"Wait until you meet Moon Puppy. Then you'll know."

"Come on, is your father really *that* bad?"

Wynn sighed deeply. "I suppose not. He's lonely without my mother. At loose ends."

"That's good." She paused, hearing what she'd said. "It's not good that he's lonely, but... Well, you know what I mean." LaVonne might seem all the more attractive to him if he craved female companionship. LaVonne deserved someone who needed her, who would appreciate her and her cats and her...psychic talents.

"You ready?" he asked.

"Let me grab my coat."

"You don't have to do this, you know."

"Wynn, I'm happy to," she assured him, and she meant it.

The airport traffic was snarled, and it took two turns through the short-term parking garage to find an available space. Thankfully they'd allotted plenty of time.

Wynn had agreed to meet his father at baggage claim. No more than five minutes after they'd staked out a place near the luggage carousel, a man wearing a Hawaiian shirt, with long dark hair tied in a ponytail, walked toward them. He didn't have a jacket or coat.

K.O. felt Wynn stiffen.

"Wynn!" The man hurried forward.

Wynn met his father halfway, with K.O. trailing behind, and briefly hugged him. "Hello, Dad." He put his hand on K.O.'s shoulder. "This is my friend Katherine O'Connor. Katherine, this is my father, Moon Puppy Jeffries."

Moon Puppy winced. "Delighted to meet you, Katherine," he said politely. "But please, call me Max. I don't go by Moon Puppy anymore."

"Welcome to Seattle," K.O. said, shaking hands. "I'm sorry you didn't arrive to sunshine and warmer weather."

"Thank you. Don't worry, I've got a jacket in my bag."

In a few minutes Max had collected his suitcase and Wynn led the way to his car. "It's been unseasonably chilly," K.O. said, making small talk as they took the escalator to the parking garage. Max had retrieved his jacket by then.

At the car, Wynn took the suitcase from his father and stored it in the trunk. This gave K.O. an opportunity to study father and son. She glanced at Wynn and then back at his father. After the description Wynn had given her, she'd expected something quite different. Yes, Max Jeffries looked like an old hippie, as Wynn had said, but his hair was neatly trimmed and combed. He wore clean, pressed clothes and had impeccable manners. He was an older version of Wynn and just as respectable looking, she thought. Well, except for the hair.

"It was a surprise to hear you were coming for Christmas," Wynn commented when he got into the car.

"I figured it would be," his father said. "I didn't mention it earlier because I was afraid you'd find a convenient excuse for me not to come."

So Max Jeffries was direct and honest, too. A lot like his son. K.O. liked him even more.

They chatted on the ride into Seattle, and K.O. casually invited him for cocktails the following afternoon.

"I'd enjoy that," Wynn's father told her.

"Katherine wants to introduce you to her neighbor, LaVonne."

"I see," Max said with less enthusiasm and quickly changed the subject. "I understand your book is selling nicely."

"Yes, I'm fortunate to have a lot of publisher support."

"He's writing a second book," K.O. said, joining the conversation. It pleased her that Max seemed proud of his son.

"So, how long have you two been seeing each other?" Max asked, looking at K.O.

"Not long," Wynn answered for them. His gaze caught K.O.'s in the rearview mirror. "We met through a psychic," he said.

"We most certainly did not." K.O. was about to argue when she realized Wynn was smiling. "We actually met through a mutual friend who believes she has psychic powers," she explained, not telling Max that her neighbor and this "psychic" were one and the same.

As they exited off the freeway and headed into downtown Seattle and toward Blossom Street, Max said, "I had no idea Seattle was this beautiful."

"Oh, just wait until nighttime," K.O. told him. It was fast becoming dark, and city lights had begun to sparkle. "There's lots to do at night. Wynn and I took a horse-drawn carriage ride last week and then on Friday night we went on a merry-go-round."

"My first such experience," Wynn said, a smile quivering at the edges of his mouth.

"Your mother and I never took you?" Max sounded incredulous.

"Never."

"I know I had some failings as a father," Max said despondently.

"Not getting to ride on a merry-go-round isn't exactly a big deal, Dad. Don't worry about it," Wynn muttered.

That seemed to ease his father's mind. "So what's on the agenda for tomorrow?" he asked brightly.

Wynn cast K.O. a look as if to say he'd told her so.

"I can take you on a tour of Pike Place Market," K.O. offered.

"That would be great." Max thanked her with a warm smile. "I was hoping to get a chance to go up the Space Needle while I'm here, too."

"We can do that on Tuesday."

Max nodded. "Do you have any free time, Wynn?" he asked.

"Some," Wynn admitted with obvious reluctance. "But not much. In addition to my appointments and writing schedule, I'm still doing promotion for my current book."

"Of course," Max murmured.

K.O. detected a note of sadness in his voice and wanted to reassure him. Unfortunately she didn't know how.

Wynn phoned K.O. early Monday morning. "I don't think this is going to work," he whispered.

"Pardon?" K.O. strained to hear.

"Meet me at the French Café," he said, his voice only slightly louder.

"When?" She had her sweats on and was ready to tackle her treadmill. After shedding the two pounds, she'd gained them again. It wasn't much, but enough to send her racing for a morning workout. She knew how quickly these things could get out of control.

"Now," he said impatiently. "Want me to pick you up?"

"No. I'll meet you there in ten minutes."

By the time she entered the café, Wynn had already

purchased two cups of coffee and procured a table. "What's wrong?" she asked as she pulled out the chair.

"He's driving me insane!"

"Wynn, I like your father. You made him sound worse than a deadbeat dad, but he's obviously proud of you and—"

"Do you mind if we don't list his admirable qualities just now?" He brought one hand to his temple, as if warding off a headache.

"All right," she said, doing her best to understand.

"The reason I called is that I don't think it's a good idea to set him up with LaVonne."

"Why not?" K.O. thought her plan was brilliant. She had everything worked out in her mind; she'd bought the liquor and intended to dust and vacuum this afternoon. As far as she was concerned, the meeting of Max and LaVonne was destiny. Christmas romances were always the best.

"Dad isn't ready for another relationship," Wynn declared. "He's still mourning my mother."

"Shouldn't he be the one to decide that?" Wynn might be a renowned child psychologist but she believed everyone was entitled to make his or her own decisions, especially in matters of the heart. She considered it all right to lend a helping hand, however. That was fair.

"I can tell my father's not ready," Wynn insisted.

"But I invited him for drinks this evening and he accepted." It looked as if her entire day was going to be spent with Max Jeffries, aka Moon Puppy. Earlier she'd agreed to take him to Pike Place Market, which was a

must-see for anyone visiting Seattle. It was always an entertaining place for tourists, but never more so than
during the holiday season. The whole market had an air
of festivity, the holiday mood infectious.

"What about LaVonne?" he asked.

"I'll give her a call later." K.O. hadn't wanted to be
obvious about this meeting. Still, when LaVonne met
Max, she'd know, the same way Wynn and K.O. had
known, that they were being set up.

"Don't," he said, cupping the coffee mug with
both hands.

"Why not?"

He frowned. "I have a bad feeling about this."

K.O. smothered a giggle. "Are you telling me you've
found your own psychic powers?"

"Hardly," he snorted.

"Wynn," she said, covering his hand with hers in
a gesture of reassurance. "It's going to work out
fine, trust me." Hmm. She seemed to be saying that
a lot these days.

He exhaled slowly, as if it went against his better judgment to agree. "All right, do whatever you think is best."

"I've decided to simplify things. I'm serving egg-
nog and cookies." And olives, if anyone wanted them.
When she'd find time to bake she didn't know, but
K.O. was determined to do this properly.

"Come around five-thirty," she suggested.

"That early?"

"Yes. You're taking care of arranging their dinner, right?"

"Ah...I don't think they'll get that far."

"But they might," she said hopefully. "You make the reservation, and if they don't want to go, then we will. Okay?"

He nodded. "I'll see what I can do." Wynn took one last swallow of coffee and stood. "I've got to get to the office." Slipping into his overcoat, he confided, "I have a patient this morning. Emergency call."

K.O. wondered what kind of emergency that would be—an ego that needed splinting? A bruised id? But she knew better than to ask. "Have a good day," was all she said. In his current mood, that was an iffy proposition. K.O. couldn't help wondering what Max had done to upset him.

"You, too," he murmured, then added, "And thank you for looking after Moon Puppy."

"His name is Max," K.O. reminded him.

"Maybe to you, but to me he'll always be the hippie surfer bum I grew up with." Wynn hurried out of the café.

By five that afternoon, K.O. felt as if she'd never left the treadmill. After walking for forty minutes on her machine, she showered, baked and decorated three dozen cookies and then met Wynn's father for a whirlwind tour of the Seattle waterfront, starting with Pike Place. She phoned LaVonne from the Seattle Aquarium. LaVonne had instantly agreed to drinks, and K.O. had a hard time getting off the phone. LaVonne chatted excitedly about the man in the soup, the man K.O. had claimed to see with her "psychic" eyes. Oh, dear, maybe this had gone a little too far....

Max was interested in absolutely everything, so they

didn't get back to Blossom Street until after four, which gave K.O. very little time to prepare for *the meeting*.

She vacuumed and dusted and plumped up the sofa pillows and set out a dish of peppermint candies, a favorite of LaVonne's. The decorated sugar cookies were arranged on a special Santa plate. K.O. didn't particularly like sugar cookies, which, therefore, weren't as tempting as shortbread or chocolate chip would've been. She decided against the olives.

K.O. was stirring the rum into the eggnog when she saw the blinking light on her phone. A quick check told her it was Zelda. She didn't have even a minute to chat and told herself she'd return the call later.

Precisely at 5:30 p.m., just after she'd put on all her Christmas CDs, Wynn arrived without his father. "Where's your dad?" K.O. demanded as she accepted the bottle of wine he handed her.

"He's never on time if there's an excuse to be late," Wynn muttered. "He'll get here when he gets here. You noticed he doesn't wear a watch?"

K.O. had noticed and thought it a novelty. LaVonne wasn't known for her punctuality, either, so they had at least that much in common. Already this relationship revealed promise—in her opinion, anyway.

"How did your afternoon go?" Wynn asked. He sat down on the sofa and reached for a cookie, nodding his head to the tempo of "Jingle Bell Rock."

"Great. I enjoyed getting to know your father."

Wynn glanced up, giving her a skeptical look.

"What is it with you two?" she asked gently, sitting beside him.

Wynn sighed. "I didn't have a happy childhood, except for the time I spent with my grandparents. I resented being dragged hither and yon, based on where the best surf could be found. I hated living with a bunch of self-absorbed hippies whenever we returned to the commune, which was their so-called home base. For a good part of my life, I had the feeling I was a hindrance my father tolerated."

"Oh, Wynn." The unhappiness he still felt was at odds with the amusing stories he'd told about his childhood at Chez Jerome and during dinner with Vickie and John. She'd originally assumed that he was reflecting his own upbringing in his "Free Child" theories, but she now saw that wasn't the case. Moon Puppy Max might have been a hippie, but he'd imposed his own regimen on his son. Not much "freedom" there.

"Well, that's my life," he said stiffly. "I don't want my father here and I dislike the way he's using you and—"

"He's not using me."

He opened his mouth to argue, but apparently changed his mind. "I'm not going to let my father come between us."

"Good, because I'd feel terrible if that happened." This would be a near-perfect relationship—if it wasn't for the fact that he was Wynn Jeffries, author of *The Free Child*. And the fact that he hadn't forgiven his father, who'd been a selfish and irresponsible parent.

His eyes softened. "I won't let it." He kissed her then, and K.O. slipped easily into his embrace. He wrapped his arms around her and they exchanged a series of deep and probing kisses that left K.O.'s head reeling.

"Katherine." Wynn breathed harshly as he abruptly released her.

She didn't want him to stop.

"You'd better answer your door," he advised.

K.O. had been so consumed by their kisses that she hadn't heard the doorbell. "Oh," she breathed, shaking her head to clear away the fog of longing. This man did things to her heart—not to mention the rest of her—that even a romance novelist couldn't describe.

Wynn's father stood on the other side of the door, wearing another Hawaiian flowered shirt, khaki pants and flip-flops. From the way he'd dressed, he could be on a tropical isle rather than in Seattle with temperatures hovering just above freezing. K.O. could tell that Max's choice of clothes irritated Wynn, but to his credit, Wynn didn't comment.

Too bad the current Christmas song was "Rudolph," instead of "Mele Kaliki Maka."

K.O. welcomed him and had just poured his eggnog when the doorbell chimed again. Ah, the moment she'd been waiting for. Her friend had arrived. K.O. glided toward the door and swept it open as if anticipating Santa himself.

"LaVonne," she said, leaning forward to kiss her friend's cheek. "How good of you to come." Her neighbor had brought Tom with her. The oversize feline was draped over her arm like a large furry purse.

"This is so kind of you," LaVonne said. She looked startled at seeing Max.

"Come in, please," K.O. said, gesturing her inside. She realized how formal she sounded—like a character in an old drawing room comedy. "Allow me to introduce Wynn's father, Max Jeffries. Max, this is La-Vonne Young."

Max stood and backed away from LaVonne. "You have a cat on your arm."

"This is Tom," LaVonne said. She glanced down lovingly at the cat as she stepped into the living room. "Would you like to say hello?" She held Tom out, but Max shook his head adamantly.

By now he'd backed up against the wall. "I don't like cats."

"What?" She sounded shocked. "Cats are magical creatures."

"Maybe to you they are," the other man protested. "I don't happen to be a cat person."

Wynn shared an I-told-you-so look with K.O.

"May I get you some eggnog?" K.O. asked, hoping to rescue the evening from a less-than-perfect beginning.

"Please," LaVonne answered just as "Have Yourself a Merry Little Christmas" began.

Eager for something to do, K.O. hurried into the kitchen and grabbed the pitcher of eggnog.

She heard Tom hiss loudly and gulped down some of her own eggnog to relax.

"Your cat doesn't like me," Max said as he carefully approached the sofa.

"Oh, don't be silly. Tom's the friendly one."

"You mean you have *more* than one?"

"Dad," Wynn said, "why don't you sit down and make yourself comfortable. You're quite safe. Tom is very well-behaved."

"I don't like cats," Max reiterated.

"Tom is gentle and loving," LaVonne said.

Max slowly approached the sofa. "Then why is he hissing at me?"

"He senses your dislike," LaVonne explained. She gave Max a dazzling smile. "Pet him, and he'll be your friend for life."

"See, Dad?" Wynn walked over to LaVonne, who sat with Tom on her lap. He ran his hand down Tom's back and the tabby purred with pleasure.

"He likes you," Max said.

"He'll like you, too, as soon as you pet him." LaVonne was still smiling happily, stroking the cat's head.

Max came a bit closer. "You live in the building?" he asked, making his way, step by careful step, toward LaVonne.

"Just across the hall," she answered.

"Your husband, too?"

"I'm single. Do you enjoy cards? Because you're welcome to stop by anytime."

K.O. delivered the eggnog. This was going even better than she'd hoped. Max was already interested and LaVonne was issuing invitations. She recognized the gleam in the other man's eyes. A sense of triumph filled her and she cast a glance in Wynn's direction. Wynn was just reaching into his pocket, withdrawing a real-looking catnip mouse.

Relaxed now, Max leaned forward to pet Tom.

At that very moment, chaos broke out. Although LaVonne claimed she'd never known Tom to take a dislike to anyone, the cat clearly detested Max. Before anyone could react, he sprang from her lap and grabbed Max's bare arm. The cat's claws dug in, drawing blood. He wasn't about to let go, either.

"Get him off," Max screamed, thrashing his arm to and fro in an effort to free himself from the cat-turned-killer. Wynn was desperately—and futilely—trying to distract Tom by waving the toy mouse. It didn't help.

"Tom, Tom!" LaVonne screeched at the top of her lungs.

Blood spurted onto the carpet.

In a panic, Max pulled at Tom's fur. The cat then sank his teeth into Max's hand and Max yelped in pain.

"Don't hurt my cat," LaVonne shrieked.

Frozen to the spot, K.O. watched in horror as the scene unfolded. Wynn dropped the mouse, and if not for his quick action, K.O. didn't know what would have happened. Before she could fully comprehend how he'd done it, Wynn had disentangled Tom from his father's arm. LaVonne instantly took her beloved cat into her embrace and cradled him against her side.

At the sight of his own blood, Max looked like he was about to pass out. K.O. hurriedly got him a clean towel, shocked at the amount of blood. The scratches seemed deep. "Call 911," Max shouted.

Wynn pulled out his cell phone. "That might not be a bad idea," he said to K.O. "Cat scratches can get infected."

"Contact the authorities, too," Max added, glaring at LaVonne. He stretched out his good arm and pointed at her. "I want that woman arrested and her animal destroyed."

LaVonne cried out with alarm and hovered protectively over Tom. "My poor kitty," she whispered.

"You're worried about the *cat?*" Max said. "I'm bleeding to death and you're worried about your cat?"

Wynn replaced his phone. "The medics are on their way."

"Oh...good." K.O. could already hear sirens in the background. She turned off her CD player. Thinking she should open the lobby door, she left the apartment, and when the aid car arrived, she directed the paramedics. Things had gotten worse in the short time she was gone. Max and LaVonne were shouting at each other as the small living room filled with people. Curious onlookers crowded the hallway outside her door.

"My cat scratched him and I'm sorry, but he provoked Tom," LaVonne said stubbornly.

"I want that woman behind bars." Max stabbed his finger in LaVonne's direction.

"Sir, sir, we need you to settle down," instructed the paramedic who was attempting to take his blood pressure.

"While she's in jail, declaw her cat," Max threw in.

Wynn stepped up behind K.O. "Yup," he whispered. "This is a match made in heaven, all right."

Then, just when K.O. was convinced nothing more could go wrong, her phone started to ring.

Chapter

12

"**D**on't you think you should answer that?" the paramedic treating Max's injuries asked.

K.O. was too upset to move. The romantic interlude she'd so carefully plotted couldn't have gone worse. At least Wynn seemed to understand her distress.

"I'll get it," Wynn said, and strode into the kitchen. "O'Connor residence," he said. At the way his eyes instantly shot to her, K.O. regretted not answering the phone herself.

"It's your sister," he said, holding the phone away from his ear.

Even above the racket K.O. could hear Zelda's high-pitched excitement. Her idol, Dr. Wynn Jeffries, had just spoken to her. The last person K.O.

wanted to deal with just then was her younger sister. However, she couldn't subject Wynn to Zelda's adoration.

She took the phone, but even before she had a chance to speak, Zelda was shrieking, "Is it *really* you, Dr. Jeffries? Really and truly?"

"Actually, no," K.O. informed her sister. "It's me."

"But Dr. Jeffries is with you?"

"Yes."

"Keep him there!"

"I beg your pardon?"

"Don't let him leave," Zelda said, sounding even more excited. "I'm calling on my cell. I'm only a few minutes away." She took a deep breath. "I need to talk to him. It's urgent. Zach and I just had the biggest argument *ever*, and I need to talk to Dr. Jeffries."

"Zelda," K.O. cut in. "Now is not the best time for you to visit."

"Didn't you hear me?" her sister cried. "This is an emergency."

With that, the phone went dead. Groaning, K.O. replaced the receiver.

"Is something wrong?" Wynn asked as he stepped around the paramedic who was still looking after Max.

"It's Zelda. She wants—no, *needs*—to talk to you. According to her it's an emergency." K.O. felt the need to warn him. "She's already on her way."

"Now? You mean she's coming now?"

K.O. nodded. "Apparently so." Zelda hadn't mentioned what this argument with Zach was about. Three guesses said it had to do with Christmas and Wynn's theories. Oh, great. Her sister was arriving at the scene of a disaster.

"Are you taking him to the h-hospital?" LaVonne sobbed, covering her mouth with both hands.

"It's just a precaution," the medic answered. "A doctor needs to look at those scratches."

"Not that dreadful man!" LaVonne cried, pointing at Max. "I'm talking about my cat."

"Oh." The paramedic glanced at his companion. "Unfortunately, in instances such as this, we're obliged to notify Animal Control."

"You're hauling my Tom to...jail?"

"Quarantine," he told her gently.

For a moment LaVonne seemed about to faint. Wynn put his arm around the older woman's shoulders and led her to the sofa so she could sit down. "This can't be happening," LaVonne wailed. "I can't believe this is happening to my Tom."

"Your cat should be—"

Wynn cast his father a look meaningful enough to silence the rest of whatever Max had planned to say.

"I'm going to be scarred for life," Max shouted. "I just hope you've got good insurance, because you're going to pay for this. And you're going to pay big."

"Don't you dare threaten me!" LaVonne had recovered enough to shout back.

With his arm stretched out in front of him, Max Jeffries followed the paramedic out of the condo and past the crowd of tenants who'd gathered in the hallway outside K.O.'s door.

"That…that terrible man just threatened me," La-
Vonne continued. "Tom's never attacked anyone like
this before."

"Please, please, let me through."

K.O. heard her sister's voice.

Meanwhile LaVonne was weeping loudly. "My poor
Tom. My poor, poor Tom. What will become of him?"

"What on earth is going on here?" Zelda demanded
as she made her way into the apartment. The second
paramedic was gathering up his equipment and getting ready to leave. The blood-soaked towels K.O.
had wrapped around Max's arm were on the floor.
The scene was completely chaotic and Zelda's arrival
only added to the mayhem.

"Your f-father wants to s-sue me," LaVonne stuttered, pleading with Wynn. "*Do* something. Promise
me you'll talk to him."

Wynn sat next to LaVonne and tried to comfort
her. "I'll do what I can," he said. "I'm sure that once
my father's settled down he'll listen to reason."

LaVonne's eyes widened, as though she had trouble believing Wynn. "I don't mean to insult you, but
your father doesn't seem like a reasonable man to me."

"Whose blood is that?" Zelda asked, hands on her
hips as she surveyed the room.

K.O. tried to waylay her sister. "As you can see,"
she said, gesturing about her, "this *really* isn't a good
time to visit."

"I don't care," Zelda insisted. "I need to talk to Dr.
Jeffries." She thrust his book at him and a pen. "Could
you sign this for me?"

Just then a man wearing a jacket that identified him as an Animal Control officer came in, holding an animal carrier. The name Walt was embroidered on his shirt.

Wynn quickly signed his name, all the while watching the man from Animal Control.

LaVonne took one look at Walt and burst into tears. She buried her face in her hands and started to rock back and forth.

"Where's the cat?" Walt asked.

"We've got him in the bathroom," the paramedic said.

"Please don't hurt him," LaVonne wept. "Please, please..."

Walt raised a reassuring hand. "I handle situations like this every day. Don't worry, Miss, I'll be gentle with your pet."

"Dr. Jeffries, Dr. Jeffries." Zelda slipped past K.O. and climbed over LaVonne's knees in order to reach Wynn. She plunked herself down on the coffee table, facing him. "I really do need to talk to you."

"Zelda!" K.O. was shocked by her sister's audacity.

"Zach and I never argue," Zelda said over her shoulder, glaring at K.O. as if that fact alone should explain her actions. "This will only take a few minutes, I promise. Once I talk to Dr. Jeffries, I'll be able to tell Zach what he said and then he'll understand."

LaVonne wailed as Walt entered the bathroom.

K.O. heard a hiss and wondered if her shower curtain was now in shreds. She'd never seen a cat react to anyone the way Tom had to Wynn's father. Even now she couldn't figure out what had set him off.

"This'll only take a minute," Zelda went on. "You see, my husband and I read your book, and it changed everything. Well, to be perfectly honest, I don't know if Zach read the whole book." A frown crossed her face.

"LaVonne, perhaps I should take you home now," K.O. suggested, thinking it might be best for her neighbor not to see Tom leave the building caged.

"I can't leave," LaVonne said. "Not until I know what's happening to Tom."

The bathroom door opened and Walt reappeared with Tom safely inside the cat carrier.

"Tom, oh, Tom," LaVonne wailed, throwing her arms wide.

"Dr. Jeffries, Dr. Jeffries," Zelda pleaded, vying for his attention.

"Zelda, couldn't this wait a few minutes?" K.O. asked.

"Where are you taking Tom?" LaVonne demanded.

"We're just going to put him in quarantine," Walt said in a soothing voice.

"Tom's had all his shots. My veterinarian will verify everything you need to know."

"Good. Still, we're legally required to do this. I guarantee he'll be well looked after."

"Thank you," K.O. said, relieved.

"Can I speak to Dr. Jeffries now?" Zelda asked impatiently. "You see, I don't think my husband really did read your book," she continued, picking up where she'd left off. "If he had, we wouldn't be having this disagreement."

"I'll see LaVonne home," K.O. said. She closed

one arm around her friend's waist and steered her out of the condo.

Wynn looked at Zelda and sent K.O. a beseeching glance.

"I'll be back as soon as I can," she promised.

He nodded and mouthed the word *hurry*.

K.O. rolled her eyes. As she escorted LaVonne, the sound of her sister's voice followed her into the hallway, which was fortunately deserted. It didn't take long to get LaVonne settled in her own place. Once she had Phillip and Martin with her, she was comforted, since both seemed to recognize her distress and lavished their mistress with affection.

When she returned to her condo, K.O. found that her sister hadn't moved. She still sat on the coffee table, so close to Wynn that their knees touched. Judging by the speed with which Zelda spoke, K.O. doubted he'd had a chance to get a word in edgewise.

"Then the girls started to cry," Zelda was saying. "They want a Christmas tree and Zach thinks we should get one."

"I don't believe—" Wynn was cut off before he could finish his thought.

"I know you don't actually condemn Christmas trees, but I didn't want to encourage the girls about this Santa thing, and I feel decorating a tree would do that. If we're going to bury Santa under the sleigh—and I'm in complete agreement with you, Dr. Jeffries—then it makes sense to downplay everything else having to do with Christmas, too. Certainly all the commercial aspects. But how do I handle the girls' reaction when they hear their friends talking about Santa?"

Wynn raised a finger, indicating that he'd like to comment. His request, however, was ignored.

"I feel as you do," Zelda rushed on breathlessly, bringing one hand to her chest in a gesture of sincerity. "It's wrong to mislead one's children with figures of fantasy. It's wrong, wrong, wrong. Zach agreed with me—but only in principle, as it turns out. Then we got into this big fight over the Christmas tree and you have to understand that my husband and I hardly ever argue, so this is all very serious."

"Where's Zach now?" K.O. asked, joining Wynn on the sofa.

As if to let her know how much he appreciated having her back, Wynn reached for her hand. At Zelda's obvious interest, he released it, but the contact, brief as it was, reassured her.

Zelda lowered her head. "Zach's at home with the girls. If you must know, I sort of left my husband with the twins."

"Zoe and Zara," K.O. said under her breath for Wynn's benefit.

"Despite my strong feelings on the matter, I suspect my husband is planning to take our daughters out to purchase a Christmas tree." She paused. "A *giant* one."

"Do you think he might even decorate it with Santa figurines and reindeer?" K.O. asked, pretending to be scandalized.

"Oh, I hope not," Zelda cried. "That would ruin

everything I've tried so hard to institute in our family."

"As I recall," Wynn finally said. He waited a moment as if to gauge whether now was a good time to insert his opinions. When no one interrupted him, he continued. "I didn't say anything in my book against Christmas trees, giant or otherwise."

"Yes, I know that, but it seems to me—"

"It seems to *me* that you've carried this a bit further than advisable," Wynn said gently. "Despite what you and K.O. think, I don't want to take Christmas away from your children or from you and your husband. It's a holiday to be celebrated. Family and traditions are important."

K.O. agreed with him. She felt gratified that there was common ground between them, an opinion on which they could concur. Nearly everything she'd heard about Wynn to this point had come from her sister. K.O. was beginning to wonder if Zelda was taking his advice to extremes.

"Besides," he said, "there's a fundamental contradiction in your approach. You're correct to minimize the element of fantasy—but your children are telling you what they want, aren't they? And you're ignoring that."

K.O. wanted to cheer. She took Wynn's hand again, and this time he didn't let go.

"By the way," Zelda said, looking from Wynn to K.O. and staring pointedly at their folded hands. "Just when did you two start dating?"

"I told you—"

"What you said," her sister broke in, "was that Dr. Jeffries lived in the same building as you."

"I told you we went to dinner a couple of times."

"You most certainly did not." Zelda stood up, an irritated expression on her face. "Well, okay, you did mention the one dinner at Chez Jerome."

"Did you know that I'm planning to join Katherine this Friday when she's watching the twins?" Wynn asked.

"She's bringing you along?" Zelda's eyes grew round with shock. "You might've said something to me," she burst out, clearly upset with K.O.

"I thought I had told you."

"You haven't talked to me in days," Zelda wailed. "It's like I'm not even your sister anymore. The last I heard, you were going to get Dr. Jeffries's autograph for me, and you didn't, although I specifically asked if you would."

"Would you prefer I not watch the twins?" Wynn inquired.

"Oh, no! It would be an honor," Zelda assured him, smiling, her voice warm and friendly. She turned to face K.O. again, her eyes narrowed. "But my own sister," she hissed, "should've told me she intended on having a famous person spend the night in my home."

"You're not to tell anyone," K.O. insisted.

Zelda glared at her. "Fine. I won't."

"Promise me," K.O. said. Wynn was entitled to his privacy; the last thing he needed was a fleet of parents in SUVs besieging him about his book.

"I promise." Without a further word, Zelda grabbed her purse and made a hasty exit.

"Zelda!" K.O. called after her. "I think we need to talk about this for a minute."

"I don't have a minute. I need to get home to my husband and children. We'll talk later," Zelda said in an ominous tone, and then she was gone.

Chapter

13

"I'd better leave now, as well," Wynn announced, getting his coat. "Dad'll need me to drive him back from the emergency room." K.O. was glad he didn't seem eager to go.

For her part, she wanted him to stay. Her nerves were frayed. Nothing had worked out as she'd planned and now everyone was upset with her. LaVonne, her dear friend, was inconsolable. Zelda was annoyed that K.O. hadn't kept her updated on the relationship with Wynn. Max Jeffries was just plain angry, and while the brunt of his anger had been directed at LaVonne, K.O. realized he wasn't pleased with her, either. Now Wynn had to go. Reluctantly K.O. walked him to the door. "Let me know how your father's doing, okay?" she asked, looking up at him.

"Of course." Wynn placed his hands on her shoulders. "You know I'd much rather be here with you."

She saw the regret in his eyes and didn't want to make matters worse. "Thank you for being so wonderful," she said and meant it. Wynn had been the voice of calm and reason throughout this entire ordeal.

"I'll call you about my father as soon as I hear."

"Thank you."

After a brief hug, he hurried out the door.

After a dinner of eggnog and peanut butter on crackers, K.O. waited up until after midnight, but no word came. Finally, when she couldn't keep her eyes open any longer, she climbed between the sheets and fell instantly asleep. This surprised her; she hadn't anticipated sleeping easily or well. When she woke the following morning, the first thoughts that rushed into her mind were of Wynn. Something must have happened, something unexpected and probably dreadful, or he would've called.

Perhaps the hospital had decided to keep Max overnight for observation. While there'd been a lot of blood involved, K.O. didn't think any of the cuts were deep enough to require stitches. But if Max had filed a police report, that would cause problems for La-Vonne and might explain Wynn's silence. Every scenario that roared through her head pointed to trouble.

Even before she made her first cup of coffee, K.O.'s stomach was in knots. As she headed into the kitchen, she discovered a sealed envelope that had been slipped under her door.

It read:

Katherine,

I didn't get back from the hospital until late and I was afraid you'd already gone to bed. Dad's home and, other than being cantankerous, he's doing fine, so don't worry on his account. The hospital cleaned and bandaged his arm and said he'd be good as new in a week or so. Please reassure LaVonne. The cuts looked worse than they actually were.

Could you stop by my office this afternoon? I'm at the corner of Fourth and Willow, Suite 1110. Does one o'clock work for you? If you can't fit it into your schedule, please contact my assistant and let her know. Otherwise, I'll look forward to seeing you, then.

Wynn

Oh, she could fit it in. She could *definitely* fit it in. K.O. was ready to climb Mount Rainier for a chance to see Wynn. With purpose now, she showered and dressed and then, on the off chance Max might need something, she phoned Wynn's condo.

His father answered right away, which made her wonder if he'd been sitting next to the phone waiting for a call.

"Good morning," she said, striving to sound cheerful and upbeat—all the while hoping Max wasn't one to hold grudges.

"Who is this?"

"It's K.O.," she told him, her voice faltering despite her effort to maintain a cheery tone.

He hesitated as if he needed time to place who she might be. "Oh," he finally said. "The woman from downstairs. The woman whose *friend* caused me irreparable distress." After another pause, he said, "I'm afraid I might be suffering from trauma-induced amnesia."

"Excuse me?" K.O. was sure she'd misunderstood.

"I was attacked yesterday by a possibly rabid beast and am fortunate to be alive. I don't remember much after that vicious animal sank its claws into my arm," he added shakily.

K.O. closed her eyes for a moment. "I'm so sorry to hear that," she said, going along with it. "But the hospital released you, I see."

"Yes." This was said with disdain; apparently, he felt the medical profession had made a serious error in judgment. "I'm on heavy pain medication."

"Oh, dear."

"I don't know where my son's gone," he muttered fretfully.

If Wynn hadn't told his father he was at the office, then K.O. wasn't about to, either. She suspected Wynn had good reason to escape.

"Since you live in the building..." Max began.

"Uh..." She could see it coming. Max wanted her to sit and hold his uninjured hand for the rest of the day.

"I do, but unfortunately I'm on my way out."

"Oh."

It took K.O. a few more minutes to wade through the guilt he was shoveling in her direction. "I'll drop by and check on you later," she promised.

"Thank you," he said, ending their conversation with a groan, a last shovelful of guilt.

K.O. hung up the phone, groaning, too. This was

even worse than she'd imagined and she had a fine imagination. Max was obviously playing this incident for all it was worth. Irreparable distress. Rabid beast. Trauma-induced amnesia! Oh, brother.

Wanting to leave before Max decided to drop by, she hurried out the door and stopped at the French Café for a mocha and bran muffin. If ever she'd deserved one, it was now. At the rate her life was going, there wouldn't be enough peppermint mochas in the world to see her through another day like yesterday.

Rather than linger as she normally did, K.O. took her drink and muffin to go and enjoyed a leisurely stroll down Blossom Street. A walk would give her exercise and clear her mind, and just then clarity was what she needed. She admired the evergreen boughs and garlands decorating the storefronts, and the inventive variations on Christmas themes in every window. The weather remained unseasonably cold with a chance of snow flurries. In December Seattle was usually in the grip of gloomy winter rains, but that hadn't happened yet this year. The sky was already a clear blue with puffy clouds scattered about.

By the time she'd finished her peppermint mocha, K.O. had walked a good mile and felt refreshed in both body and mind. When she entered her building, LaVonne—wearing a housecoat—was stepping out of her condo to grab the morning paper. Her eyes were red and puffy and it looked as if she hadn't slept all night. She bent over to retrieve her paper.

"LaVonne," K.O. called out.

Her friend slowly straightened. "I thought I should

see if there's a report in the police blotter about Tom scratching that...that man," she spat out.

"I doubt it."

"Is he...back from the hospital?"

"Max Jeffries is alive and well. He sustained a few scratches, but it isn't nearly as bad as we all feared." Wynn's father seemed to be under the delusion that he'd narrowly escaped with his life, but she didn't feel the need to mention that. Nor did K.O. care to enlighten LaVonne regarding Max's supposed amnesia.

"I'm so glad." LaVonne sounded tired and sad.

"Is there anything I can get you?" K.O. asked, feeling partially to blame.

"Thanks for asking, but I'm fine." She gave a shuddering sob. "Except for poor Tom being in jail..."

"Call if you need me," K.O. said before she returned to her own apartment.

The rest of the morning passed quickly. She worked for a solid two hours and accomplished more in that brief time than she normally did in four. She finished a medical report, sent off some résumés by e-mail and drafted a Christmas letter for a woman in Zach's office who'd made a last-minute request. Then, deciding she should check on Max Jeffries, she went up for a quick visit. At twelve-thirty, she grabbed her coat and headed out the door again. With her hands buried deep in her red wool coat and a candy-cane striped scarf doubled around her neck, she walked to Wynn's office.

This was her first visit there, and she wasn't sure what to expect. When she stepped inside, she found a comfortable waiting room and thought it looked like any doctor's office.

A middle-aged receptionist glanced up and smiled warmly. "You must be Katherine," she said, extending her hand. "I'm Lois Church, Dr. Jeffries's assistant."

"Hello," K.O. said, returning her smile.

"Come on back. Doctor is waiting for you." Lois led her to a large room, lined with bookshelves and framed degrees. A big desk dominated one end, and there was a sitting area on the other side, complete with a miniature table and chairs and a number of toys.

Wynn stood in front of the bookcase, and when K.O. entered the room, he closed the volume he'd been reading and put it back in place.

Lois slipped quietly out of the room and shut the door.

"Hi," K.O. said tentatively, wondering at his mood.

He smiled. "I see you received my note."

"Yes," she said with a nod. She remained standing just inside his office.

"I asked you to come here to talk about my father. I'm afraid he's going a little overboard with all of this."

"I got that impression myself."

Wynn arched his brows. "You've spoken to him?"

She nodded again. "I stopped by to see how he's doing. He didn't seem to remember me right away. He says he's suffering from memory loss."

Wynn groaned.

"I hate to say this, but I assumed that hypochondria's what he's really suffering from." She paused. "Either that or he's faking it," she said boldly.

Wynn gave a dismissive shrug. "I believe your second diagnosis is correct. It's a recurring condition of his," he said with a wry smile.

K.O. didn't know quite what to say.

"He's exaggerating, looking for attention." Wynn motioned for her to sit down, which she did, sinking into the luxurious leather sofa. Wynn took the chair next to it. "I don't mean to sound unsympathetic, but for all his easygoing hippie ways, Moon Puppy—Max—can be quite the manipulator."

"Well, it's not like LaVonne did it on purpose or anything."

There was a moment's silence. "In light of what happened yesterday, do you still want me to accompany you to your sister's?" he asked.

K.O. would be terribly disappointed if he'd experienced a change of heart. "I hoped you would, but if you need to bow out because of your father, I understand."

"No," he said decisively. "I want to do this. It's important for us both, for our relationship."

K.O. felt the same way.

"I've already told my father that I have a business appointment this weekend, so he knows I'll be away."

That made K.O. smile. This *was* business. Sort of.

"I'd prefer that Max not know the two of us will be together. He'll want to join us and, frankly, dealing with him will be more work than taking care of the kids."

"All right." Despite a bit of residual guilt, K.O. was certainly willing to abide by his wishes. She was convinced that once Wynn spent time with Zoe and Zara, he'd know for himself that his theories didn't work. The twins and their outrageous behavior would speak more eloquently than she ever could.

"I'm afraid we might not have an opportunity to get together for the rest of the week."

She was unhappy about it but understood. With his injuries and need for attention, Max would dominate Wynn's time.

"Are you sure your father will be well enough by Friday for you to leave?" she asked.

"He'd better be," Wynn said firmly, "because I'm going. He'll survive. In case you hadn't already figured this out, he's a little...immature."

"Really?" she asked, feigning surprise. Then she laughed out loud.

Wynn smiled, too. "I'm going to miss you, Katherine," he said with a sigh. "I wish I could see you every day this week, but between work and Max..."

"I'll miss you, too."

Wynn checked his watch and K.O. realized that was her signal to go. Wynn had appointments.

They both stood.

"Before I forget," he said casually. "A friend of mine told me his company's looking for a publicist. It's a small publisher, Apple Blossom Books, right in the downtown area, not far from here."

"They are?" K.O.'s heart raced with excitement. A small publishing company would be ideal. "Really?"

"I mentioned your name, and Larry asked if you'd be willing to send in a résumé." Wynn picked up a business card from his desk and handed it to her. "You can e-mail it directly to him."

"Oh, Wynn, thank you." In her excitement, she hugged him.

That seemed to be all the encouragement he needed to keep her in his arms and kiss her. She responded with equal fervor, and it made her wonder how she could possibly go another three days until she saw him again.

They smiled at each other. Wynn threaded his fingers through her hair and brought his mouth to hers for another, deeper kiss.

A polite knock at the door was followed by the sound of it opening.

Abruptly Wynn released her, taking a step back. "Yes, Lois," he said, still looking at K.O.

"Your one-thirty appointment has arrived."

"I'll be ready in just a minute," he said. As soon as the door was shut, he leaned close, touching his forehead to hers. "I'd better get back to work."

"Me, too." But it was with real reluctance that they drew apart.

As K.O. left, glancing at the surly teen being ushered into his office, she felt that Friday couldn't come soon enough.

On Thursday afternoon, LaVonne invited K.O. for afternoon tea, complete with a plate of sliced fruitcake. "I'm feeling much better," her neighbor said as she poured tea into mugs decorated with cats in Santa costumes. "I've been allowed to visit Tom, and he's doing so well. In a couple of days, he'll be back home where he belongs." She frowned as if remembering Wynn's father. "No thanks to that dreadful man who had Tom taken away from me."

K.O. sat on the sofa and held her mug in one hand and a slice of fruitcake in the other. "I'm so pleased to hear Tom will be home soon." Her conscience had been bothering her, and for the sake of their friendship, K.O. felt the need to confess what she'd done.

"The best part is I haven't seen that maniac all week," LaVonne was saying.

K.O. gave her neighbor a tentative smile and lowered her gaze. She hadn't seen Max, either. Or Wynn, except for that brief visit to his office, although they'd e-mailed each other a couple of times. He'd kept her updated on his father and the so-called memory loss, from which Max had apparently made a sudden recovery. In fact, he now remembered a little too much, according to Wynn. But the wounds on his arm appeared to be healing nicely and Max seemed to enjoy the extra attention Wynn paid him. Wynn, meanwhile, was looking forward to the reprieve offered by their visit to Zelda's.

"I owe you an apology," K.O. said to LaVonne.

"Nonsense. You had no way of knowing how Tom would react to Mr. Jeffries."

"True, but..." She swallowed hard. "You should know..." She started again. "I didn't really have a psychic experience."

LaVonne set down her mug and stared at K.O. "You didn't actually see a man for me in the soup? You mean to say there *wasn't* any message in the cracker crumbs?"

"No," K.O. admitted.

"Oh."

"It might seem like I was making fun of you and your psychic abilities, but I wasn't, LaVonne, I truly wasn't. I thought that if you believed a man was coming into your life, you'd be looking for one, and if you were expecting to meet a man, then you just might, and I hoped that man would be Wynn's father, but clearly it wasn't...isn't." This was said without pausing for breath.

A short silence ensued, followed by a disappointed, "Oh."

"Forgive me if I offended you."

LaVonne took a moment to think this through. "You didn't," she said after a while. "I've more or less reached the same conclusion about my psychic abilities. But—" she smiled brightly "—guess what? I've signed up for another class in January." She reached for a second slice of fruitcake and smiled as Martin brought K.O. the catnip mouse Wynn had given Tom that ill-fated evening.

"Another one at the community college?" K.O. asked.

LaVonne shook her head. "No, I walked across the street into A Good Yarn and decided I'd learn how to knit."

"That sounds good."

"Want to come, too?" LaVonne asked.

Every time her friend enrolled in a new course, she urged K.O. to take it with her. Because of finances and her job search, K.O. had always declined. This time, however, she felt she might be able to swing it. Not to mention the fact that she owed LaVonne… "I'll see."

"Really?" Even this little bit of enthusiasm seemed to delight LaVonne. "That's wonderful."

"I had a job interview on Wednesday," K.O. told her, squelching the desire to pin all her hopes on this one interview. Apple Blossom Books, the publisher Wynn had recommended, had called her in almost immediately. She'd met with the president and the marketing manager, and they'd promised to get back to her before Christmas. For the first time in a long while, K.O. felt optimistic. A publishing company, even a small one, would be ideal.

"And?" LaVonne prompted.

"And..." K.O. said, smiling. "I'm keeping my fingers crossed."

"That's just great! I know you've been looking for ages."

"The Christmas letters are going well, too," she added. "I wrote another one this week for a woman in Zach's office. She kept thinking she had time and then realized she didn't, so it was a rush job."

"You might really be on to something, you know. A little sideline business every Christmas."

"You aren't upset with me about what I did, are you?" K.O. asked, returning to her apology. "You've been such a good friend, and I wouldn't do anything in the world to hurt you."

"Nah," LaVonne assured her, petting Phillip, who'd jumped into her lap. "If anyone's to blame it's that horrible man. As far as I'm concerned, he's a fruitcake." That said, she took another bite of the slice she'd been enjoying.

Wynn had devised a rather complicated plan of escape. On Friday afternoon he would leave his office at three-thirty and pick K.O. up on the corner of Blossom Street and Port Avenue. Because he didn't want to risk going inside and being seen by his father, she'd agreed to wait on the curb with her overnight bag.

K.O. was packed and ready long before the time

they'd arranged. At three, her phone rang. Without checking caller ID, she knew it had to be her sister.

"I can't believe Dr. Wynn Jeffries is actually coming to the house," she said and gave a shrill cry of excitement. "You can't *imagine* how jealous my friends are."

"No one's supposed to know about this," K.O. reminded her.

"No one knows exactly when he'll be here, but I did mention it to a few close friends."

"Zelda! You promised."

"I know, I know. I'm sorry, but I couldn't keep this to myself. You just don't understand what an honor it is to have Dr. Jeffries in my home."

"But…"

"Don't worry, no one knows it's this weekend," Zelda told her.

"You're *sure*?"

"I swear, all right?"

It would be a nightmare if a few dozen of Zelda's closest friends just happened to drop by the house unannounced. Unfortunately, K.O. didn't have any choice but to believe her.

"How are the girls?" K.O. asked, hoping the twins were up to their usual antics. She didn't want Zoe and Zara to be on their best behavior. That would ruin all her plans.

"They're fine. Well, mostly fine. Healthwise, they're both getting over ear infections."

Oh, dear. "You might've told me this before!" K.O. cried. Her mind shifted into overdrive. If the girls were sick, it would throw everything off. Wynn would insist their behavior was affected by how they were feeling.

"They've been on antibiotics for the last two weeks," Zelda said, breaking into her thoughts. "The doctor explained how important it is to finish the medicine, and they only have a couple of doses left. I wrote it all down for you and Dr. Jeffries, so there's no need to worry."

"Fine," K.O. said, relieved. "Anything else you're not telling me?"

Her sister went silent for a moment. "I can't think of anything. I've got a list of instructions for you and the phone numbers where we can be reached. I do appreciate this, you know."

K.O. in turn appreciated the opportunity to spend this time with the twins—and to share the experience with Wynn. At least they'd be able to stop tiptoeing around the subject of the Free Child movement.

"We have a Christmas tree," Zelda murmured as if she were admitting to a weakness of character. "Zach felt we needed one, and when I spoke to Dr. Jeffries last Monday he didn't discourage it. So I gave in, although I'm still not sure it's such a good idea."

"You made the right choice," K.O. told her.

"I hope so."

K.O. noticed the clock on her microwave and was shocked to see that it was time to meet Wynn. "Oh, my goodness, I've got to go. I'll see you in about thirty minutes."

K.O. hung up the phone and hurried to put on her long wool coat, hat and scarf. Grabbing her purse and overnight bag, she rushed outside. Traffic was heavy, and it was already getting dark. She'd planned to be waiting at the curb so when Wynn pulled up, she could quickly hop inside his car. Then they'd be on their way, with no one the wiser.

No sooner had she stepped out of the building than she saw Max Jeffries walking toward her. His cheeks were ruddy, as if he'd been out for a long stroll.

"Well, hello there, Katherine," he said cheerfully. "How are you this fine cold day?"

"Ah…" She glanced furtively around. "I'm going to my sister's tonight," she said when he looked pointedly at her small suitcase.

"Wynn's away himself."

"Pure coincidence," she told him and realized how guilty she sounded.

Max chuckled. "Business trip, he said."

She nodded, moving slowly toward the nearby corner of Blossom and Port. She kept her gaze focused on the street, fearing she was about to give everything away.

"I'm healing well," Max told her conversationally. "I had a couple of rough days, but the pain is much better now."

"I'm glad to hear it."

"Yes, me, too. I never want to see that crazy cat woman again as long as I live."

It demanded restraint not to immediately defend her friend, but K.O. managed. "I see your memory's back," she said instead, all the while keeping a lookout for Wynn.

"Oh, yes, it returned within a day or two. In some ways," he sighed, "I wished it hadn't. Because now all I can think about is how that vicious feline latched on to my arm."

Not wanting to give Max an excuse to continue the conversation, K.O. threw him a vague smile.

"Have you ever seen so much blood in your life?" he said with remarkable enthusiasm.

"Uh, no," she murmured. Since it was her towels that had cleaned it up, she had to confess there'd been lots.

"My son seems to be quite taken with you," Max said next.

As badly as she wanted to urge Max to go about his business, K.O. couldn't ignore that particular comment. Not when Max dropped this little morsel at her feet—much as Martin had presented her with the catnip mouse. "He does? Really?"

Max nodded.

"He talks about me?"

"Hmm. It's more a question of what he doesn't say than what he does. He was always an intense child. As a youngster... Well, I'm sure you don't have time to go into that right now."

K.O. thought she could see Wynn's car. "I don't... I'm sorry."

"Take my word for it, Wynn's interested in you."

K.O. felt like dancing in the street. "I'm interested in him, too," she admitted.

"Good, good," Max said expansively. "Well, I'd better get back inside. Have a nice weekend."

"I will. Thank you." It did look like Wynn's car. His timing was perfect—or almost. She hoped that when he reached the curb, his father would be inside the building.

Just then the front doors opened and out stepped LaVonne. She froze in midstep when she saw Wynn's father. He froze, too.

K.O. watched as LaVonne's eyes narrowed. She couldn't see Max's face, but from LaVonne's reaction, she assumed he shared her resentment. They seemed unwilling to walk past each other, and both stood there, looking wildly in all directions except ahead. If it hadn't been so sad, it would've been laughable.

K.O. could see that it was definitely Wynn's car. He smiled when he saw her and started to ease toward the curb. At the same moment, he noticed his father and LaVonne and instantly pulled back, merging into traffic again. He drove straight past K.O.

Now LaVonne and Max were staring at each other. They still hadn't moved, and people had to walk around them as they stood in the middle of the sidewalk.

K.O. had to find a way to escape without being detected. As best as she could figure, Wynn had to drive around the block. With one-way streets and heavy traffic, it might take him ten minutes to get back to Blossom. If she hurried, she might catch him on Port Avenue or another side street and avoid letting Max see them together.

"I think my ride's here," she said, backing away and dragging her suitcase with her.

They ignored her.

"Bye," she said, waving her hand.

This, too, went without comment. "I'll see you both later," she said, rushing past them and down the sidewalk.

Again there was no response.

K.O. didn't dare look back. Blossom Street had never seemed so long. She rounded the corner and walked some distance down Port, waiting until she saw Wynn's car again. Raising her arm as if hailing a taxi, she managed to catch his attention.

Wynn pulled up to the curb, reached over and opened the passenger door. "That was a close call," he murmured as she climbed inside.

"You have no idea," she said, shaking her head.

"Is everything all right?" he asked.

"I don't know and, frankly, I don't want to stick around and find out."

Wynn chuckled. "I don't, either," he said, rejoining the stream of traffic.

They were off on what she hoped would be a grand adventure in the land of Z.

"This is Zoe," K.O. said as her niece wrapped one arm around her leg. After a half-hour of instructions, Zelda was finally out the door, on her way to meet Zach at the hotel. The twins stood like miniature statues, dressed in jean coveralls and red polka-dot shirts, with their hair in pigtails. They each stared up at Wynn.

"No, I'm Zara."

K.O. narrowed her eyes, unsure whether to believe the child. The twins were identical and seemed to derive great satisfaction from fooling people, especially their parents.

"Zoe," K.O. challenged. "Tell the truth."

"I'm hungry."

"It'll be dinnertime soon," K.O. promised.

Zoe—and she felt sure it *was* Zoe—glared up at her. "I'm hungry *now*. I want to eat *now*." She punctuated her demand by stamping her foot. Her twin joined in, shouting that she, too, was hungry.

"I want dinner *now*," Zara insisted.

Wynn smiled knowingly. "Children shouldn't be forced to eat on a schedule. If they're hungry, we should feed them no matter what the clock says."

Until then, the girls had barely acknowledged Wynn. All of a sudden, he was their best friend. Both beamed brilliant smiles in his direction, then marched over and stood next to him, as though aligning themselves with his theories.

"What would you like for dinner?" he asked, squatting down so he was at eye level with them.

"Hot dogs," Zoe said, and Zara agreed. The two Yorkies, Zero and Zorro, seemed to approve, because they barked loudly and then scampered into the kitchen.

"I'll check the refrigerator," K.O. told him. Not long ago, Zelda hadn't allowed her daughters anywhere near hot dogs. She considered them unhealthy, low-quality fare that was full of nitrates and other preservatives. But nothing was off limits since Zelda had read *The Free Child* and become a convert.

"I'll help you look," Zara volunteered and tearing into the kitchen, threw open the refrigerator door and peered inside.

Not wanting to be left out, Zoe dragged over a kitchen chair and climbed on top. She yanked open the freezer and started tossing frozen food onto the floor. Zero and Zorro scrambled to get out of the way of flying frozen peas and fish.

"There aren't any hot dogs," K.O. said after a few minutes. "Let's choose something else." After all, it was only four o'clock and she was afraid that if the girls ate too early, they'd be hungry again later in the evening.

"I *want* a hot dog," Zara shouted.

"Me, too," Zoe chimed in, as though eating wieners was a matter of eternal significance.

Wynn stood in the kitchen doorway. "I can run to the store."

K.O. couldn't believe her ears. She hated to see him cater to the whims of Zoe and Zara, but far be it from her to object. If he was willing to go to those lengths to get the twins the meal they wanted, she'd let him do it.

"Isn't that nice of Dr. Jeffries?" K.O. asked her nieces.

Both girls ignored her and Wynn.

K.O. followed him into the other room, where Wynn retrieved his jacket from the hall closet. "I'll be back soon," he said.

"I'll put together a salad and—"

"Let the girls decide if they want a salad," Wynn interrupted. "Given the option, children will choose a well-balanced diet on their own. We as adults shouldn't be making these decisions for them."

K.O. had broken down and bought a copy of *The Free Child* at a small bookstore that had recently opened on Blossom Street. She'd skimmed it last night, so she knew this advice was in the book, stated in exactly those words. She might not approve, but for tonight she was determined to follow his lead. So she kept her mouth shut. Not that it was easy.

While the girls were occupied, he planted a gentle kiss on her lips, smiled and then was out the door.

It was now three days since they'd been able to spend time together. With that one short kiss, a lovely warmth spread through her. She closed the door after him and was leaning against it when she noticed that the twins had turned to stare at her. "While we're waiting for Wynn to get back, would you like me to read you a story?" she asked. The salad discussion could wait.

The girls readily agreed, and the three of them settled on the sofa. She was only a few pages into the book when both Zoe and Zara slumped over, asleep. Before Zelda left, she'd said the twins had been awake since five that morning, excited about Katherine's visit. Apparently they no longer took naps. This was something else Wynn had advised. Children would sleep when they needed to, according to him. Regimented naptimes stifled children's ability to understand their internal clocks. Well, Zoe and Zara's clocks had obviously wound down—and K.O. was grateful.

The quiet was so blissful that she leaned her head back and rested her own eyes. The tranquility didn't last long, however. In less than fifteen minutes, Wynn was back from the store, carrying a plastic bag with wieners and fresh buns. The dogs barked frantically as he entered the house, waking both children.

"Here they are," he announced as if he brandished an Olympic gold medal.

Zara yawned. "I'm not hungry anymore."

"Me, neither," Zoe added.

It probably wasn't the most tactful thing to do, but K.O. smiled triumphantly.

"That's okay. We can wait until later," Wynn said, completely unfazed.

He really was good with the girls and seemed to enjoy spending time with them. While K.O. set the kitchen table and cleared away the clutter that had accumulated everywhere, Wynn sat down and talked to the twins. The girls showed him the Christmas tree and the stockings that hung over the fireplace and the nativity scene set up on the formal dining room table.

K.O. heard Zoe mention her imaginary horse named Blackie. Not to be outdone, Zara declared that *her* imaginary horse was named Brownie. Wynn listened to them seriously and even scooted over to make room for the horses on the sofa. K.O. was grateful that Wynn was sharing responsibility for the girls, whose constant demands quickly drained her.

"I'm hungry now," Zoe informed them half an hour later.

"I'll start the hot dogs," K.O. said, ready for dinner herself.

"I want pancakes."

"With syrup," Zara said. Zoe nodded.

K.O. looked at Wynn, who shrugged as if it was no big deal.

"Then pancakes it is," K.O. agreed. She'd let him

cope with the sugar high. For the next ten minutes she was busy mixing batter and frying the pancakes. The twins wanted chocolate syrup and strawberry jam on top, with bananas and granola. Actually, it didn't taste nearly as bad as K.O. had feared.

According to her sister's instructions, the girls were to be given their medication with meals. After dinner, Zoe and Zara climbed down from their chairs. When K.O. asked them to take their plates to the sink, they complied without an argument or even a complaint.

"Time for your medicine," K.O. told them next. She removed two small bottles filled with pink antibiotic from the refrigerator.

The two girls raced about the kitchen, shrieking, with the dogs yapping at their heels. They seemed incapable of standing still.

"Girls," K.O. ordered sternly. "Take your medicine and then you can run around." The way they were dashing back and forth, it was difficult to see who was who.

Zara skidded to a stop and dutifully opened her mouth. Carefully measuring out the liquid, K.O. filled the spoon and popped it into the child's mouth. Immediately afterward, the twins took off in a frenzied race around the kitchen table.

"Zoe," K.O. said, holding the second bottle and a clean spoon and waiting for the mayhem to die down so she could dispense the correct dose to her other niece. "Your turn."

The twin appeared in front of her, mouth open. K.O. poured medicine onto the spoon. About to give it to Zoe, she hesitated. "You're not Zoe. You're Zara."

"I'm Zoe," she insisted. Although the girls were identical, K.O. could usually tell one from the other, partly by their personalities. Zara had the stronger, more dominant nature. "Are you sure?" she asked.

The little girl nodded vigorously. Uncertain, K.O. reluctantly gave her the medication. The twins continued to chase each other about the kitchen, weaving their way around and between Wynn and K.O. The dogs dashed after them, yapping madly.

Wynn asked, "Is everything all right?"

K.O. still held the empty spoon. "I have a horrible feeling I just gave two doses to the same girl."

"You can trust the twins to tell you the truth," Wynn pronounced. "Children instinctively know when it's important to tell the truth."

"Really?" K.O. couldn't help worrying.

"Of course. It's in the book," Wynn said as if quoting Scripture.

"You didn't feed Blackie and Brownie," Zara cried when K.O. tossed the leftover pancakes in the garbage.

"Then we must." Wynn proceeded to remove the cold pancakes and tear them into small pieces. Zero and Zorro leaped off the ground in an effort to snatch up the leftovers. Zoe and Zara sat on the floor and fed the dogs and supposedly their imaginary pets, as well.

The yapping dogs were giving K.O. a headache. "How about if I turn on the television," she suggested, shouting to be heard above the racket made by the girls and the dogs.

The twins hollered their approval, but the show that flashed onto the screen was a Christmas cartoon featuring none other than Santa himself. Jolly old soul that he was, Santa laughed and loaded his sleigh while the girls watched with rapt attention. Knowing how her sister felt, K.O. figured this was probably the first time they'd seen Santa all season. K.O. glanced at Wynn, who was frowning back.

"Let's see what else is on," K.O. said quickly.

"I want to watch Santa," Zoe shouted.

"Me, too," Zara muttered.

Wynn sat on the sofa between them and wrapped his arms around their small shoulders. "This show is about a character called Santa Claus," he said in a solicitous voice.

Both girls were far too involved in the program to be easily distracted by adult conversation.

"Sometimes mommies and daddies like to make believe, and while they don't mean to lie, they can mislead their children," he went on.

Zoe briefly tore her gaze away from the television screen. "Like Santa, you mean?"

Wynn smiled. "Like Santa," he agreed.

"We know he's not real," Zoe informed them with all the wisdom of a five-year-old.

"Santa is really Mommy and Daddy," Zara explained. "*Everyone* knows that."

"They do?"

Both girls nodded.

Zoe's eyes turned serious. "We heard Mommy and

Daddy fighting about Santa and we almost told them it doesn't matter 'cause we already know."

"We like getting gifts from him, though," Zara told them.

"Yeah, I like Santa," Zoe added.

"But he's not real," Wynn said, sounding perfectly logical.

"Mommy's real," Zara argued. "And Daddy, too."

"Yes, but…" Wynn seemed determined to argue further, but stopped when he happened to glance at K.O. He held her gaze a moment before looking away.

K.O. did her best to keep quiet, but apparently Wynn realized how difficult that was, because he clammed up fast enough.

The next time she looked at the twins, Zara had slumped over to one side, eyes drooping. K.O. gently shook the little girl's shoulders but Zara didn't respond. Still fearing she might have given one twin a double dose of the antibiotic, she knelt down in front of the other child.

"Zoe," she asked, struggling to keep the panic out of her voice. "Did you get your medicine or did Zara swallow both doses?"

Zoe grinned and pantomimed zipping her mouth closed.

"Zoe," K.O. said again. "This is important. We can't play games when medicine is involved." So much for Wynn's theory that children instinctively knew when it was necessary to tell the truth.

"Zara likes the taste better'n me."

"Did you take your medicine or did Zara take it for you?" Wynn asked.

Zoe smiled and shook her head, indicating that she wasn't telling.

Zara snored, punctuating the conversation.

"Did you or did you not take your medicine?" Wynn demanded, nearly yelling.

Tears welled in Zoe's eyes. She buried her face in K.O.'s lap and refused to answer Wynn.

"This isn't a joke," he muttered, clearly losing his patience with the twins.

"Zoe," K.O. cautioned. "You heard Dr. Jeffries. It's important for us to know if you took your medication."

The little girl raised her head, then slowly nodded. "It tastes bad, but I swallowed it all down."

"Good." Relief flooded K.O. "Thank you for telling the truth."

"I don't like your friend," she said, sticking her tongue out at Wynn. "He yells."

"I only yelled because...you made me," Wynn countered. He marched to the far side of the room, and K.O. reflected that he didn't sound so calm and reasonable anymore.

"Why don't we all play a game?" she suggested.

Zara raised her head sleepily from the sofa edge. "Can we play Old Maid?" she asked, yawning.

"I want to play Candyland," Zoe mumbled.

"Why don't we play both?" K.O. said, and they did. In fact, they played for two hours straight, watched television and then drank hot chocolate.

"Shall we take a bath now?" K.O. asked, hoping that would tire the girls out enough to want to go to bed. She didn't know where they got their stamina, but her own was fading rapidly.

The twins were eager to do something altogether different and instantly raced out of the room.

Wynn looked like he could use a break—and he hadn't even seen them at their most challenging. All in all, the girls were exhibiting good behavior, or what passed for good in the regime of the Free Child.

"I'll run the bath water," K.O. told Wynn as he gathered up the cards and game pieces. Had she been on her own, K.O. would have insisted the twins pick up after themselves.

While the girls were occupied in their bedroom, she put on a Christmas CD she particularly liked and started the bath. When she glanced into the living room, she saw Wynn collapsed on the sofa, legs stretched out.

"It hasn't been so bad," he said, as though that was proof his theories were working well. "As soon as the twins are down, we can talk," he murmured, "about us…"

K.O. wasn't ready for that, feeling he should spend more time with the girls. She felt honor-bound to remind Wynn of what he'd written in his book. "Didn't you say that children know when they need sleep and we as adults should trust them to set their own schedules?"

He seemed about to **argue** with her, but then abruptly sat up and pointed across the room. "What's that?"

A naked dog strolled into the living room. Rather, a hairless dog.

"Zero? Zorro?" K.O. asked. "Oh, my goodness!" She dashed into the bathroom to discover Zara sitting on the floor with Wynn's electric shaver. A pile of brown-and-black dog hair littered the area.

"What happened?" Wynn cried, hard on her heels. His mouth fell open when he saw the girls intent on their task. They'd gone through his toiletries, which were spread across the countertop next to the sink. K.O. realized that the hum of the shaver had been concealed by the melodious strains of "Silent Night." "What are you doing?"

"We're giving haircuts," Zara announced. "Do you want one?"

Chapter

16

Two hours later, at ten-thirty, both Zoe and Zara were in their beds and asleep. This was no small accomplishment. After half a dozen stories, the girls were finally down for the night. K.O. tiptoed out of the room and as quietly as possible closed the door. Wynn was just ahead of her and looked as exhausted as she felt.

Zero regarded K.O. forlornly from the hallway. The poor dog had been almost completely shaved. He stared up at her, hairless and shivering. Zorro still had half his hair. The Yorkshire terrier's left side had been sheared before K.O. managed to snatch the razor out of her niece's hand. Last winter Zelda had knit tiny dog sweaters, which K.O. found, and with Wynn's help slipped over the two terriers. At least they'd be warm, although neither dog seemed especially grateful.

K.O. sank down on the sofa beside Wynn, with the dogs nestled at their feet. Breathing out a long, deep sigh, she gazed up at the ceiling. Wynn was curiously quiet.

"I feel like going to bed myself," she murmured when she'd recovered enough energy to speak.

"What time are your sister and brother-in-law supposed to return?" Wynn asked with what seemed to require an extraordinary amount of effort.

"Zelda said they should be home by three."

"That late?"

K.O. couldn't keep the grin off her face. It was just as she'd hoped. She wouldn't have to argue about the problem with his Free Child theories, since he'd been able to witness for himself the havoc they caused.

Straightening, K.O. suggested they listen to some more music.

"That won't disturb them, will it?" he asked when she got up to put on another CD. Evidently he had no interest in anything that might wake the girls.

"I should hope not." She found the Christmas CD she'd given to Zelda two years earlier, and inserted it in the player. It featured a number of pop artists. Smiling over at Wynn, she lowered the volume. John Denver's voice reached softly into the room, singing "Joy to the World."

Wynn turned off the floor lamp, so the only illumination came from the Christmas-tree lights. The mood was cheerful and yet relaxed.

For the first time in days they were alone. The incident with Wynn's father and the demands of the twins were the last things on K.O.'s mind.

Wynn placed his arm across the back of the sofa and she sat close to him, resting her head against his shoulder. All they needed now was a glass of wine and a kiss or two. Romance swirled through the room with the music and Christmas lights. Wynn must've felt it, too, because he turned her in his arms. K.O. started to close her eyes, anticipating his kiss, when she caught a movement from the corner of her eye.

She gasped.

A mouse…a rodent ran across the floor.

Instantly alarmed, K.O. jerked away from Wynn.

He bolted upright. "What is it?"

"A mouse." She hated mice. "There," she cried, covering her mouth to stifle a scream. She pointed as the rodent scampered under the Christmas tree.

Wynn leaped to his feet. "I see it."

Apparently so did Zero, because he let out a yelp and headed right for the tree. Zorro followed.

K.O. brought both feet onto the sofa and hugged her knees. It was completely unreasonable—and so clichéd—to be terrified of a little mouse. But she was. While logic told her a mouse was harmless, that knowledge didn't help.

"You have to get it out of here," she whimpered as panic set in.

"I'll catch it," he shouted and dived under the Christmas tree, toppling it. The tree slammed against the floor, shattering several bulbs. Ornaments rolled in all directions. The dogs ran for cover. Fortunately the tree was still plugged in because it offered what little light was available.

Unable to watch, K.O. hid her eyes. She wondered what Wynn would do if he did manage to corner the rodent. The thought of him killing it right there in her sister's living room was intolerable.

"Don't kill it," she insisted and removed her hands from her eyes to find Wynn on his hands and knees, staring at her.

The mouse darted across the floor and raced under the sofa, where K.O. just happened to be sitting.

Zero and Zorro ran after it, yelping frantically.

K.O. screeched and scrambled to a standing position on the sofa. Not knowing what else to do, she bounced from one cushion to the other.

Zero had buried his nose as far as it would go under the sofa. Zorro dashed back and forth on the carpet. As hard as she tried, K.O. couldn't keep still and began hopping up and down, crying out in abject terror. She didn't care if she woke the girls or not, there was a mouse directly beneath her feet…somewhere. For all she knew, it could have crawled into the sofa itself.

That thought made her jump from the middle of the sofa, over the armrest and onto the floor, narrowly missing Zero. The lamp fell when she landed, but she was able to catch it seconds before it crashed to the floor. As she righted the lamp, she flipped it on, provided a welcome circle of light.

Meanwhile, Barry Manilow crooned out "The Twelve Days of Christmas."

Still on all fours, Wynn crept across the carpet to the sofa, which he overturned. As it pitched onto its back, the mouse shot out.

Directly at K.O.

She screamed.

Zero yelped.

Zorro tore fearlessly after it.

K.O. screamed again and grabbed a basket in which Zelda kept her knitting. She emptied the basket and, more by instinct than anything else, flung it over the mouse, trapping him.

Wynn sat up with a shocked look. "You got him!"

Both dogs stood guard by the basket, sniffing at the edges. Zero scratched the carpet.

Zelda's yarn and needles were a tangled mess on the floor but seemed intact. Breathless, K.O. stared at the basket, not knowing what to do next. "It had a brown tail," she commented.

Wynn nodded. "I noticed that, too."

"I've never seen a mouse with a brown tail before."

"It's an African brown-tailed mouse," he said, sounding knowledgeable. "I saw a documentary on them."

"African mice are here in the States?" She wondered if Animal Control knew about this.

He nodded again. "So I gather."

"What do we do now?" Because Wynn seemed to know more about this sort of thing, she looked to him for the answer.

"Kill it," he said without a qualm.

Zero and Zorro obviously agreed, because they both growled and clawed at the carpet, asking for the opportunity to do it themselves.

"No way!" K.O. objected. She couldn't allow him to kill it. The terriers, either. Although mice terrified her,

K.O. couldn't bear to hurt any of God's creatures. "All I want you to do is get that brown-tailed mouse out of here." As soon as Zelda returned, K.O. planned to suggest she call a pest control company to inspect the entire house. Although, if there were other mice around, she didn't want to know it....

"All right," Wynn muttered. "I'll take it outside and release it."

He got a newspaper and knelt down next to the dogs. Carefully, inch by inch, he slid the paper beneath the upended basket. When he'd finished that, he stood and carried the whole thing to the front door. Zero and Zorro followed, leaping up on their hind legs and barking wildly.

K.O. hurried to open first the door and then the screen. The cold air felt good against her heated face.

Wynn stepped onto the porch while K.O. held back the dogs by closing the screen door. They both objected strenuously and braced their front paws against the door, watching Wynn's every movement.

K.O. turned her back as Wynn released the African brown-tailed mouse into the great unknown. She wished the critter a pleasant life outside.

"Is it gone?" she asked when Wynn came back into the house, careful to keep Zero and Zorro from escaping and racing after the varmint.

"It's gone, and I didn't even need to touch it," he assured her. He closed the door.

K.O. smiled up at him. "My hero," she whispered.

Wynn playfully flexed his muscles. "Anything else I can do for you, my fair damsel?"

Looping her arms around his neck, K.O. backed him up against the front door and rewarded him with a warm, moist kiss. Wynn wrapped his arms about her waist and half lifted her from the carpet.

"You *are* my hero," she whispered between kisses. "You saved me from that killer mouse."

"The African brown-tailed killer rat."

"It was a *rat?*"

"A small one," he murmured, and kissed her again before she could ask more questions.

"A baby rat?" That meant there must be parents around and possibly siblings, perhaps any number of other little rats. "What makes you think it was a rat?" she demanded, fast losing interest in kissing.

"He was fat. But perhaps he was just a fat mouse."

"Ah…"

"You're still grateful?"

"Very grateful, but—"

He kissed her again, then abruptly broke off the kiss. His eyes seemed to focus on something across the room.

K.O. tensed, afraid he'd seen another mouse. Or rat. Or rodent of some description.

It took genuine courage to glance over her shoulder, but she did it anyway. Fortunately she didn't see anything—other than an overturned Christmas tree, scattered furniture and general chaos brought about by the Great Brown-Tailed Mouse Hunt.

"The fishbowl has blue water," he said.

"Blue water?" K.O. dropped her arms and stared at the counter between the kitchen and the living room, where the fishbowl sat. Sure enough, the water was a deep blue.

Wynn walked across the room.

Before K.O. could ask what he was doing, Wynn pushed up his sweater sleeve and thrust his hand into the water. "Just as I thought," he muttered, retrieving a gold pen.

After she'd found the twins with Wynn's electric shaver, she realized, they'd opened his overnight case.

"This is a gold fountain pen," he told her, holding up the dripping pen. "As it happens, this is a *valuable* gold fountain pen."

"With blue ink," K.O. added. She didn't think it could be too valuable, since it was leaking.

She picked up the bowl with both hands and carried it into the kitchen, setting it in the sink. Scooping out the two goldfish, she put them in a temporary home—a coffee cup full of fresh, clean water—and refilled the bowl.

Wynn was pacing the kitchen floor behind her.

"Does your book say anything about situations like this?" she couldn't resist asking.

He glared at her and apparently that was all the answer he intended to give.

"Aunt Katherine?" one of the twins shouted. "Come quick." K.O. heard unmistakable panic in the little girl's voice.

Soon the two girls were both crying out.

Hurrying into the bedroom with Wynn right behind her, K.O. found Zoe and Zara weeping loudly.

"What's wrong?" she asked.

"Freddy's gone," Zoe wailed.

"Freddy?" she repeated. "Who's Freddy?"

"Our hamster," Zoe explained, pointing at what K.O. now recognized as a cage against the far wall. "He must've figured out how to open his cage."

A chill went through her. "Does Freddy have a brown tail and happen to be a little chubby?" she asked the girls.

Hope filled their eyes as they nodded eagerly.

K.O. scowled at Wynn. African brown-tailed mouse, indeed.

Chapter 17

Thankfully, Wynn rescued poor Freddy, who was discovered shivering in a corner of the porch. The girls were relieved to have their hamster back, and neither mentioned the close call Freddy had encountered with certain death. After calming the twins, it took K.O. and Wynn an hour to clean up the living room. By then, they were both cranky and tired.

Saturday morning, Zoe and Zara decided on wieners for breakfast. Knowing Wynn would approve, K.O. cooked the hot dogs he'd purchased the night before. However, the unaccustomed meat didn't settle well in Zoe's tummy and she threw up on her breakfast plate. Zara insisted that all she wanted was orange juice poured over dry cereal. So that was what she got.

For the rest of the morning, Wynn remained pensive and remote. He helped her with the children but didn't want to talk. In fact, he seemed more than eager to get back to Blossom Street. When Zelda and Zach showed up that afternoon, he couldn't quite hide his relief. The twins hugged K.O. goodbye and Wynn, too.

While Wynn loaded the car, K.O. talked to Zelda about holiday plans. Zelda asked her to join the family for Christmas Eve dinner and church, but not Christmas Day, which they'd be spending with Zach's parents. K.O. didn't mind. She'd invite LaVonne to dinner at her place. Maybe she'd include Wynn and his father, too, despite the disastrous conclusion of the last social event she'd hosted for this same group. Still, when she had the chance, she'd discuss it with Wynn.

On the drive home, Wynn seemed especially quiet.

"The girls are a handful, aren't they?" she asked, hoping to start a conversation.

He nodded.

She smiled to herself, remembering Wynn's expression when Zoe announced that their hamster had escaped. Despite his reproachful silence, she laughed. "I promise not to mention that rare African brown-tailed mouse again, but I have to tell LaVonne."

"I never said it was rare."

"Oh, sorry, I thought you had." One look told her Wynn wasn't amused. "Come on, Wynn," she said, as they merged with the freeway traffic. "You have to admit it was a little ridiculous."

He didn't appear to be in the mood to admit anything. "Are you happy?" he asked.

"What do you mean?"

"You proved your point, didn't you?"

So that was the problem. "If you're referring to how the girls behaved then, yes, I suppose I did."

"You claimed that after your sister read my book, they changed into undisciplined hellions."

"Well…" Wasn't it obvious? "They're twins," she said, trying to sound conciliatory, "and as such they've always needed a lot of attention. Some of what happened on Friday evening might have happened without the influence of your child-rearing theories. Freddy would've escaped whether Zelda read your book or not."

"Very funny."

"I wasn't trying to be funny. Frankly, rushing to the store to buy hot dogs because that's what the girls wanted for dinner is over the top, in my opinion. I feel it teaches them to expect that their every whim must be met."

"I beg to differ. My getting the dinner they wanted showed them that I cared about their likes and dislikes."

"Two hours of sitting on the floor playing Old Maid said the same thing," she inserted.

"I let you put them to bed even though they clearly weren't ready for sleep."

"I beg to differ," she said, a bit more forcefully than she'd intended. "Zoe and Zara were both yawning when they came out of the bath. I asked them if they wanted to go to bed."

"What you asked," he said stiffly, "was if they were *ready* for bed."

"And the difference is?"

"Two hours of storytime while they wore us both out."

"What would you have done?" she asked.

His gaze didn't waver from the road. "I would've allowed them to play quietly in their room until they'd tired themselves out."

Quietly? He had to be joking. Wynn seemed to have conveniently forgotten that during the short time they were on their own, Zoe and Zara had gotten into his overnight bag. Thanks to their creative use of his personal things, the goldfish now had a bluish tint. The two Yorkies were nearly hairless. She could argue that because the girls considered themselves *free*, they didn't see anything wrong with opening his bag. The lack of boundaries created confusion and misunderstanding.

"Twins are not the norm," he challenged. "They encourage ill behavior in each other."

"However, before Zelda read your book, they were reasonably well-behaved children."

"Is that a fact?" He sounded as though he didn't believe her.

"Yes," she said swiftly. "Zoe and Zara were happy and respectful and kind. Some would even go so far as to say they were well-adjusted. Now they constantly demand their own way. They're unreasonable, selfish and difficult." She was only getting started and dragged in another breath. "Furthermore, it used to be a joy to spend time with them and now it's a chore. And if you must know, I blame you and that blasted book of yours." There, she'd said it.

A stark silence followed.

"You don't mince words, do you?"

"No…"

"I respect that. I wholeheartedly disagree, but I respect your right to state your opinion."

The tension in the car had just increased by about a thousand degrees.

"After this weekend, you still disagree?" She was astonished he'd actually said that, but then she supposed his ego was on the line.

"I'm not interested in arguing with you, Katherine."

She didn't want to argue with him, either. Still, she'd hoped the twins would convince him that while his theories might look good on paper, in reality they didn't work.

After Wynn exited the freeway, it was only a few short blocks to Blossom Street and the parking garage beneath their building. Wynn pulled into his assigned slot and turned off the engine.

Neither moved.

K.O. feared that the minute she opened the car door, it would be over, and she didn't want their relationship to end, not like this. Not now, with Christmas only nine days away.

She tried again. "I know we don't see eye to eye on everything—"

"No, we don't," he interrupted. "In many cases, it doesn't matter, but when it comes to my work, my livelihood, it does. Not only do you not accept my theories, you think they're ludicrous."

She opened her mouth to defend herself, then realized he was right. That was exactly what she thought.

"You've seen evidence that appears to contradict them and, therefore, you discount the years of research I've done in my field. The fact is, you don't respect my work."

Feeling wretched, she hung her head.

"I expected there to be areas in which we disagree, Katherine, but this is more than I can deal with. I'm sorry, but I think it would be best if we didn't see each other again."

If that was truly how he felt, then there was nothing left to say.

"I appreciate that you've been honest with me," he continued. "I'm sorry, Katherine—I know we both would've liked this to work, but we have too many differences."

She made an effort to smile. If she thought arguing with him would do any good, she would have. But the hard set of his jaw told her no amount of reasoning would reach him now. "Thank you for everything. Really, I mean that. You've made this Christmas the best."

He gave her a sad smile.

"Would it be all right—would you mind if I gave you a hug?" she asked. "To say goodbye?"

He stared at her for the longest moment, then slowly shook his head. "That wouldn't be a good idea," he whispered, opening the car door.

By the time K.O. was out of the vehicle, he'd already retrieved her overnight bag from the trunk.

She waited, but it soon became apparent that he had no intention of taking the elevator with her. It seemed he'd had about as much of her company as he could stand.

She stepped into the elevator with her bag and turned around. Before the doors closed, she saw Wynn leaning against the side of his car with his head down, looking dejected. K.O. understood the feeling.

It had been such a promising relationship. She'd never felt this drawn to a man, this attracted. If only she'd been able to keep her mouth shut—but, oh, no, not her. She'd wanted to prove her point, show him the error of his ways. She still believed he was wrong— well, mostly wrong—but now she felt petty and mean.

When the elevator stopped at the first floor, the doors slid open and K.O. got out. The first thing she did was collect her mail and her newspapers. She eyed the elevator, wondering if she'd ever see Wynn again, other than merely in passing, which would be painfully unavoidable.

After unpacking her overnight case and sorting through the mail, none of which interested her, she walked across the hall, hoping to talk to LaVonne.

Even after several long rings, LaVonne didn't answer her door. Perhaps she was doing errands.

Just as K.O. was about to walk away, her neighbor opened the door just a crack and peered out.

"LaVonne, it's me."

"Oh, hi," she said.

"Can I come in?" K.O. asked, wondering why LaVonne didn't immediately invite her inside. She'd never hesitated to ask her in before.

"Ah…now isn't really a good time."

"Oh." That was puzzling.

"How about tomorrow?" LaVonne suggested.

"Sure." K.O. nodded. "Is Tom back?" she asked.

"Tom?"

"Your cat."

"Oh, oh...that Tom. Yes, he came home this morning."

K.O. was pleased to hear that. She dredged up a smile. "I'll talk to you tomorrow, then."

"Yes," she agreed. "Tomorrow."

K.O. started across the hall, then abruptly turned back. "You might care to know that the Raisin Bran got it all wrong."

"I beg your pardon?" LaVonne asked, narrowing her gaze.

"I think you might've read the kitty litter wrong, too. But then again, that particular box accurately describes my love life."

LaVonne opened the door a fraction of an inch wider. "Do you mean to tell me you're no longer seeing Wynn?"

K.O. nodded. "Apparently we were both wrong in thinking Wynn was the man for me."

"He is," LaVonne said confidently.

K.O. sighed. "I wish he was. I genuinely like Wynn. When I first discovered he was the author of that loony book my sister read..." Realizing what she'd just said, K.O. began again. "When I discovered he wrote the book she'd read, I had my doubts."

"It *is* a loony book," LaVonne said.

"I should never have told him how I felt."

"You were honest."

"Yes, but I was rude and hurtful, too." She shook her head mournfully. "We disagree on just about every aspect of child-rearing. He doesn't want to see me again and I don't blame him."

LaVonne stared at her for an intense moment. "You're falling in love with him."

"No, I'm not," she said, hoping to make light of her feelings, but her neighbor was right. K.O. had known it the minute Wynn dived under the Christmas tree to save her from the not-so-rare African brown-tailed mouse. The minute he'd waved down the horse-drawn carriage and covered her knees with a lap robe and slipped his arm around her shoulders.

"Don't try to deny it," LaVonne said. "I don't really know what I saw in that Raisin Bran. Probably just raisins. But all along I've felt that Wynn's the man for you."

"I wish that was true," she said as she turned to go home. "But it's not."

As she opened her own door, she heard LaVonne talking. When she glanced back, she could hear her in a heated conversation with someone inside the condo. Unfortunately LaVonne was blocking the doorway, so K.O. couldn't see who it was.

"LaVonne?"

The door opened wider and out stepped Max Jeffries. "Hello, Katherine," he greeted her, grinning from ear to ear.

K.O. looked at her neighbor and then at Wynn's father. The last she'd heard, Max was planning to sue

LaVonne for everything she had. Somehow, in the past twenty-four hours, he'd changed his mind.

"Max?" she said in an incredulous voice.

He grinned boyishly and placed his arm around La-Vonne's shoulders.

"You see," LaVonne said, blushing a fetching shade of red. "My psychic talents might be limited, but you're more talented than you knew."

Chapter 18

K.O. was depressed. Even the fact that she'd been hired by Apple Blossom Books as their new publicist hadn't been enough to raise her spirits. She was scheduled to start work the day after New Year's and should've been thrilled. She was, only...nothing felt right without Wynn.

It was Christmas Eve and it should have been one of the happiest days of the year, but she felt like staying in bed. Her sister and family were expecting her later that afternoon, so K.O. knew she couldn't mope around the condo all day. She had things to do, food to buy, gifts to wrap, and she'd better get moving.

Putting on her coat and gloves, she walked out of

her condo wearing a smile. She refused to let anyone know she was suffering from a broken heart.

"Katherine," LaVonne called the instant she saw her. She stood at the lobby mailbox as if she'd been there for hours, just waiting for K.O. "Merry Christmas!"

"Merry Christmas," K.O. returned a little too brightly. She managed a smile and with her shoulders squared, made her way to the door.

"Do you have any plans for Christmas?" her neighbor called after her.

K.O.'s mouth hurt from holding that smile for so long. She nodded. "I'm joining Zelda, Zach and the girls this evening, and then I thought I'd spend a quiet Christmas by myself." Needless to say, she hadn't issued any invitations, and she'd hardly seen LaVonne in days. Tomorrow she'd cook for herself. While doing errands this morning, she planned to purchase a small—very small—turkey. She refused to mope and feel lonely, not on Christmas Day.

"Have dinner with me," LaVonne said. "It'll just be me and the boys."

When K.O. hesitated, she added, "Tom, Phillip and Martin would love to see you. I'm cooking a turkey and all the fixings, and I'd be grateful for the company."

"Are you sure?"

"Of course I'm sure!"

K.O. didn't take long to consider her friend's invitation. "I'd love to, then. What would you like me to bring?"

"Dessert," LaVonne said promptly. "Something yummy and special for Christmas."

"All right." They agreed on a time and K.O. left, feeling better than she had in days. Just as she was about to step outside, she turned back.

"How's Max?" she asked, knowing her neighbor was on good terms with Wynn's father. Exactly how good those terms were remained to be seen. She wondered fleetingly what the Jeffrieses were doing for Christmas, then decided it was none of her business. Still, the afternoon K.O. had found Max in LaVonne's condo, she'd been shocked to say the least. Their brief conversation the following day hadn't been too enlightening but maybe over Christmas dinner LaVonne would tell her what had happened—and what was happening now.

Flustered, LaVonne lowered her eyes as she sorted through a stack of mail that seemed to be mostly Christmas cards. "He's completely recovered. And," she whispered, "he's apologized to Tom."

A sense of pleasure shot through K.O. at this...and at the way LaVonne blushed. Apparently this was one romance that held promise. Her own had fizzled out fast enough. She'd come to truly like Wynn. More than like... At the thought of him, an aching sensation pressed down on her. In retrospect, she wished she'd handled the situation differently. Because she couldn't resist, she had to ask, "Have you seen Wynn?"

Her friend nodded but the look in LaVonne's eyes told K.O. everything she dreaded.

"He's still angry, isn't he?"

LaVonne gave her a sad smile. "I'm sure everything will work out. I know what I saw in that Raisin Bran." She attempted a laugh.

"When you see him again, tell him..." She paused. "Tell him," she started again, then gave up. Wynn had made his feelings clear. He'd told her it would be best if they didn't see each other again, and he'd meant it. Nine days with no word told her he wasn't changing his mind. Well, she had her pride, too.

"What would you like me to tell him?" LaVonne asked.

"Nothing. It's not important."

"You could write him a letter," LaVonne suggested.

"Perhaps I will," K.O. said on her way out the door, but she knew she wouldn't. It was over.

Blossom Street seemed more alive than at any other time she could remember. A group of carolers performed at the corner, songbooks in their hands. An elderly gentleman rang a bell for charity outside the French Café, which was crowded with customers. Seeing how busy the place was, K.O. decided to purchase her Christmas dessert now, before they completely sold out.

After adding a donation to the pot as she entered the café, she stood in a long line. When her turn finally came to order, she saw that one of the bakers was helping at the counter. K.O. knew Alix Townsend or, at least, she'd talked to her often enough to know her by name.

"Merry Christmas, K.O.," Alix said.

"Merry Christmas to you, too." K.O. surveyed the sweet delicacies behind the glass counter. "I need something that says Christmas," she murmured. The decorated cookies were festive but didn't seem quite right. A pumpkin pie would work, but it wasn't really special.

"How about a small Bûche de Noël," Alix said. "It's a traditional French dessert—a fancy cake decorated with mocha cream frosting and shaped to look like a Yule log. I baked it myself from a special recipe of the owner's."

"Bûche de Noël," K.O. repeated. It sounded perfect.

"They're going fast," Alix pointed out.

"Sold," K.O. said as the young woman went to collect one from the refrigerated case. It was then that K.O. noticed Alix's engagement ring.

"Will there be anything else?" Alix asked, setting the pink box on the counter and tying it with string.

"That diamond's new, isn't it?"

Grinning, Alix examined her ring finger. "I got it last week. Jordan couldn't wait to give it to me."

"Congratulations," K.O. told her. "When's the wedding?"

Alix looked down at the diamond as if she could hardly take her eyes off it. "June."

"That's fabulous."

"I'm already talking to Susannah Nelson—she owns the flower shop across the street. Jacqueline, my friend, insists we hold the reception at the Country Club. If it was up to me, Jordan and I would just elope, but his family would never stand for that." She shrugged in a resigned way. "I love Jordan, and I don't care what I have to do, as long as I get to be his wife."

The words echoed in K.O.'s heart as she walked out of the French Café with a final "Merry Christmas." She didn't know Alix Townsend all that well, but she liked her. Alix was entirely without pretense. No one need doubt how she felt about any particular subject; she spoke her mind in a straightforward manner that left nothing to speculation.

K.O. passed Susannah's Garden, the flower shop, on her way to the bank. The owner and her husband stood out front, wishing everyone a Merry Christmas. As K.O. walked past, Susannah handed her a sprig of holly with bright red berries.

"Thank you—this is so nice," K.O. said, tucking the holly in her coat pocket. She loved the flower shop and the beauty it brought to the street.

"I want to let the neighborhood know how much I appreciate the support. I've only been in business since September and everyone's been so helpful."

"Here, have a cup of hot cider." Susannah's husband was handing out plastic cups from a small table set up beside him. "I'm Joe," he said.

"Hello, Joe. I'm Katherine O'Connor."

Susannah slid one arm around her husband's waist and gazed up at him with such adoration it was painful for K.O. to watch. Everywhere she turned, people were happy and in love. A knot formed in her throat. Putting on a happy, carefree face was getting harder by the minute.

Just then the door to A Good Yarn opened and out came Lydia Goetz and a man K.O. assumed must be her husband. They were accompanied by a young boy, obviously their son. Lydia paused when she saw K.O.

Lydia was well-known on the street.

"Were you planning to stop in here?" she asked, and cast a quick glance at her husband. "Brad convinced me to close early today. I already sent my sister home, but if you need yarn, I'd be happy to get it for you. In fact, you could even pay me later." She looked at her husband again, as if to make sure he didn't object to the delay. "It wouldn't take more than a few minutes. I know what it's like to run out of yarn when you only need one ball to finish a project."

"No, no, that's fine," K.O. said. She'd always wanted to learn to knit and now that LaVonne was taking a class, maybe she'd join, too.

"Merry Christmas!" Lydia tucked her arm in her husband's.

"Merry Christmas," K.O. returned. Soon they hurried down the street, with the boy trotting ahead.

Transfixed, K.O. stood there unmoving. The lump that had formed in her throat grew huge. The whole world was in love, and she'd let the opportunity of her life slip away. She'd let Wynn go with barely a token protest, and that was wrong. If she believed in their love, she needed to fight for it, instead of pretending everything was fine without him. Because it wasn't. In fact, she was downright miserable, and it was time she admitted it.

She knew what she had to do. Afraid that if she didn't act quickly, she'd lose her nerve, K.O. ran back across the street and into her own building. Marching to the elevator, she punched the button and waited.

She wasn't even sure what she'd tell Wynn; she'd figure that out when she saw him. But seeing him was a necessity. She couldn't spend another minute like this. She'd made a terrible mistake, and so had he. If there was any chance of salvaging this relationship, she had to try.

Her heart seemed to be pounding at twice its normal rate as she rode the elevator up to Wynn's penthouse condominium. She'd only been inside once, and then briefly.

By the time she reached his front door, she was so dizzy she'd become light-headed. That didn't deter her from ringing the buzzer and waiting for what felt like an eternity.

Only it wasn't Wynn who opened the door. It was Max.

"Katherine," he said, obviously surprised to find her at his son's door. "Come in."

"Is Wynn available?" she asked, as winded as if she'd climbed the stairs instead of taking the elevator. Talking to Wynn—*now*—had assumed a sense of urgency.

Wynn stepped into the foyer and frowned when he

saw her. "Katherine?" She could see the question in his eyes.

"Merry Christmas," Max said. He didn't seem inclined to leave.

"Could we talk?" she asked. "Privately?" She was terrified he'd tell her that everything had already been said, so she rushed to add, "Really, this will only take a moment and then I'll leave."

Wynn glanced at his father, who took the hint and reluctantly left the entryway.

K.O. remained standing there, clutching her purse with one hand and the pink box with the other. "I was out at the French Café and I talked to Alix."

"Alix?"

"She's one of the bakers and a friend of Lydia's—and Lydia's the lady who owns A Good Yarn. But that's not important. What *is* important is that Alix received an engagement ring for Christmas. She's so happy and in love, and Lydia is, too, and Susannah from the flower shop and just about everyone on the street. It's so full of Christmas out there, and all at once it came to me that…that I couldn't let this Christmas pass with things between us the way they are." She stopped to take a deep breath.

"Katherine, I—"

"Please let me finish, otherwise I don't know if I'll have the courage to continue."

He motioned for her to speak.

"I'm so sorry, Wynn, for everything. For wanting

to be right and then subjecting you to Zoe and Zara. Their behavior *did* change after Zelda read your book and while I can't say I agree with everything you—"

"This is an apology?" he asked, raising his eyebrows.

"I'm trying. I'm sincerely trying. Please hear me out."

He crossed his arms and looked away. In fact, he seemed to find something behind her utterly fascinating.

This wasn't the time to lose her courage. She went on, speaking quickly, so quickly that the words practically ran together. "Basically, I wanted to tell you it was rude of me to assume I knew more than you on the subject of children. It was presumptuous and self-righteous. I was trying to prove how wrong you were…are, and that I was right. To be honest, I don't know what's right or wrong. All I know is how much I miss you and how much it hurts that you're out of my life."

"I'm the one who's been presumptuous and self-righteous," Wynn said. "You *are* right, Katherine, about almost everything. It hasn't been easy for me to accept that, let alone face it."

"Oh, for heaven's sake, aren't you two going to kiss and make up?" Max demanded, coming back into the foyer. Apparently he'd been standing in the living room, out of sight, and had listened in on every word. "Wynn, if you let this woman walk away, then you're a fool. An even bigger fool than you know."

"I—I…" Wynn stuttered.

"You've been in love with her for weeks." Max shook his head as if this was more than obvious.

Wynn pinned his father with a fierce glare.

"You love me?" K.O. asked, her voice rising to a squeak. "Because I'm in love with you, too."

A light flickered in his eyes at her confession. "Katherine, I appreciate your coming. However, this is serious and it's something we both need to think over. It's too important—we can't allow ourselves to get caught up in emotions that are part of the holidays. We'll talk after Christmas, all right?"

"I can't do that," she cried.

"Good for you," Max shouted, encouraging her. "I'm going to phone LaVonne. This calls for champagne."

"What does?" Wynn asked.

"Us," she explained. "You and me. I love you, Wynn, and I can't bear the thought that I won't see you again. It's tearing me up. I don't *need* time to think about us. I already know how I feel, and if what your father says is true, you know how you feel about me."

"Well, I do need to think," he insisted. "I haven't figured out what I'm going to do yet, because I can't continue promoting a book whose theories I can no longer wholly support. Let me deal with that first."

"No," she said. "Love should come first." She stared into his eyes. "Love changes everything, Wynn." Then, because it was impossible to hold back for another second, she put down her purse and the Yule log and threw her arms around him.

Wynn was stiff and unbending, and then his arms circled her, too. "Are you always this stubborn?" he asked.

"Yes. Sometimes even more than this. Ask Zelda."

Wynn kissed her. His arms tightened around her, as if he found it hard to believe she was actually there in his embrace.

"That's the way to handle it," Max said from somewhere behind them.

Wynn and K.O. ignored him.

"He's been a real pain these last few days," Max went on. "But this should improve matters."

Wynn broke off the kiss and held her gaze. "We'll probably never agree on everything."

"Probably."

"I can be just as stubborn as you."

"That's questionable," she said with a laugh.

His lips found hers again, as if he couldn't bear not to kiss her. Each kiss required a bit more time and became a bit more involved.

"I don't believe in long courtships," he murmured, his eyes still closed.

"I don't, either," she said. "And I'm going to want children."

He hesitated.

"We don't need all the answers right this minute, do we, Dr. Jeffries?"

"About Santa—"

She interrupted him, cutting off any argument by kissing him. What resistance there was didn't last.

"I was about to suggest we could bring Santa out from beneath that sleigh," he whispered, his eyes briefly fluttering open.

"Really?" This was more than she'd dared hope.

"Really."

She'd been more than willing to forgo Santa as long as she had Wynn. But Santa *and* Wynn was better yet.

"No hamsters, though," he said firmly.

"Named Freddy," she added.

Wynn chuckled. "Or anything else."

The doorbell chimed and Max hurried to answer it, ushering LaVonne inside. The instant she saw Wynn and K.O. in each other's arms, she clapped with delight. "Didn't I tell you everything would work out?" she asked Max.

"You did, indeed."

LaVonne nodded sagely. "I think I may have psychic powers, after all. I saw it all plain as day in the leaves of my poinsettia," she proclaimed. "Just before Max called, two of them fell to the ground—together."

Despite herself, K.O. laughed. Until a few minutes ago, her love life had virtually disappeared. Now there was hope, real hope for her and Wynn to learn from each other and as LaVonne's prophecy—real or imagined—implied, grow together instead of apart.

"Champagne, anyone?" Max asked, bringing out a bottle.

Wynn still held K.O. and she wasn't objecting. "I need to hire you," he whispered close to her ear.

"Hire me?"

"I'm kind of late with my Christmas letter this year and I wondered if I could convince you to write one for me."

"Of course. It's on the house." With his arms around her waist, she leaned back and looked up at him. "Is there anything in particular you'd like me to say?"

"Oh, yes. You can write about the success of my first published book—and explain that there'll be a retraction in the next edition." He winked. "Or, if you prefer, you could call it a compromise."

K.O. smiled.

"And then I want you to tell my family and friends that I'm working on a new book that'll be called *The Happy Child*, and it'll be about creating appropriate boundaries within the Free Child system of parenting."

K.O. rewarded him with a lengthy kiss that left her knees weak. Fortunately, he had a firm hold on her, and she on him.

"You can also mention the fact that there's going to be a wedding in the family."

"Two weddings," Max inserted as he handed LaVonne a champagne glass.

"Two?" LaVonne echoed shyly.

Max nodded, filling three more glasses. "Wynn and K.O.'s isn't the only romance that started out rocky.

The way I figure it, if I can win Tom over, his mistress shouldn't be far behind."

"Oh, Max!"

"Is there anything else you'd like me to say in your Christmas letter?" K.O. asked Wynn.

"Oh, yes, there's plenty more, but I think we'll leave it for the next Christmas letter and then the one after that." He brought K.O. close once more and hugged her tight.

She loved being in his arms—and in his life. Next year's Christmas letter would be from both of them. It would be all about how happy they were…and every word would be true.

Rainy Day Kisses

Prologue

"Is it true, Michelle?" Jolyn Johnson rolled her chair from her cubicle across the aisle and nearly caught the wheel on a drooping length of plastic holly. The Marketing Department had won the Christmas decoration contest for the third year in a row.

Michelle Davidson glanced away from her computer screen and immediately noticed her neighbor's inquisitive expression. It certainly hadn't taken long for the rumors to start. She realized, of course, that it was unusual for a high school senior to be accepted as an intern at a major company like Windy Day Toys, one of the most prestigious toy manufacturers in the country. She'd be working here during the Christmas and summer breaks—and she'd actually be getting paid!

Michelle had connections—*good* connections. She'd

been a bit naive, perhaps, to assume she could keep her relationship to Uncle Nate under wraps. Still, she'd hoped that with the Christmas season in full swing, her fellow workers would be too preoccupied with the holidays to pay any attention to her. Apparently that wasn't the case.

"Whatever you heard is probably true," she answered, doing her best to look busy.

"Then you *are* related to Mr. Townsend?" Jolyn's eyes grew large.

"I'm his niece."

"Really?" the other girl said in awe. "Wow."

"I'm the one who introduced my aunt Susannah to my uncle Nate." If the fact that Michelle was related to the company owner and CEO impressed Jolyn, then this piece of information should send her over the moon.

"You've got to be kidding! When was that? I thought the Townsends have been married for years and years. I heard they have three children!"

"Tessa, Junior and Emma Jane." When she left the office this afternoon, Michelle would be heading over to her aunt and uncle's home on Lake Washington to babysit. She didn't think it would be good form to mention that, however. She figured interns for Windy Day Toys didn't usually babysit on the side.

"*You* were responsible for introducing your aunt and uncle?" Jolyn repeated, sounding even more incredulous. "When?" she asked again.

"I was young at the time," Michelle answered evasively.

"You must have been."

Michelle grinned and gave in to Jolyn's obvious curiosity. Might as well tell the truth, which was bound to emerge anyway. "I think that might be why Uncle Nate agreed to let me intern here." He loved to tease her about her—admittedly inadvertent—role as matchmaker, but Michelle knew he was grateful. So was her aunt Susannah.

Michelle planned to major in marketing when she enrolled in college next September, and doing an internship this winter and during the summer holidays was the perfect opportunity to find out whether she liked the job. It was only her second day, but already Michelle could see that she was going to love it.

A couple of the other workers had apparently been listening in on the conversation and rolled their chairs toward her cubicle, as well. "You can't stop the story there," Karen said.

Originally Michelle had hoped to avoid this kind of attention, but she accepted that it was inevitable. "When my aunt was almost thirty, she was absolutely sure she'd never marry or have a family."

"Susannah Townsend?"

This news astonished the small gathering, as Michelle had guessed it would. Besides working with Nate, her mother and aunt had started their own company, Motherhood, Inc., about ten years ago and they'd done incredibly well. It seemed that everything the Townsend name touched turned to gold.

"I know it sounds crazy, considering everything that's happened since."

"*Exactly,*" Jolyn murmured.

"Aunt Susannah's a great mother. But," Michelle added, "at one time, she couldn't even figure out how to change a diaper." Little did the others know that the diaper Susannah had such difficulty changing had been Michelle's.

"This is a joke, right?"

"I swear it's true. Hardly anyone knows the whole story."

"What really happened?" the third woman, whom Michelle didn't know, asked.

Michelle shrugged. "Actually, I happened."

"What do you mean?"

"My mother was desperate for a babysitter and asked her sister, my aunt Susannah, to look after me."

"How old were you?"

"About nine months," she admitted.

"So how did everything turn out the way it did?" Jolyn asked.

"I'd love to hear, too," Karen said, and the third woman nodded vigorously.

Michelle leaned back in her chair. "Make yourselves comfortable, my friends, because I have a story to tell," she began dramatically. "A story in which I play a crucial part."

The three women scooted their chairs closer.

"It all started seventeen years ago..."

1

Susannah Simmons blamed her sister, Emily, for this. As far as she was concerned, her weekend was going to be the nightmare on Western Avenue. Emily, a nineties version of the "earth mother," had asked Susannah, the dedicated career woman, to babysit nine-month-old Michelle.

"Emily, I don't think so." Susannah had balked when her sister first phoned. What did she, a twenty-eight-year-old business executive, know about babies? The answer was simple—not much.

"I'm desperate."

Her sister must have been to ask her. Everyone knew what Susannah was like around babies—not only Michelle, but infants in general. She just wasn't the motherly type. Interest rates, negotiations, troubleshooting, staff motivation, these were her strong points. Not formula, teething and diapers.

It was nothing short of astonishing that the same two parents could have produced such completely different daughters. Emily baked her own oat-bran muffins, subscribed to *Organic Gardening* and hung her wash to dry on a clothesline—even in winter.

Susannah, on the other hand, wasn't the least bit domestic and had no intention of ever cultivating the trait. She was too busy with her career to let such tedious tasks disrupt her corporate lifestyle. She was currently a director in charge of marketing for H&J Lima, the nation's largest sporting goods company. The position occupied almost every minute of her time.

Susannah Simmons was a woman on the rise. Her name appeared regularly in trade journals as an up-and-coming achiever. None of that mattered to Emily, however, who needed a babysitter.

"You know I wouldn't ask you if it wasn't an emergency," Emily had pleaded.

Susannah felt herself weakening. Emily was, after all, her younger sister. "Surely, there's got to be someone better qualified."

Emily had hesitated, then tearfully blurted, "I don't know what I'll do if you won't take Michelle." She began to sob pitifully. "Robert's left me."

"What?" If Emily hadn't gained her full attention earlier, she did now. If her sister was an earth mother, then her brother-in-law, Robert Davidson, was Abraham Lincoln, as solid and upright as a thirty-foot oak. "I don't believe it."

"It's true," Emily wailed. "He...he claims I give Michelle all my attention and that I never have enough energy left to be a decent wife." She paused to draw in a quavery breath. "I know he's right...but being a good mother demands so much time and effort."

"I thought Robert wanted six children."

"He does...or did." Emily's sobbing began anew.

"Oh, Emily, it can't be that bad," Susannah had murmured in a soothing voice, thinking as fast as she could. "I'm sure you misunderstood Robert. He loves you and Michelle, and I'm positive he has no intention of leaving you."

"He does," Emily went on to explain between hiccuping sobs. "He asked me to find someone to look after Michelle for a while. He says we have to have some time to ourselves, or our marriage is dead."

That sounded pretty drastic to Susannah.

"I swear to you, Susannah, I've called everyone who's ever babysat Michelle before, but no one's available. No one—not even for one night. When I told Robert I hadn't found a sitter, he got so angry...and that's not like Robert."

Susannah agreed. The man was the salt of the earth. Not once in the five years she'd known him could she recall him even raising his voice.

"He told me that if I didn't take this weekend trip to San Francisco with him he was going alone. I *tried* to find someone to watch Michelle," Emily said. "I honestly tried, but there's no one else, and now Robert's home and he's loading up the car and, Susannah, he's serious. He's going to leave without me

and from the amount of luggage he's taking, I don't
think he plans to come back."

The tale of woe barely skimmed the surface of
Susannah's mind. The key word that planted itself in
fertile ground was *weekend*. "I thought you said you
only needed me for one night?" she asked.

At that point, Susannah should've realized she
wasn't much brighter than a brainless mouse, inno-
cently nibbling away at the cheese in a steel trap.

Emily sniffled once more, probably for effect,
Susannah mused darkly.

"We'll be flying back to Seattle early Sunday afternoon. Robert's got some business in San Francisco
Saturday morning, but the rest of the weekend is
free...and it's been such a long time since we've been
alone."

"Two days and two nights," Susannah said slowly,
mentally tabulating the hours.

"Oh, please, Susannah, my whole marriage is at
stake. You've always been such a good big sister. I know
I don't deserve anyone as good as you."

Silently Susannah agreed.

"Somehow I'll find a way to repay you," Emily continued.

Susannah closed her eyes. Her sister's idea of
repaying her was usually freshly baked zucchini bread
shortly after Susannah announced she was watching
her weight.

"Susannah, please!"

It was then that Susannah had caved in to the
pressure. "All right. Go ahead and bring Michelle over."

Somewhere in the distance, she could've sworn she heard the echo of a mousetrap slamming shut.

By the time Emily and Robert had deposited their offspring at Susannah's condominium, her head was swimming with instructions. After planting a kiss on her daughter's rosy cheek, Emily handed the clinging Michelle to a reluctant Susannah.

That was when the nightmare began in earnest.

As soon as her sister left, Susannah could feel herself tense up. Even as a teenager, she hadn't done a lot of babysitting; it wasn't that she didn't like children, but kids didn't seem to take to her.

Holding the squalling infant on her hip, Susannah paced while her mind buzzed with everything she was supposed to remember. She knew what to do in case of diaper rash, colic and several other minor emergencies, but Emily hadn't said one word about how to keep Michelle from crying.

"Shhh," Susannah cooed, jiggling her niece against her hip. She swore the child had a cry that could've been heard a block away.

After the first five minutes, her calm cool composure began to crack under the pressure. She could be in real trouble here. The tenant agreement she'd signed specifically stated "no children."

"Hello, Michelle, remember me?" Susannah asked, doing everything she could think of to quiet the baby. Didn't the kid need to breathe? "I'm your auntie Susannah, the business executive."

Her niece wasn't impressed. Pausing only a few seconds to gulp for air, Michelle increased her volume and glared at the door as if she expected her mother to miraculously appear if she cried long and hard enough.

"Trust me, kid, if I knew a magic trick that'd bring your mother back, I'd use it now."

Ten minutes. Emily had been gone a total of ten minutes. Susannah was seriously considering giving the state Children's Protective Services a call and claiming that a stranger had abandoned a baby on her doorstep.

"Mommy will be home soon," Susannah murmured wistfully.

Michelle screamed louder. Susannah started to worry about her stemware. The kid's voice could shatter glass.

More tortured minutes passed, each one an eternity. Susannah was desperate enough to sing. Not knowing any appropriate lullabies, she began with a couple of ditties from her childhood, but quickly exhausted those. Michelle didn't seem to appreciate them anyway. Since Susannah didn't keep up with the current top twenty, the best she could do was an old Christmas favorite. Somehow singing "Jingle Bells" in the middle of September didn't feel right.

"Michelle," Susannah pleaded, willing to stand on her head if it would keep the baby from wailing, "your mommy will be back, I assure you."

Michelle apparently didn't believe her.

"How about if I buy municipal bonds and put them in your name?" Susannah tried next. "Tax-free bonds, Michelle! This is an offer you shouldn't refuse.

All you need to do is stop crying. Oh, please stop crying."

Michelle wasn't interested.

"All right," Susannah cried, growing desperate. "I'll sign over my Microsoft stock. That's my final offer, so you'd better grab it while I'm in a generous mood."

Michelle answered by gripping Susannah's collar with both of her chubby fists and burying her wet face in a once spotless white silk blouse.

"You're a tough nut to crack, Michelle Margaret Davidson," Susannah muttered, gently patting her niece's back as she paced. "You want blood, don't you, kid? You aren't going to be satisfied with anything less."

A half hour after Emily had left, Susannah was ready to resort to tears herself. She'd started singing again, returning to her repertoire of Christmas songs. "You'd better watch out,/ you'd better not cry,/ Aunt Susannah's here telling you why...."

She was just getting into the lyrics when someone knocked heavily on her door.

Like a thief caught in the act, Susannah whirled around, fully expecting the caller to be the building superintendent. No doubt there'd been complaints and he'd come to confront her.

Expelling a weary sigh, Susannah realized she was defenseless. The only option she had was to throw herself on his mercy. She squared her shoulders and walked across the lush carpet, prepared to do exactly that.

Only it wasn't necessary. The building superintendent wasn't the person standing on the other side of her door. It was her new neighbor, wearing a baseball cap and a faded T-shirt, and looking more than a little disgruntled.

"The crying and the baby I can take," he said, crossing his arms and relaxing against the doorframe, "but your singing has got to go."

"Very funny," she grumbled.

"The kid's obviously distressed."

Susannah glared at him. "Nothing gets past you, does it?"

"Do something."

"I'm trying." Apparently Michelle didn't like this stranger any more than Susannah did because she buried her face in Susannah's collar and rubbed it vigorously back and forth. That at least helped muffle her cries, but there was no telling what it would do to white silk. "I offered her my Microsoft stock and it didn't do any good," Susannah explained. "I was even willing to throw in my municipal bonds."

"You offered her stocks and bonds, but did you suggest dinner?"

"Dinner?" Susannah echoed. She hadn't thought of that. Emily claimed she'd fed Michelle, but Susannah vaguely remembered something about a bottle.

"The poor thing's probably starving."

"I think she's supposed to have a bottle," Susannah said. She turned and glanced at the assorted bags Emily and Robert had deposited in her condominium, along with the necessary baby furniture. From the number of things stacked on the floor, it must seem as if she'd been granted permanent guardianship. "There's got to be one in all this paraphernalia."

"I'll find it—you keep the kid quiet."

Susannah nearly laughed out loud. If she was able to keep Michelle quiet, he wouldn't be here in the first place. She imagined she could convince CIA agents to hand over top-secret documents more easily than she could silence one distressed nine-month-old infant.

Without waiting for an invitation, her neighbor moved into the living room. He picked up one of the three overnight bags and rooted through that. He hesitated when he pulled out a stack of freshly laundered diapers, and glanced at Susannah. "I didn't know anyone used cloth diapers anymore."

"My sister doesn't believe in anything disposable."

"Smart woman."

Susannah made no comment, and within a few seconds noted that he'd come across a plastic bottle. He removed the protective cap and handed the bottle to Susannah, who looked at it and blinked. "Shouldn't the milk be heated?"

"It's room temperature, and frankly, at this point I don't think the kid's going to care."

He was right. The instant Susannah placed the rubber nipple in her niece's mouth, Michelle grasped the bottle with both hands and sucked at it greedily.

For the first time since her mother had left, Michelle stopped crying. The silence was pure bliss. Susannah's tension eased, and she released a sigh that went all the way through her body.

"You might want to sit down," he suggested next.

Susannah did, and with Michelle cradled awkwardly in her arms, leaned against the back of the sofa, trying not to jostle her charge.

"That's better, isn't it?" Her neighbor pushed the baseball cap farther back on his head, looking pleased with himself.

"Much better." Susannah smiled shyly up at him. They hadn't actually met, but she'd certainly noticed her new neighbor. As far as looks went, he was down-right handsome. She supposed most women would find his mischievous blue eyes and dark good looks appealing. He was tanned, but she'd have wagered a month's pay that his bronzed features weren't the result of any machine. He obviously spent a great deal of time outdoors, which led her to the conclusion that he didn't work. At least not in an office. And frankly, she doubted he was employed outside of one, either. The clothes he wore and the sporadic hours he kept had led her to speculate about him earlier. If he had money, which apparently he did or else he wouldn't be living in this complex, then he'd inherited it.

"I think it's time I introduced myself," he said conversationally, sitting on the ottoman across from her. "I'm Nate Townsend."

"Susannah Simmons," she said. "I apologize for all the racket. My niece and I are just getting acquainted and—oh, boy—it's going to be a long weekend, so bear with us."

"You're babysitting for the weekend?"

"Two days and two nights." It sounded like a whole lifetime to Susannah. "My sister and her husband are off on a second honeymoon. Normally my parents would watch Michelle and love doing it, but they're visiting friends in Florida."

"It was kind of you to offer."

Susannah thought it best to correct this impression. "Trust me, I didn't volunteer. In case you hadn't noticed, I'm not very maternal."

"You've got to support her back a little more," he said, watching Michelle.

Susannah tried, but it felt awkward to hold on to her niece *and* the bottle.

"You're doing fine."

"Sure," Susannah muttered. She felt like someone with two left feet who'd been unexpectedly ushered onto center stage and told to perform the lead in *Swan Lake*.

"Relax, will you?" Nate encouraged.

"I told you already I'm not into this motherhood business," she snapped. "If you think you can do better, you feed her."

"You're doing great. Don't worry about it."

She wasn't doing great at all, and she knew it, but this was as good as she got.

"When's the last time you had anything to eat?" he asked.

"I beg your pardon?"

"You sound hungry to me."

"Well, I'm not," Susannah said irritably.

"I think you are, but don't worry, I'll take care of

that." He walked boldly into her kitchen and paused in front of the refrigerator. "Your mood will improve once you have something in your stomach."

Shifting Michelle higher, Susannah stood and followed him. "You can't just walk in here and—"

"I'll say I can't," he murmured, his head inside her fridge. "Do you realize there's nothing in here except an open box of baking soda and a jar full of pickle juice?"

"I eat out a lot," Susannah said defensively.

"I can see that."

Michelle had finished the bottle and made a slurping sound that prompted Susannah to remove the nipple from her mouth. The baby's eyes were closed. Little wonder, Susannah thought. She was probably exhausted. Certainly Susannah was, and it was barely seven on Friday evening. The weekend was just beginning.

Setting the empty bottle on the kitchen counter, Susannah awkwardly lifted Michelle onto her shoulder and patted her back until she produced a tiny burp. Feeling a real sense of accomplishment, Susannah smiled proudly.

Nate chuckled and when Susannah glanced in his direction, she discovered him watching her, his grin warm and appraising. "You're going to be fine."

Flustered, Susannah lowered her gaze. She always disliked it when a man looked at her that way, examining her features and forming a judgment about her by the size of her nose, or the direction in which her eyebrows grew. Most men seemed to believe they'd been granted a rare gift of insight and could determine a woman's entire character just by looking at her face. Unfortunately, Susannah's was too austere by conventional standards to be classified as beautiful. Her eyes were deep-set and dark, her cheekbones high. Her nose came almost straight from her forehead and together with her full mouth made her look like a classic Greek sculpture. Not pretty, she thought. Interesting perhaps.

It was during Susannah's beleaguered self-evaluation that Michelle stirred and started jabbering cheerfully, reaching one hand toward a strand of Susannah's dark hair.

Without her realizing it, her chignon had come undone. Michelle had somehow managed to loosen the pins and now the long dark tresses fell haphazardly over Susannah's shoulder. If there was one thing Susannah was meticulous about, and actually there were several, it was her appearance. She must look a rare sight, in an expensive business suit with a stained white blouse and her hair tumbling over her shoulder.

"Actually I've been waiting for an opportunity to introduce myself," Nate said, leaning against the counter. "But after the first couple of times we saw each other, our paths didn't seem to cross again."

"I've been working a lot of overtime lately." If the truth be known, Susannah almost always put in extra hours. Often she brought work home with her. She was dedicated, committed and hardworking. Her neighbor, however, didn't seem to possess any of those qualities. She strongly suspected that everything in life had come much too easily for Nate Townsend. She'd never seen him without his baseball cap or his T-shirt. Somehow she doubted he even owned a suit. And if he did, it probably wouldn't look right on him. Nate Townsend was definitely a football-jersey type of guy.

He seemed likable—friendly and outgoing—but from what she'd seen, he lacked ambition. Apparently there'd never been anything he'd wanted badly enough to really strive for.

"I'm glad we had the chance to introduce ourselves," Susannah added, walking back into the living room and toward her front door. "I appreciate the help, but as you said, Michelle and I are going to be fine."

"It didn't sound that way when I arrived."

"I was just getting my feet wet," she returned, defending herself, "and why are you arguing with me? You're the one who said I was doing all right."

"I lied."

"Why would you do that?"

Nate shrugged nonchalantly. "I thought a little self-confidence would do you good, so I offered it."

Susannah glared at him, resenting his attitude. So much for the nice-guy-who-lives-next-door image she'd had of him. "I don't need any favors from you."

"You may not," he agreed, "but unfortunately Michelle does. The poor kid was starving and you didn't so much as suspect."

"I would've figured it out."

Nate gave her a look that seemed to cast doubt on her intelligence, and Susannah frowned right back. She opened the door with far more force than necessary and flipped her hair over her shoulder with flair a Paris model would have envied. "Thanks for stopping in," she said stiffly, "but as you can see everything's under control."

"If you say so." He grinned at her and without another word was gone.

Susannah banged the door shut with her hip, feeling a rush of satisfaction as she did so. She knew this was petty, but her neighbor had annoyed her in more ways than one.

Soon afterward Susannah heard the soft strains of an Italian opera drifting from Nate's condominium. At least she thought it was Italian, which was unfortunate because that made her think of spaghetti and how hungry she actually was.

"Okay, Michelle," she said, smiling down on her niece. "It's time to feed your auntie." Without too much trouble, Susannah assembled the high chair and set her niece in that while she scanned the contents of her freezer.

The best she could come up with was a frozen Mexican entrée. She gazed at the picture on the front of the package, shook her head and tossed it back inside the freezer.

Michelle seemed to approve and vigorously slapped the tray on her high chair.

Crossing her arms and leaning against the freezer door, Susannah paused. "Did you hear what he said?"

she asked, still irate. "I guess he was right, but he didn't have to be so superior about it."

Michelle slapped her hands in approval once again. The music was muted by the thick walls, and wanting to hear a little more, Susannah cracked open the sliding glass door to her balcony, which was separated from Nate's by a concrete partition. It bestowed privacy, but didn't muffle the beautiful voices raised in triumphant song.

Susannah opened the glass door completely and stepped outside. The evening was cool, but pleasantly so. The sun had just started to set and had cast a wash of golden shadows over the picturesque waterfront.

"Michelle," she muttered when she came back in, "he's cooking something that smells like lasagna or spaghetti." Her stomach growled and she returned to the freezer, taking out the same Mexican entrée she'd rejected earlier. It didn't seem any more appetizing than it had the first time.

A faint scent of garlic wafted into her kitchen. Susannah turned her classic Greek nose in that direction, then followed the aroma to the open door like a puppet drawn there by a string. She sniffed loudly and turned eagerly back to her niece. "It's definitely Italian, and it smells divine."

Michelle pounded the tray again.

"It's garlic bread," Susannah announced and whirled around to face her niece, who clearly wasn't impressed. But then, thought Susannah, she wouldn't be. She'd eaten.

Under normal conditions, Susannah would've reached for her jacket and headed to Mama Mataloni's, a fabulous Italian restaurant within easy walking distance. Unfortunately Mama Mataloni's didn't deliver.

Against her better judgment, Susannah stuck the frozen entrée into her microwave and set the timer. When there was another knock on her door, she stiffened and looked at Michelle as if the nine-month-old would sit up and tell Susannah who'd come by *this* time.

It was Nate again, holding a plate of spaghetti and a glass of red wine. "Did you fix yourself something to eat?" he asked.

For the life of her Susannah couldn't tear her gaze away from the oversize plate, heaped high with steaming pasta smothered in a thick red sauce. Nothing had ever looked—or smelled—more appetizing. The fresh Parmesan cheese he'd grated over the top had melted onto the rich sauce. A generous slice of garlic bread was balanced on the side.

"I, ah, was just heating up a...microwave dinner." She pointed behind her toward the kitchen as if that would explain what she was trying to say. Her tongue seemed to be stuck to the roof of her mouth.

"I shouldn't have acted like such a know-it-all earlier," he said, pushing the plate toward her. "I'm bringing you a peace offering."

"This...is for me?" She raised her eyes from the

plate, wondering if he knew how hungry she felt and was toying with her.

He handed her the meal and the wine. "The sauce has been simmering most of the afternoon. I like to pretend I'm a bit of a gourmet chef. Every once in a while I get creative in the kitchen."

"How...nice." She conjured up a picture of Nate standing in his kitchen stirring sauce while the rest of the world struggled to make a living. Her attitude wasn't at all gracious and she mentally apologized. Without further ado, she marched into her kitchen, reached for a fork and plopped herself down at the table. She might as well eat this feast while it was hot!

One sample told her everything she needed to know. "This is great." She took another bite, pointed her fork in his direction and rolled her eyes. "Marvelous. Wonderful."

Nate pulled a bread stick out of his shirt pocket and gave it to Michelle. "Here's looking at you, kid."

As Michelle chewed contentedly on the bread stick, Nate pulled out a chair and sat across from Susannah, who was too busy enjoying her dinner to notice anything out of the ordinary until Nate's eyes narrowed.

"What's wrong?" Susannah asked. She wiped her mouth with a napkin and sampled the wine.

"I smell something."

Judging by his expression, whatever it was apparently wasn't pleasant. "It might be the microwave dinner," she suggested hopefully, already knowing better.

"I'm afraid not."

Susannah carefully set the fork beside her plate as uneasiness settled over her.

"It seems," Nate said, covering his nose with one hand, "that someone needs to change Michelle's diaper."

Chapter
2

Holding a freshly diapered Michelle on her hip, Susannah rushed out of the bathroom into the narrow hallway and gasped for breath.

"Are you all right?" Nate asked, his brow creased with a concerned frown.

She nodded and sagged against the wall, feeling light-headed. Once she'd dragged several clean breaths through her lungs, she straightened and even managed a weak smile.

"That wasn't so bad now, was it?"

Susannah glared at him. "I should've been wearing an oxygen mask."

Nate's responding chuckle did little to improve her mood.

"In light of what I just experienced," she muttered,

"I can't understand why the population continues to grow." To be on the safe side, she opened the hall linen closet and took out a large can of disinfectant spray. Sticking her arm inside the bathroom, she gave a generous squirt.

"While you were busy I assembled the crib," Nate told her, still revealing far too much amusement to suit Susannah. "Where would you like me to put it?"

"The living room will be fine." His action had been thoughtful, but Susannah wasn't accustomed to depending on others, so when she thanked him, the words were forced.

Susannah followed him into the living room and found the bed ready. She laid Michelle down on her stomach and covered her with a handknit blanket. The baby settled down immediately, without fussing.

Nate walked toward the door. "You're sure everything's okay?" he said softly.

"Positive." Susannah wasn't, but Michelle was her niece and their problems weren't his. Nate had done more than enough already. "Thanks for dinner."

"Anytime." He paused at the door and turned back. "I left my phone number on the kitchen counter. Call if you need me."

"Thanks."

He favored her with a grin on his way out the door, and Susannah stood a few moments after he'd left the apartment, thinking about him. Her feelings were decidedly mixed.

She began sorting through the various bags her sister had brought, depositing the jars of baby food in the cupboard and putting the bottles of formula in the fridge. As Nate had pointed out, there was plenty of room—all she had to do was scoot the empty pickle jar aside.

She supposed she should toss the jar in the garbage, but one of the guys from the office had talked about making pickled eggs. It sounded so simple—all she had to do was peel a few hard-boiled eggs and keep them refrigerated in the jar for a week or so. Susannah had been meaning to try it ever since. But she was afraid that when the mood struck her, she wouldn't have any pickle juice around, so she'd decided to keep it on hand.

Once she'd finished in the kitchen, Susannah soaked in a hot bath, leaving the door ajar in case Michelle woke and needed her. She felt far more relaxed afterward.

Walking back into the living room on the tips of her toes, she brought out her briefcase and removed a file. She glanced down at her sleeping niece and gently patted her back. The little girl looked so angelic, so content.

Suddenly a powerful yearning stirred within Susannah. She felt real affection for Michelle, but the feeling was more than that. This time alone with her niece had evoked a longing buried deep in Susannah's heart, a longing she'd never taken the time to fully examine. And with it came an aching restless sensation that she promptly submerged.

When Susannah had chosen a career in business, she'd realized she was giving up the part of herself that hungered for husband and children. There was nothing that said she couldn't marry, couldn't raise a child, but she knew herself too well. From the time she was in high school it had been painfully apparent that she was completely inadequate in the domestic arena. Especially when she compared herself to Emily, who seemed to have been born with a dust rag in one hand and a cookbook in the other.

Susannah had never regretted the decision she'd made to dedicate herself to her career, but then she was more fortunate than some. She had Emily, who was determined to supply her with numerous nieces and nephews. For Susannah, Michelle and the little ones who were sure to follow would have to be enough.

Reminding herself that she was comfortable with her choices, Susannah quietly stepped away from the crib. For the next hour, she sat on her bed reading the details of the proposed marketing program the department had sent her. The full presentation was scheduled for Monday morning and she wanted to be informed and prepared.

When she finished reading the report, she tiptoed back to her desk, situated in the far corner of the living room, and replaced the file in her briefcase.

Once more she paused to check on her niece. Feeling just a little cocky, she returned to the bedroom convinced this babysitting business wasn't going to be so bad after all.

Susannah changed her mind at one-thirty when a piercing wail startled her out of a sound sleep. Not knowing how long Michelle had been at it, Susannah nearly fell out of bed in her rush to reach her niece.

"Michelle," she cried, stumbling blindly across the floor, her arms stretched out in front of her. "I'm coming.... There's no need to panic."

Michelle disagreed vehemently.

Turning on a light only made matters worse. Squinting to protect her eyes from the glare, Susannah groped her way to the crib, then let out a cry herself when she stubbed her toe on the leg of the coffee table.

Michelle was standing, holding on to the bars and looking as if she didn't have a friend in the world.

"What's the matter, sweetheart?" Susannah asked softly, lifting the baby into her arms.

A wet bottom told part of the story. And the poor kid had probably woken and, finding herself in a strange place, felt scared. Susannah couldn't blame her.

"All right, we'll try this diapering business again."

Susannah spread a thick towel on the bathroom counter, then gently placed Michelle on it. She was halfway through the changing process when the phone rang. Straightening, Susannah glanced around her, wondering what she should do. She couldn't leave Michelle, and picking her up and carrying her into the kitchen would be difficult. Whoever was calling at this time of night should know better! If it was important they could leave a message on her answering machine.

But after three rings, the phone stopped, followed almost immediately by a firm knock at her door.

Hauling Michelle, newly diapered, Susannah squinted and checked the peephole to discover a disgruntled Nate on the other side.

"Nate," she said in surprise as she opened the door. She couldn't even guess what he wanted. And she wasn't too keen about letting him into her apartment at this hour.

He stood just inside the condo, barefoot and dressed in a red plaid housecoat. His hair was mussed, which made Susannah wonder about her own disheveled appearance. She suspected she looked like someone who'd walked out of a swamp.

"Is Michelle all right?" he barked, despite the evidence before him. Not waiting for a reply, he continued in an accusing tone, "You didn't answer the phone."

"I couldn't. I was changing her diaper."

Nate hesitated, then studied her closely. "In that case, are *you* all right?"

She nodded and managed to raise one hand. It was difficult when her arms were occupied with a baby. "I lived to tell about it."

"Good. What happened? Why was Michelle crying?"

"I'm not sure. Maybe when she woke up and didn't recognize her surroundings, she suffered an anxiety attack."

"And, from the look of us, caused a couple more."

Susannah would rather he hadn't mentioned that. Her long, tangled hair spilled over her shoulders and she, too, was barefoot. She'd been so anxious to get to Michelle that she hadn't bothered to reach for her slippers or her robe.

Michelle, it seemed, was pleased with all the unexpected attention, and when she leaned toward Nate, arms outstretched, Susannah marveled at how fickle an infant could be. After all, she was the one who'd fed and diapered her. Not Nate.

"It's my male charm," he explained delightedly.

"More likely, it's your red housecoat."

Whatever it was, Michelle went into his arms as if he were a long-lost friend. Susannah excused herself to retrieve her robe from the foot of her bed. By the time she got back, Nate was sitting on the sofa with his feet stretched out, supported by Susannah's mahogany coffee table.

"Make yourself at home," she muttered. Her mood wasn't always the best when she'd been abruptly wakened from a sound sleep.

He glanced up at her and grinned. "No need to be testy."

"Yes, there is," she said, but destroyed what remained of her argument by yawning loudly. Covering her mouth with the back of her hand, she slumped down on the chair across from him and flipped her hair away from her face.

His gaze followed the action. "You should wear your hair down more often."

She glared at him. "I always wear my hair up."

"I noticed. And frankly, it's much more flattering down."

"Oh, for heaven's sake," she cried, "are you going to tell me how to dress next?"

"I might."

He said it with such a charming smile that any sting there might have been in his statement was diluted.

"You don't have to stick with business suits every day, do you? Try jeans sometime. With a T-shirt."

She opened her mouth to argue with him, then decided not to bother. The arrogance he displayed seemed to be characteristic of handsome men in general, she'd noted. Because a man happened to possess lean good looks and could smile beguilingly, he figured he had the right to say anything he pleased to a woman—to comment on how she styled her hair, how she chose to dress or anything else. These were things he wouldn't dream of discussing if he were talking to another man.

"You aren't going to argue?"

"No," she said, and for emphasis shook her head.

That stopped him short. He paused and blinked, then sent her another of his captivating smiles. "I find that refreshing."

"I'm gratified to hear there's something about me you approve of." There were probably plenty of other things that didn't please him. Given any encouragement, he'd probably be glad to list them for her.

Sweet little traitor that she was, Michelle had curled up in Nate's arms, utterly content just to sit there and study his handsome face, which no doubt had fascinated numerous other females before her. The least Michelle could do was show some signs of going back to sleep so Susannah could return her to the crib and usher Nate out the door.

"I shouldn't have said what I did about your hair and clothes."

"Hey," she returned flippantly, "you don't need to worry about hurting my feelings. I'm strong. I've got a lot of emotional fortitude."

"Strong," he repeated. "You make yourself sound like an all-weather tire."

"I've had to be tougher than that."

His face relaxed into a look of sympathy. "Why?"

"I work with men just like you every day."

"Men just like me?"

"It's true. For the past seven years, I've found myself up against the old double standard, but I've learned to keep my cool."

He frowned as if he didn't understand what she was talking about. Susannah felt it was her obligation to tell him. Apparently Nate had never been involved in office politics. "Let me give you a few examples. If a male coworker has a cluttered desk, then everyone assumes he's a hard worker. If my desk is a mess, it's a sign of disorganization."

Nate looked as if he wanted to argue with her, but Susannah was just warming to her subject and she forged ahead before he had a chance to speak. "If a man in an office marries, it's good for the company because he'll settle down and become a more productive employee. If a woman marries, it's almost the kiss of death because management figures she'll get pregnant and quit. If a man leaves because he's been offered a better job, everyone's pleased for him because he's taking advantage of an excellent career opportunity.

But if the same position is offered to a woman and she takes it, then upper management shrugs and claims women aren't dependable."

When she'd finished there was a short pause. "You have very definite feelings on the subject," he said at last.

"If you were a woman, you would, too."

His nod of agreement was a long time coming. "You're right, I probably would."

Michelle seemed to find the toes of her sleeper fascinating and was examining them closely. Personally, Susannah didn't know how anyone could be so wide-awake at this ungodly hour.

"If you turn down the lights, she might get the hint," Nate said, doing a poor job of smothering a yawn.

"You're beat," said Susannah. "There's no need for you to stay. I'll take her." She held out her arms to Michelle, who whimpered and clung all the more tightly to Nate. Susannah's feelings of inadequacy were reinforced.

"Don't worry about me. I'm comfortable like this," Nate told her.

"But..." She could feel the warmth invading her cheeks. She lowered her eyes, regretting her outburst of a few minutes ago. She'd been standing on her soapbox again. "Listen, I'm sorry about what I said. What goes on at the office has nothing to do with our being neighbors."

"Then we're even."

"Even?"

"I shouldn't have commented on your hair and

clothes." He hesitated long enough to envelop her in his smile. "Friends?"

Despite the intolerable hour, Susannah found herself smiling back. "Friends."

Michelle seemed to concur because she cooed loudly, kicking her feet.

Susannah stood and turned the lamp down to its lowest setting, then reached for Michelle's blanket, covering the baby. Feeling slightly chilled herself, she fetched the brightly colored afghan at the foot of the sofa, which Emily had crocheted for her last Christmas.

The muted light created an intimate atmosphere, and suddenly self-conscious, Susannah suggested, "Maybe I'll sing to her. That should help her go to sleep."

"If anyone sings, it'll be me," he said much too quickly.

Susannah's pride was a little dented, but remembering her limited repertoire of songs, she gestured toward him and said, "All right, Frank Sinatra, have a go."

To Susannah's surprise, Nate's singing voice was soothing and melodious. Even more surprisingly, he knew exactly the right kind of songs. Not lullabies, but easy-listening songs, the kind she'd heard for years on the radio. She felt her own eyes drifting closed and battled to stay awake. His voice dropped to a mere whisper that felt like a warm caress. Much too warm. And cozy, as if the three of them belonged together, which was ridiculous since she'd only just met Nate. He was her neighbor and nothing more. There hadn't

been time for them to get to know each other, and
Michelle was her *niece*, not her daughter.

But the domestic fantasy continued, no matter how
hard she tried to dispel it. She couldn't stop thinking
about what it would be like to share her life with a
husband and children—and she could barely manage
to keep her eyes open for more than a second or two.
Perhaps if she rested them for a moment…

The next thing Susannah knew, her neck ached.
She reached up to secure her pillow, then realized she
didn't have one. Instead of being in bed, she was
curled up in the chair, her head resting uncomfort-
ably against the arm. Slowly, reluctantly, she opened
her eyes and discovered Nate across from her, head
tilted back, sleeping soundly. Michelle was resting
peacefully in his arms.

It took Susannah a minute or so to orient herself.
When she saw the sun breaking across the sky and
spilling through her large windows, she closed her
eyes again. It was morning. Morning! Nate had spent
the night at her place.

Flustered, Susannah twisted her body into an
upright position and rubbed the sleep from her face,
wondering what she should do. Waking Nate was
probably not the best idea. He was bound to be as
unnerved as she was to discover he'd fallen asleep in
her living room. To complicate matters, the afghan
she'd covered herself with had somehow become
twisted around her hips and legs. Muttering under her
breath, Susannah yanked it about in an effort to stand.

Her activity disturbed Nate's restful slumber. He stirred, glanced in her direction and froze for what seemed the longest moment of Susannah's life. Then he blinked several times and glared at her as though he hoped she'd vanish into thin air.

Standing now, Susannah did her best to appear dignified, which was nearly impossible with the comforter still twisted around her.

"Where am I?" Nate asked dazedly.

"Ah...my place."

His eyes drifted shut. "I was afraid of that." The mournful look that came over Nate's face would have been comical under other circumstances. Only neither of them was laughing.

"I, ah, must've fallen asleep," she said, breaking the embarrassed silence. She took pains to fold the afghan, and held it against her stomach like a shield.

"Me, too, apparently," Nate muttered.

Michelle woke and struggled into a sitting position. She looked around her and evidently didn't like what she saw, either. Her lower lip started to tremble.

"Michelle, it's okay," Susannah said quickly, hoping to ward off the scream she feared was coming. "You're staying with Auntie Susannah this weekend, remember?"

"I think she might be wet," Nate offered when Michelle began to whimper softly. He let out a muffled curse and hastily lifted the nine-month-old from his lap. "I'm positive she's wet. Here, take her."

Susannah reached for her niece and a dry diaper in one smooth movement, but it didn't help. Michelle was intent on letting them both know, in no uncertain terms, that she didn't like her schedule altered. Nor did she appreciate waking up in a stranger's arms. She conveyed her displeasure in loud boisterous cries.

"I think she might be hungry, too," Nate suggested, trying to brush the dampness from his housecoat.

"Brilliant observation," Susannah said sarcastically on her way to the bathroom, Michelle in her arms.

"My, my, you certainly get testy in the mornings," he said.

"I need coffee."

"Fine. I'll make us both a cup while I'm heating a bottle for Michelle."

"She's supposed to eat her cereal first," Susannah shouted. At least that was what Emily had insisted when she'd outlined her daughter's schedule.

"I'm sure she doesn't care. She's hungry."

"All right, all right," Susannah yelled from the bathroom. "Heat her bottle first if you want."

Yelling was a mistake, she soon discovered. Michelle clearly wasn't any keener on mornings than Susannah was. Punching the air with her stubby legs, her niece made diapering a nearly impossible task. Susannah grew more frustrated by the minute. Finally her hair, falling forward over her shoulders, caught Michelle's attention. She grasped it, pausing to gulp in a huge breath.

"Do you want me to get that?" she heard Nate shout.

"Get what?"

Apparently it wasn't important because he didn't

answer her. But a moment later he was standing at the bathroom door.

"It's for you," he said.

"What's for me?"

"The phone."

The word bounced around in her mind like a ricocheting bullet. "Did...did they say who it was?" she asked, her voice high-pitched and wobbly. No doubt it was someone from the office and she'd be the subject of gossip for months.

"Someone named Emily."

"Emily," she repeated. That was even worse. Her sister was sure to be full of awkward questions.

"Hi," Susannah said as casually as possible into the receiver.

"Who answered the phone?" her sister demanded without preamble.

"My neighbor. Nate Townsend. He, ah, lives next door." That awkward explanation astonished even her. Worse, Susannah had been ready to blurt out that Nate had spent the night, but she'd stopped herself just in time.

"I haven't met him, have I?"

"My neighbor? No, you haven't."

"He sounds cute."

"Listen, if you're phoning about Michelle," Susannah hurried to add, anxious to end the conversation, "there's no need for concern. Everything's under control." That was a slight exaggeration, but what Emily didn't know couldn't worry her.

"Is that Michelle I hear crying in the background?" Emily asked.

"Yes. She just woke up and she's a little hungry." Nate was holding the baby and pacing the kitchen, waiting impatiently for Susannah to get off the phone.

"My poor baby," Emily moaned. "Tell me when you met your neighbor. I don't remember you ever mentioning anyone named Nate."

"He's been helping me out," Susannah said quickly. Wanting to change the subject, she asked, "How are you and Robert?"

Her sister sighed audibly. "Robert was so right. We needed this weekend alone. I feel a thousand times better and so does he. Every married couple should get away for a few days like this—but then everyone doesn't have a sister as generous as you to fill in on such short notice."

"Good, good," Susannah said, hardly aware of what she was supposed to think was so fantastic. "Uh-oh," she said, growing desperate. "The bottle's warm. I hate to cut you off, but I've got to take care of Michelle. I'm sure you understand."

"Of course."

"I'll see you tomorrow afternoon then. What time's your flight landing?"

"One-fifteen. We'll drive straight to your place and pick up Michelle."

"Okay, I'll expect you sometime around two." Another day with Michelle. She could manage for another twenty-four hours, couldn't she? What could possibly go wrong in that small amount of time?

Losing patience, Nate took the bottle and Michelle and returned to the living room. Susannah watched through the doorway as he turned on her television and plopped himself down as if he'd been doing it for years. His concentration moved from the TV long enough to place the rubber nipple in Michelle's eager mouth.

Her niece began greedily sucking, too hungry to care who was feeding her. Good heavens, Susannah thought, Michelle had spent the night in his arms. A little thing like letting this man feed her paled in comparison.

Emily was still chatting, telling her sister how romantic her first night in San Francisco had been. But Susannah barely heard. Her gaze settled on Nate, who looked rumpled, crumpled and utterly content, sitting in her living room, holding an infant in his arms.

That sight affected Susannah as few ever had, and she was powerless to explain its impact on her senses. She'd dated a reasonable number of men—debonair, rich, sophisticated ones. But the feeling she had now, this attraction, had taken her completely by surprise. Over the years, Susannah had always been careful to guard her heart. It hadn't been difficult, since she'd never met anyone who truly appealed to her. Yet this disheveled, disgruntled male, who sat in her living room feeding her infant niece with enviable expertise, attracted her more profoundly than anyone she'd ever met. It wasn't the least bit logical. Nothing could ever develop between them—they were as different as…as gelatin and concrete. The last thing she wanted was to become involved in a serious relationship. With some effort, she forced her eyes away from the homey scene.

When at last she was able to hang up the phone, Susannah moved into the living room, feeling weary. She brushed the tangled curls from her face, wondering if she should take Michelle from Nate so he could return to his own apartment. No doubt her niece would resist and humiliate her once more.

"Your sister isn't flying with Puget Air, is she?" he asked, frowning. His gaze remained on the television screen.

"Yes, why?"

Nate's mouth thinned. "You...we're in trouble here. Big trouble. According to the news, maintenance workers for Puget Air are going on strike. By six tonight, every plane they own will be grounded."

Chapter

3

"**I**f this is a joke," Susannah told him angrily, "it's in poor taste."

"Would I kid about this?" Nate asked mildly.

Susannah slumped down on the edge of the sofa and gave a ragged sigh. This couldn't be happening, it just couldn't. "I'd better call Emily." She assumed her sister was blissfully unaware of the strike.

Susannah was back a few minutes later.

"Well?" Nate demanded. "What did she say?"

"Oh, she knew all along," Susannah replied disparagingly, "but she didn't want to say anything because she was afraid I'd worry."

"How exactly does she intend to get home?"

"Apparently they booked seats on another airline on the off chance something like this might happen."

"That was smart."

"My brother-in-law's like that. I'm not to give the matter another thought," she said, quoting Emily. "My sister will be back Sunday afternoon as promised." If the Fates so decreed—and Susannah said a fervent prayer that they would.

But the Fates had other plans.

Sunday morning, there were bags under Susannah's eyes. She was mentally and physically exhausted, and convinced anew that motherhood was definitely not for her. Two nights into the ordeal, Susannah had noticed that the emotional stirring for a husband and children came to her only when Michelle was sleeping or eating. And with good reason.

Nate arrived around nine bearing gifts. He brought freshly baked cinnamon rolls still warm from the oven. He stood in her doorway, tall and lean, with a smile bright enough to dazzle the most dedicated career woman. Once more, Susannah was shocked by her overwhelming reaction to him. Her heart leaped to her throat, and she immediately wished she'd taken time to dress in something better than her faded housecoat.

"You look terrible."

"Thanks," she said, bouncing Michelle on her hip.

"I take it you had a bad night."

"Michelle was fussing. She didn't seem the least bit interested in sleeping." She wiped a hand over her face.

"I wish you'd called me," Nate said, taking her by the elbow and leading her into the kitchen. He actually looked guilty because he'd had a peaceful night's rest. Ridiculous, Susannah thought.

"Call you? Whatever for?" she asked. "So you could have paced with her, too?" As it was, Nate had spent a good part of Saturday in and out of her apartment helping her. Spending a second night with them was above and beyond the call of duty. "Did I tell you," Susannah said, yawning, "Michelle's got a new tooth coming in—I felt it myself." Deposited in the high chair, Michelle was content for the moment.

Nate nodded and glanced at his watch. "When does your sister's flight get in?"

"One-fifteen." No sooner had the words left her lips than the phone rang. Susannah's and Nate's eyes met, and as it rang a second time she wondered how a telephone could sound so much like a death knell. Even before she answered it, Susannah knew it would be what she most dreaded hearing.

"Well?" Nate asked when she'd finished the call.

Covering her face with both hands, Susannah sagged against the wall.

"Say something."

Slowly she lowered her hands. "Help."

"Help?"

"Yes," she cried, struggling to keep her voice from cracking. "All Puget Air flights are grounded just the way the news reported, and the other airline Robert and Emily made reservations with is overbooked. The earliest flight they can get is tomorrow morning."

"I see."

"Obviously you don't!" she cried. "Tomorrow is Monday and I've got to be at work!"

"Call in sick."

"I can't do that," she snapped, angry with him for even suggesting such a thing. "My marketing group is giving their presentation and I've got to be there."

"Why?"

She frowned at him. It was futile to expect someone like Nate to understand something as important as a sales presentation. Nate didn't seem to have a job; he didn't worry about a career. For that matter, he couldn't possibly grasp that a woman holding a management position had to strive twice as hard to prove herself.

"I'm not trying to be cute, Susannah," he said with infuriating calm. "I honestly want to know why that meeting is so important."

"Because it is. I don't expect you to appreciate this, so just accept the fact that I *have* to be there."

Nate cocked his head and idly rubbed the side of his jaw. "First, answer me something. Five years from now, will this meeting make a difference in your life?"

"I don't know." She pressed two fingers to the bridge of her nose. She'd had less than three hours' sleep, and Nate was asking impossible questions. Michelle, bless her devilish little heart, had fallen asleep in her high chair. Why shouldn't she? Susannah reasoned. She'd spent the entire night fussing, and was exhausted now. By the time Susannah had discovered the new tooth, she felt as if she'd grown it herself.

"If I were you, I wouldn't sweat it," Nate said with that same nonchalant attitude. "If you aren't there to hear their presentation, your marketing group will give it Tuesday morning."

"In other words," she muttered, "you're saying I don't have a thing to worry about."

"Exactly."

Nate Townsend knew next to nothing about surviving in the corporate world, and he'd obviously been protected from life's harsher realities. It was all too obvious to Susannah that he was a man with a baseball-cap mentality. He couldn't be expected to fully comprehend her dilemma.

"So," he said now, "what are you going to do?"

Susannah wasn't sure. Briefly, she closed her eyes in an effort to concentrate. *Impose discipline,* she said to herself. *Stay calm.* That was crucial. *Think slowly and analyze your objectives.* For every problem there was a solution.

"Susannah?"

She glanced at him; she'd almost forgotten he was there. "I'll cancel my early-morning appointments and go in for the presentation," she stated matter-of-factly.

"What about Michelle? Are you going to hire a sitter?"

A babysitter hired by the babysitter. A novel thought, perhaps even viable, but Susannah didn't know anyone who sat with babies.

Then she made her decision. She would take Michelle to work with her.

And that was exactly what she did.

* * *

As she knew it would, Susannah's arrival at H&J Lima caused quite a stir. At precisely ten the following morning, she stepped off the elevator. Her black leather briefcase was clutched in one hand and Michelle was pressed against her hip with the other. Head held high, Susannah marched across the hardwood floor, past the long rows of doorless cubicles and shelves of foot-thick file binders. Several employees moved away from their desks to view her progress. A low rumble of hushed whispers followed her.

"Good morning, Ms. Brooks," Susannah said crisply as she walked into her office, the diaper bag draped over her shoulder like an ammunition pouch.

"Ms. Simmons."

Susannah noted that her assistant—to her credit—didn't so much as bat an eye. The woman was well trained; to all outward appearances, Susannah regularly arrived at the office with a nine-month-old infant attached to her hip.

Depositing the diaper bag on the floor, Susannah took her place behind a six-foot-wide walnut desk. Content for the moment, Michelle sat on her lap, gleefully viewing her aunt's domain.

"Would you like some coffee?" Ms. Brooks asked.

"Yes, please."

Her assistant paused. "Will your, ah…"

"This is my niece, Michelle, Ms. Brooks."

The woman nodded. "Will Michelle require anything to drink?"

"No, but thanks anyway. Is there anything urgent in the mail?"

"Nothing that can't wait. I canceled your eight and nine o'clock appointments," her assistant went on to explain. "When I spoke to Mr. Adams, he asked if you could join him for drinks tomorrow night at six."

"That'll be fine." The old lecher would love to do all their business outside the office. On this occasion, she'd agree to his terms, since she'd been the one to cancel their appointment, but she wouldn't be so willing a second time. She'd never much cared for Andrew Adams, who was overweight, balding and a general nuisance.

"Will you be needing me for anything else?" Ms. Brooks asked when she delivered the coffee.

"Nothing. Thank you."

As she should have predicted, the meeting was an unmitigated disaster. The presentation took twenty-two minutes, and in that brief time Michelle managed to dismantle Susannah's Cross pen, unfasten her blouse and pull her hair free from her carefully styled French twist. The baby clapped her hands at various inappropriate points and made loud noises. At the low point of the meeting, Susannah had been forced to leave her seat and dive under the conference table to retrieve her niece, who was cheerfully crawling over everyone's feet.

By the time she got home, Susannah felt like climbing back into bed and staying there. It was the type of day that made her crave something chocolate and excessively sweet. But there weren't enough chocolate chip cookies in the world to see her through another morning like that one.

To Susannah's surprise, Nate met her in the foyer outside the elevator. She took one look at him and resisted the urge to burst into tears.

"I take it things didn't go well."

"How'd you guess?" she asked sarcastically.

"It might be the fact you're wearing your hair down when I specifically remember you left wearing it up. Or it could be that your blouse is buttoned wrong and there's a gaping hole in the middle." His smile was mischievous. "I wondered if you were the type to wear a lacy bra. Now I know."

Susannah groaned and slapped a hand over her front. He could have spared her that comment.

"Here, kiddo," he said, taking Michelle out of Susannah's arms. "It looks like we need to give your poor aunt a break."

Turning her back, Susannah refastened her blouse and then brought out her key. Her once orderly, immaculate apartment looked as if a cyclone had gone through it. Blankets and baby toys were scattered from one end of the living room to the other. She'd slept on the couch in order to be close to Michelle, and her pillow and blankets were still there, along with her blue suit jacket, which she'd been forced to change when Michelle had tossed a spoonful of plums on the sleeve.

"What happened here?" Nate asked, looking in astonishment at the scene before him.

"Three days and three nights with Michelle and you need to ask?"

"Sit down," he said gently. "I'll get you a cup of coffee." Susannah did as he suggested, too grateful to argue with him.

Nate stopped just inside the kitchen. "What's this purple stuff all over the walls?"

"Plums," Susannah informed him. "I discovered the hard way that Michelle hates plums."

The scene in the kitchen was a good example of how her morning had gone. It had taken Susannah the better part of three hours to get herself and Michelle ready for the excursion to the office. And that was just the beginning.

"What I need is a double martini," she told Nate when he carried in two cups of coffee.

"It's not even noon."

"I know," she said, slowly lowering herself to the sofa. "Can you imagine what I'd need if it was two o'clock?"

Chuckling, Nate handed her the steaming cup. Michelle was sitting on the carpet, content to play with the very toys she'd vehemently rejected that morning.

Nate unexpectedly sat down next to her and looped his arm over her shoulder. She tensed, but if he noticed, he chose to ignore it. He stretched his legs out on the coffee table and relaxed.

Susannah felt her tension mount. The memory of the meeting with marketing was enough to elevate her blood pressure, but when she analyzed the reasons for this anxiety, she discovered it came from being so close to Nate. It wasn't that Susannah objected to his touch;

in reality, quite the opposite was true. They'd spent three days in close quarters, and contrary to everything she'd theorized about her neighbor, she'd come to appreciate his happy-go-lucky approach to life. But it was diametrically opposed to her own, and the fact that she could be so attracted to him was something of a shock.

"Do you want to talk about marketing's presentation?"

She released her breath. "No, I think this morning is best forgotten by everyone involved. You were right, I should have postponed the meeting."

Nate sipped his coffee and said, "It's one of those live-and-learn situations."

Pulling herself to a standing position at the coffee table, Michelle cheerfully edged her way around until she was stopped by Nate's outstretched legs. Then she surprised them both by reaching out one arm and granting him a smile that would have melted concrete.

"Oh, look," Susannah said proudly, "you can see her new tooth!"

"Where?" Lifting the baby onto his lap, Nate peered inside her mouth. Susannah was trying to show him where to look when someone, presumably her sister, rang impatiently from the lobby.

Susannah opened her door a minute later, and Emily flew in as if she'd sprouted wings. "My baby!" she cried. "Mommy missed you so-o-o much."

Not half as much as I missed you, Emily, she mused, watching the happy reunion.

Robert followed on his wife's heels, obviously pleased. The weekend away had apparently done them both good. Never mind that it had nearly destroyed Susannah's peace of mind *and* her career.

"You must be Nate," Emily said, claiming the seat beside Susannah's neighbor. "My sister couldn't say enough about you."

"Coffee anyone?" Susannah piped up eagerly, rubbing her palms together. The last thing she needed was her sister applying her matchmaking techniques to her and Nate. Emily strongly believed it was unnatural for Susannah to live the way she did. A career was fine, but choosing to forgo the personal satisfaction of a husband and family was beyond her sister's comprehension. Being fulfilled in that role herself, Emily assumed that Susannah was missing an essential part of life.

"Nothing for me," Robert answered.

"I'll bet you're eager to pack everything up and head home," Susannah said hopefully. Her eye happened to catch Nate's, and it was obvious that he was struggling not to laugh at her less-than-subtle attempt to usher her sister and family on their way.

"Susannah's right," Robert announced, glancing around the room. It was clear he'd never seen his orderly, efficient sister-in-law's home in such a state of disarray.

"But I've hardly had a chance to talk to Nate," Emily protested. "And I was looking forward to getting to know him better."

"I'll be around," Nate said lightly.

His gaze settled on Susannah, and the look he gave her made her insides quiver. For the first time she realized how much she wanted this man to kiss her. Susannah wasn't the type of person who looked at a handsome male and wondered how his mouth would feel on hers. She was convinced this current phenomenon had a lot to do with sheer exhaustion, but whatever the cause she found her eyes riveted to his.

Emily suddenly noticed what was happening. "Yes, I think you may be right, Robert," she said, and her voice contained more than a hint of amusement. "I'll pack Michelle's things."

Susannah's cheeks were pink with embarrassment by the time she tore her gaze away from Nate's. "By the way, did you know Michelle has an aversion to plums?"

"I can't say I did," Emily said, busily throwing her daughter's things together.

Nate helped disassemble the crib and the high chair, and it seemed no more than a few minutes had passed before Susannah's condo was once more her own. She stood in the middle of the living room savoring the silence. It was pure bliss.

"They're off," she said when she saw that Nate had stayed behind.

"Like a herd of turtles."

Susannah had heard that saying from the time she was a kid. She didn't find it particularly funny anymore, but she shared a smile with him.

"I have my life back now," she sighed. It would probably take her a month to recover, though.

"Your life is your own," Nate agreed, watching her closely.

Susannah would've liked to attribute the tears that

flooded her eyes to his close scrutiny, but she knew better. With her arms cradling her middle, she walked over to the window, which looked out over Elliott Bay. A green-and-white ferry glided peacefully over the darker green waters. Rain tapped gently against the window, and the sky, a deep oyster-gray, promised drizzle for most of the afternoon.

Hoping Nate wouldn't notice, she wiped the tears from her face and drew in a deep calming breath.

"Susannah?"

"I...I was just looking at the Sound. It's so lovely in the fall." She could hear him approach her from behind, and when he placed his hands on her shoulders it was all she could do to keep from leaning against him.

"You're crying."

She nodded, sniffling because it was impossible to hold it inside any longer.

"It's not like you to cry, is it? What's wrong?"

"I don't know..." she said and hiccuped on a sob. "I can't believe I'm doing this. I love that little kid...we were just beginning to understand each other...and... dear heaven, I'm glad Emily came back when...she did." Before Susannah could recognize how much she was missing without a husband and family.

Nate ran his hands down her arms in the softest of caresses.

He didn't say anything for a long time, and Susannah was convinced she was making an absolute idiot of herself. Nate was right; it wasn't like her to dissolve into tears. This unexpected outburst must've been a result of the trauma she'd experienced that morning in her office, or the fact that she hadn't had a decent night's sleep in what felt like a month and, yes, she'd admit it, of meeting Nate.

Without saying another word, Nate turned her around and lifted her chin with his finger, raising her eyes to his. His look was so tender, so caring, that Susannah sniffled again. Her shoulders shook and she wiped her nose.

He brushed away the hair that clung to the sides of her damp face. His fingertips slid over each of her features as though he were a blind man trying to memorize her face. Susannah was mesmerized, unable to pull away. Slowly, as if denying himself the pleasure for as long as he could, he lowered his mouth.

When his lips settled on hers, Susannah released a barely audible sigh. She'd wondered earlier what it would be like when Nate kissed her. Now she knew. His kiss was soft and warm. Velvet smooth and infinitely gentle, and yet it was undeniably exciting.

As if one kiss wasn't enough, he kissed her again. This time it was Nate who sighed. Then he dropped his hands and stepped back.

Startled by his abrupt action, Susannah swayed slightly. Nate's arms righted her. Apparently he'd come to his senses at the same time she had. For a brief moment they'd decided to ignore their differences. The only thing they had in common was the fact that they lived in the same building, she reminded herself. Their values and expectations were worlds apart.

"Are you all right?" he asked, frowning.

She blinked, trying to find a way to disguise that she wasn't. Everything had happened much too fast; her heart was galloping like a runaway horse. She'd never been so attracted to a man in her life. "Of course I'm all right," she said with strained bravado. "Are you?"

He didn't answer for a moment. Instead, he shoved his hands in his pants pocket and moved away from her, looking annoyed.

"Nate?" she whispered.

He paused, scowling in her direction. Rubbing his hand across his brow, he twisted the ever-present baseball cap until it faced backward. "I think we should try that again."

Susannah wasn't sure what he meant until he reached for her. His first few kisses had been gentle, but this one was meant to take charge of her senses. His mouth slid over hers until she felt the starch go out of her knees. In an effort to maintain her balance, she gripped his shoulders, and although she fought it, she quickly surrendered to the swirling excitement. Nate's kiss was debilitating. She couldn't breathe, couldn't think, couldn't move.

Nate groaned, then his hands shifted to the back of her head. He slanted his mouth over hers. At length he released a jagged breath and buried his face in the soft curve of her neck. "What about now?"

"You're a good kisser."

"That's not what I meant, Susannah. You feel it, too, don't you? You must! There's enough electricity between us to light up a city block."

"No," she lied, and swallowed tightly. "It was nice as far as kisses go—"

"Nice!"

"Very nice," she amended, hoping to appease him, "but that's about it."

Nate didn't say anything for a long minute, a painfully long minute. Then, scowling at her again, he turned and walked out of the apartment.

Trembling, Susannah watched him go. His kiss had touched a chord within her, notes that had been long-silent, and now she feared the music would forever mark her soul. But she couldn't let him know that. They had nothing in common. They were too mismatched.

Now that she was seated in the plush cocktail lounge with her associate, Andrew Adams, Susannah regret-ted having agreed to meet him after hours. It was apparent from the moment she stepped into the dimly lit room that he had more on his mind than business. Despite the fact that Adams was balding and over-weight, he would have been attractive enough if he hadn't seen himself as some kind of modern-day Adonis. Although Susannah struggled to maintain a businesslike calm, it was becoming increasingly dif-ficult, and she wondered how much longer her good intentions would hold.

"There are some figures I meant to show you," Adams said, holding the stem of his martini glass with both hands and studying Susannah with undisguised admiration. "Unfortunately I left them at my apart-ment. Why don't we conclude our talk there?"

Susannah made a point of looking at her watch and frowning, hoping he'd get the hint. Something told her differently. "I'm afraid I won't have the time," she said. It was almost seven and she'd already spent an hour with him.

"My place is only a few blocks from here," he coaxed.

His look was much too suggestive, and Susannah was growing wearier by the minute. As far as she could see, this entire evening had been a waste of time.

The only thing that interested her was returning to her own place and talking to Nate. He'd been on her mind all day and she was eager to see him again. The truth was, she felt downright nervous after their last meeting, and wondered how they'd react to each other now. Nate had left her so abruptly, and she hadn't talked to him since.

"John Hammer and I are good friends," Adams claimed, pulling his chair closer to her own. "I don't know if you're aware of that."

He didn't even bother to veil his threat—or his bribe, whichever it was. Susannah worked directly under John Hammer, who would have the final say on the appointment of a new vice president. Susannah and two others were in the running for the position. And Susannah wanted it. Badly. She could achieve her five-year goal if she got it, and in the process make H&J Lima history—by being the first female vice president.

"If you're such good friends with Mr. Hammer," she said, "then I suggest you give those figures to him directly, since he'll need to review them anyway."

"No, that wouldn't work," he countered sharply. "If you come with me it'll only take a few minutes. We'd be in and out of my place in, say, half an hour at the most."

Susannah's immediate reaction to situations such as this was a healthy dose of outrage, but she managed to control her temper. "If your apartment is so convenient, then I'll wait here while you go back for those sheets." As she spoke, a couple walked past the tiny table where she was seated with Andrew Adams. Susannah didn't pay much attention to the man, who wore a gray suit, but the blonde with him was striking. Susannah followed the woman with her eyes and envied the graceful way she moved.

"It would be easier if you came with me, don't you think?"

"No," she answered bluntly, and lowered her gaze to her glass of white wine. It was then that she felt an odd sensation prickle down her spine. Someone was staring at her; she could feel it as surely as if she were being physically touched. Looking around, Susannah was astonished to discover Nate sitting two tables away. The striking blonde was seated next to him and obviously enjoying his company. She laughed softly and the sound was like a melody, light and breezy.

Susannah's breath caught in her chest, trapped there until the pain reminded her it was time to breathe again. When she did, she reached for her wineglass and succeeded in spilling some of the contents.

Nate's gaze centered on her and then moved to her companion. His mouth thinned and his eyes, which had been so warm and tender a day earlier, now looked hard. Almost scornful.

Susannah wasn't exactly thrilled herself. Nate was dating a beauty queen while she was stuck with Donald Duck.

Chapter
4

Susannah vented her anger by pacing the living room carpet. Men! Who needed them?

Not her. Definitely not her! Nate Townsend could take his rainy day kisses and stuff them in his baseball cap for all she cared. Only he hadn't been wearing it for Miss Universe. Oh no, with the other woman, he was dressed like someone out of *Gentlemen's Quarterly*. Susannah, on the other hand, rated worn football jerseys or faded T-shirts.

Susannah hadn't been home more than five minutes when there was a knock at her door. She whirled around. Checking the peephole, she discovered that her caller was Nate. She pulled back, wondering what she should do. He was the last person she wanted to see. He'd made a fool of her... Well, that wasn't strictly true. He'd only made her *feel* like a fool.

"Susannah," he said, knocking impatiently a second time. "I know you're in there."

"Go away."

Her shout was followed by a short pause. "Fine. Have it your way."

Changing her mind, she turned the lock and yanked open the door. She glared at him with all the fury she could muster—which just then was considerable.

Nate glared right back. "Who was that guy?" he asked with infuriating calm.

She was tempted to inform Nate that it wasn't any of his business. But she decided that would be churlish.

"Andrew Adams," she answered and quickly followed her response with a demand of her own. "Who was that woman?"

"Sylvia Potter."

For the longest moment, neither spoke.

"That was all I wanted to know," Nate finally said.

"Me, too," she returned stiffly.

Nate retreated two steps, and like precision clockwork Susannah shut the door. "Sylvia Potter," she echoed in a low-pitched voice filled with disdain. "Well, Sylvia Potter, you're welcome to him."

It took another fifteen minutes for the outrage to work its way through her system, but once she'd watched a portion of the evening news and read her mail, she was reasonably calm.

When Susannah really thought about it, what did she have to be so furious about? Nate Townsend didn't mean anything to her. How could he? Until a week ago, she hadn't even known his name.

Okay, so he'd kissed her a couple of times, and sure, there'd been electricity, but that was all. Electricity did not constitute a lifetime commitment. If Nate Townsend chose to date every voluptuous blonde between Seattle and New York it shouldn't matter to her.

But it did. And that infuriated Susannah more than anything. She didn't *want* to care about Nate. Her career goals were set. She had drive, determination and a positive mental attitude. But she didn't have Nate.

Jutting out her lower lip, she expelled her breath forcefully, ruffling the dark wisps of hair against her forehead. Maybe it was her hair color—perhaps Nate preferred blondes. He obviously did, otherwise he wouldn't be trying to impress Sylvia Potter.

Refusing to entertain any more thoughts of her neighbor, Susannah decided to fix herself dinner. An inspection of the freezer revealed a pitifully old chicken patty. Removing it from the cardboard box, Susannah took one look at it and promptly tossed it into the garbage.

Out of the corner of her eye she caught a movement on her balcony. She turned and saw a sleek Siamese cat walking casually along the railing as if he were strolling across a city park.

Although she remained outwardly calm, Susannah's

heart lunged to her throat. Her condo was eight floors up. One wrong move and that cat would be history. Walking carefully to her sliding glass door, Susannah eased it open and called, "Here, kitty, kitty, kitty."

The cat accepted her invitation and jumped down from the railing. With his tail pointing skyward, he walked directly into her apartment and headed straight for the garbage pail, where he stopped.

"I bet you're hungry, aren't you?" she asked softly. She retrieved the chicken patty and stuck it in her microwave. While she stood waiting for it to cook, the cat, with his striking blue eyes and dark brown markings, wove around her legs, purring madly.

She'd just finished cutting the patty into bite-size pieces and putting it on a plate when someone pounded at her door. Wiping her fingers clean, she moved into the living room.

"Do you have my cat?" Nate demanded when she opened the door. He'd changed from his suit into jeans and a bright blue T-shirt.

"I don't know," she fibbed. "Describe it."

"Susannah, this isn't the time for silly games. Chocolate Chip is a valuable animal."

"Chocolate Chip," she repeated with a soft snicker, crossing her arms and leaning against the doorjamb. "Obviously you didn't read the fine print in the tenant's agreement, because it specifically states in section 12, paragraph 13, that no pets are allowed." Actually she didn't have a clue what section or what paragraph that clause was in, but she wanted him to think she did.

"If you don't tattle on me, then I won't tattle on you."

"I don't have any pets."

"No, you had a baby."

"But only for three days," she said. Talk about nit-picking people! He was flagrantly disregarding the rules and had the nerve to throw a minor infraction in her face.

"The cat belongs to my sister. He'll be with me for less than a week. Now, is Chocolate Chip here, or do I go into cardiac arrest?"

"He's here."

Nate visibly relaxed. "Thank God. My sister dotes on that silly feline. She flew up from San Francisco and left him with me before she left for Hawaii." As if he'd heard his name mentioned, Chocolate Chip casually strolled across the carpet and paused at Nate's feet.

Nate bent down to retrieve his sister's cat, scolding him with a harsh look.

"I suggest you keep your balcony door closed," she told him, striving for a flippant air.

"Thanks, I will." Chocolate Chip was tucked under his arm as Nate's gaze casually caught Susannah's. "You might be interested to know that Sylvia Potter's my sister." He turned and walked out her door.

"'Sylvia Potter's my sister,'" Susannah mimicked. It wasn't until she'd closed and locked her door that she recognized the import of what he'd said. "His sister," she repeated. "Did he really say that?"

Susannah was at his door before she stopped to judge the wisdom of her actions. When Nate answered her furious knock, she stared up at him, her eyes confused. "What was that you just said?"

"I said Sylvia Potter's my sister."

"I was afraid of that." Her thoughts were tumbling over one another like marbles in a bag. She'd imagined…she'd assumed….

"Who's Andrew Adams?"

"My brother?" she offered, wondering if he'd believe her.

Nate shook his head. "Try again."

"An associate from H&J Lima," she said, then hurried to explain. "When I canceled my appointment with him Monday morning, he suggested we get together for a drink to discuss business this evening. It sounded innocent enough at the time, but I should've realized it was a mistake. Adams is a known sleazeball."

An appealing smile touched the edges of Nate's mouth. "I wish I'd had a camera when you first saw me in that cocktail lounge. I thought your eyes were going to fall out of your face."

"It was your sister—she intimidated me," Susannah admitted. "She's lovely."

"So are you."

The man had obviously been standing out in the sun too long, Susannah decided. Compared to Sylvia, who was tall, blond and had curves in all the right places, Susannah felt about as pretty as a professional wrestler.

"I'm flattered that you think so." Susannah wasn't comfortable with praise. She was much too levelheaded to let flattery affect her. When men paid her compliments, she smiled and thanked them, but she treated their words like water running off a slick surface.

Except with Nate. Everything was different with him. She seemed to be accumulating a large stack of exceptions because of Nate. As far as Susannah could see, he had no ambition, and if she'd met him anyplace other than her building, she probably wouldn't have given him a second thought. Instead she couldn't stop thinking about him. She knew better than to allow her heart to be distracted this way, and yet she couldn't seem to stop herself.

"Do you want to come in?" Nate asked and stepped aside. A bleeping sound drew Susannah's attention to a five-foot-high television screen across the room. She'd apparently interrupted Nate in the middle of an action-packed video game. A video game!

"No," she answered quickly. "I wouldn't want to interrupt you. Besides I was...just about to make myself some dinner."

"You cook?"

His astonishment—no, shock—was unflattering, to say the least.

"Of course I do."

"I'm glad to hear it, because I seem to recall that you owe me a meal."

"I—"

"And since we seem to have gotten off on the wrong foot tonight, a nice quiet dinner in front of the fireplace sounds like exactly what we need."

Susannah's thoughts were zooming at the speed of light. Nate was inviting himself to dinner—one she was supposed to whip up herself! Why did she so glibly announce that she could cook? Everything she'd ever attempted in the kitchen had been a disaster. Other than toast. Toast was her specialty. Her mind whirled with all the different ways she could serve it. Buttered? With honey? Jam? Cheese? The list was endless.

"You fix dinner and I'll bring over the wine," Nate said in a low seductive voice. "It's time we sat down together and talked. Deal?"

"I, ah, I've got some papers I have to read over tonight."

"No problem. I'll make it a point to leave early so you can finish whatever you need to."

His eyes held hers for a long moment, and despite everything Susannah knew about Nate, she still wanted time alone with him. She had some papers to review and he had to get back to his video game. A relationship like theirs was not meant to be. However, before she was even aware of what she was doing, Susannah nodded.

"Good. I'll give you an hour. Is that enough time?"

Once more, like a remote-controlled robot, she nodded.

Nate smiled and leaned forward to lightly brush his lips over hers. "I'll see you in an hour then."

He put his hand at her lower back and guided her out the door. For a few seconds she did nothing more than stand in the hallway, wondering how she was going to get herself out of this one. She reviewed her options and discovered there was only one.

The Western Avenue Deli.

Precisely an hour later, Susannah was ready. A tossed green salad rested in the middle of the table in a crystal bowl, which had been a gift when she graduated from college. Her aunt Gerty had given it to her. Susannah loved her aunt dearly, but the poor soul had her and Emily confused. Emily would have treasured the fancy bowl. As it happened, this was the first occasion Susannah had even used it and now that she looked at it, she thought the bowl might have been meant for punch. Maybe Nate wouldn't notice. The stroganoff was simmering in a pan and the noodles were in a foil-covered dish, keeping warm in the oven.

Susannah drew in a deep breath, then frantically waved her hands over the simmering food to disperse the scent around the condo before she opened her door.

"Hi," Nate said. He held a bottle of wine.

His eyes were so blue, it was like looking into a clear, deep lake. When she spoke, her voice trembled slightly. "Hi. Dinner's just about ready."

He sniffed the air appreciatively. "Will red wine do?"

"It's perfect," she told him, stepping aside so he could come in.

"Shall I open it now?"

"Please." She led him into the kitchen.

He cocked an eyebrow. "It looks like you've been busy."

For good measure, Susannah had stacked a few pots and pans in the sink and set out an array of spices on the counter. In addition, she'd laid out several books. None of them had anything to do with cooking—she didn't own any cookbooks—but they looked impressive.

"I hope you like stroganoff," she said cheerfully.

"It's one of my favorites."

Susannah swallowed and nodded. She'd never been very good at deception, but then she'd rarely put her pride on the line the way she had this evening.

While she dished up the stroganoff, Nate expertly opened the wine and poured them each a glass. When everything was ready, they sat across the table from each other.

After one taste of the buttered noodles and the rich sauce, Nate said, "This is delicious."

Susannah kept her eyes lowered. "Thanks. My mother has a recipe that's been handed down for years." It was a half-truth that was stretched about as far it could go without snapping back and hitting her in the face. Yes, her mother did have a favorite family recipe, but it was for Christmas candies.

"The salad's excellent, too. What's in the dressing?"

This was the moment Susannah had dreaded. "Ah…" Her mind faltered before she could remember exactly what usually went into salad dressings. "Oil!" she cried, as if black gold had just been discovered in her living room.

"Vinegar?"

"Yes," she agreed eagerly. "Lots of that."

Planting his elbows on the table, he smiled at her. "Spices?"

"Oh, yes, those, too."

His mouth was quivering when he took a sip of wine.

Subterfuge had never been Susannah's strong suit. If Nate hadn't started asking her these difficult questions, she might've been able to pull off the ruse. But he obviously knew, and there wasn't any reason to continue it.

"Nate," she said, after fortifying herself with a sip of wine, "I...I didn't exactly cook this meal myself."

"The Western Avenue Deli?"

She nodded, feeling wretched.

"An excellent choice."

"H-how'd you know?" Something inside her demanded further abuse. Anyone else would have dropped the matter right then.

"You mean other than the fact that you've got enough pots and pans in your sink to have fed a small army? By the way, what could you possibly have used the broiler pan for?"

"I...was hoping you'd think I'd warmed the dinner rolls on it."

"I see." He was doing an admirable job of not laughing outright, and Susannah supposed she should be grateful for that much.

After taking a bite of his—unwarmed—roll, he asked, "Where'd you get all the spices?"

"They were a Christmas gift from Emily one year. She continues to hold out hope that a miracle will happen and I'll suddenly discover I've missed my calling in life and decide to chain myself to the stove."

Nate grinned. "For future reference, I can't see how you'd need poultry seasoning or curry powder for stroganoff."

"Oh." She should've quit when she was ahead. "So...you knew right from the first?"

Nate nodded. "I'm afraid so, but I'm flattered by all the trouble you went to."

"I suppose it won't do any more harm to admit that I'm a total loss in the kitchen. I'd rather analyze a profit-and-loss statement any day than attempt to bake a batch of cookies."

Nate reached for a second dinner roll. "If you ever do, my favorite are chocolate chip."

Perhaps he was the one who'd named his sister's cat, she mused. Or maybe chocolate chip cookies were popular with his whole family. "I'll remember that." An outlet for Rainy Day Cookies had recently opened on the waterfront and they were the best money could buy.

Nate helped her clear the table once they'd finished. While she rinsed the plates and put them in the dishwasher, Nate built a fire. He was seated on the floor in front of the fireplace waiting for her when she entered the room.

"More wine?" he asked, holding up the bottle.

"Please." Inching her straight skirt slightly higher, Susannah carefully lowered herself to the carpet beside him. Nate grinned and reached for the nearby lamp, turning it to the lowest setting. Shadows from the fire flickered across the opposite wall. The atmosphere was warm and cozy.

"All right," he said softly, close to her ear. "Ask away."

Susannah frowned, not sure what he meant.

"You've been dying of curiosity about me from the moment we met. I'm simply giving you the opportunity to ask me anything you want."

Susannah gulped her wine. If he could read her so easily, then she had no place in the business world. Yes, she was full of questions about him and had been trying to find a subtle way to bring some of them into the conversation.

"First, however," he said, "let me do this."

Before she knew what was happening, Nate had pressed her down onto the carpet and was kissing her. Kissing her deeply, drugging her senses with a mastery that was just short of arrogant. He'd caught her unprepared, and before she could raise any defenses, she was captured in a dizzying wave of sensation.

When he lifted his head, Susannah stared up at him, breathless and amazed at her own ready response. Before she could react, Nate slid one hand behind her. He unpinned her hair, then ran his fingers through it.

"I've been wanting to do that all night," he murmured.

Still she couldn't speak. He'd kissed and held her, but it didn't seem to affect his power of speech, while she felt completely flustered and perplexed.

"Yes, well," she managed to mutter, scrambling to a sitting position. "I...forget what we were talking about."

Nate moved behind her and pulled her against his chest, wrapping his arms around her and nibbling on the side of her neck. "I believe you were about to ask me something."

"Yes...you're right, I was...Nate, do you work?"

"No."

Delicious shivers were racing up and down her spine. His teeth found her earlobe and he sucked on it gently, causing her insides to quake in seismic proportions.

"Why not?" she asked, her voice trembling.

"I quit."

"But why?"

"I was working too hard. I wasn't enjoying myself anymore."

"Oh."

His mouth had progressed down the gentle slope of her neck to her shoulder, and she closed her eyes to the warring emotions churning inside her. Part of her longed to surrender to the thrill of his touch, yet she hungered to learn all she could about this unconventional man.

Nate altered his position so he was in front of her again. His mouth began exploring her face with soft kisses that fell like gentle raindrops over her eyes, nose, cheeks and lips.

"Anything else you want to know?" he asked, pausing.

Unable to do more than shake her head, Susannah sighed and reluctantly unwound her arms from around his neck.

"Do you want more wine?" he asked.

"No...thank you." It demanded all the fortitude she possessed not to ask him to keep kissing her.

"Okay," he said, making himself comfortable. He raised his knees and wrapped his arms around them. "My turn."

"Your turn?"

"Yes," he said with a lazy grin that did wicked things to her equilibrium. "I have a few questions for you."

Susannah found it difficult to center her attention on anything other than the fact that Nate was sitting a few inches away from her and could lean over and kiss her again at any moment.

"You don't object?"

"No," she said, gesturing with her hand.

"Okay, tell me about yourself."

Susannah shrugged. For the life of her, she couldn't think of a single thing that would impress him. She'd worked hard, climbing the corporate ladder, inching her way toward her long-range goals.

"I'm up for promotion," she began. "I started working for H&J Lima five years ago. I chose this company, although the pay was less than I'd been offered by two others."

"Why?"

"There's opportunity with them. I looked at the chain of command and saw room for steady advancement. Being a woman is both an asset and a detriment, if you know what I mean. I had to prove myself, but I was also aware of being the token woman on the staff."

"You mean you were hired because you were female?"

"Exactly. But I swallowed my pride and set about proving I could handle anything asked of me, and I have."

Nate looked proud of her.

"Five years ago, I decided I wanted to be the vice president in charge of marketing," she said, her voice gaining strength and conviction. "It was a significant goal, because I'd be the first woman to hold a position that high within the company."

"And?"

"And I'll find out in the next few weeks if I'm going to get it. I'll derive a great deal of satisfaction from knowing I earned it. I won't be their token female in upper management anymore."

"What's the competition like?"

Susannah slowly expelled her breath. "Stiff. Damn stiff. There are two men in the running, and both have been with the company as long as me, in one case longer. Both are older, bright and dedicated."

"You're bright and dedicated, too."

"That may not be enough," she murmured. Now that her dream was within reach, she yearned for it even more. She could feel Nate's eyes studying her.

"This promotion means a lot to you, doesn't it?"

"Yes. It's everything. From the moment I was hired, I've striven toward this very thing. And it's happening faster than I dared hope."

Nate was silent for a moment. He put another log on the fire, and although she hadn't asked for it, he replenished her wine.

"Have you ever stopped to think what would happen if you achieved your dreams and then discovered you weren't happy?"

"How could I not be happy?" she asked. She honestly didn't understand. For years she'd worked toward obtaining this vice presidency. Of course she was going to be happy! She'd be thrilled, elated, jubilant.

Nate's eyes narrowed. "Aren't you worried about there being a void in your life?"

Oh, no, he was beginning to sound like Emily. "No," she said flatly. "How could there be? Now before you start, I know what you're going to say, so please don't. Save your breath. Emily has argued with me about this from the time I graduated from college."

Nate looked genuinely puzzled. "Argued with you about what?"

"Getting married and having a family. But the roles of wife and mother just aren't for me. They never have been and they never will be."

"I see."

Susannah was convinced he didn't. "If I were a man, would everyone be pushing me to marry?"

Nate chuckled and his eyes rested on her for a tantalizing moment. "Trust me, Susannah, no one's going to mistake you for a man."

She grinned and lowered her gaze. "It's the nose, isn't it?"

"The nose?"

"Yes." She turned sideways and held her chin at a lofty angle so he could view her classic profile. "I think it's my best feature." The wine had obviously gone to her head. But that was all right because she felt warm and comfortable and Nate was sitting beside her. Rarely had she been more content.

"Actually I wasn't thinking about your nose at all. I was remembering that first night with Michelle."

"You mean when we both fell asleep in the living room?"

Nate nodded and reached for her shoulder, his eyes trapping hers. "It was the only time in my life I can remember having one woman in my arms and wanting another."

Chapter

5

"I've decided not to see him again," Susannah announced.

"I beg your pardon?" Ms. Brooks stopped in her tracks and looked at her boss.

Unnerved, Susannah made busywork at her desk. "I'm sorry, I didn't realize I'd spoken out loud."

Her assistant brought a cup of coffee to her desk and hesitated. "How late did you end up staying last night?"

"Not long," Susannah lied. It had, in fact, been past ten when she left the building.

"And the night before?" Ms. Brooks pressed.

"Not so late," Susannah fibbed again.

Eleanor Brooks walked quietly out of the room, but not before she gave Susannah a stern look that said she didn't believe her for one moment.

As soon as the door closed, Susannah pressed the tips of her fingers to her forehead and exhaled a slow steady breath. Dear heaven, Nate Townsend had her so twisted up inside she was talking to the walls.

Nate hadn't left her condo until almost eleven the night he'd come for dinner, and by that time he'd kissed her nearly senseless. Three days had passed and Susannah could still taste and feel his mouth on hers. The scent of his aftershave lingered in her living room to the point that she looked for him whenever she entered the room.

The man didn't even hold down a job. Oh, he'd had one, but he'd quit and it was obvious, to her at least, that he wasn't in any hurry to get another. He'd held her and kissed her and patiently listened to her dreams. But he hadn't shared any of his own. He had no ambition, and no urge to better himself.

And Susannah was falling head over heels for him.

Through the years, she had assumed she was immune to falling in love. She was too sensible for that, too practical, too career-oriented. Not once did she suspect she'd fall so hard for someone like Nate. Nate, with his no-need-to-rush attitude and tomorrow-will-take-care-of-itself lifestyle.

Aware of what was happening to her, Susannah had done the only thing she could—gone into hiding. For three days she'd managed to avoid Nate. He'd left a couple of messages on her answering machine, which she'd ignored. If he confronted her, she had a perfect excuse. She was working. And it was true: she spent

much of her time holed up in the office. She headed
out early in the morning and arrived home late at
night. The extra hours she was putting in served two
distinct purposes: they showed her employer that she
was dedicated, and they kept her from having to deal
with Nate.

Her intercom buzzed, pulling Susannah from her
thoughts. She reached over and hit the speaker button.
"Yes?"

"Mr. Townsend is on the phone."

Susannah squeezed her eyes shut and her throat
muscles tightened. "Take a message, please," she said,
her voice little more than a husky whisper.

"He insists on speaking to you."

"Tell him I'm in a meeting and...unavailable."

It wasn't like Susannah to lie, and Eleanor Brooks
knew it. She finally asked, "Is this the man you plan
never to see again?"

The abruptness of her question caught Susannah
off guard. "Yes..."

"I assumed as much. I'll tell him you're not available."

"Thank you." Susannah's hand was trembling as
she released the intercom button. She hadn't dreamed
Nate would call her at the office.

By eleven, a feeling of normalcy had returned.
Susannah was gathering her notes for an executive
meeting with the finance committee when her assistant came in. "Mr. Franklin phoned and canceled his
afternoon appointment."

Susannah glanced up. "Did he want to reschedule?"

"Friday at ten."

She nodded. "That'll be fine." It was on the tip of her tongue to ask how Nate had responded earlier when told she was unavailable, but she resisted the temptation.

"Mr. Townsend left a message. I wrote it out for you."

Her assistant knew her too well, it seemed. "Leave it on my desk."

"You might want to read it," the older woman urged.

"I will. Later."

Halfway through the meeting, Susannah wished she'd followed her assistant's advice. Impatience filled her. She wanted this finance meeting over so she could hurry back to her desk and read the message from Nate. Figures flew overhead—important ones with a bearing on the outcome of the marketing strategy she and her department had planned. Yet, again and again, Susannah found her thoughts drifting to Nate.

That wasn't typical for her. When the meeting ended, she was furious with herself. She walked briskly back to her office, her low heels making staccato taps against the polished hardwood floor.

"Ms. Brooks," she said, as she went into the outer office. "Could you—"

Susannah stopped dead in her tracks. The last person she'd expected to see was Nate. He was sitting on the corner of her assistant's desk, wearing a Mariners

T-shirt, faded jeans and a baseball cap. He tossed a baseball in the air and deftly caught it in his mitt.

Eleanor Brooks looked both unsettled and inordinately pleased. No doubt Nate had used some of his considerable male charm on the gray-haired grandmother.

"It's about time," Nate said, grinning devilishly. He leaped off the desk. "I was afraid we were going to be late for the game."

"Game?" Susannah repeated. "What game?"

Nate held out his right hand to show her his baseball mitt and ball—just in case she hadn't noticed them. "The Mariners are playing, and I've got two of the best seats in the place reserved for you and me."

Susannah's heart sank to the pit of her stomach. It was just like Nate to assume she could take off in the middle of the day on some lark. He obviously had no understanding of what being a responsible employee meant. It was bad enough that he'd dominated her thoughts during an important meeting, but suggesting they escape for an afternoon was too much.

"You don't honestly expect me to leave, do you?"

"Yes."

"I can't. I won't."

"Why not?"

"I'm working," she said, deciding that was sufficient explanation.

"You've been at the office every night this week. You need a break. Come on, Susannah, let your hair down long enough to have a good time. It isn't going to hurt. I promise."

He was so casual about the whole thing, as if obligation and duty were of little significance. It proved more than anything that he didn't grasp the concept of hard work being its own reward.

"It *will* hurt," she insisted.

"Okay," he said forcefully. "What's so important this afternoon?" To answer his own question, he walked around her assistant's desk. Then he leaned forward and flipped open the pages of her appointment schedule.

"Mr. Franklin canceled his three o'clock appointment," Ms. Brooks reminded her primly. "And you skipped lunch because of the finance meeting."

Susannah frowned at the older woman, wondering what exactly Nate had said or done that had turned her into a traitor on such short acquaintance.

"I have more important things to do," Susannah told them both stiffly.

"Not according to your appointment schedule," Nate said confidently. "As far as I can see, you haven't got an excuse in the world not to attend that baseball game with me."

Susannah wasn't going to stand there and argue with him. Instead she marched into her office and dutifully sat down at her desk.

To her chagrin both Nate and Ms. Brooks followed her inside. It was all Susannah could do not to bury her face in her hands and demand that they leave.

"Susannah," Nate coaxed gently, "you need a break. Tomorrow you'll come back rejuvenated and refreshed. If you spend too much time at the office, you'll begin to lose perspective. An afternoon away will do you good."

Her assistant seemed about to comment, but Susannah stopped her with a scalding look. Before she could say anything to Nate, someone else entered her office.

"Susannah, I was just checking over these figures and I—" John Hammer stopped midsentence when he noticed the other two people in her office.

If there'd been an open window handy, Susannah would gladly have hurled herself through it. The company director smiled benignly, however, looking slightly embarrassed at having interrupted her. Now, it seemed, he was awaiting an introduction.

"John, this is Nate Townsend...my neighbor."

Ever the gentleman, John stepped forward and extended his hand. If he thought it a bit odd to find a man in Susannah's office dressed in jeans and a T-shirt, he didn't show it.

"Nate Townsend," he repeated, pumping his hand. "It's a pleasure, a real pleasure."

"Thank you," Nate said. "I'm here to pick up Susannah. We're going to a Mariners game this afternoon."

John removed the glasses from the end of his nose, and nodded thoughtfully. "An excellent idea."

"No, I really don't think I'll go. I mean..." She stopped when it became obvious that no one was paying any attention to her protests.

"Nate's absolutely right," John said, setting the file on her desk. "You've been putting in a lot of extra hours lately. Take the afternoon off. Enjoy yourself."

"But—"

"Susannah, are you actually going to argue with your boss?" Nate prompted.

Her jaw sagged. "I...guess not."

"Good. Good." John looked as pleased as if he'd made the suggestion himself. He was smiling at Nate and nodding as if the two were longtime friends.

Her expression more than a little smug, Eleanor Brooks returned to her own office.

Nate glanced at his watch. "We'd better go now or we'll miss the opening pitch."

With heavy reluctance, Susannah scooped up her purse. She'd done everything within her power to avoid Nate, yet through no fault of her own, she was spending the afternoon in his company. They didn't get a chance to speak until they reached the elevator, but once the door glided shut, Susannah tried again. "I can't go to a baseball game dressed like this."

"You look fine to me."

"But I've got a business suit on."

"Hey, don't sweat the small stuff." His hand clasped hers and when the elevator door opened on the bottom floor, he led her out of the building. Once outside, he quickened his pace as he headed toward the stadium.

"I want you to know I don't appreciate this one bit," she said, forced to half run to keep pace with his long-legged stride.

"If you're going to complain, wait until we're inside and settled. As I recall, you get testy on an empty stomach." His smile could have caused a nuclear meltdown, but she was determined not to let it influence her. Nate had a lot of nerve to come bursting into her office, and as soon as she could catch her breath, she'd tell him so.

"Don't worry, I'm going to feed you," he promised as they waited at a red light.

His words did nothing to reassure her. Heaven only knew what John Hammer thought—although she had to admit that her employer's reaction had baffled her. John was as hardworking and dedicated as Susannah herself. It wasn't like him to fall in with Nate's offbeat idea of attending a ball game in the middle of the afternoon. In fact, it almost seemed as if John knew Nate, or had heard of him. Hardly ever had she seen her employer show such enthusiasm when introduced to anyone.

The man at the gate took their tickets and Nate directed her to a pair of seats right behind home plate. Never having attended a professional baseball game before, Susannah didn't realize how good these seats were—until Nate pointed it out.

She'd no sooner sat down in her place than he leaped to his feet and raised his right hand, glove and all. Susannah slouched as low as she could in the uncomfortable seat. The next thing she knew, a bag of peanuts whizzed past her ear.

"Hey!" she cried, and jerked around.

"Don't panic," Nate said, chuckling. "I'm just playing catch with the vendor." Seconds after the words left his mouth he expertly caught another bag.

"Here." Nate handed her both bags. "The hot dog guy will be by in a minute."

Susannah had no intention of sitting still while food was being tossed about. "I'm getting out of here. If you want to play ball, go on the field."

Once more Nate laughed, the sound husky and rich. "If you're going to balk at every little thing, I know a good way to settle you down."

"Do you think I'm a complete idiot? First you drag me away from my office, then you insist on throwing food around like some schoolboy. I can't even begin to guess what's going to happen next and—"

She didn't get any further, although her outrage was mounting with every breath she drew. Before she could guess his intention, Nate planted his hands on her shoulders, pulled her against him and gave her one of his dynamite-packed kisses.

Completely unnerved, she numbly lowered herself back into her seat and closed her eyes, her pulse roaring in her ears.

A little later, Nate was pressing a fat hot dog into her lifeless hands. "I had them put everything on it," he said.

A glance at the overstuffed bun informed her that "everything" included pickles, mustard, ketchup, onions and sauerkraut and one or two other items she wasn't sure she could identify.

"Now eat it before I'm obliged to kiss you again."

His warning was all the incentive she needed. Several minutes had passed since he'd last kissed her and she was still so bemused she could hardly think. On cue, she lifted the hot dog to her mouth, prepared for the worst. But to her surprise, it didn't taste half bad. In fact, it was downright palatable. When she'd polished it off, she started on the peanuts, which were still warm from the roaster. Warm and salty, and excellent.

Another vendor strolled past and Nate bought them each a cold drink.

The first inning was over by the time Susannah finished eating. Nate reached for her hand. "Feel better?" His eyes were fervent and completely focused on her.

One look certainly had an effect on Susannah. Whenever her eyes met his she felt as though she was caught in a whirlpool and about to be sucked under. She'd tried to resist the pull, but it had been impossible.

"Susannah?" he asked. "Are you okay?"

She managed to nod. After a moment she said, "I still feel kind of foolish...."

"Why?"

"Come on, Nate. I'm the only person here in a business suit."

"I can fix that."

"Oh?" Susannah had her doubts. What did he plan to do? Undress her?

He gave her another of his knowing smiles and casually excused himself. Puzzled, Susannah watched as he made his way toward the concession stand. Then he was back—with a Mariners T-shirt in one hand, a baseball cap in the other.

Removing her suit jacket, Susannah slipped the T-shirt over her head. When she'd done that, Nate set the baseball cap on her head, adjusting it so the bill dipped low over her forehead.

"There," he said, satisfied. "You look like one of the home team now."

"Thanks." She smoothed the T-shirt over her straight skirt and wondered how peculiar she looked. Funny, but it didn't seem to matter. She was having a good time with Nate, and it felt wonderful to laugh and enjoy life.

"You're welcome."

They both settled back in their seats to give their full attention to the game. The Seattle Mariners were down by one run at the bottom of the fifth inning.

Susannah didn't know all that much about baseball, but the crowd was lending vociferous support to the home team and she loved the atmosphere, which crackled with excitement, as if everyone was waiting for something splendid to happen.

"You've been avoiding me," Nate said halfway through the sixth inning. "I want to know why."

She couldn't very well tell him the truth, but lying seemed equally unattractive. Pretending to concentrate on the game, Susannah shrugged, hoping he'd accept that as explanation enough.

"Susannah?"

She should've known he'd force the issue. "Because I don't like what happens when you kiss me," she blurted out.

"What happens?" he echoed. "The first time we kissed, you nearly dealt my ego a fatal blow. As I recall, you claimed it was a pleasant experience. I believe you described it as 'nice,' and said that was about it."

Susannah kicked at the litter on the cement floor with the toes of her pumps, her eyes downcast. "Yes, I do remember saying something along those lines."

"You lied?"

He didn't need to drill her to prove his point. "All right," she admitted, "I lied. But you knew that all along. You must have, otherwise..."

"Otherwise what?"

"You wouldn't be kissing me every time you want to coerce me into doing something I don't want to do."

Crow's-feet fanned out beside his eyes as he grinned, making him look naughty and angelic at once.

"You knew all along," she repeated, "so don't give me that injured-ego routine!"

"There's electricity between us, Susannah, and it's about time you recognized that. I did, from the very first."

"Sure. But there's a big difference between standing next to an electrical outlet and fooling around with a high-voltage wire. I prefer to play it safe."

"Not me." He ran a knuckle down the side of her face. Circling her chin, his finger rested on her lips, which parted softly. "No," he said in a hushed voice, studying her. "I always did prefer to live dangerously."

"I've noticed." Nerve endings tingled at his touch, and Susannah held her breath until he removed his hand. Only then did she breathe normally again.

The cheering crowd alerted her to the fact that something important had taken place on the field. Glad to have her attention diverted from Nate, she watched as a Mariner rounded the bases for a home run. Pleased, she clapped politely, her enthusiasm far more restrained than that of the spectators around her.

That changed, however, at the bottom of the ninth. The bases were loaded and Susannah sat on the edge of her seat as the designated hitter approached home plate.

The fans chanted, "Grand slam, grand slam!" and Susannah soon joined in. The pitcher tossed a fastball, and unable to watch, she squeezed her eyes shut. But the sound of the wood hitting the ball was unmistakable. Susannah opened her eyes and jumped to her feet as the ball flew into left field and over the wall. The crowd went wild, and after doing an impulsive jig, Susannah threw her arms around Nate's neck and hugged him.

Nate appeared equally excited, and when Susannah had her feet back on the ground, he raised his fingers to his mouth and let loose a piercing whistle.

She was laughing and cheering and even went so far as to cup her hands over her mouth and boisterously yell her approval. It was then that she noticed Nate watching her. His eyes were wide with feigned shock, as if he couldn't believe the refined and businesslike Susannah Simmons would lower herself to such uninhibited behavior.

His apparent censure instantly cooled her reactions, and she returned to her seat and demurely folded her hands and crossed her ankles, embarrassed now by her response to something as mindless as a baseball game. When she dared to glance in Nate's direction, she discovered him watching her intently.

"Nate," she whispered, disconcerted by his attention. The game was over and the people around them had started to leave their seats. Susannah could feel the color in her cheeks. "Why are you looking at me like that?"

"You amaze me."

More likely, she'd disgraced herself in his eyes by her wild display. She was mortified.

"You're going to be all right, Susannah Simmons," he said cryptically. "We both are."

"Susannah, I didn't expect to find you home on a Saturday," Emily said as she stepped inside her sister's apartment. "Michelle and I are going to the Pike Place Market this morning and decided to drop by and see you first. You don't mind, do you?"

"No. Of course not. Come in." Susannah brushed the disheveled hair from her face. "What time is it anyway?"

"Eight-thirty."

"That late, huh?"

Emily chuckled. "I forgot. You like to sleep in on the weekends, don't you?"

"Don't worry about it," she said on the tail end of a yawn. "I'll put on a pot of coffee and be myself in no time."

Emily and Michelle followed her into the kitchen. Once the coffee was brewing, Susannah took the chair across from her sister. Michelle gleefully waved her arms, and despite the early hour, Susannah found herself smiling at her niece's enthusiasm for life. She held out her arms to the baby and was pleasantly surprised when Michelle came happily into them.

"She remembers you," Emily said.

"Of course she does," Susannah said as she nuzzled her niece's neck. "We had some great times, didn't we, kiddo? Especially when it came to feeding you plums."

Emily chuckled. "I don't think I'll ever be able to thank you enough for keeping Michelle that weekend. It was just what Robert and I needed."

"Don't mention it." Susannah dismissed Emily's appreciation with a weak gesture of her hand. She was the one who'd profited from that zany weekend. It might've been several more weeks before she met Nate if it hadn't been for Michelle.

Emily sighed. "I've been trying to get hold of you, but you're never home."

"Why didn't you leave a message?"

Emily shook her head and her long braid swung

back and forth. "You know I hate doing that. I get all tongue-tied and I can't seem to talk. You might phone *me* sometime, you know."

Over the past couple of weeks, Susannah had considered it, but she'd been avoiding her sister because she knew that the minute she called, Emily was going to ply her with questions about Nate.

"Have you been working late every night?" Emily asked.

Susannah dropped her gaze. "Not exactly."

"Then you must've been out with Nate Townsend." Emily didn't give her time to respond, but immediately started jabbering away. "I don't mind telling you, Susannah, both Robert and I were impressed with your new neighbor. He was wonderful with Michelle, and from the way he was looking at you, I think he's interested. Now, please don't tell me to keep my nose out of this. You're twenty-eight, for heaven's sake, and that biological clock is ticking away. If you're ever going to settle down and get serious about a man, the time is now. And personally, I don't think you'll find anyone better than Nate. Why, he's…"

She paused to breathe, giving Susannah the chance she'd been waiting for. "Coffee?"

Emily blinked, then nodded. "You didn't listen to a word I said, did you?"

"I listened."

"But you didn't *hear* a single word."

"Sure I did," Susannah countered. "You're saying I'd be a fool not to put a ring through Nate Townsend's nose. You want me to marry him before I lose my last chance at motherhood."

"Exactly," Emily said, looking pleased that she'd conveyed her message so effectively.

Michelle squirmed and Susannah set her on the floor to crawl around and explore.

"Well?" Emily pressed. "What do you think?"

"About marrying Nate? It would never work," she said calmly, as though they were discussing something as mundane as stock options, "for more reasons than you realize. But to satisfy your curiosity I'll list a few. First and foremost I've got a career and he doesn't, and furthermore—"

"Nate's unemployed?" her sister gasped. "But how can he not work? I mean, this is an expensive complex. Didn't you tell me the condominium next to yours is nearly twice as large? How can he afford to live there if he doesn't have a job?"

"I have no idea."

Susannah forgot about Nate for the moment as her eyes followed Michelle, astonished by how much she'd missed her. She stood and got two cups from the cupboard.

"That's not decaffeinated, is it?" Emily asked.

"No."

"Then don't bother pouring me a cup. I gave up caffeine years ago."

"Right." Susannah should have remembered. Michelle crawled across the kitchen floor toward her and, using Susannah's nightgown for leverage, pulled herself into a standing position. She smiled proudly at her achievement.

"Listen," Susannah said impulsively, leaning over to pick up her niece. "Why don't you leave Michelle with me? We'll take this morning to become reacquainted and you can do your shopping without having to worry about her."

There was a shocked silence. "Susannah?" Emily said. "Did I hear you correctly? I thought I just heard you volunteer to babysit."

Chapter

6

The morning was bright and sunny, and unable to resist, Susannah opened the sliding glass door and let the salty breeze off Elliott Bay blow into her apartment. Sitting on the kitchen floor with a saucepan and a wooden spoon, Michelle proceeded to demonstrate her musical talents by pounding out a loud enthusiastic beat.

When the phone rang, Susannah knew it was Nate.

"Good morning," she said, pushing her hair behind her ears. She hadn't pinned it up when she got dressed, knowing Nate preferred it down, and she didn't try to fool herself with excuses for leaving it that way.

"Morning," he breathed into the phone. "Do you have a drummer visiting?"

"No, a special friend. I think she'd like to say hello.

Wait a minute." Susannah put down the receiver and lifted Michelle from the floor. Holding the baby on her hip, she pressed the telephone receiver to the side of Michelle's face. Practically on cue, the child spouted an excited flow of gibberish.

"I think she said good-morning," Susannah explained.

"Michelle?"

"How many other babies would pay me a visit?"

"How many Simmons girls are there?"

"Only Emily and me," she answered with a soft laugh, "but trust me, the two of us were enough for any one set of parents to handle."

Nate's responding chuckle was warm and seductive. "Are you in the mood for more company?"

"Sure. If you bring the Danish, I'll provide the coffee."

"You've got yourself a deal."

It wasn't until several minutes had passed that Susannah realized how little resistance she'd been putting up lately when it came to Nate. Since the baseball game, she'd given up trying to avoid him; she simply didn't have the heart for it, although deep down, she knew anything beyond friendship was impossible. Yet despite her misgivings, after that one afternoon with him she'd come away feeling exhilarated. Being with Nate was like recapturing a part of her youth that had somehow escaped her. But even though seeing him was fun, it wasn't meant to last, and Susannah reminded herself of that every time they were together. Nate Townsend was like an unexpected burst of sunshine on an overcast day, but soon the rain

would come, the way it always did. Susannah wasn't
going to be fooled into believing there could ever be
anything permanent between them.

When Nate arrived, the reunion was complete. He
lifted Michelle high in the air and Susannah smiled
at the little girl's squeals of delight.

"Where's Emily?" he wanted to know.

"Shopping. She won't be more than an hour or
so."

With Michelle in one arm, Nate moved into the
kitchen, where Susannah was dishing up the pastries
and pouring coffee. "She's grown, hasn't she?" she
said.

"Is that another new tooth?" he asked, peering
inside the baby's mouth.

"It might be," Susannah replied, taking a look herself.

Nate slipped his free arm around her shoulder and
smiled at her. "Your hair's down," he murmured, his
smile caressing her upturned face.

She nodded, not knowing how else to respond,
although a dozen plausible excuses raced through her
mind. But none of them would have been true.

"For me?"

Once more, she answered him with a slight nod.

"Thank you," he whispered, his face so close to her
own that his words were like a kiss.

Susannah leaned into him, pressing herself against
his solid length. When he kissed her, she could hardly
stop herself from melting into his arms.

Michelle thought it was great fun to have two adults for

company. She wove her fingers into Susannah's hair and yanked until Susannah was forced to pull away from Nate.

Smiling, Nate disengaged the baby's hand from her aunt's hair and kissed Susannah again. "Hmm," he said when he lifted his head. "You taste better than any sweet roll ever could."

Unnerved, and suddenly feeling shy, Susannah busied herself setting the pastries on the table.

"Do you have plans for today?" he asked, taking a chair, Michelle gurgling happily on his lap.

Michelle was content for now, but from experience Susannah knew she'd want to be back on the floor soon. "I...I was planning to go to the office for an hour or so."

"I don't think so," Nate said flatly.

"You don't?"

"I'm taking you out." He surveyed her navy-blue slacks and the winter-white sweater she wore. "I don't suppose you have any jeans."

Susannah nodded. She knew she did, somewhere, but it was years since she'd worn them. As long ago as college, and maybe even her last year of high school. "I don't know if they'll fit, though."

"Go try them on."

"Why? What are you planning? Knowing you, I could end up on top of Mount Rainier looking over a crevasse, with no idea how I got there."

"We're going to fly a kite today," he said casually, as if it was something they'd done several times.

Susannah thought she'd misunderstood him. Nate

obviously loved this kind of surprise. First a baseball game in the middle of a workday, and now kites?

"You heard me right. Now go find your jeans."

"But...kites...that's for kids. Frankly, Nate," she said, her voice gaining conviction, "I don't happen to have one hidden away in a closet. Besides, isn't that something parents do with their children?"

"No, it's for everyone. Adults have been known to have fun, too. Don't worry about a thing. I built a huge one and it's ready for testing."

"A kite?" she repeated, holding in the desire to laugh outright. She'd been in grade school when she'd last attempted anything so...so juvenile.

By the time Susannah had rummaged in her closet and found an old pair of jeans, Emily had returned for Michelle. Nate let her sister inside, but the bedroom door was cracked open, and Susannah could hear the conversation. She held her breath, first because her hips were a tiny bit wider than the last time she'd worn her jeans, and also because Susannah could never be sure what her sister was going to say. Or do.

It'd be just like Emily to start telling Nate how suitable Susannah would be as a wife. That thought was sobering and for a moment Susannah stopped wriggling into her pants.

"Nate," she heard her sister say, "it's so good of you to help with Michelle." In her excitement, her voice was a full octave higher than usual.

"No problem. Susannah will be out in a minute—she's putting on a pair of jeans. We're going to Gas Works Park to fly a kite."

There was a short pause. "Susannah wearing jeans and flying a kite? You mean she's actually going with you?"

"Of course I am. Don't look so shocked," Susannah said, walking into the room. "How did the shopping go?"

Emily couldn't seem to close her mouth. She stared at her sister to the point of embarrassment, then swung her gaze to Nate and back to Susannah again.

Susannah realized she must look different, wearing jeans and with her hair down, but it certainly didn't warrant this openmouthed gawking.

"Emily?" Susannah waved her hand in front of her sister's face in an effort to bring her back to earth.

"Oh...the shopping went just fine. I was able to get the fresh herbs I wanted. Basil and thyme and...some others." As though in a daze, Emily lifted the home-sewn bag draped over her arm as evidence of her successful trip to the market.

"Good," Susannah said enthusiastically, wanting to smooth over her sister's outrageous reaction. "Michelle wasn't a bit of trouble. If you need me to watch her again, just say so."

Her sister's eyes grew wider. She swallowed and nodded. "Thanks. I'll remember that."

The sky was as blue as Nate's eyes, Susannah thought, sitting with her knees tucked under her chin on the lush green grass of Gas Works Park. The wind whipped Nate's box kite back and forth as he scrambled from one hill to the next, letting the brisk breeze carry the multicolored crate in several directions. As it was late September, Susannah didn't expect many more glorious Indian summer days like this one.

She closed her eyes and soaked up the sun. Her spirits raced with the kites that abounded in the popular park. She felt like tossing back her head and laughing triumphantly, for no other reason than that it felt good to be alive.

"I'm beat," Nate said, dropping down on the grass beside her. He lay on his back, arms and legs spread-eagle.

"Where's the kite?"

"I gave it to one of the kids who didn't have one."

Susannah smiled. That sounded exactly like something Nate would do. He'd spent hours designing and constructing the box kite, and yet he'd impulsively given it away without a second thought.

"Actually I begged the kid to take it, before I keeled over from exhaustion," he amended. "Don't let anyone tell you otherwise. Flying a kite is hard work."

Work was a subject Susannah stringently avoided with Nate. From the first he'd been completely open with her. Open and honest. She was confident that if she quizzed him about his profession or lack of one, he'd answer her truthfully.

Susannah had decided that what she didn't know about him couldn't upset her. Nate apparently had plenty of money. He certainly didn't seem troubled by financial difficulties. But it was his attitude that worried her. He seemed to see life as a grand adventure; he leaped from one interest to another without rhyme or reason. Nothing appeared to be more important or vital than the moment.

"You're frowning," he said. He slipped a hand around her neck and pulled her down until her face was within inches of his own. "Aren't you having fun?"

She nodded, unable to deny the obvious.

"Then what's the problem?"

"Nothing."

He hesitated and the edges of his mouth lifted sensuously. "It's a good thing you didn't become an attorney," he said with a roguish grin. "You'd never be able to fool a jury."

Susannah was astonished that Nate knew she'd once seriously considered going into law.

He grinned at her. "Emily told me you'd thought about entering law school."

Susannah blinked a couple of times, then smiled, too. She was determined not to ruin this magnificent afternoon with her concerns.

"Kiss me, Susannah," he whispered. The humor had left his face and his gaze searched hers.

Her breath caught. She lifted her eyes and quickly glanced around. The park was crowded and children were everywhere.

"No," he said, cradling the sides of her face. "No fair peeking. I want you to kiss me no matter how many spectators there are."

"But—"

"If you don't kiss me, I'll simply have to kiss you. And, honey, if I do, watch out because—"

Not allowing him to finish, she lowered her mouth

and gently skimmed her lips over his. Even that small sample was enough to send the blood racing through her veins. Whatever magic quality this man had should be bottled and sold over the counter. Susannah knew she'd be the first one in line to buy it.

"Are you always this stingy?" he asked when she raised her head.

"In public, yes."

His eyes were smiling and Susannah swore she could have drowned in his look. He exhaled, then bounded to his feet with an energy she had to envy.

"I'm starved," he announced, reaching out for her. Susannah placed her hand in his and he pulled her to her feet. "But I hope you realize," he whispered close to her ear, wrapping his arm around her waist, "my appetite isn't for food. I'm crazy about you, Susannah Simmons. Eventually we're going to have to do something about that."

"I hope I'm not too early," Susannah said as she entered her sister's home on Capitol Hill. When Emily had called to invite her to Sunday dinner, she hadn't bothered to disguise her intentions. Emily was dying to grill Susannah about her budding relationship with Nate Townsend. A week ago, Susannah would've found an excuse to get out of tonight's dinner. But after spending an entire Saturday with Nate, she was so confused that she was willing to talk this out with her sister, who seemed so much more competent in dealing with male/female relationships.

"Your timing's perfect," Emily said, coming out of

the kitchen to greet her. She wore a full-length skirt with a bib apron, and her long hair was woven into a single braid that fell halfway down her back.

"Here." Susannah handed her sister a bottle of chardonnay, hoping it was appropriate for the meal.

"How thoughtful," Emily murmured, leading her back into the kitchen. The house was an older one, built in the early forties, with a large family kitchen. The red linoleum countertop was crowded with freshly canned tomatoes. Boxes of jars were stacked on the floor, along with a wicker basket filled with sun-dried diapers. A rope of garlic dangled above the sink and a row of potted plants lined the windowsill.

"Whatever you're serving smells wonderful."

"It's lentil soup."

Emily opened the oven and pulled out the rack, wadding up the skirt of her apron to protect her fingers. "I made a fresh apple pie. Naturally I used organically grown apples so you don't need to worry."

"Oh, good." That hadn't been a major concern of Susannah's.

"Where's Michelle?" Father and daughter were conspicuously absent.

Emily turned around, looking mildly guilty, and Susannah realized that her sister had gone to some lengths to provide time alone with her. No doubt she was anxious to wring out as much information about Nate as possible. Not that Susannah had a lot to tell.

"How was your day in the park?"

Susannah took a seat on the stool and made herself

comfortable for the coming inquisition. "Great. I really enjoyed it."

"You like Nate, don't you?"

Like was the understatement of the year. Contrary to every ounce of sense she possessed, Susannah was falling in love with her neighbor. It wasn't what she wanted, but she hadn't been able to stop herself.

"Yes, I like him," she answered after a significant pause.

Emily seemed thrilled by her admission. "I thought as much," she said, nodding profoundly. She pushed a stool next to Susannah and sat down. Emily's hands were rarely idle, and true to form, she reached for her crocheting.

"I'm waiting," Susannah said, growing impatient.

"For what?"

"For the lecture."

Emily cracked a knowing smile. "I was gathering my thoughts. You were always the one who could evaluate things so well. I always had trouble with that and you aced every paper."

"School reports have very little to do with real life," Susannah reminded her. How much simpler it would be if she could just look up everything she needed to know about dealing with Nate.

"I knew that, but I wasn't sure you did."

Perhaps Susannah hadn't until she met Nate. "Emily," she said, her stomach tightening, "I need to ask you something…important. How did you know you loved Robert? What was it that told you the two of you were meant to share your lives?" Susannah understood that she was practically laying her cards faceup on the table, but she was past the point of subtlety. She wanted hard facts.

Her sister smiled and tugged at her ball of yarn before she responded. "I don't think you're going to like my answer," she murmured, frowning slightly. "It was the first time Robert kissed me."

Susannah nearly toppled from her perch on the stool, remembering her experience with Nate. "What happened?"

"We'd gone for a nature walk in the rain forest over on the Olympic Peninsula and had stopped to rest. Robert helped me remove my backpack, then he looked into my eyes and leaned over and kissed me." She sighed softly at the memory. "I don't think he intended to do it because he looked so shocked afterward."

"Then what?"

"Robert took off his own backpack and asked if I minded that he'd kissed me. Naturally I told him I rather liked it, and he sat down next to me and did it again—only this time it wasn't a peck on the lips but a full-blown kiss." Emily's shoulders sagged a little in a sigh. "The moment his lips touched mine I couldn't think, I couldn't breathe, I couldn't even move. When he finished I was trembling so much I thought something might be physically wrong with me."

"So would you say you felt...electricity?"

"Exactly."

"And you never had that with any of the other men you dated?"

"Never."

Susannah wiped a hand down her face. "You're right," she whispered. "I don't like your answer."

Emily paused in her crocheting to glance at her. "Nate kissed you and you felt something?"

Susannah nodded. "I was nearly electrocuted."

"Oh, Susannah, you poor thing!" She patted her sister's hand. "You don't know what to do, do you?"

"No," she admitted, feeling wretched.

"You never expected to fall in love, did you?"

Slowly Susannah shook her head. And it couldn't be happening at a worse time. The promotion was going to be announced within the next week, and the entire direction of her life could be altered if she became involved with Nate. She didn't even know if that was what either of them wanted. Susannah felt mystified by everything going on in her life, which until a few short weeks ago had been so straightforward and uncluttered.

"Are you thinking of marriage?" Emily asked outright.

"Marriage," Susannah echoed weakly. It seemed the natural conclusion when two people were falling in love. She was willing to acknowledge her feelings, but she wasn't completely confident Nate felt the same things she did. Nor was she positive that he was ready to move into something as permanent as a lifelong commitment. She knew *she* wasn't, and the very thought of all this was enough to throw her into a tizzy.

"I don't…know about marriage," Susannah said. "We haven't discussed anything like that." The fact was, they hadn't even talked about dating regularly.

"Trust me, if you leave it to Nate the subject of marriage will never come up. Men never want to talk about getting married. The topic is left totally up to us women."

"Oh, come on—"

"No, it's true. From the time Eve slipped Adam the apple, we've been stuck with the burden of taming men, and it's never more difficult than when it comes to convincing one he should take a wife."

"But surely Robert wanted to get married?"

"Don't be silly. Robert's like every other man alive. I had to convince him this was what he wanted. Subtlety is the key, Susannah. In other words, I chased Robert until he caught me." She stopped working her crochet hook to laugh at her own wit.

From the first day she met her brother-in-law, Susannah had assumed he'd taken one look at her sister and dropped to his knees to propose. It had always seemed obvious to Susannah that they were meant for each other, far more obvious than it was that Nate was right for her.

"I don't know, Emily," she said with a deep sigh. "Everything's so confused in my mind. How could I possibly be so attracted to this man? It doesn't make any sense! Do you know what we did yesterday afternoon when we'd finished at the park?" She didn't wait for a response. "Nate brought over his Nintendo game and Super Mario Brothers cartridge, and we played video games. Me! I can't believe it even now. It was a pure waste of time."

"Did you have fun?"

That was a question Susannah wanted to avoid. She'd laughed until her stomach hurt. They'd challenged each other to see who could achieve the higher score, and then had done everything possible to sabotage each other.

Nate had discovered a sensitive area behind her ear and taken to kissing her there just when she was about to outscore him. Fair was fair, however, and Susannah soon discovered that Nate had his own area of vulnerability. Without a qualm, she'd used it against him, effectively disrupting his game. Soon they both forgot Nintendo and became far more interested in learning about each other.

"We had fun" was all Susannah was willing to admit.

"What about the kite flying?"

Her sister didn't know when to quit. "Then, too," she said reluctantly. "And at the baseball game Thursday, as well."

"He took you to a Mariners game...on Thursday? But they played in the middle of the afternoon. Did you actually leave the office?"

Susannah nodded, without explaining the details of how Nate had practically kidnapped her. "Back to you and Robert," she said, trying to change the subject.

"You want to know how I convinced him he wanted to get married? It wasn't really that difficult."

For Emily it wouldn't have been, but for Susannah it would be another story entirely. The biggest problem was that she wasn't sure she *wanted* Nate to be convinced. However, she should probably learn these things for future reference. She'd listen to what her sister had to say and make up her mind later.

"Remember that old adage—the way to a man's heart is through his stomach? It's true. Men equate food with comfort and love—that's a well-known fact."

"Then I'm in trouble," Susannah said flatly. Good grief, she thought, Nate could cook far better than she could any day of the week. She couldn't attract him with her cooking. All she had in the way of looks was her classic profile. Painful as it was to accept, men simply weren't attracted to her.

"Now don't overreact. Just because you can't whip up a five-course meal doesn't mean your life is over before it even begins."

"My married life is. I can't put together soup and a sandwich and you know it."

"Susannah, I wish you'd stop demeaning yourself. You're bright and pretty, and Nate would be the luckiest man in the world if he were to marry you."

Now that they were actually discussing marriage, Susannah was having mixed feelings. "I...don't know if Nate's the marrying kind," she muttered. "For that matter, I don't know if I am."

Emily ignored that. "I'll start you out on something simple and we'll work our way up."

"I don't understand."

"Cookies," Emily explained. "There isn't a man alive who doesn't appreciate homemade cookies. There's something magical about them—really," she added when Susannah cast her a doubtful glance. "Cookies create an aura of domestic bliss—it sounds crazy, but it's true. A man can't resist a woman who bakes him cookies. They remind him of home and mother and a fire crackling in the fireplace." Emily paused and sighed. "Now, it's also true that men have been fighting this feeling since the beginning of time."

"What feeling?"

Emily rolled her eyes. "Domestic contentment. It's exactly what they need and want, but they fight it."

Susannah mulled over her sister's words. "Now that you mention it, Nate did say chocolate chip's his favorite."

"See what I mean?"

Susannah couldn't believe she was pursuing this subject with her sister. Okay, so she and Nate had shared some good times. But lots of people had good times together. She was also willing to admit there was a certain amount of chemistry between them. But that wasn't any reason to run to the nearest altar.

For the past few minutes, she'd been trying to sensibly discuss this situation between Nate and her with her sister, and before she even knew how it'd happened, Emily had her talking about weddings and chocolate chip cookies. At this rate Emily would have her married and pregnant by the end of the week.

"So how did dinner with your sister go?" Nate asked her later that same night. He'd been on the Seattle waterfront earlier in the day and had brought her back a polished glass paperweight made of ash from the Mount St. Helens volcano.

"Dinner was fine," she said quickly, perhaps too quickly. "Emily and I had a nice talk."

Nate put his arms around her, trapping her against the kitchen counter. "I missed you."

Swallowing tensely, she murmured, "I missed you, too."

He threaded his fingers though the length of her hair, pulling it away from her face and holding it there. "You wore it down again today," he whispered against her neck.

"Yes…Emily says she likes it better that way, too." Talking shouldn't be this difficult, but every time Nate touched her it was. Susannah's knees had the consistency of pudding and her resolve was just as weak. After analyzing her talk with Emily, Susannah had decided to let the situation between her and Nate cool for a while. Things were happening much too quickly. She wasn't ready, and she doubted Nate was, either.

When he kissed her lightly at the hollow of her throat, it was all she could do to remain in an upright position. As she braced her hands against his chest, she began to push him gently away. But when his lips traveled up the side of her neck, blazing a trail of moist kisses, she was lost. His mouth grazed the line of her jaw, slowly edging its way toward her lips, prolonging the inevitable until Susannah thought she'd dissolve at his feet.

When he finally kissed her mouth, they both sighed, caught in a swelling tide of longing. His mouth moved hungrily over hers. Then he tugged at her lower lip with his teeth, creating a whole new wave of sensation.

By the time Nate went back to his own apartment, Susannah was shaking from the inside out. She'd walked all the way to the kitchen before she was conscious of her intent. She stared at the phone for a long moment. Calling Emily demanded every ounce of courage she had. With a deep calming breath, she punched out her sister's number.

"Emily," she said when her sister answered on the second ring, "do you have a recipe for chocolate chip cookies?"

Chapter

7

The recipe for chocolate chip cookies was safely tucked away in a kitchen drawer. The impulse to bake them had passed quickly and reason had returned.

Monday morning, back at the office, Susannah realized how close she'd come to the edge of insanity. The vice presidency was almost within her grasp, and she'd worked too long and too hard to let this promotion slip through her fingers simply because she felt a little weak in the knees when Nate Townsend kissed her. To even contemplate anything beyond friendship was like…like amputating her right hand because she had a sliver in her index finger. She'd been overreacting, which was understandable, since she'd never experienced such a strong attraction to a man before.

"There's a call for you on line one," Ms. Brooks told her. She paused, then added dryly, "It sounds like that nice young man who stopped by last week."

Nate. Squaring her shoulders—and her resolve—Susannah picked up the phone. "This is Susannah Simmons."

"Good morning, beautiful."

"Hello, Nate," she said stiffly. "What can I do for you?"

He chuckled. "That's a leading question if there ever was one. Trust me, honey, you don't want to know."

"Nate," she breathed, briefly closing her eyes. "Please. I'm busy. What do you want?"

"Other than your body?"

Hot color leaped into her cheeks and she gave a distressed gasp. "We'd better put an end to this conversation—"

"All right, all right, I'm sorry. I just woke up and I was lying here thinking how nice it would be if we could escape for the day. Could I tempt you with a drive to the ocean? We could dig for clams, build a sand castle, and then make a fire and sing our favorite camp songs."

"As a matter of interest, I've been up for several hours. And since you've obviously forgotten, I do have a job—an important one. At least it's important to me. Now exactly what is the purpose of this call, other than to embarrass me?"

"Lunch."

"I can't today. I've got an appointment."

"Okay." He sighed, clearly frustrated. "How about dinner, just you and me?"

"I'm working late and was planning on sending out for something. Thanks, anyway."

"Susannah," he said in a burst of impatience, "are we going to go through this again? You should've figured out by now that avoiding me won't change anything."

Perhaps not, she reasoned, but it would certainly help. "Listen, Nate, I really am busy. Perhaps we should continue this conversation another time."

"Like next year—I know you. You'd be willing to bury your head in the sand for the next fifteen years if I didn't come and prod you along. I swear, I've never met a more stubborn woman."

"Goodbye, Nate."

"Susannah," he persisted, "what about dinner? Come on, change your mind. We have a lot to talk about."

"No. I wasn't lying—I do have to work late. The fact is, I can't go outside and play today—or tonight."

"Ouch," Nate cried. "That hurt."

"Perhaps it hit too close to home."

A short silence followed. "Maybe it did," he murmured thoughtfully. "But before we hang up, I do want to know when I can see you again."

Susannah leaned forward and stretched her arm across the desk to her calendar, flipping the pages until she found a blank space. "How about lunch on Thursday?"

"All right," he said, "I'll see you Thursday at noon."

For a long moment after they'd hung up, Susannah

kept her hand on the receiver. As crazy as it seemed, spending the afternoon with Nate at the beach sounded far too appealing. The way he made her think and feel was almost frightening. The man was putting her whole career in jeopardy. Something had to be done, only Susannah wasn't sure what.

An hour later, Ms. Brooks tapped on her door and walked inside, carrying a huge bouquet of red roses. "These just arrived."

"For me?" Surely there was some mistake. No one had ever sent her flowers. There'd never been any reason. There wasn't now.

"The card has your name on it," her assistant informed her. She handed the small white envelope to Susannah.

Not until Eleanor had left the room did Susannah read the card. The roses were from Nate, who wrote that he was sorry for having disturbed her earlier. She was right, he told her, now wasn't the time to go outside and play. He'd signed it with his love. Closing her eyes, Susannah held the card to her breast and fought down a swelling surge of emotion. The least he could do was stop being so damn wonderful. Then everything would be easier.

As it turned out, Susannah finished work relatively early that evening and returned home a little after seven. Her apartment was dark and empty—but it was that way every night and she didn't understand why it should matter to her now. Yet it did.

It was when she stood outside Nate's door and knocked that she realized how impulsive her behavior

had become since she'd met him. She was doing everything in her power to avoid him, and yet she couldn't
stay away.

"Susannah," he said when he opened the door.
"This is a pleasant surprise."

She laced her fingers together. "I...I just wanted
you to know how much I appreciated the roses. They're
lovely and the gesture was so thoughtful."

"Come in," he said, stepping inside. "I'll put on
some coffee."

"No, thanks. I've got to get back, but I wanted to
thank you for the flowers...and to apologize if I
sounded waspish on the phone. Monday mornings
aren't exactly my best time."

Grinning, he leaned against the doorjamb and
crossed his arms over his broad chest. "Actually, I'm the
one who owed you an apology. I should never have
phoned you this morning. I was being selfish. You do
have an important job and these are anxious days for
you. Didn't you tell me you'd hear about that promotion within the next week or two?"

Susannah nodded.

"You might find this hard to believe, but I don't want
to say or do anything to take that away from you. You're
a dedicated, hardworking employee and you deserve to
be the first female vice president of H&J Lima."

His confidence in her was reassuring, but it confused her, too. From everything she'd witnessed about
Nate, she could only conclude that he didn't appreciate hard work and its rewards.

"If I do get the promotion," she said, watching him

closely, "things will change between you and me. I...I won't have a lot of free time for a while."

"Does that mean you won't be able to go outside and play as often?" he asked, his mouth curving into a sensuous smile. He was taunting her with the words she'd used earlier that day.

"Exactly."

"I can accept that. Just..." He hesitated.

"What?" Nate was frowning and that wasn't like him. He wore a saucy grin as often as he donned a baseball cap. "Tell me," she demanded.

"I want you to do everything possible to achieve your dreams, Susannah, but there are plenty of pitfalls along the way."

Now it was her turn to frown. She wasn't sure she understood what he was talking about.

"All I'm saying," he elaborated, "is that you shouldn't lose sight of who you are because this vice presidency means so much to you. And most important, count the cost." With that he stepped forward, gazed hungrily into her eyes and kissed her lightly on the lips. Then he stepped back reluctantly.

For a second Susannah teetered, then she moved forward into his arms as if that was the most natural place in the world for her to be. Even now, she didn't entirely understand what he meant, but she couldn't mistake the tenderness she heard in his voice. Once her head had cleared and she wasn't wrapped up in this incredible longing he created every time he touched her, she'd mull over his words.

* * *

Susannah woke around midnight, and rolling over, adjusted her pillow. The illuminated dial on her clock radio told her she'd only been sleeping for a couple of hours. She yawned, wondering what had woken her out of a sound peaceful slumber. Closing her eyes, she tucked the blankets more securely over her shoulders, determined to sleep. She tried visualizing herself accepting the promotion to vice president. Naturally, there'd be a nice write-up about her in the evening paper and possibly a short piece in a business journal or two.

Susannah's eyes drifted open as she recalled Nate's words reminding her not to forget who she was. Who *was* she? A list of possible replies skipped easily through her mind. She was Susannah Simmons, future vice president in charge of marketing for the largest sporting-goods store in the country. She was a daughter, a sister, an aunt... And then it hit her. *She was a woman.* That was what Nate had been trying to tell her. It was the same message Emily had tried to get across to her on Sunday. From the time Susannah had set her goals, she'd dedicated her life to her career and pushed aside every feminine part of herself. Now was the time for her to deal with that aspect of her life.

It was the following evening after work. Susannah was leaning against the kitchen counter, struggling to remove the heavy food mixer from its reinforced cardboard box. Emily's recipe for chocolate chip cookies made three dozen. After her trip to the grocery, plus a jaunt to the hardware store for the mixer, cookie sheets and measuring utensils, these cookies were costing her $4.72 apiece.

Price be damned. She was setting out to prove something important—although she wasn't sure exactly what. She would've preferred to dismiss all her sister's talk about cookies being equated with warmth and love as a philosophy left over from an earlier generation. Susannah didn't actually believe Emily's theory, but she wanted to give it a try. Susannah didn't know why she was doing this anymore. All she knew was that she had this urge to bake chocolate chip cookies.

Emily had eagerly given her the recipe, and Susannah had read it carefully. Just how difficult could baking cookies be?

Not very, she determined twenty minutes later when everything was laid out on her extended counter. Pushing up the sleeves of her shirt, she turned on the radio to keep her company. Next she tied the arms of an old shirt around her waist, using that as an apron. Emily always seemed to wear one when she worked in the kitchen and if her sister did, then it must be the thing to do.

The automatic mixer was blending the butter and white sugar nicely and, feeling extraordinarily proud of herself, Susannah cracked the eggs on the edge of the bowl with a decided flair.

"Damn," she cried when half the shell fell into the swirling blades. She glared at it a moment, watching helplessly as the beater broke the fragile shell into a thousand bits. Shrugging, she figured a little extra protein—or was it calcium?—wasn't going to hurt anyone. Finally she turned off the mixer and stirred in the flour, then the chocolate chips.

The oven was preheated exactly as the recipe required when Susannah slipped the shiny new cookie sheet inside. She closed the oven door with a swing of her hip and set the timer for twelve minutes.

Sampling a blob of dough from the end of her finger, she had to admit it was tasty. At least as good as Emily's. But Susannah considered it best not to let anyone know her secret ingredient was eggshell.

With a sense of genuine satisfaction, she poured herself a cup of coffee and sat down at the table with the evening paper.

A few minutes later she smelled smoke. Suspiciously sniffing the air, she set the paper aside. It couldn't possibly be her cookies—they'd been in the oven less than five minutes. To be on the safe side, however, she reached for a towel and opened the oven door.

She was immediately assaulted by billowing waves of smoke, followed by flames that licked out at her. Gasping in horror, she dropped the towel and gave a piercing scream. "Fire! Fire!"

The smoke alarm blared, and she thought she'd never heard anything louder in her life. Like a madwoman, Susannah raced for the door, throwing it open in an effort to allow the smoke to escape. Then she ran back to the table and hurled her coffee straight into the belly of the oven. Coughing hoarsely, she slammed the door shut.

"Susannah!" Breathless, Nate burst into her condominium.

"I started a fire," she shouted above the deafening din of the smoke alarm. Her voice still sounded raspy.

"Where?" Nate circled her table several times, looking frantically for the source of her panic.

"In the oven." Standing aside, she covered her face with her hands, not wanting to look.

A few minutes later, Nate took her in his arms. The smoke alarm was off. Two blackened sheets of charred cookies were angled into the sink. "Are you all right?"

Somehow she managed a nod.

"You didn't burn yourself?"

She didn't have so much as a blister and told him so.

Gently he brushed the hair away from her face, and expelled his breath, apparently to ease his tension. "Okay, how did the fire get started?"

"I don't know," she said dismally. "I...I did everything the recipe said, but when I put the cookies in the oven they...they caught on fire." Her voice quavered as she spoke.

"The cookies weren't responsible for the fire," he corrected her. "The cookie sheets were the culprits. They must've been new—it seems, ah, you forgot to remove the paper covering."

"Oh," she whispered. Her shoulders were shaking with the effort to repress her sobs.

"Susannah, there's no reason to cry. It was a reasonable mistake. Here, sit down." Gently he lowered her onto the kitchen chair and knelt in front of her, taking her hands in his and rubbing them. "It isn't the biggest disaster in the world."

"I know that," she wailed, unable to stop herself. "You don't understand. It was sort of a test...."

"A test?"

"Yes. Emily claims men love cookies...and I was baking them for you." She didn't go on to add that Emily also claimed that men loved the women who baked those cookies. "I can't cook...I started a fire... and I dropped part of the eggshell in the batter and...and left it.... I wasn't going to tell anyone."

Her confession must have shocked Nate because he stood up and left the room. Burying her face in her hands, Susannah endeavored to regain her composure and was doing an admirable job of it when Nate returned, holding a box of tissue.

Effortlessly lifting her into his arms, he pulled out the chair and sat down, holding her securely on his lap. "Okay, Betty Crocker, explain yourself."

She wiped her face dry with the tissue, feeling rather silly at the way she was reacting. So she'd burned a couple of cookie sheets and ruined a batch of chocolate chip cookies. Big deal, she told herself with as much bravado as she could muster. "Explain what?"

"The comment about men loving cookies. Were you trying to prove something to me?"

"Actually it was Emily I wanted to set straight," she whispered.

"You said you were baking them for my benefit."

"I was. Yesterday you said I shouldn't forget who I was, I should find myself, and...I think this sudden urge to bake was my response to that." Susannah suspected she wasn't making much sense. "Believe me, after today, I know I'm never going to be worth a damn in the kitchen."

"I don't remember suggesting you 'find yourself' in the kitchen," Nate said, looking confused.

"Actually that part was Emily's idea," she admitted. "She's the one who gave me the recipe. My sister seems to believe a woman can coerce a man into giving up his heart and soul if she can bake chocolate chip cookies."

"And you want my heart and soul?"

"Of course not! Don't be ridiculous."

He hesitated for a moment and seemed to be considering her words. "Would it come as a surprise if I said I wanted yours?"

Susannah barely heard him; she wasn't in the mood to talk about heart and soul right now. She'd just shown how worthless she was in the kitchen. Her lack in that area hadn't particularly troubled her—until now. She'd made a genuine effort and fallen flat on her face. Not only that, having Nate witness her defeat had badly dented her pride. "When I was born something must've been missing from my genes," she murmured thoughtfully. "Obviously. I can't cook, and I don't sew, and I can hardly tell one end of a knitting needle from the other. I can't do any of the things that...normal people associate with the female gender."

"Susannah." He said her name on a disgruntled sigh. "Did you hear what I just said?"

She shook her head. She understood the situation perfectly. Some women had it and others didn't. Unfortunately, she was in the latter group.

"I was telling you something important. But I can see you're going to force me to say it without words." Cupping her face, Nate directed her mouth to his. But he didn't only kiss her. The hot moist tip of his tongue traced the sensitive line of her lips until she shivered with a whole new realm of unexplored sensations. All her disheartened thoughts dissolved instantly. She forgot to think, to breathe, to do anything but tremble in his arms. The fire in her oven was nothing compared to the one Nate had started in her body. Without conscious volition, she wrapped her arms around his neck and slanted her mouth over his, surrendering to the hot currents of excitement he'd created. She opened herself to him, granting him anything he wanted. His tongue found hers, and Susannah whimpered at the shock of pleasure she received. Her response was innocent and abandoned, unskilled and unknowing, yet eager.

"There," he whispered, supporting his forehead against hers, while he drew in deep breaths. His husky voice was unsteady.

He seemed to think their kiss was enough to prove everything. Susannah slowly opened her eyes. She took a steadying breath herself, one that made her tremble all the way to her toes. If she was going to say anything, it would be to whisper his name repeatedly and ask why he was doing this and then plead with him never to stop.

He threaded his fingers through her hair and kissed her again with a mastery that caused her to cling to him as if he were a life raft in a stormy sea. Unable to keep still, Susannah ran her palms along his neck and onto his shoulders and down the length of his arms. He must have liked her touch because he groaned and deepened the kiss even more.

"Unfortunately I don't think you're ready to hear it yet," he said.

"Hear what?" she asked, when she could find her voice.

"What I was telling you."

She puckered her brow. "What was that?"

"Forget the cookies. You're more than enough woman for any man."

She blinked, not understanding him. She barely understood herself.

"I never meant for you to test who you are. All I suggested was that you take care not to lose sight of your own personality. Goals are all well and good, even necessary, but you should always calculate the cost."

"Oh." Her mind was still too hazy to properly assimilate his meaning.

"Are you going to be all right?" he asked, as he grazed her cheek with his fingertips. He kissed Susannah's eyelids, closing them.

All she could do was nod.

* * *

"John Hammer would like to see you right away," Ms. Brooks told Susannah when she walked into her office Thursday morning.

Susannah's heart flew into her throat and stayed there for an uncomfortable moment. This was it. The day for which she'd been waiting five long years.

"Did he say what he wanted?" she asked, making an effort to appear at least outwardly calm.

"No," Ms. Brooks replied. "He just asked me to tell you he wanted to talk to you at your convenience."

Susannah slumped into her high-backed office chair. She propped her elbows on the desk and hid her face in her hands, trying to put some order to her muddled thoughts. "At my convenience," she repeated in a ragged whisper. "I didn't get the promotion. I just know it."

"Susannah," her assistant said sternly, calling her by her first name—something she rarely did. "I think you might be jumping to conclusions."

Susannah glared at her, annoyed by the woman's obtuseness. "If he planned to appoint me vice president, he would've called me into his office late in the afternoon. That's how it's done. Then he'd go through this long spiel about me being a loyal employee and what an asset I am to the company and all that stuff. Wanting to talk to me *now* means... Well, you know what it means."

"I can't say I do," Ms. Brooks said primly. "My suggestion is that you pull yourself together and get over to Mr. Hammer's office before he changes his mind."

Susannah got to her feet and stiffened her spine. But no matter how hard she tried she couldn't seem to stop shaking.

"I'll be waiting here when you get back," Ms. Brooks told her on her way out the door. She smiled then, an encouraging gesture that softened her austere features. "Break a leg, kid."

"I probably will, whatever happens," she muttered. If she didn't get this promotion, she was afraid she'd fall apart. Assuming a calm manner, she decided not to worry until she knew for sure.

John Hammer stood when she was announced. Susannah walked into his office, and the first thing she noticed was that the two men who were her competition hadn't been called. The company president smiled benignly and motioned toward a chair. Susannah sat on the edge of the cushion, doing her best to disguise how nervous she was.

A smile eased over her boss's face. "Good morning, Susannah…"

True to her word, Susannah's assistant was waiting for her when she strolled back to her office.

"Well?"

Eleanor Brooks followed her to her desk and watched as Susannah carefully sat down.

"What happened?" she demanded a second time. "Don't just sit there. Talk!"

Susannah's gaze slowly moved from the phone to her assistant. Then she started to chuckle. The laughter came from deep within her and she had to cover her mouth with her palms. When she could talk, she wiped the tears from the corners of her eyes.

"The first thing he did was ask me if I wanted to trade offices while mine was being repainted."

"What?"

Susannah thought Ms. Brooks's expression probably reflected her own when Mr. Hammer had asked that question. "That was my reaction, too," Susannah exclaimed. "I didn't understand what he meant. Then he said he was going to have my office redone, because he felt it was only right that the vice president in charge of marketing have a brand-new office."

"You got the promotion?" Eleanor Brooks clapped her hands in sheer delight, then pressed them over her lips.

"I got it," Susannah breathed, squeezing her eyes shut. "I actually got it."

"Congratulations."

"Thank you, thank you." Already she was reaching for the phone. She had to tell Nate. Only a few days before, he'd said she should go after her dreams, and now everything was neatly falling into place.

There was no answer at his apartment and, dejected, she replaced the receiver. But the need to talk to him consumed her, and she tried again every half hour until she thought she'd go crazy.

At noon, she was absorbed in her work when Ms. Brooks announced that her luncheon date had arrived.

"Send him in," Susannah said automatically, irritated that her concentration had been broken.

Nate strolled casually into her office and plopped himself down in the chair opposite her desk.

"Nate," she cried, leaping to her feet. "I've been trying to get hold of you all morning. What are you doing here?"

"We're going out to lunch, remember?"

Chapter

8

"**N**ate!" Susannah ran around her desk until she stood directly in front of him. "John Hammer called me into his office this morning," she explained breathlessly. "I got the promotion! You're looking at the vice president in charge of marketing for H&J Lima."

For a moment Nate said nothing. Then he slowly repeated, "You got the promotion?"

"Yes," she told him. "I got it." In her enthusiasm, Susannah nodded several times, with a vigor that almost dislocated her neck. She was smiling so hard, her face ached.

Throwing back his head, Nate let out a shout that must have shaken the ceiling tile. Then he locked his arms around her waist, picked her up and swung her around, all the while howling with delight.

Susannah laughed with him. She'd never experienced joy more profoundly. The promotion hadn't seemed real to her until she'd shared it with Nate. The first person she'd thought to tell had been him. He'd become the very center of her world, and it was time to admit she was in love with him.

Nate had stopped whirling her around, but he continued to clasp her middle so that her face was elevated above his own.

Breathless with happiness, Susannah smiled down on him and on impulse buried her fingers in his hair. She couldn't resist him, not now, when she was filled with such exhilaration. Her mouth was trembling when she kissed him. She made a soft throaty sound of discovery and pleasure. Her gaze fell to the sensual lines of his mouth, and she remembered how she'd felt when he'd held and reassured her after the cookie disaster. She lowered her lips once more, lightly rocking her head back and forth, creating a friction that was so hot, she thought she'd catch fire.

In an unhurried movement, Nate lowered her to the ground and slid his arms around her. "Susannah," he moaned, kissing the corner of her mouth with exquisite care.

With a shudder, she opened her mouth to him. She wanted him to kiss her the way he had in the past. Deep, slow, moist, kisses that made her forget to breathe. She yearned for the taste and scent of him. This was the happiest moment of her life, and only a small part of it could be attributed to the promotion. Everything else was Nate and the growing love she felt for him each time they were together.

Someone coughed nervously in the background, and Nate broke off the kiss and glanced past her to the open door.

"Ms. Simmons," her assistant said, smiling broadly.

"Yes?" Breaking away from Nate, Susannah smoothed the hair at the sides of her head and struggled to replace her business facade.

"I'll be leaving now. Ms. Andrews will be answering your calls."

"Thank you, Ms. Brooks," Nate muttered, but there was little appreciation in his tone.

Susannah chastised him with a look. "We'll...I'll be leaving directly for my lunch appointment."

"I'll tell Ms. Andrews."

"This afternoon, I'd like you to call a meeting of my staff," Susannah said, "and I'll announce the promotion."

Eleanor Brooks nodded, but her smiling eyes landed heavily on Nate. "I believe everyone's already guessed from the...commotion that came from here a few minutes ago."

"I see." Susannah couldn't help smiling, too.

"There isn't an employee here who isn't happy about your news."

"I can think of two," Susannah said under her breath, considering the men she'd been competing against. Nate squeezed her hand, and she knew he'd heard her sardonic remark.

Her assistant closed the door on her way out, and
the minute she did, Nate reached for Susannah to
bring her back into the shelter of his arms. "Where
were we?"

"About to leave for lunch, as I recall."

Nate frowned. "That's not the way I remember it."

Susannah laughed and hugged him tightly. "We
both forgot ourselves for a while there." She broke
away again and reached for her purse, hooking the
long strap over her shoulder. "Are you ready?"

"Anytime you are." But the eager look in his eyes told
her he was talking about something other than lunch.

Susannah could feel the color working its way up
her neck and suffusing her face. "Nate," she whispered, "behave yourself. Please."

"I'm doing the best I can under the circumstances,"
he whispered back, his eyes filled with mischief. "In
case you haven't figured it out yet, I'm crazy about
you, woman."

"I...I'm pretty keen on you myself."

"Good." He tucked his arm around her waist and
led her out of the office and down the long hallway to
the elevator. Susannah was sure she could feel the
stares of her staff, but for the first time, she didn't care
what image she projected. Everything was right in her
world, and she'd never been happier.

Nate chose the restaurant, Il Bistro, which was one
of the best in town. The atmosphere was festive, and
playing the role of gentleman to the hilt, Nate wouldn't
allow her to even look at the menu, insisting that he'd
order for her.

"Nate," she said once the waiter had left the table, "I want to pay for this. It's a business lunch."

His thick brows arched upward. "And how are you going to rationalize *that* when your boss questions you about it, my dear?" He wiggled his eyebrows suggestively.

"There's a reason I agreed to go to lunch with you— other than celebrating my promotion, which I didn't even know about until this morning." As she'd explained to Nate earlier, her life was going to change with this promotion. New responsibility would result in a further commitment of time and energy to the company, and could drastically alter her relationship with Nate. If anything, she wanted them to grow closer, not apart. This advancement had the potential to make or break them, and Susannah was looking for a way to keep them together. She thought she'd found it.

"A reason?" Nate questioned.

They were interrupted by the waiter as he produced a bottle of expensive French wine for their inspection. He removed the cork and poured a sample into Nate's glass to taste. When Nate nodded in approval, the waiter filled their glasses and discreetly retreated.

"Now, you were saying?" Nate continued, studying her. His mouth quirked up at the edges.

Gathering her resolve, Susannah reached across the table and took Nate's hand. "You've always been open and honest with me. I want you to know how much I value that. When I asked you if you had a job, you told me you'd had one until recently and that you'd quit." She waited for him to elaborate on his circumstances, but he didn't, so she went on. "It's obvious you don't need the money, but there's something else that's obvious, too."

Nate removed his fingers from hers and twirled the stem of the wineglass between his open palms. "What's that?"

"You lack purpose."

His eyes rose to meet hers and his brow creased in query.

"You have no direction," she said. "Over the past several weeks, I've watched you flit from one interest to another. First it was baseball, then it was video games and kite flying, and tomorrow, no doubt, it'll be something completely different."

"Traveling," he concluded for her. "I was thinking of doing some serious sightseeing. I have a hankering to stroll the byways of Hong Kong."

"Hong Kong," she repeated, gesturing with one hand. "That's exactly what I mean." Her heart slowed to a sluggish beat at the thought of his being gone for any length of time. She'd become accustomed to having Nate nearby, to sharing bits and pieces of her day with him. Not only had she fallen in love with Nate Townsend, he'd quickly become her best friend.

"Do you think traveling is wrong?" he asked.

"Not wrong," she returned swiftly. "But what are you going to do once you've run out of ways to entertain yourself and places to travel? What are you going to do when you've spent all your money?"

"I'll face that when the time comes."

"I see." She lowered her gaze, wondering if she was

only making matters worse. There wasn't much she could say to counter his don't-worry attitude.

"Susannah, you make it sound like the end of the world. Trust me, wealth isn't all that great. If I run out of money, fine. If I don't, that's all right, too."

"I see," she murmured miserably.

"Why are you so worried?" he asked in a gentle voice.

"It's because I care about you, I guess." She paused to take a deep breath. "We may live in the same building, but our worlds are totally opposite. My future is charted, right down to the day I retire. I know what I want and how to get there."

"I thought I did once, too, but then I learned how unimportant it all was."

"It doesn't have to be like that," she told him, her voice filled with determination. "Listen, there's something important I'm going to propose, but I don't want you to answer me now. I want you to give yourself time to think about it. Promise me you'll at least do that."

"Are you suggesting we get married?" he teased.

"No." Flustered, she smoothed out the linen napkin in her lap, her fingers lingering there to disguise her nervousness. "I'm offering you a job."

"You're doing what?" He half rose out of his seat.

Embarrassed, Susannah glanced nervously around and noted that several people had stopped eating and were gazing in their direction. "Don't look so aghast. A job would make a lot of difference in your attitude toward life."

"And exactly what position are you offering me?" Now that the surprise had worn off, he appeared amused.

"I don't know yet. We'd have to figure something out. But I'm sure there'd be a position that would fit your qualifications."

The humor drained from his eyes, and for a long moment Nate said nothing. "You think a job would give me purpose?"

"I believe so." In her view, it would help him look beyond today and toward the future. Employment would give Nate a reason to get out of bed in the morning, instead of sleeping in until nine or ten every day.

"Susannah—"

"Before you say anything," she interrupted, holding up her hand, "I want you to think it over seriously. Don't say anything until you've had a chance to consider my offer."

His eyes were more serious than she could ever remember seeing them—other than just before he kissed her. His look was almost brooding.

Their meal arrived, and the lamb was as delicious as Nate had promised. He was unusually quiet during the remainder of the meal, but that didn't alarm her. He was reflecting on her job offer, which was exactly what she wanted. She hoped he'd come to the right decision. Loving him the way she did, she longed to make his world as right as her own.

Despite Nate's protests, Susannah paid for their lunch. He walked her back to her office, standing with her on the sidewalk while they exchanged a few words of farewell. Susannah kissed him on the cheek and asked once more that he consider her offer.

"I will," he promised, running his finger lightly down the side of her face.

He left her then, and Susannah watched as he walked away, letting her gaze linger on him for several minutes.

"Any messages?" she asked Dorothy Andrews, who was sitting in her assistant's place.

"One," Dorothy said, without looking up. "Emily—she didn't leave her full name. She said she'd catch you later."

"Thanks." Susannah went into her office and, sitting down at her desk, punched out her sister's telephone number.

"Emily, this is Susannah. You phoned?"

"I know I probably shouldn't have called you at the office, but you never seem to be home and I had something important to ask you," her sister said, talking so fast she ran her words together.

"What's that?" Already Susannah was reaching for a file, intending to read while her sister spoke. It sometimes took Emily several minutes to get around to the reason for any call.

Her sister hesitated. "I've got a bunch of zucchini left from my garden, and I was wondering if you wanted some."

"About as much as I want a migraine headache." After her disaster with the chocolate chip cookies, Susannah planned to never so much as read a recipe again.

"The zucchini are excellent," Emily prompted, as

if that would be enough to induce Susannah into agreeing to take a truckload.

Her sister hadn't phoned her to ask about zucchini; Susannah would have staked her promotion on it. That was merely a lead-in for some other request, and no doubt Susannah would have to play a guessing game. Mentally, she scanned a list of possible favors and decided to jump in with both feet.

"Zucchini are out, but I wouldn't mind looking after Michelle again, if you need me to."

"Oh, Susannah, would you? I mean, it'd work out so well if you could take her two weeks from this Saturday."

"All night?" As much as she loved her niece, another overnight stretch was more than Susannah wanted to contemplate. Still, Nate would probably be more than willing to lend a hand. No doubt she'd need it.

"Oh, no, not for the night, just for dinner. Robert's boss is taking us out to eat, and it wouldn't be appropriate if we brought Michelle along. Robert got a big promotion."

"Congratulate him for me, okay?"

"I'm so proud of him," Emily said. "I think he must be the best accountant in Seattle."

Susannah toyed with the idea of letting her sister in on her own big news, but she didn't want to take anything away from her brother-in-law. She could tell them both in two weeks when they dropped off Michelle.

"I'll be happy to keep Michelle for you," Susannah said, and discovered, as she marked the date on her calendar, how much she actually meant that. She might be a disaster waiting to happen in the kitchen, but she didn't do half badly with her niece. The time might yet come when she'd consider having a child of her own— not now, of course, but sometime in the future. "All right, I've got you down for the seventeenth."

"Susannah, I can't tell you how much this means to me," Emily said.

When Susannah arrived home that evening she was tipsy. The staff meeting that afternoon had gone wonderfully well. After five, she'd been taken out for a drink by her two top aides, to celebrate. Several others from her section had unexpectedly dropped by the cocktail lounge and insisted on buying her drinks, too. By seven, Susannah was flushed and excited, and from experience, she knew it was time to call it quits and phone for a taxi.

Dinner probably would have cut the effects of the alcohol, but she was more interested in getting home. After a nice hot bath, she'd fix herself some toast and be done with it.

She hadn't been back more than half an hour when her phone rang. Dressed in her robe and sipping tea in the kitchen, she grabbed the receiver.

"Susannah, it's Nate. Can I come over?"

Glancing down at her robe and fuzzy slippers, she decided it wouldn't take her long to change.

"Give me five minutes."

"All right."

Dressed in slacks and a sweater, she opened the

door at his knock. "Hi," she said cheerfully, aware that her mouth had probably formed a crooked grin despite her efforts to smile naturally.

Nate barely looked at her. His hands were thrust deep in his pockets, and his expression was disgruntled as he marched into her apartment. He didn't take a seat but paced the carpet in front of her fireplace. Obviously something was going on.

She sat on the edge of the sofa, watching him, feeling more than a little reckless and exhilarated from her promotion and the celebration afterward. She was amused, too, at Nate's peculiar agitation.

"I suppose you want to talk to me about the job offer," she said, surprised by how controlled her voice sounded.

He paused, splayed his fingers through his thick hair and nodded. "That's exactly what I want to talk about."

"Don't," she said, smiling up at him.

His forehead puckered in a frown. "Why not?"

"Because I'd like you to give long and careful consideration to the proposal."

"I need to explain something to you first."

Susannah wasn't listening. There were far more important things she had to tell him. "You're personable, bright and attractive," she began enthusiastically. "You could be anything you wanted, Nate. Anything."

"Susannah..."

She waved a finger at him and shook her head. "There's something else you should know."

"What?" he demanded.

"I'm in love with you." Her glorious confession was followed by a loud yawn. Unnerved, she covered her mouth with the tips of her fingers. "Oops, sorry."

Nate's eyes narrowed suspiciously. "Have you been drinking?"

She pressed her thumb and index finger together and held them up for his inspection. "Just a little, but I'm more happy than anything else."

"Susannah!" He dragged her name out into the sigh. "I can't believe you."

"Why not? Do you want me to shout it to all of Seattle? Because I will. Watch!" She waltzed into the kitchen and jerked open the sliding glass door.

Actually, some of the alcohol had worn off, but she experienced this irrepressible urge to tell Nate how much she'd come to care for him. They'd skirted around the subject long enough. He didn't seem to want to admit it, but she did, especially now, fortified as she was with her good fortune. This day had been one of the most fantastic of her life. After years of hard work, everything was falling into place, and she'd found the most wonderful man in the world to love— even if he *was* misguided.

The wind whipped against her on the balcony, and the multicolored lights from the waterfront below resembled those on a Christmas tree. Standing at the railing, she cupped her hands around her mouth and shouted, "I love Nate Townsend!" Satisfied, she whirled to face him and opened her arms as wide as she could. "See? I announced it to the world."

He joined her outside and slid his arms around her

and closed his eyes. Susannah had expected him to show at least *some* emotion.

"You don't look very happy about it," she challenged.

"You're not yourself," he said as he released her.

"Then who am I?" Fists digging into her hips, she glared up at him, her eyes defiant. "I feel like me. I bet you think I'm drunk, but I'm not."

He didn't reply. Instead he threw an arm over her shoulder and urged her into the kitchen. Then, quickly and efficiently, he started to make coffee.

"I gave up caffeine," she muttered.

"When was this? You had regular coffee today at lunch," he said.

"Just now." She giggled. "Come on, Nate," she cried, bending forward and snapping her fingers. "Loosen up."

"I'm more concerned about sobering *you* up."

"You could kiss me."

"I could," he agreed, "but I'm not going to."

"Why not?" She pouted, disappointed by his refusal.

"Because if I do, I may not be able to stop."

Sighing, she closed her eyes. "That's the most romantic thing you've ever said to me."

Nate rubbed his face and leaned against the kitchen counter. "Have you had anything to eat since lunch?"

"One stuffed mushroom, a water chestnut wrapped in a slice of bacon and a piece of celery filled with cheese."

"But no dinner?"

"I was going to make myself some toast, but I wasn't hungry."

"After a stuffed mushroom, a celery stick and a water chestnut? I can see why not."

"Are you trying to be cute with me? Oh, just a minute, there was something I was supposed to ask you." She pulled herself up short and covered one eye, while she tugged at her memory for the date her sister had mentioned. "Are you doing anything on the seventeenth?"

"The seventeenth? Why?"

"Michelle's coming over to visit her auntie Susannah and I know she'll want to see you, too."

Nate looked even more disturbed, but he hadn't seemed particularly pleased about anything from the moment he'd arrived.

"I've got something else that night."

"Oh, well, I'll make do. I have before." She stopped abruptly. "No, I guess I haven't, but Michelle and I'll be just fine, I think..."

The coffee had finished dripping into the glass pot. Nate poured a cup and, scowling, handed it to her.

"Oh, Nate, what's wrong with you? You've been cranky since you got here. We should be kissing by now and all you seem to do is ignore me."

"Drink your coffee."

He stood over her until she'd taken the first sip. She grimaced at the heat. "You know what I drank tonight? I've never had them before and they tasted so good. Shanghai Slungs."

"They're called Singapore Slings."

"Oh." Maybe she was more confused than she thought.

"Come on, drink up, Tokyo Rose."

Obediently Susannah did as he said. The whole time she was sipping her coffee, she was watching Nate, who moved restlessly about her kitchen, as if unable to stand still. He was disturbed about something, and she wished she knew what.

"Done," she announced when she'd finished her coffee, pleased with herself and this minor accomplishment. "Nate," she said, growing concerned, "do you love me?"

He turned around to face her, his eyes serious. "So much I can't believe it myself."

"Oh, good," she said with an expressive sigh. "I was beginning to wonder."

"Where are your aspirin?" He was searching through her cupboards, opening and closing the ones closest to the sink.

"My aspirin? Did telling me how you feel give you a headache?"

"No." He answered her with a gentle smile. "I want to have it ready for you in the morning because you're going to need it."

Her love for him increased tenfold. "You are so thoughtful!"

"Take two tablets when you wake up. That should help." He crouched in front of her and took both her hands in his. "I'm leaving tomorrow and I won't be back for a couple of days. I'll call you, all right?"

"You're going away to think about my job offer, aren't you? That's a good idea—when you come back

you can tell me your decision." She was forced to stop
in order to yawn, a huge jaw-breaking yawn that
depleted her strength. "I think I should go to bed,
don't you?"

The next thing Susannah knew, her alarm was buzzing
angrily. With the noise came a piercing pain that shot
straight through her temple. She groped for the clock,
turned it off and sighed with relief. Sitting up in bed
proved to be equally overwhelming and she groaned.

When she'd managed to maneuver herself into the
kitchen, she saw the aspirin bottle and remembered
that Nate had insisted on setting it out the night
before.

"Bless that man," she said aloud and winced at the
sound of her own voice.

By the time she arrived at the office, she was oper-
ating on only three cylinders. Eleanor Brooks didn't
seem to be any better off than Susannah was. They
took one look at each other and smiled knowingly.

"Your coffee's ready," her assistant informed her.

"Did you have a cup yourself?"

"Yes."

"Anything in the mail?"

"Nothing that can't wait. Mr. Hammer was in
earlier. He told me to give you this magazine and said
you'd be as impressed as he was." Susannah glanced at
the six-year-old issue of *Business Monthly*, a trade
magazine that was highly respected in the industry.

"It's several years old," Susannah noted, wondering why her employer would want her to read it now.

"Mr. Hammer said there was a special feature in there about your friend."

"My friend?" Susannah didn't understand.

"Your friend," Eleanor Brooks repeated. "The one with the sexy eyes—Nathaniel Townsend."

Susannah waited until Eleanor had left the office before opening the magazine. The article on Nathaniel Townsend was the lead feature. The picture showed a much younger Nate standing in front of a shopping-mall outlet for Rainy Day Cookies, the most successful cookie chain in the country. He was holding a huge chocolate chip cookie.

Rainy Day Cookies were Susannah's absolute favorite. There were several varieties, but the chocolate chip ones were fantastic.

Two paragraphs into the article, Susannah thought she was going to be physically ill. She stopped reading and closed her eyes to the waves of nausea that lapped against her. Pressing a hand to her stomach, she resolutely focused her attention on the article, storing away the details of Nate's phenomenal success in her numb mind.

He had started his cookie company in his mother's kitchen while still in college. His specialty was chocolate chip cookies, and they were so popular, he soon found himself caught up in a roller-coaster ride that had led him straight to the top of the corporate world. By age twenty-eight, Nate Townsend was a multimillionaire.

Now that she thought about it, an article she'd read six or seven months ago in the same publication had said the company was recently sold for an undisclosed sum, which several experts had estimated to be a figure so staggering Susannah had gasped out loud.

Bracing her elbows on the desk, Susannah took several calming breaths. She'd made a complete idiot of herself over Nate, and worse, he had let her. She suspected this humiliation would stay with her for the rest of her life.

To think she'd baked the cookie king of the world chocolate chip cookies, and in the process nearly set her kitchen on fire. But that degradation couldn't compare to yesterday's little pep talk when she'd spoken to him about drive, ambition and purpose, before—dear heaven, it was too much—she'd offered him a job. How he must have laughed at that.

Eleanor Brooks brought in the mail and laid it on the corner of Susannah's desk. Susannah looked up at her and knew then and there that she wasn't going to be able to cope with the business of the day.

"I'm going home."

"I beg your pardon?"

"If anyone needs me, tell them I'm home sick."

"But..."

Susannah knew she'd shocked her assistant. In all the years she'd been employed by H&J Lima, Susannah had never used a single day of her sick leave. There'd been a couple of times she probably *should* have stayed home, but she'd insisted on working anyway.

"I'll see you Monday morning," she said on her way out the door.

"I hope you're feeling better then."

"I'm sure I will be." She needed some time alone to lick her wounds and gather the scattered pieces of her pride. To think that only a few hours earlier she'd drunkenly declared her undying love to Nate Townsend!

That was the worst of it.

When Susannah walked into her apartment she felt as if she was stumbling into a bomb shelter. For the moment she was hidden from the world outside. Eventually she'd have to go back and face it, but for now she was safe.

She picked up the afghan her sister had crocheted for her, wrapped it around her shoulders and sat staring sightlessly into space.

What an idiot she'd been! What a fool! Closing her eyes, she leaned her head against the back of the sofa and drew in several deep breaths, releasing the anger and hurt before it fermented into bitterness. She refused to dwell on the might-have-beens and the if-onlys, opting instead for a more positive approach. *Next time*, she would know enough not to involve her heart. *Next time*, she'd take care not to make such a fool of herself.

It astonished her when she awoke an hour later to realize she'd fallen asleep. Tucking the blanket more securely around her, she analyzed her situation.

Things weren't so bad. She'd achieved her primary goal and was vice president in charge of marketing. The first female in the company's long history to hold such a distinguished position, she reminded herself. Her life was good. If on occasion she felt the yearning for a family of her own, there was always Emily, who was more than willing to share. Heaving a sigh, Susannah told herself that she lacked for nothing. She was respected, hardworking and healthy. Yes, life was good.

Her head ached and her stomach didn't feel much better, but at noon, Susannah heated some chicken noodle soup and forced that down. She was putting the bowl in the dishwasher when the telephone rang. Ms. Brooks was the only one who knew she was home, and her assistant would call her only if it was important. Susannah answered the phone just as she would in her office.

"Susannah Simmons."

"Susannah, it's Nate."

She managed to swallow a gasp. "Hello, Nate," she said as evenly as possible. "What can I do for you."

"I called the office and your assistant said you'd gone home sick."

"Yes. I guess I had more to drink last night than I realized. I had one doozy of a hangover when I woke up this morning." But she didn't add how her malady had worsened once she read the article about him.

"Did you find the aspirin on the kitchen counter?"

"Yes. Now that I think about it, you were by last night, weren't you?" She was thinking fast, wanting to cover her tracks. "I suppose I made a fool of myself," she said, instilling a lightness in her tone. "I didn't say anything to embarrass you—or me, did I?"

He chuckled softly. "You don't remember?"

She did, but she wasn't going to admit it. "Some of it, but most of the evening's kind of fuzzy."

"Once I'm back in Seattle I'll help you recall every single word." His voice was low, seductive and filled with promise.

That was one guarantee, however, that Susannah had no intention of accepting.

"I...probably made a complete idiot of myself," she mumbled. "If I were you, I'd forget anything I said. Obviously, I can't be held responsible for it."

"Susannah, Susannah, Susannah," Nate said gently. "Let's take this one step at a time."

"I...think we should talk about it later, I really do...because it's all too obvious I wasn't myself." Tears pooled at the corners of her eyes. Furious at this display of emotion, she wiped them aside with the back of her hand.

"You're feeling okay now?"

"Yes...no. I was about to lie down."

"Then I'll let you," Nate said. "I'll be back Sunday. My flight should arrive early afternoon. I'd like us to have dinner together."

"Sure," she said, without thinking, willing to agree to just about anything in order to end this conversation. She was still too raw, still bleeding. By Sunday, she'd be able to handle the situation far more effectively. By Sunday, she could disguise her pain.

"I'll see you around five then."

"Sunday," she echoed, feeling like a robot programmed to do exactly as its master requested. She had no intention of having dinner with Nate, none whatsoever. He'd find out why soon enough.

The only way Susannah made it through Saturday was by working. She went to her office and sorted through the mail Ms. Brooks had left on her desk. News of her promotion was to be announced in the Sunday business section of the *Seattle Times*, but apparently word had already leaked out, probably through her boss; there was a speaking invitation in the mail, for a luncheon at a conference of local salespeople who had achieved a high level of success. The request was an honor and Susannah sent a note of acceptance to the organizer. She considered it high praise to have been asked. The date of the conference was the seventeenth, which was only two weeks away, so she spent a good part of the morning making notes for her speech.

On Sunday, Susannah woke feeling sluggish and out of sorts. She recognized the source of her discomfort almost instantly. This afternoon, she would confront Nate. For the past two days, she'd gone over in her mind exactly what she planned to say, how she'd act.

Nate arrived at four-thirty. She answered his knock, dressed in navy blue slacks and a cream shell-knit sweater. Her hair was neatly rolled into a chignon.

"Susannah." His gaze was hungry as he stepped across the threshold and reached for her.

It was too late to hide her reaction by the time she realized he intended to kiss her. He swept her into his arms and eagerly pressed his mouth over hers. Despite everything that he'd failed to tell her, Susannah felt an immediate excitement she couldn't disguise.

Nate slipped his fingers into her hair, removing the pins that held it in place, while he leisurely moved his mouth over hers.

"Two days have never seemed so long," he breathed, then nibbled on her lower lip.

Regaining her composure, she broke away, her shoulders heaving. "Would you like some coffee?"

"No. The only thing I want is you."

She started to walk away from him, but Nate caught her, hauling her back into the warm shelter of his arms. He linked his hands at the small of her back and gazed down at her, his eyes soft and caressing. Gradually, his expression altered.

"Is everything all right?" he asked.

"Yes...and no," she admitted dryly. "I happened upon an article in an old issue of *Business Monthly*. Does that tell you anything?"

He hesitated, and for a moment Susannah wondered if he was going to say anything or not.

"So you know?"

"That you're the world's cookie king, or once were— yes, I know."

His eyes narrowed slightly. "Are you angry?"

She sighed. A good deal depended on her delivery, and although she'd practiced her response several times, it was more difficult than she'd expected. She was determined, however, to remain calm and casual.

"I'm more embarrassed than amused," she said. "I wish you'd said something before I made such a fool of myself."

"Susannah, you have every right to be upset." He let her go and rubbed the back of his neck as he began to walk back and forth between the living room and kitchen. "It isn't like it was a deep dark secret. I sold the business almost six months ago, and I was taking a sabbatical—hell, I needed one. I'd driven myself as far as I could. My doctor thinks I was on the verge of a complete physical collapse. When I met you, I was just coming out of it, learning how to enjoy life again. The last thing I wanted to do was sit down and talk about the past thirteen years. I'd put Rainy Day Cookies behind me, and I was trying to build a new life."

Susannah crossed her arms. "Did you ever intend to tell me?"

"Yes!" he said vehemently. "Thursday. You were so sweet to have offered me a job and I knew I had to say something then, but you were..."

"Tipsy," she finished for him.

"All right, tipsy. You have to understand why I didn't. The timing was all wrong."

"You must have got a good laugh from the cookie disaster," she said, surprised at how steady her voice remained. Her poise didn't even slip, and she was proud of herself.

The edges of his mouth quivered, and it was apparent that he was struggling not to laugh.

"Go ahead," she said, waving her hand dramatically. "I suppose those charred cookies and the smoldering cookie sheets were pretty comical. I don't blame you. I'd probably be in hysterics if the situation were reversed."

"It isn't that. The fact that you made those cookies was one of the sweetest things anyone's ever done for me. I want you to know I was deeply touched."

"I didn't do it for you," she said, struggling to keep the anger out of her voice. "It was a trial by fire—" Hearing what she'd said, Susannah closed her eyes.

"Susannah—"

"You must've got a real kick out of that little pep talk I gave you the other day, too. Imagine *me* talking to *you* about drive, motivation and goals."

"That touched me, too," he insisted.

"Right on the funny bone, I'll bet." She faked a laugh herself just to prove what a good sport she was. Still, she wasn't exactly keen on being the brunt of one.

Nate paused, then gestured at her. "I suppose it looks bad considered from your point of view."

"Looks bad," she echoed, with a short hysterical laugh. "That's one way of putting it!"

Nate strode from one end of the room to the other. If he didn't stop soon, he was going to wear a path in the carpet.

"Are you willing to put this misunderstanding behind us, Susannah, or are you going to hold it against me? Are you willing to ruin what we have over a mistake?"

"I don't know yet." Actually she did, but she didn't want him to accuse her of making snap decisions. It would be so easy for Nate to talk his way out of this. But Susannah had been humiliated. How could she possibly trust him now? He'd thought nothing of hiding an important portion of his life from her.

"How long will it be before you come to a conclusion about us?"

"I don't know that, either."

"I guess dinner is out?"

She nodded, her face muscles so tight, they ached.

"Okay, think everything through. I trust you to be completely fair and unbiased. All I want you to do is ask yourself one thing. If the situation were reversed, how would you have handled it?"

"All right." She'd grant him that much, although she already knew what she would have done—and it wasn't keep up a charade the way he had.

"There's something else I want you to think about," he said when she held open the door for him.

"What?" Susannah was frantic to get him out of her home. The longer he stayed, the more difficult it was to remain angry with him.

"This." He kissed her then and it was the type of kiss that drove to the very depths of her soul. His mouth on hers was hot, the kiss deep and moist and so filled with longing that her knees almost buckled. Tiny sounds interrupted the moment, and Susannah realized she was the one making them.

When Nate released her, she backed away and nearly stumbled. Breathing hard, she leaned against the doorframe and heaved in giant gulps of oxygen.

Satisfied, Nate smiled infuriatingly. "Admit it, Susannah," he whispered and ran his index finger over her collarbone. "We were meant for each other."

"I...I'm not willing to admit anything."

His expression looked forlorn. It was no doubt calculated to evoke sympathy, but it wouldn't work. Susannah wouldn't be fooled a second time.

"You'll phone me?" he pressed.

"Yes." When the moon was in the seventh house, which should be somewhere around the time the government balanced the budget. Perhaps a decade from now.

For two days, Susannah's life returned to a more normal routine. She went in to the office early and worked late, doing everything she could to avoid Nate, although she was sure he'd wait patiently for some signal from her. After all, he, too, had his pride; she was counting on that.

When she arrived home on Wednesday, there was a folded note taped to her door. Susannah stared at it for several thundering heartbeats, then finally reached for it.

She waited until she'd put her dinner in the microwave before she read it. Her heart was pounding painfully hard as she opened the sheet and saw three words: "Call me. Please."

Susannah gave a short hysterical laugh. Ha! Nate Townsend could tumble into a vat of melted chocolate chips before she'd call him again. Guaranteed he'd say or do something that would remind her of what a fool she'd been! And yet... Damn, but it was hard to stay angry with him!

When the phone rang she was still ambivalent. Jumping back, she glared at it before answering.

"Hello," she said cautiously, quaveringly.

"Susannah? Is that you?"

"Oh, hi, Emily."

"Good grief, you scared me. I thought you were sick. You sounded so weak."

"No. No, I'm fine."

"I hadn't talked to you in a while and I was wondering how you were doing."

"Fine," she repeated.

"Susannah!" Her sister's tone made her name sound like a warning. "I know you well enough to realize something's wrong. I also know it probably has to do with Nate. You haven't mentioned him the last few times we've talked, but before you seemed to be overflowing with things you wanted to say about him."

"I'm not seeing much of Nate these days."

"Why not?"

"Well, being a multimillionaire keeps him busy."

Emily paused to gulp in a breath, then gasped, "I think there must be a problem with the phone. I thought you just said—"

"Ever been to Rainy Day Cookies?"

"Of course. Hasn't everyone?"

"Have you made the connection yet?"

"You mean Nate…"

"…is Mr. Chocolate Chip himself."

"But that's marvelous! That's wonderful. Why, he's famous…I mean his cookies are. To think that the man who developed Rainy Day Cookies actually helped Robert carry out Michelle's crib. I can't wait until he hears this."

"Personally, I wasn't all that impressed." It was difficult to act indifferent when her sister was bubbling over with such enthusiasm. Emily usually only got excited about something organic.

"When did you find out?" Emily asked, her voice almost accusing, as if Susannah had been holding out on her.

"Last Friday. John Hammer gave me a magazine that had an article about Nate in it. The issue was a few years old, but the article told me everything Nate should have."

A brief sound of exclamation followed. "So you just found out?"

"Right."

"And you're angry with him?"

"Good heavens, no. Why should I be?" Susannah was afraid Emily wouldn't appreciate the sarcasm.

"He probably planned on telling you," Emily argued, defending Nate. "I don't know him all that well, but he seemed straightforward enough to me. I'm sure he intended to explain the situation when the time was right."

"Perhaps," Susannah said, but as far as she was concerned, that consolation was too little, too late. "Listen, I've got something in the microwave, so I've got to scoot." The excuse was feeble, but Susannah didn't want to continue discussing Nate. "Oh, before I forget," she added quickly. "I've got a speaking engagement on the seventeenth, but I'll be finished before five-thirty so you can count on me watching Michelle."

"Great. Listen, if you want to talk, I'm always here. I mean that. What are sisters for if not to talk?"

"Thanks, I'll remember that."

Once she replaced the receiver, Susannah was left to deal, once more, with Nate's three-word note. By all rights, she should crumple it up and toss it in the garbage. She did, feeling a small—very small—sense of satisfaction.

Out of sight, out of mind, or so the old adage went. Only this time it wasn't working. Whenever she turned around, the sight of the telephone seemed to pull at her.

Her dinner was ready, but as she gazed down at the unappetizing entrée, she considered throwing it out and going to the Western Avenue Deli for a pastrami on rye instead. That would serve two purposes; first, it would take her away from the phone, which seemed to be luring her to its side; and second, she'd at least have a decent meal.

Having made her decision, she was already in the living room when there was a knock at the door. Susannah groaned, knowing even before she answered it that her visitor had to be Nate.

"You didn't call," he snapped the minute she opened the door.

He stormed inside without waiting for an invitation, looking irritated but in control. "Just how long were you planning to keep me waiting? It's obvious you're going to make me pay for the error of my ways, which to a certain point I can understand. But we've gone well past that point. So what are you waiting for? An apology? Okay—I'm sorry."

"Ah—"

"You have every reason to be upset, but what do you want? Blood? Enough is enough. I'm crazy about you, Susannah, and you feel the same about me, so don't try to fool me with this indifference routine, because I can see right through it. Let's put this foolishness behind us and get back on track."

"Why?" she demanded.

"Why what?"

"Why did you wait to tell me? Why couldn't you have said something sooner?"

He gave her a frown that suggested they were rehashing old news, then started his usual pacing. "Because I wanted to put Rainy Day Cookies out of my mind. I'd made the business my entire world." He stopped and whirled to face her. "I recognized a kindred spirit in you. Your entire life is wrapped up in some sporting goods company—"

"Not just *some* sporting goods company" she returned, indignant. "H&J Lima is the largest in the country."

"Forgive me, Susannah, but that doesn't really impress me. What about your *life?* Your whole world revolves around how far you can climb up the corporate ladder. Let me tell you that once you're at the top, the view isn't all that great. You forget what it means to appreciate the simple things in life. I did."

"Are you telling me to stop and smell the flowers? Well, I've got news for you, Nate Townsend. I like my life just the way it is. I consider it insulting that you think you can casually walk into my world and my career and tell me I'm headed down the road to destruction, because I'll tell you right now—" she paused to take a deep breath "—I don't appreciate it."

Nate's expression tightened. "I'm not talking about flowers, Susannah. I want you to look out this window at Puget Sound and see the lovely view with ferryboats and snowcapped mountains. Life, abundant life, is more than that. It's meaningful relationships. Connecting with other people. Friends. Fun. We'd both lost sight of that. It happened to me first, and I can see you going in the same direction."

"That's fine for you, but I—"

"You need the same things I do. We need each other."

"Correction," she said heatedly. "As I told you, I like my life just the way it is, thank you. And why shouldn't I? My five-year goals have been achieved, and there are more in the making. I can go straight to the top with this company, and that's exactly what I want. As for needing relationships, you're wrong about that, too. I got along fine before I met you, and the same will be true when you're out of my life."

The room went so still that for a second Susannah was convinced Nate had stopped breathing.

"*When* I'm out of your life," he echoed. "I see. So you've made your decision."

"Yes," she said, holding her head high. "It was fun while it lasted, but if I had to choose between you and the vice presidency, the decision wouldn't be difficult at all. I'm sure you'll encounter some other young woman who needs to be saved from herself and her goals. As far as I can see, from your perspective our relationship was more of a rescue mission. Now that you know how the cookie crumbles—the pun's intended—perhaps you'll leave me to my sorry lot."

"Susannah, would you listen to me?"

"No." She held up her hand for effect. "I'll try to be happy," she said, a heavy note of mockery in her voice.

For a moment, Nate said nothing. "You're making a mistake, but that's something you're going to have to learn on your own."

"I suppose you're planning on being around to pick up the pieces when I fall apart?"

His blue eyes bored into hers. "I might be, but then again, I might not."

"Well, you needn't worry, because either way, you've got a long wait."

"Ms. Simmons, Mr. Hammer, it's an honor to meet you."

"Thank you," Susannah said, smiling politely at the young man who'd been sent to greet her and her boss. The Seattle Convention Center was filled to capacity. The moment Susannah realized her audience was going to be so large, her stomach was attacked by a bad case of nerves. Not the most pleasant conditions under which to be eating lunch.

"If you'll come this way, I'll show you to the head table."

Susannah and John Hammer followed the young executive toward the front of the crowded room. There were several other people already seated on the stage. Susannah recognized the mayor and a couple of city councillors, along with the King County executive and two prominent local businessmen.

She was assigned the chair to the right of the podium. John was assigned the place beside her. After shaking hands with the conference coordinator, she greeted the others and took her seat. Almost immediately, the caterers started serving lunch, which consisted of an elegantly prepared salad tossed with a raspberry vinaigrette, wild rice and broiled fresh salmon with a teriyaki glaze.

She didn't think she could manage even a bite while sitting in front of so many people. Glancing out over the sea of unfamiliar faces, she forced herself to remain calm and collected. She was, after all, one of the featured speakers for the afternoon, and she'd come well prepared.

There was a slight commotion to her right, but the podium blocked her view.

"Hi, gorgeous. No one told me you were going to be here."

Nate. Susannah nearly swallowed her forkful of salmon whole. It stuck in her throat and she would've choked had she not reached for her water and hurriedly gulped some down.

Twisting around in her chair, she came eye to eye with him. "Hello, Nate," she said as nonchalantly as she could. Her smile was firmly in place.

"I thought Nate Townsend might be here," John whispered, looking pleased with himself.

"I see you've taken to following me around now," Nate taunted as he took his seat, two chairs down from John's.

Susannah ignored his comment and both men, studiously returning to her salmon, hoping to suggest that her meal was far more appealing than their conversation.

"Have you missed me?"

It was ten agonizing days since she'd last seen Nate. Avoiding him hadn't been easy. He'd made sure of that. The first night she'd come home to an Italian opera played just loud enough to be heard through her kitchen wall. The sound of the music was accompanied by the tangy scent of his homemade spaghetti sauce. The aroma of simmering tomatoes and herbs mingled with the pungent scent of hot garlic and butter.

Evidently Nate assumed the way to *her* heart was through her stomach. She'd nearly succumbed then, but her conviction was strong and she'd hurried to a favorite Italian restaurant to alleviate her sudden craving for pasta.

By the weekend, Susannah could've sworn Nate had whipped up every recipe in an entire cookbook, each one more enticing than the last. Susannah had never eaten as many restaurant meals as she had in the past week.

When Nate realized she couldn't be bought so easily with fine food, wine and song, he'd tried another tactic, this one less subtle.

A single red rose was waiting outside her door when she arrived home from the office. There wasn't any note with it, just a perfect fresh flower. She picked it up and against her better judgment took it inside with her, inhaling the delicate scent. The only person who

could have left it was Nate. Then, in a flurry of righteousness, she'd taken the rose and put it back where
she found it. Five minutes later, she jerked open her
door and to her dismay discovered the flower was still
there, looking forlorn and dejected.

Deciding to send him her own less than subtle
message, Susannah dropped the rose outside Nate's
door. She hoped he'd understand once and for all that
she refused to be bought!

Nate, however, wasn't dissuaded. The rose was
followed the next evening by a small box of luscious
chocolates. This time Susannah didn't even bring
them inside, but marched them directly to Nate's
door.

"No," she said now, forcing her thoughts back to
the present and the conference. She surveyed the
crowded, noisy room. "I haven't missed you in the
least."

"You haven't?" He looked dashed. "But I thought
you were trying to make it up to me. Why else would
you leave those gifts outside my door?"

For just a second her heart thumped wildly. Then she
gave him a fiery glare and diligently resumed her meal,
making sure she downed every bite. If she didn't, Nate
would think she was lovesick for want of him.

Her boss tilted his head toward her, obviously
pleased with himself. "I thought it would be a nice
surprise for you to be speaking with Nate. Fact is, I
arranged it myself."

"How thoughtful," Susannah murmured.

"You have missed me, haven't you?" Nate asked

again, balancing on two legs of his chair in an effort
to see her.

Okay, she was willing to admit she'd been a bit
lonely, but that was to be expected. For several weeks,
Nate had filled every spare moment of her time with
silliness like baseball games and kite flying. But she'd
lived a perfectly fine life before she met him, and now
she'd gone back to that same serene lifestyle without
a qualm. Her world was wonderful. Complete. She
didn't need him to make her a whole person. Nate was
going to a lot of trouble to force her to admit she was
miserable without him. She wasn't about to do that.

"I miss you," he said, batting his baby blues at her.
"The least you could do is concede that you're as lonely
and miserable as me."

"But I'm not," she answered sweetly, silently ac-
knowledging the lie. "I have a fantastic job and a
promising career. What else could I want?"

"Children?"

She leaned forward and spoke across the people
between them. "Michelle and I have loads of fun
together, and when we get bored with each other, she
goes home to her mother. In my opinion that's the
perfect way to enjoy a child."

The first speaker approached the podium, and
Susannah's attention was diverted to him. He was five
minutes into his greeting when Susannah felt something hit her arm. She darted a glance at Nate, who
was holding up a white linen napkin. *"What about a
husband?"* was inked across the polished cloth.

Groaning, Susannah prayed no one else had seen

his note, especially her boss. She rolled her eyes and emphatically shook her head. It was then that she noticed how everyone was applauding and looking in her direction. She blinked, not understanding, until she realized that she'd just been introduced and they were waiting for her to stand up and give her talk.

Scraping back her chair, she stood abruptly and approached the podium, not daring to look at Nate. The man was infuriating! A lesser woman would have dumped the contents of her water glass over his smug head. Instead of venting her irritation, she drew in a deep calming breath and gazed out over her audience. That was a mistake. There were so many faces, and they all had their eyes trained on her.

Her talk had been carefully planned and memorized. But to be on the safe side, she'd brought the typed sheets with her. She had three key points she intended to share, and had illustrated each one with several anecdotes. Suddenly her mind was blank. It took all her courage not to bolt and run from the stage.

"Go get 'em, Susannah," Nate mouthed, smiling up at her.

His eyes were so full of encouragement and faith that the paralysis started to leave her. Although she'd memorized her speech, she stared down at the written version. The instant she read the first sentence she knew she was going to be fine.

For the next twenty minutes she spoke about the importance of indelibly marking a goal on one's mind and how to minimize difficulties and maximize strengths. She closed by explaining the significance of building a mental ladder to one's dreams. She talked about using determination, discipline, dedication and demeanor as the rungs of this ladder to success.

Despite Nate's earlier efforts to undermine her dignity and poise, she was pleased by the way her speech was received. Many of her listeners nodded at key points in her talk, and Susannah knew she was reaching them. When she came to the end, she felt good, satisfied with her speech and with herself.

As she turned to go back to her seat, her gaze caught Nate's. He was smiling as he applauded, and the gleam in his eyes was unmistakably one of respect and admiration. The warm, caressing look he sent her nearly tripped her heart into overdrive. Yet he'd maddened her with his senseless questions, distracted her, teased and taunted her with his craziness and then written a note on a napkin. But when she finished her speech, the first person she'd looked at, whether consciously or unconsciously, was Nate.

Once Susannah was seated, she saw that her hands were trembling. But she couldn't be sure if it was a release from the tension that had gripped her when she first started to speak, or the result of Nate's tender look.

Nate was introduced next, and he walked casually to the podium. It would serve him right, Susannah thought, if she started writing messages on her napkin and holding them up for him to read while he gave his talk. She was immediately shocked by the childishness of the idea. Five minutes with Nate seemed to reduce her mentality to that of a ten-year-old.

With a great deal of ceremony, or so it seemed to Susannah, Nate retrieved his notes from inside his suit jacket. It was all she could do to keep from laughing out loud when she saw that everything he planned to say had been jotted on the back of a single index card. So this was how seriously he'd taken that afternoon's address. It looked as if he'd scribbled a couple of notes while she was delivering her speech. He hadn't given his lecture a second thought until five minutes before he was supposed to stand at the podium.

But Nate proved her wrong, as seemed to be his habit. The minute he opened his mouth, he had the audience in the palm of his hand. Rarely had she heard a more dynamic speaker. His strong voice carried to the farthest corners of the huge hall, and although he used the microphone, Susannah doubted he really needed it.

Nate told of his own beginnings, of how his father had died the year he was to enter college, so that the funds he'd expected to further his education were no longer available. It was the lowest point of his life and out of it had come his biggest success. Then he explained that his mother's chocolate chip cookies had always been everyone's favorite. Because of his father's untimely death, she'd taken a job in a local factory, and Nate, eager to find a way to attend university in the fall, had started baking the cookies and selling them to tourists for fifty cents each.

Halfway through the summer he'd made more

than enough money to see him through his first year of school. Soon a handful of local delis had contacted him, wanting to include his cookies as part of their menus. These requests were followed by others from restaurants and hotels.

Nate went to school that first year and took every business course available to him. By the end of the following summer, he had set up a kitchen with his mother's help and opened his own business, which thrived despite his mistakes. The rest was history. By the time he graduated from college, Nate was already a millionaire and his mother was able to retire comfortably. To his credit, he'd resisted the temptation to abandon his education. It had served him well since, and he was glad he'd stuck with it, even though everyone around him seemed to be saying he knew more, from personal experience, than most of the authors of the textbooks did. A fact he was quick to dispute.

Susannah was enthralled. She'd assumed Nate would be telling this audience what he'd been beating her over the head with from the moment they'd met—that the drive to succeed was all well and good, but worthless if in the process one forgot to enjoy life. However, if that thought was on Nate's mind, he didn't voice it. Susannah suspected he'd reserved that philosophy for her and her alone.

When he returned to his seat, the applause was thunderous. The first thing he did was look at Susannah, who smiled softly, as touched by his story as the rest of the audience was. Not once had he patted himself on the back, or taken credit for the phenomenal success of

Rainy Day Cookies. Susannah would almost have preferred it if his talk had been a boring rambling account
of his prosperous career. She didn't want to feel so much
admiration for him. It would be easier to get Nate out
of her life and her mind if she didn't.

The luncheon ended a few minutes later. Gathering
up her things, Susannah hoped to make a speedy escape.
She should've known Nate wouldn't allow that. Several
people had hurried up to the podium to talk to him, but
he excused himself and moved to her side.

"Susannah, could we talk for a minute?"

She made a show of glancing at her watch, then at her
boss. "I have another appointment," she said stiffly.
She secured the strap of her purse over her shoulder and
offered him what she hoped was a regretful smile.

"Your speech was wonderful."

"Thank you. So was yours," she said, then mentioned the one thing that had troubled her. "You
never told me about your father's death."

"I've never told you I love you, either, but I do."

His words, so casual, so calm and serene, were like
a blow to her solar plexus. Susannah felt the tears
form in her eyes and tried to blink them back. "I...I
wish you hadn't said that."

"The way I feel about you isn't going to change."

"I...really have to go," she said, turning anxiously
toward John Hammer. All she wanted to do was escape
with her heart intact.

"Mr. Townsend," a woman bellowed from the
audience. "You're going to be at the auction tonight,
aren't you?"

Nate's gaze slid reluctantly from Susannah to the well-dressed woman on the floor. "I'll be there," he called back.

"I'll be looking for you," she said and laughed girlishly.

Susannah decided the other woman's laugh resembled the sound an unwell rooster would make. She was tempted to ask Nate exactly what kind of auction he planned to attend where he expected to run into someone who yelled questions across a crowded room. But she ignored the urge, which was just as well.

"Goodbye, Nate," she said, moving away.

"Goodbye, my love." It wasn't until she was walking out of the Convention Center that Susannah realized how final his farewell had sounded.

It was what she wanted, wasn't it? As far as she was concerned, Nate had proved he wasn't trustworthy; he had an infuriating habit of keeping secrets. So now that he wasn't going to see her again, there was absolutely no reason for her to complain. At least that was what Susannah told herself as she headed home, making a short side trip to the Seattle waterfront.

Within a couple of hours, Emily and Robert would be dropping off Michelle before they went to dinner with Robert's employer. Once the baby was with her, Susannah reminded herself, she wouldn't have a chance to worry about Nate or anyone else.

By the time Emily arrived with her family, Susannah was in a rare mood. She felt light-headed and witty, as though she'd downed something alcoholic, but the strongest thing she'd had all day was coffee.

"Hi," she said cheerfully, opening the door.

Michelle looked at her with large round eyes and grabbed for her mother's collar.

"Sweetheart, this is your auntie Susannah, remember?"

"Emily, the only thing she remembers is that every time you bring her here, you leave," Robert said, carrying in the diaper bag and a sack full of blankets and toys.

"Hello, Robert," Susannah murmured, kissing him on the cheek. The action surprised her as much as it did her brother-in-law. "I understand congratulations are in order."

"For you, too."

"Yes, well, it wasn't that big a deal," she said, playing down her own success.

"Not according to the article in the paper."

"Oh," Emily said, whirling around. "Speaking of the paper, I read Nate's name today."

"Yes...we were both speakers at a conference this afternoon."

Emily seemed impressed, but Susannah couldn't be sure if it was because of her or Nate.

"That wasn't what I read about him," Emily continued, focusing her attention on removing the jacket from Michelle's arms. The child wasn't being cooperative. "Nate's involved in the auction."

"Da-da!" Michelle cried once her arms were free.

Robert looked on proudly. "She finally learned my name. Michelle's first and only word," he added, beaming. "Da-da loves his baby, yes, he does."

It was so unusual to hear Robert using baby talk that for an instant, Susannah didn't catch what her sister was saying. "What was that?"

"I'm trying to tell you about the auction," Emily said again, as if that should explain everything. At Susannah's puzzled look, she added, "His name was in an article about the auction to benefit the Children's Home Society."

The lightbulb that clicked on inside Susannah's head was powerful enough to search the night sky. "Not the *bachelor* auction?" Her question was little more than a husky murmur. No wonder the woman who'd shouted to Nate at the luncheon had been so brazen! She was going to bid on him.

Slowly, hardly conscious of what she was doing, Susannah lowered herself onto the sofa next to her sister.

"He didn't tell you?"

"No, but then why should he? We're nothing more than neighbors."

"Susannah!"

Her sister had the annoying ability to turn Susannah's name into an entire statement just by the way she said it.

"Honey," Robert said, studying his watch, "it's quarter to seven. We'd better leave now if we're going to be at the restaurant on time. I don't want to keep my boss waiting."

Emily's glance at Susannah promised a long talk later. At least Susannah had several hours during which to come up with a way of warding off her sister's questions.

"Have a good time, you two," Susannah said light-heartedly, guiding them toward the door, "and don't worry about a thing."

"Bye, Michelle," Emily said as she waved from the doorway.

"Tell Mommy goodbye." Since the baby didn't seem too inclined to do so, Susannah held up the chubby hand and waved it for her.

As soon as Emily and Robert had left, Michelle started whimpering softly. Susannah took one look at her niece and her spirits plummeted. Who was she trying to fool? Herself? She'd been miserable and lonely from the moment she'd rejected Nate. Michelle sniffled, and Susannah felt like crying right along with her.

So the notorious Nate Townsend had done it again—he hadn't even bothered to mention the bachelor auction. Obviously he'd agreed to this event weeks in advance and it had never even occurred to him to tell her. Oh, sure, he swore undying love to her, but he was willing to let some strange woman buy him. Men, she was quickly learning, were not to be trusted.

The more Susannah thought back to their previous conversations, the angrier she became. When she'd asked Nate about helping her out with Michelle, he'd casually said he had "something else" this evening. He sure did. Auctioning off his body to the highest bidder!

"I told him I didn't want to see him again," Susannah announced to her niece, her fervor causing her to raise her voice. "That man was trouble from the night we met. You were with me at the time, remember? Don't we wish we'd known then what we know now?"

Michelle's shoulders began to shake, with the effort to either cry or keep from crying. Susannah didn't know which.

"He has this habit of hiding things from me—important information. But I'm telling you right now that I'm completely over that man. Any woman who wants him tonight can have him, because I'm not interested."

Michelle buried her face against Susannah's neck.

"I know exactly how you feel, kid," she said, stalking the carpet in front of the large picture window. She stared out at the lights and sounds of the city at night. "It's like you've lost your best friend, right?"

"Da-da."

"He's with your mommy. I thought Nate was my friend once," she said sadly to the baby. "But I learned the hard way what he really is—nothing earth-shattering, don't misunderstand me. But he let me make a complete idiot of myself. And…and he doesn't trust me enough to tell me anything important."

Michelle looked at Susannah wide-eyed, apparently enthralled with her speech. In an effort to keep the baby appeased, she continued chattering. "I hope he feels like a fool on the auction block tonight," she said as she imagined him standing in front of an auditorium full of screaming women. She slowly released a sigh, knowing that with his good looks, Nate would probably bring in top money. In past auctions, several of the men had gone for thousands of dollars. All for an evening in the company of one of Seattle's eligible bachelors.

"So much for love and devotion," she muttered. Michelle watched her solemnly, and Susannah felt it was her duty as the baby's aunt to give her some free advice. "Men aren't all they're cracked up to be. You'd be wise to figure that out now."

Michelle gurgled cheerfully, obviously in full agreement.

"I for one don't need a man. I'm totally happy living on my own. I've got a job, a really good job, and a few close friends—mostly people I work with—and of course your mother." Michelle raised her hand to Susannah's face and rubbed her cheek where a tear had streaked a moist trail.

"I know what you're thinking," Susannah added, although it was unnecessary to explain all that to anyone so young. "If I'm so happy, then why am I crying? Darned if I know. The problem is I can't help loving him and that's what makes this so difficult. Then he had to go and write that note on a napkin." She brought her fingers to her mouth, trying to calm herself. "He asked me if I was willing to live my life without a husband…on a napkin he asked me that. Can you imagine what the caterers are going to think when they read it? And we were sitting at the head table, no less."

"Da-da."

"He asked about that, too," Susannah said, sniffling as she spoke. She was silent a moment and when she began again her voice trembled slightly. "I never thought I'd want children, but then I didn't realize how much I could love a little one like you." Holding the baby against her breast, Susannah closed her eyes to the pain that clawed at her. "I'm so mad at that man."

Fascinated by Susannah's hair, Michelle reached up and tugged it free from the confining pins.

"I wore it up this afternoon to be contrary—and to prove to myself that I'm my own woman. Then he was there and the whole time I was speaking I wished I'd left it down—just because Nate prefers it that way. Oh, honestly, Michelle, I think I may be ready to go off the deep end here. Any advice you'd care to give me?"

"Da-da."

"That's what I thought you'd say." Forcing in a deep breath, Susannah tried to control the tears that sprang to her eyes. She hadn't expected to cry.

"I really believed that once I was promoted to vice president everything would be so wonderful and, well, it *has* been good, but I feel…empty inside. Oh, Michelle, I don't know if I can explain it. The nights are so long and there are only so many hours I can work without thinking about getting home and the possibility of seeing Nate. I…I seem to have lost my drive. Here I was talking to all these people today about determination and drive and discipline, and none of it seemed real. Then…then on the way home I was walking along the waterfront and I saw an old college friend. She's married and has a baby a little older than you and she looked so happy." She paused long enough to rub the back of her hand under her nose. "I told her all about my big promotion and Sally seemed genuinely happy for me, but I felt this giant hole inside."

"Da-da."

"Michelle, can't you learn another word? Please. How about Auntie? It's not so difficult. Say it after me. Auntie."

"Da-da."

"Nate's probably going to meet some gorgeous blonde and fall madly in love with her. She'll bid thousands of dollars for him and he'll be so impressed he won't even mind when she—" Susannah stopped, her mind whirling. "You won't believe what I was thinking," she said to Michelle, who was studying her curiously. "It's completely crazy, but...perhaps not."

Michelle waved her arms and actually seemed interested in hearing about this insane idea that had popped into Susannah's head. It was impossible. Absurd. But then she'd made a fool of herself over Nate so many times that once more certainly wasn't going to hurt.

It took several minutes to get Michelle back into her coat. Susannah would've sworn the thing had more arms than an octopus.

After glancing at the balance in her checkbook, she grabbed her savings-account records and, carrying Michelle, headed to the parking garage. She'd been saving up to pay cash for a new car, but bidding for Nate was more important.

The parking lot outside the theater where the bachelor auction was being held was full, and Susannah had a terrible time finding a place to leave her car. Once she was inside the main entrance, the doorman was hesitant to let her into the auditorium, since Michelle was with her and neither one of them had a ticket.

"Ma'am, I'm sorry, I can't let you in there without a ticket and a bidding number—besides I don't think married women are allowed."

"I'll buy one and this is my niece. Now, either you let me in there or...or you'll...I'll...I don't know what I'll do. Please," she begged. "This is a matter of life and death." Okay, so that was a slight exaggeration.

While the doorman conferred with his supervisor, Susannah looked through the swinging doors that led into the theater. She watched as several women raised their hands, and leaped enthusiastically to their feet to show their numbers. A television crew was there taping the proceedings, as well.

Susannah was impatiently bouncing Michelle on her hip when the doorman returned.

"Ma'am, I'm sorry, but my supervisor says the tickets are sold out."

Susannah was about to argue with him when she heard the master of ceremonies call out Nate's name. A fervent murmur rose from the crowd.

Desperate times demanded desperate measures, and instead of demurely going back outside, Susannah rushed to the swinging doors, shoved them open and hurried down the narrow aisle.

As soon as the doorman saw what she'd done, he ran after her, shouting, "Stop that woman!"

The master of ceremonies ceased speaking, and a hush fell over the room as every head in the place turned toward Susannah, who was clutching Michelle protectively to her chest. She'd made it halfway down the center aisle before the doorman caught up with her. Susannah cast a wretched pleading glance at Nate, who had shielded his eyes from the glare of the lights and was staring at her.

Michelle cooed and with her pudgy hand, pointed toward Nate.

"Da-da! Da-da!" she cried, and her voice echoed loudly in the auditorium.

An immediate uproar rose from the theater full of women. Nothing Susannah did could distract Michelle from pointing toward Nate and calling him Da-da. For his part, Nate appeared to be taking all the commotion in his stride. He walked over to the master of ceremonies, whom Susannah recognized as Cliff Dolittle, a local television personality, and whispered something in his ear.

"What seems to be the problem?" Cliff asked the doorman.

"This lady doesn't have a ticket or a bidding number," he shouted back. He clutched Susannah's upper arm and didn't look any too pleased with this unexpected turn of events.

"I may not have a number, but I've got $6010.12 I'd like to bid for this man," she shouted.

Her announcement was again followed by a hubbub of whispering voices, which rolled over the theater like a wave crashing onto the shore. That six thousand was the balance in Susannah's savings account, plus all the cash she had with her.

A noise from the back of the room distracted her, and that was when she realized the television crew had the cameras rolling. Every single detail of this debacle was being documented.

"I have a bid of $6010.12," Cliff Dolittle announced, sounding a little shocked. "Going once, going twice—" he paused and scanned the female audience "—sold to the lady who gate-crashed this auction. The one with the baby in her arms."

The doorman released Susannah and reluctantly directed her to where she was supposed to pay. It seemed that everyone was watching her and whispering. Several of the women were bold enough to shout bits of advice to her.

A man with a camera balanced on his shoulder hurried toward her. Loving the attention, Michelle pointed her finger at the lens and cried "Da-da" once more for all the people who would soon be viewing this disaster at home.

"Susannah, what are you doing here?" Nate whispered, joining her when she'd reached the teller's booth.

"You know what really irritates me about this?"

she said, her face bright with embarrassment. "I probably could've had you for three thousand, only I panicked and offered every penny I have. Me, the marketing wizard. I'll never be able to hold my head up again."

"You're not making any sense."

"And you are? One moment you're saying you love me and the next you're on the auction block, parading around for a bunch of women."

"That comes to $6025.12," the white-haired woman in the teller's booth told her.

"I only bid $6010.12," Susannah protested.

"The extra money is the price of the ticket. You weren't supposed to bid without one."

"I see."

Unzipping her purse and withdrawing her checkbook while balancing Michelle on her hip proved to be difficult.

"Here, I'll take her." Nate reached for Michelle, who surprised them both by protesting loudly.

"What have you been telling her about me?" Nate teased.

"The truth." With considerable ceremony, Susannah wrote out the check and ripped it from her book. Reluctantly she slid it across the counter to the woman collecting the fees.

"I'll write you a receipt."

"Thank you," Susannah said absently. "By the way, what exactly am I getting for my hard-earned money?"

"One evening with this young man."

"One evening," Susannah repeated grimly. "If we go out to dinner does he pay or do I?"

"I do," Nate answered for her.

"It's a good thing, because I don't have any money left."

"Have you eaten?"

"No, and I'm starved."

"Me, too," he told her, smiling sheepishly, but the look in his eyes said he wasn't talking about snacking on crêpes suzette. "I can't believe you did this."

"I can't, either," she said, shaking her head in wonder. "I'm still reeling with the shock." Later, she'd probably start trembling and not be able to stop. Never in her life had she done anything so bold. Love apparently did things like that to a woman. Before she met Nate she'd been a sound, logical, dedicated businesswoman. Six weeks later, she was smelling orange blossoms and thinking about weddings and babies—all because she was head over heels in love!

"Come on, let's get out of here," Nate said, tucking his arm around her waist and leading her toward the theater doors.

Susannah nodded. The doorman seemed relieved that she was leaving his domain.

"Susannah," Nate said, once they were in the parking lot. He turned and placed his hands on her shoulders, then closed his eyes as if gathering his thoughts. "You were the last person I expected to see tonight."

"Obviously," she returned stiffly. "When we're

married, I'm going to have to insist that you keep me informed of your schedule."

Nate's head snapped up. "When we're married?"

"You don't honestly believe I just spent six thousand dollars for one dinner in some fancy restaurant, did you?"

"But—"

"And there'll be children, as well. I figure that two are about all I can handle, but we'll play that by ear."

For the first time since she'd met him, Nate Townsend seemed speechless. His mouth made several movements in an attempt to talk, but nothing came out.

"I suppose you're wondering how I plan to manage my career," she said, before he could ask the question. "I'm not sure what I'm going to do yet. Since I'm looking at the good side of thirty, I suppose we could delay having children for a few more years."

"I'm thirty-three. I want a family soon."

Nate's voice didn't sound at all like it normally did, and Susannah peered at him carefully, wondering if the shock had been too much for him. It had been for her! And she was going to end up on the eleven-o'clock news. "Fine, we'll plan on starting our family right away," she agreed. "But before we do any more talking about babies, I need to ask you something important. Are you willing to change messy diapers?"

A smile played at the edges of his mouth as he nodded.

"Good." Susannah looked at Michelle, who'd laid

her head against her aunt's shoulder and closed her eyes. Apparently the events of the evening had tired her out.

"What about dinner?" Nate asked, tenderly brushing the silky hair from the baby's brow. "I don't think Michelle's going to last much longer."

"Don't worry about it. I'll buy something on the way home." She paused, then gestured weakly with her hand. "Forget that. I...I don't have any money left."

Nate grinned widely. "I'll pick up some takeout and meet you back at your place in half an hour."

Susannah smiled her appreciation. "Thanks."

"No," Nate whispered, his eyes locked with hers. "Thank _you._"

He kissed her then, slipping his hand behind her neck and tilting her face up to meet his. His touch was so potent Susannah thought her heart would beat itself right out of her chest.

"Nate." Her eyes remained shut when his name parted her lips.

"Hmm?"

"I really do love you."

"Yes, I know. I love you, too. I knew it the night you bought the stroganoff from the Western Avenue Deli and tried to make me think you'd whipped it up yourself."

She opened her eyes and raised them to his. "But I didn't even realize it then. We barely knew each other."

He kissed the tip of her nose. "I was aware from the

first time we met that my life was never going to be the same."

His romantic words stirred her heart and she wiped a tear from the corner of her eye. "I...I'd better take Michelle home," she said, and sniffled.

Nate's thumb stroked the moisture from her cheek before he kissed her again. "I won't be long," he promised.

He wasn't. Susannah had no sooner got Michelle home and into her sleeper when there was a light knock at the door.

Hurriedly, she tiptoed across the carpet and opened it. She brought her finger to her lips as she let Nate inside.

"I got Chinese."

She nodded. "Great."

She paused on her way into the kitchen and showed him Michelle, who was sleeping soundly on the end of the sofa. Susannah had taken the opposite cushion and braced it against the side so there wasn't any chance she could fall off.

"You're going to be a good mother," he whispered, kissing her forehead.

It was silly to get all misty-eyed over Nate's saying that, but she did. She succeeded in disguising her emotion by walking into the kitchen and getting two plates from the cupboard. Opening the silverware drawer, she took out forks.

Nate set the large white sack on the table and lifted out five wire-handled boxes. "Garlic chicken, pan-fried noodles, ginger beef and two large egg rolls. Do you think that'll be enough?"

"Were you planning on feeding the Seventh Infantry?" she teased.

"You said you were hungry." He opened all the boxes but one.

Susannah filled her plate and sat next to Nate, propping her feet on the chair opposite hers. The food was delicious, and after the first few mouthfuls she decided if Nate could eat with chopsticks she should try it, too. Her efforts had a humbling effect on her.

Watching her artless movements, Nate laughed, then leaned over and kissed the corner of her mouth.

"What's in there?" she asked pointing a chopstick at the fifth box.

He shrugged. "I forget."

Curious, Susannah picked up the container and opened it. Her breath lodged in her throat as she raised her eyes to Nate's. "It's a black velvet box."

"Oh, yes, now that you mention it I remember the chef saying something about black velvet being the special of the month." He went on expertly delivering food to his mouth with the chopsticks.

Susannah continued to stare at the velvet box as if it would leap out and open itself. It was the size of a ring box.

Nate waved a chopstick in her direction. "You might as well take it out and see what's inside."

Wordlessly she did as he suggested. Once the box

was free, she set the carton aside and lifted the lid. She gasped when she saw the size of the diamond. For one wild moment she couldn't breathe.

"I picked it up when I was in San Francisco," Nate told her, with no more emotion than if he'd been discussing the weather.

The solitary diamond held her gaze as effectively as a magnet. "It's the most beautiful ring I've ever seen."

"Me, too. I took one look at it and told the jeweler to wrap it up."

He acted so casual, seeming far more interested in eating his ginger beef and noodles than talking about anything as mundane as an engagement ring.

"I suppose I should tell you that while I was in San Francisco, I made an offer for the Cougars. They're a professional baseball team, in case you don't know."

"The baseball team? You're going to own a professional baseball team?" Any news he hit her with, it seemed, was going to be big.

He nodded. "I haven't heard back yet, but if that doesn't work out, I might be able to interest the owner of the New York Wolves in selling."

He made it all sound as if he were buying a car instead of something that cost millions of dollars.

"But whatever happens, we'll make Seattle our home."

Susannah nodded, although she wasn't sure why.

"Here." He set his plate aside and took the ring box from her limp hand. "I suppose the thing to do would be to place this on your finger."

Once again, Susannah nodded. Her meal was sitting like a ton of lead in the pit of her stomach. From habit, she held out her right hand. He grinned and reached for her left one.

"I had to guess the size," he said, deftly removing the diamond from its lush bed. "I had the jeweler make it a size five, because your fingers are dainty." The ring slipped on easily, the fit perfect.

Susannah couldn't stop staring at it. Never in all her life had she dreamed she'd ever have anything so beautiful. "I...don't dare go near the water with this," she whispered, looking down at her hand. Lowering her eyes helped cover her sudden welling up of tears. The catch in her voice was telltale enough.

"Not go near the water...why?"

"If I accidentally fell in," she said, managing a light laugh, "I'd sink from the weight of the diamond."

"Is it too big?"

Quickly she shook her head. "It's perfect."

Catching her unawares, Nate pressed his mouth to her trembling lips, kissing what breath she had completely away. "I planned to ask you to marry me the night I came back from the trip. We were going out for dinner, remember?"

Susannah nodded. That had been shortly after she'd read the article in *Business Monthly* about Nate. The day it felt as though her whole world was rocking beneath her feet.

"I know we talked briefly about your career, but I have something else I need to tell you."

Susannah nodded, because commenting at this point was becoming increasingly impossible.

"What would it take to lure you away from H&J Lima?"

The diamond on her ring finger seemed incentive enough, but she wasn't going to let him know that quite yet. "Why?"

"Because I'm starting a kite company. Actually, it's going to be a nationwide franchise. I've got plans to open ten stores in strategic cities around the country to see how it flies." He stopped to laugh at his pun. "But from the testing we're doing, this is going to be big. However—" he drew in a deep breath "—I'm lacking one important member of my team. I need a marketing expert, and was wondering if you'd like to apply for the job."

"I suppose," she said, deciding to play his game. "But I'd want top salary, generous bonuses, a four-day week, a health and retirement plan and adequate maternity leave."

"The job's yours."

"I don't know, Nate, there could be problems," she said, cocking her head to one side, implying that she was already having second thoughts. "People are going to talk."

"Why?"

"Because I intend to sleep with the boss. And some old fuddy-duddy's bound to think that's how I got the job."

"Let them." He laughed, reaching for her and pulling her into his lap. "Have I told you I'm crazy about you?"

Smiling into his eyes, she nodded. "There's one thing I want cleared up before we go any further, Nate Townsend. No more secrets. Understand?"

"I promise." He spit on the end of his fingertips and used the same fingers to cross his heart. "I used to do that when I was a kid. It meant I was serious."

"Well," Susannah murmured, "since you seem to be in a pledging mood, there are a few other items I'd like to have you swear to."

"Such as?"

"Such as..." she whispered, and lowered her mouth to a scant inch above his. Whatever thoughts had been in her mind scattered like autumn leaves in a brisk wind. Her tongue outlined his lips, teasing and taunting him as he'd taught her to do.

"Susannah..."

Whatever he meant to say was interrupted by the door. Susannah lifted her head. It took a moment to clear her muddled thoughts before she realized it must be her sister and brother-in-law returning from their celebration dinner with Robert's boss.

She tried to move from Nate's lap, but he groaned in protest and tightened his arms around her. "Whoever it is will go away," he said close to her ear.

"Nate—"

"Go back to doing what you were just doing and forget whoever's at the door."

"It's Emily and Robert."

Nate moaned and released her.

Susannah had no sooner unlocked the door than

Emily flew in as though she were being pursued by a banshee. She marched into the living room and stopped suddenly. Robert followed her, looking nearly as frenzied as his wife. Sane sensible Robert!

"What's wrong?" Susannah asked, her heart leaping with concern.

"You're asking *us* that?" Robert flared.

"Now, Robert," Emily said, gently placing her hand on her husband's forearm. "There's no need to be so angry. Stay calm."

"Me? Angry?" he cried, facing his wife. "In the middle of our after-dinner drink you let out a shriek that scared me out of ten years of my life and now you're telling me not to be angry?"

"Emily," Susannah tried again, "what's wrong?"

"Where's Nate?" Robert shouted. One corner of her brother-in-law's mouth curved down in a snarl. He raised his clenched fist. "I'd like ten minutes alone with that man. Give me ten minutes."

"Robert!" Emily and Susannah cried simultaneously.

"Did someone say my name?" Nate asked, as he strolled out of the kitchen.

Emily threw herself in front of her husband, patting his heaving chest with her hands. "Now, honey, settle down. There's no need to get so upset."

Susannah was completely confused. She'd never heard her brother-in-law raise his voice before. Whatever had happened had clearly unsettled him to the point of violence.

"He's not getting away with this," Robert shouted, straining against his wife's restricting hands.

"Away with what?" Nate said with a calm that seemed to inflame Robert even more.

"Taking my daughter away from me!"

"What?" Susannah cried. It astonished her that Michelle could be sleeping through all this commotion. But fortunately the baby seemed oblivious to what was happening.

"You'd better start at the beginning," Susannah said, leading everyone into the kitchen. "There's obviously been some kind of misunderstanding. Now sit down and I'll put on some decaffeinated coffee and we can sort this out in a reasonable manner."

Her brother-in-law pulled out a chair and put his elbows on the table, supporting his head in his hands.

"Why don't you start?" Susannah said, looking at her sister.

"Well," Emily began, taking in a deep breath, "as I told you, we were having dinner with Robert's boss and—"

"They know all that," Robert interrupted. "Tell them about the part when we were having a drink in the cocktail lounge."

"Yes," Emily said, heaving a great sigh. "That does seem to be where the problem started, doesn't it?"

Susannah shared a look with Nate, wondering if he was as lost as she was. Neither Emily nor Robert was making any sense.

"Go on," Susannah encouraged.

"As I explained, we were all sitting in the cocktail lounge having a drink. There was a television set in the corner of the room. I hadn't been paying much attention to it, but I looked up and I saw you and Michelle on the screen."

"Then she gave a scream that was loud enough to curdle a Bloody Mary," Robert explained. "I got everyone to be quiet while the announcer came on. He said you'd taken *my daughter* to this...this bachelor auction. They showed Michelle pointing her finger at Nate and calling him Da-da."

"That was when Robert let out a fierce yell," Emily said.

"Oh, no." Susannah slumped into a chair, wanting to find a hole to crawl into and hibernate for the next ten years. Maybe by then Seattle would have forgotten how she'd disgraced herself.

"Did they say anything else?" Nate wanted to know, doing a poor job of disguising his amusement.

"Only that the details would follow at eleven."

"I demand an explanation!" Robert said, frowning at Nate.

"It's all very simple," Susannah rushed to explain. "See...Nate's wearing a suit that's very similar to yours. Same shade of brown. From the distance, Michelle obviously mistook him for you."

"She did?" Robert muttered.

"Of course," Susannah went on. "Besides, Da-da is the only word she can say...." Her voice trailed off.

"Michelle knows who her daddy is," Nate said matter-of-factly. "You don't need to worry that—"

"Susannah," Emily broke in, "when did you get that diamond? It looks like an engagement ring."

"It is," Nate said, reaching to the middle of the table for the last egg roll. He looked at Susannah. "You don't mind, do you?"

"No. Go ahead."

"What channel was it?" Nate asked between bites. Emily told him.

"Must be a slow news day," Susannah mumbled.

"Gee, Susannah," said Emily, "I always thought if you were going to make the television news it would be because of some big business deal. I never dreamed it would be over a man. Are you going to tell me what happened?"

"Someday," she said, expelling her breath. She'd never dreamed it would be over a man, either, but this one was special. More than special.

"Well, since we're going to be brothers-in-law I guess I can forget about this unfortunate incident," Robert said generously, having regained his composure.

"Good. I'd like to be friends," Nate said, holding out his hand for Robert to shake.

"You're going to be married?" Emily asked her sister.

Susannah exchanged a happy smile with Nate and nodded.

"When?"

"Soon," Nate answered for her. His eyes told her the sooner the better.

She felt the heat crawl into her face, but she was as eager as Nate to get to the altar.

"Not only has Susannah agreed to be my wife, she's also decided to take on the position of marketing director for Windy Day Kites."

"You're leaving H&J Lima?" Robert asked, as if he couldn't believe his ears.

"Had to," she said. She moved to Nate's side, wrapped her arms around his waist and smiled up at him. "The owner made me an offer I couldn't refuse."

Nate's smile felt like a summer's day. Susannah closed her eyes, basking in the warmth of this man who'd taught her about love and laughter and rainy day kisses.

Epilogue

Michelle Davidson arrived at her aunt and uncle's waterfront home just before six. Although she'd been to the house countless times, its beauty never failed to impress her. The place was even lovelier at Christmas, illuminated by string upon string of sparkling lights. The figures on the lawn—the reindeer and St. Nick and everything else—were downright magical.

Michelle's favorite was the young boy running with his kite flying high above his head. Her uncle's kites were what had launched Windy Day Toys all those years ago. Michelle didn't have any memory of those early days, of course. She'd been much too young.

Her aunt Susannah had worked with Uncle Nate for seven years. In that time, the company had gone from one successful venture to another. The first major success had been with kites, and then there was a series of outdoor games, geared toward getting kids outside instead of sitting in front of a TV or a computer screen. Buried Treasure came next and then a game called Bugs that caught national attention.

In the meantime Aunt Susannah had three children in quick succession and became a stay-at-home mother for a while. Despite her initial doubts, she'd loved it. Michelle's own mother had three children in addition to her, all born within a few months of their Townsend cousins. When her youngest sibling, Glory, entered kindergarten, Michelle's mother and Aunt Susannah had formed Motherhood, Inc.

The two sisters had introduced a series of baby products that were environmentally friendly, starting with cloth diapers and organic baby food. They'd recognized the desire of young mothers all across the country for alternatives to disposable diapers and ways to feed their babies wholesome food.

"Michelle! Michelle!"

Ten-year-old Junior was out the door and racing toward her even before Michelle had made it up the driveway. Eight-year-old Emma Jane was directly behind him. Tessa, who was twelve, was far too aloof, too cool, to show any excitement over Michelle's visit. That was all right, because Michelle knew exactly how Tessa felt. Michelle had hated it when her parents had insisted on hiring a sitter, so she couldn't very well blame Tessa now.

"Michelle." Aunt Susannah waited for her by the entrance. "I really appreciate your doing this," she said. Two large evergreen wreaths decorated the front doors, and a fifteen-foot-high Christmas tree dominated the entry, with gifts stacked all around.

Her aunt finished fastening an earring. "How'd it go at the office today?"

"People heard that we're related," Michelle confessed.

Junior and Emma Jane sat down beneath the massive Christmas tree and began sorting through the gifts—obviously an activity they indulged in often.

"I suppose everyone was likely to find out sooner or later," Aunt Susannah said, turning toward the stairs. "Nate, hurry up or we're going to be late for dinner."

"I ended up telling everyone that it was because of me that you met Uncle Nate."

At that, Tessa came out of the library. "You were?"

"It's true," Michelle said, accustomed to looks of astonishment after her coworkers' reactions earlier in the day.

"How come no one's ever mentioned *this* before?" Tessa demanded.

Aunt Susannah glanced at Michelle, frowning slightly. "It was a long time ago, sweetie."

"All you said was that you met Dad when you lived in that condo building in downtown Seattle."

"That's how we did meet." Susannah called upstairs again. "Nate!"

"I'll be right down," Nate shouted from the landing.

"Michelle?" Tessa asked, looking to her for the explanation that wasn't being offered by her mother.

"I'll tell you all about it," Michelle whispered.

"Us, too," Emma Jane said.

"Of course," Michelle promised.

Nate Townsend bounded down the stairs, looking as handsome and debonair as always. He really
was a wonderful uncle—energetic, funny and a
terrific cook.

"Honey, we need to leave right now."

"I know." He opened the hall closet and took out
Susannah's coat and his own. He helped Susannah on
with hers, then reached over to kiss each of the kids.

"Be good," he said. "And Michelle, if you're going
to tell them the story of your aunt and me, don't leave
out the part about how you nearly ruined my reputa-
tion at the Seattle Bachelor Auction."

"Or the fact that I spent far too much money to buy
you," Susannah muttered. "I could've got you for half
of what I paid."

Nate chuckled. "That's what you think. And, hey,
I was worth every penny."

"Honey, we—"

"Have fun," Michelle interrupted, steering her
aunt and uncle toward the entrance. Once they were
on their way, she closed the door—and found her three
cousins watching her expectantly.

"Now, where were we?" she murmured.

"Tell us everything," Tessa insisted.

"Can we have dinner first?" Junior asked.

"No," Tessa answered.

"Can you tell us while we eat?" Emma Jane asked.

"I do believe I can," Michelle said and the three
followed her into the kitchen. "This is one of the most
romantic and wonderful love stories I've ever heard—
and to think it all started because of me."

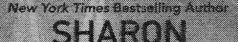

New York Times Bestselling Author

SHARON SALA

He killed her once...

Throat slashed and left for dead next to her murdered father,
a thirteen-year-old girl vows to hunt down the man who did
this to them—Solomon Tutuola. Now grown, bounty hunter
Cat Dupree lets nothing—or no one—stand in the way of
that deadly promise. Not even her lover, Wilson McKay.

Suspecting that Tutuola is still alive, despite witnessing
the horrific explosion that should have killed him, Cat
follows a dangerous money trail to Mexico, swearing not to
return until she's certain Tutuola is dead—even if it means
destroying her very soul....

CUT THROAT

"The perfect entertainment for those looking for a suspense
novel with emotional intensity."
—*Publishers Weekly* on *Out of the Dark*

*Available the first week of November 2007
wherever paperbacks are sold!*

MIRA® 　　　www.MIRABooks.com

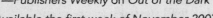

MSS2507

ICE STORM

NEW YORK TIMES
BESTSELLING AUTHOR

ANNE STUART

The powerful head of the covert mercenary organization
The Committee, Isobel Lambert is a sleek, sophisticated
professional who comes into contact with some of the
most dangerous people in the world. But beneath Isobel's
cool exterior a ghost exists, haunting her with memories
of another life…a life that ended long ago.

But Isobel's past and present are about to collide when
Serafin, mercenary, assassin and the most dangerous
man in the world, makes a deal with the Committee.
Seventeen years ago she shot him and left him for dead,
and now he's tracked her down for revenge.…

"Stuart knows how to take chances, and this edgy thriller
shows how well they can pay off."
—*Publishers Weekly* on *Cold As Ice*

*Available the first week of November 2007
wherever paperbacks are sold!*

MIRA®

www.MIRABooks.com

MAS2500

REQUEST YOUR
FREE BOOKS!

2 FREE NOVELS
FROM THE ROMANCE/SUSPENSE
COLLECTION PLUS 2 FREE GIFTS!

YES! Please send me 2 FREE novels from the Romance/Suspense Collection and my 2 FREE gifts. After receiving them, if I don't wish to receive any more books, I can return the shipping statement marked "cancel." If I don't cancel, I will receive 4 brand-new novels every month and be billed just $5.49 per book in the U.S., or $5.99 per book in Canada, plus 25¢ shipping and handling per book plus applicable taxes, if any*. That's a savings of at least 20% off the cover price! I understand that accepting the 2 free books and gifts places me under no obligation to buy anything. I can always return a shipment and cancel at any time. Even if I never buy another book from the Reader Service, the two free books and gifts are mine to keep forever.

185 MDN EF5Y   385 MDN EF6C

Name	(PLEASE PRINT)

Address		Apt. #

City	State/Prov.	Zip/Postal Code

Signature (if under 18, a parent or guardian must sign)

Mail to **The Reader Service:**
IN U.S.A.: P.O. Box 1867, Buffalo, NY 14240-1867
IN CANADA: P.O. Box 609, Fort Erie, Ontario L2A 5X3

Not valid to current subscribers to the Romance Collection,
the Suspense Collection or the Romance/Suspense Collection.

Want to try two free books from another line?
Call 1-800-873-8635 or visit www.morefreebooks.com.

* Terms and prices subject to change without notice. NY residents add applicable sales tax. Canadian residents will be charged applicable provincial taxes and GST. This offer is limited to one order per household. All orders subject to approval. Credit or debit balances in a customer's account(s) may be offset by any other outstanding balance owed by or to the customer. Please allow 4 to 6 weeks for delivery.

Your Privacy: Harlequin is committed to protecting your privacy. Our Privacy Policy is available online at www.eHarlequin.com or upon request from the Reader Service. From time to time we make our lists of customers available to reputable firms who may have a product or service of interest to you. If you would prefer we not share your name and address, please check here. ☐

DEBBIE MACOMBER